THE VAMPYRE

and

ERNESTUS BERCHTOLD

broadview editions
series editor: L.W. Conolly

John William Polidori, by F.G. Gainsford (c. 1816).
National Portrait Gallery, London.

THE VAMPYRE: A TALE

and

ERNESTUS BERCHTOLD; OR, THE MODERN ŒDIPUS

John William Polidori

edited by D.L. Macdonald and Kathleen Scherf

broadview editions

Library and Archives Canada Cataloguing in Publication

Polidori, John William, 1795-1821.

The vampyre : a tale, and Ernestus Berchtold, or, The modern Oedipus / John William Polidori ; edited by D.L. Macdonald and Kathleen Scherf.

Includes bibliographical references.
ISBN 978-1-55111-745-4

I. Macdonald, D.L. (David Lorne), 1955–   II. Scherf, Kathleen, 1960–
III. Polidori, John William, 1795–1821 Ernestus Berchtold. IV. Title.

PR5187.P5V35 2007   823'.7   C2007-903665-1

Broadview Editions

The Broadview Editions series represents the ever-changing canon of literature in English by bringing together texts long regarded as classics with valuable lesser-known works.

Advisory editor for this volume: Morgan Rooney

Broadview Press is an independent, international publishing house, incorporated in 1985. Broadview believes in shared ownership, both with its employees and with the general public; since the year 2000 Broadview shares have traded publicly on the Toronto Venture Exchange under the symbol BDP.

We welcome comments and suggestions regarding any aspect of our publications—please feel free to contact us at the addresses below or at broadview@broadviewpress.com.

North America
Post Office Box 1243, Peterborough, Ontario, Canada K9J 7H5
3576 California Road, Post Office Box 1015, Orchard Park, NY, USA 14127
Tel: (705) 743-8990; Fax: (705) 743-8353;
email: customerservice@broadviewpress.com

UK, Ireland, and continental Europe
NBN International, Estover Road, Plymouth PL6 7PY UK
Tel: 44 (0) 1752 202300   Fax: 44 (0) 1752 202330
email: enquiries@nbninternational.com

Australia and New Zealand
UNIREPS, University of New South Wales
Sydney, NSW, 2052 Australia
Tel: 61 2 9664 0999; Fax: 61 2 9664 5420
email: info.press@unsw.edu.au

www.broadviewpress.com

Broadview Press acknowledges the financial support of the Government of Canada through the Book Publishing Industry Development Program (BPIDP) for our publishing activities.

This book is printed on paper containing 100% post-consumer fibre.

Typesetting and assembly: True to Type Inc., Claremont, Canada.

PRINTED IN CANADA

Contents

Acknowledgements

Although this is a new edition of Polidori's fiction, it is closely based on the one published by the University of Toronto Press in 1994, and we are still grateful to the persons and institutions that made that edition possible, especially the Houghton Library, Harvard University, for permission to quote from manuscript marginalia in a copy of *The Vampyre*, by John William Polidori (1819), call number *EC8.P7598.819va, by permission of the Houghton Library, Harvard University. We are grateful to the staff of the following institutions for their assistance: the Bodleian Library, Oxford University, especially William Hodges; the British Library, especially P. Karmic and A. Summers; the Cambridge University Library, especially J.J. Hall; the Houghton Library, Harvard University, especially Jennie Rathbun; the Leeds University Library, especially C.D.W. Sheppard; the Pennsylvania State University Library; and the Harry Ransom Humanities Research Center, University of Texas at Austin, especially Heather Moore. Anne Yandle and George Brandak of the Special Collections Division of the University of British Columbia Library were, as usual, extremely helpful, as were Margaret Allen, Suzanne Rancourt, Prudence Tracy, and the anonymous readers for the University of Toronto Press.

We are grateful to our research assistants, David Deaton, Stephanie Kepros, and Helena Petkau, and to Bill Matheson of Matheson Graphics Services, Calgary, who prepared the map of the Switzerland of *Ernestus Berchtold*. Finally, we are grateful to Ian Balfour, Ian Fairclough, James Hume, Alec Globe, Janice El-Bayoumi, Roberta Jackson, Jay Macpherson, Anne McWhir, Andrew Nicholson, Rob Scherf-Silk, and Dan Silk.

In preparing this edition, we are grateful to the National Portrait Gallery, London, for permission to reprint the portrait of Polidori by F.G. Gainsford (c. 1816); to Terry Hale, for permission to reprint two stories from his edition of *Tales of the Dead*; and to our research assistant, Jay Gamble, and Broadview copy editor, Morgan Rooney, whose keen eyes saved us from innumerable errors.

Our part in this book is dedicated to our parents, Helga Scherf, Doreen Macdonald Zaharuk, and Peter Zaharuk; and to the memory of Frank Macdonald and George Scherf.

Introduction

The Modern Vampire

Halfway through Anne Rice's *Interview with the Vampire* (1976), her hero, Louis, travels to Transylvania in search of his roots. Louis is a familiar vampire, articulate, aristocratic, and seductive; Rice lingers on his finely tailored coat, his silk tie, and the collar as white as his flesh (3). His travelling companion, Claudia, is an equally elegant child-vampire, "a vision of lace and loveliness," an exquisite, lethal doll (130). The vampire they find in Transylvania is shockingly different: "The two huge eyes bulged from naked sockets and two small, hideous holes made up his nose; only a putrid, leathery flesh enclosed his skull, and the rank, rotting rags that covered his frame were thick with earth and slime and blood. I was battling a mindless, animated corpse. But no more" (191-92). Louis and Claudia kill it in disgust.

Despite its horror, the incident is an intellectual joke, designed to emphasize the differences between the vampires of Eastern European folklore and the vampires of modern Western popular culture.[1] The vampires of folklore, insofar as one can generalize about them, are more or less as Rice describes them[2]—corpses reanimated not by their own spirits but by an external, and often impersonal, evil force.[3] Like many revenants, they are usually confined to haunting a specific locale; often, they prey only on members of their own family. The vampires of popular culture are human beings, though usually sinister or horrible ones; they are aristocrats, wanderers, and seducers. In short, they are a combi-

---

1   For a discussion of the vampires of folklore, see Paul Barber, *Vampires, Burial, and Death: Folklore and Reality* (1988). For the vampires of popular culture, see Nina Auerbach, *Our Vampires, Ourselves* (1995); William Patrick Day, *Vampire Legends in Contemporary American Culture* (2002); and Gregory A. Waller, *The Living and the Undead* (1986).

2   Rice does get one thing wrong: the vampires of folklore are not usually described as decomposing—indeed, an unnatural preservation is one of their defining characteristics.

3   Of course, the vampires of folklore are no more consistent than the vampires of popular culture; sometimes vampires were believed to be reanimated by their own souls (Barber 26). Our other three points might be similarly qualified, but, as differences of emphasis, they still seem striking.

nation of the Byronic hero and of a caricature of Byron himself—
not surprisingly, since these differences are largely the consequence of a single literary event: the publication of "The
Vampyre: A Tale by Lord Byron" in the *New Monthly Magazine*
on 1 April 1819.

Before Byron left England forever in April 1816, he hired John
William Polidori (1795-1821) as his personal physician. Polidori
had received his MD the year before, at the age of only nineteen,
and thus was too young to apply for a licence to practise in
London (Macdonald 46). Moreover, he had literary ambitions,
so a trip with the most famous poet of the age must have seemed
like a wonderful opportunity. It turned out to be a bitter disappointment. Byron would fire him before the end of the summer.
Polidori would then try and fail to find work in Italy; he would
return to England, fail to make a living either as a physician or as
a writer, and kill himself in 1821.

The two men first travelled to Geneva, where they met Percy
Shelley; his lover, Mary Godwin; and her stepsister (Byron's
current lover), Claire Clairmont. It was a rainy summer, and the
travellers passed the time reading "Some volumes of ghost
stories, translated from the German into French" (Shelley,
Frankenstein 1831, 354).[1] These were entitled *Fantasmagoriana,
ou recueil d'histoires d'apparitions de spectres, revenans, fantômes, etc.*;
they had been translated by Jean-Baptiste-Benoit Eyriès, in 1812,
from the first two volumes of the five-volume *Gespensterbuch*
(1811-15), edited by Friedrich Schulze and Johann Apel. Eyriès's
translation had in its turn been translated into English, as *Tales of
the Dead* (1813), by Sarah Elizabeth Brown Utterson (1782?-
1851), but this version does not seem to have been available in
Geneva.

Eventually, Byron suggested that the members of the group
write ghost stories of their own. Mary Godwin wrote one that was
published as *Frankenstein; or, The Modern Prometheus* in 1818.
Polidori wrote one that was published under the strikingly similar
title *Ernestus Berchtold; or, The Modern Œdipus* in 1819. Byron
began one but became bored with it and gave it up; Polidori
appropriated his idea and based another tale on it. Somehow, the
manuscript of this tale made its way back to England, where it

---

1 We cite throughout our edition of *Frankenstein*, which is based on the
   1818 text but includes the 1823 and 1831 variants in Appendices F and
   G.

was published, without Polidori's knowledge, under Byron's name. Despite the protests of the critics, it was an astonishing success. It went through seven English editions in the first year. By the next year, plays based on it were running in London and Paris.[1] Vampires were never the same again.

Polidori does not seem to have realized what he was starting. He did not expect the tale to be published and did not write it very carefully. (After it had been published, he did revise it carefully, perhaps to make it worthy of its fame or to reclaim it as his own. This edition incorporates all his revisions.) His initial intention was primarily to caricature his employer; the two were already on terrible terms. It was this intention that made his tale so innovative: the modern vampire is essentially a Byronic vampire. Because this was his primary intention, however, he did not realize the full potential of some of his innovations. *The Vampyre* is not *Dracula* (1897), but it made Bram Stoker's masterpiece possible.

Polidori changes the vampire in four ways. Some of these changes are anticipated in the few earlier literary treatments of the monster, but Polidori takes them all further, and, more importantly, he combines them. First, he makes the vampire a real, though monstrous, human being, not the mindless animated corpse of folklore, and of Robert Southey's *Thalaba the Destroyer* (1801), the earliest English literary treatment of the motif, in which the body of Thalaba's beloved Oneiza is possessed by a "fiendish tenant" (8.10). Byron exploits this folkloric conception of the vampire in his scandalous epigram "Windsor Poetics: Lines composed on the occasion of His Royal Highness the Prince Regent being seen standing between the coffins of Henry VIII and Charles I, in the royal vault at Windsor" (1813):

FAMED for contemptuous breach of sacred ties,
By headless Charles see heartless Henry lies;
Between them stands another sceptred *thing*—
It moves, *it* reigns—in all but name, a king:

Charles to his people, Henry to his wife,
—In him the double tyrant starts to life:

---

1 As Katie Harse shows, the theatrical success of the vampire was achieved at the expense of a certain domestication. The plays kept him in circulation, however, until Stoker could re-feralize him in 1897.

Justice and death have mix'd their dust in vain,
Each royal vampire wakes to life again....
(1-8; emphasis added)[1]

Polidori seems to have decided on this change only in the course
of writing. Lord Strongmore begins the tale with the "dead grey
eye" of a corpse (39).[2] But by the end, he has acquired a consciousness of his own, and a small part of the tale is even told
from his point of view (57). Readers can feel sympathy for him,
in addition to fear and detestation. Polidori may be thinking of
the Byronic hero, that object of both sympathy and detestation,
who "left a Corsair's name to other times, / Linked with one
virtue, and a thousand crimes" (*The Corsair* 3.695-96). He may
be thinking particularly of the terrific curse of vampirism in
Byron's *The Giaour* (written, like "Windsor Poetics," in 1813), a
curse that condemns the vampire to a transitional condition of
consciousness without volition, so that he can know and loathe
what he is doing but not resist it:

But first, on earth as Vampire sent,
Thy corse shall from its tomb be rent;
Then ghastly haunt thy native place,
And suck the blood of all thy race;
There from thy daughter, sister, wife,
At midnight drain the stream of life;
Yet loathe the banquet which perforce
Must feed thy livid living corse.... (755-62; cf. Barber 57-58)

Perhaps the most important precursor of Polidori's vampire, the
highly ambiguous Geraldine in Coleridge's "Christabel" (1816)[3]
seems to be conscious, but she claims to be acting under a kind
of compulsion—though by the powers of good, not evil (221-26).

---

1 Since Byron may well have recited this poem to his travelling companion, it may have contributed to the politicization of the vampire discussed below.
2 For a discussion of the vampire's gaze, see J.P. Telotte, "A Parasitic Perspective."
3 It is not even clear that she is a vampire (Polidori calls her a witch), but
  the folklore itself does not always clearly distinguish between vampires
  and other kinds of revenants (Barber 2-3). Byron recited part of
  Coleridge's poem after midnight on 18 June, giving P.B. Shelley hyster-
  ics (Polidori, *Diary* 127-28).

Polidori makes the transition complete and unambiguous. There is nothing compulsive about his vampirism. Lord Strongmore is not only a conscious vampire but a perfectly willing one. Both the *Edinburgh Monthly Review* (Appendix B.1.a) and the *Monthly Review* (Appendix B.1.b) noted this innovation, the first referring to the vampire as "'the dead and alive' monster" (243), the second calling him "a bustling inhabitant of the world" (248).

Second, as the *Monthly Review* also noticed (248), Polidori makes his Lord Strongmore an aristocrat, like Lord Byron.[1] (In the original version of the tale, to make the point more obvious, he calls him Lord Ruthven, after Clarence de Ruthven, Lord Glenarvon, the Byronic villain of *Glenarvon* [1816], the autobiographical novel by Byron's former lover Lady Caroline Lamb.)[2] As David Punter puts it, "He is dead yet not dead, as the power of the aristocracy in the early nineteenth century was dead and not dead; he requires blood because blood is the business of an aristocracy, the blood of warfare and the blood of the family" (104). The vampires of folklore and of earlier literary treatments tend to be from modest backgrounds; Southey's Oneiza is the daughter of a nomad who is "Nor rich, nor poor" (3.21). Again, Coleridge's Geraldine is an exception: she is "of a noble line" (77). Admittedly, as the *Monthly Review* makes clear (246), writers had exploited the political implications of the vampire long before Polidori, and, compared to later writers like Stoker and Rice, Polidori does little to exploit the political possibilities of the new status he has given his vampire. Lord Strongmore is addicted to the aristocratic vice of gambling, and he drains some of his victims of cash at the faro table much as he drains others of blood after dark. Polidori may have taken the gambling motif from "The Death-Bride" (Appendix A.1.b), one of the stories in *Fantasmagoriana*, in which the central character is a mysterious "Italian marquis" who breaks all the banks at all the gambling tables at a spa. Like Strongmore, he carelessly loses his money as soon as he wins it. Unlike Strongmore, however, he has a moral purpose: he wants to wipe out gambling at the resort. Strong-

---

1   For a more detailed discussion of this point, see Gavin Budge, "'The Vampyre': Romantic Metaphysics and the Aristocratic Other."
2   Lamb, in turn, may have named her villain after Lord Grey de Ruthyn, Byron's former tenant at Newstead Abbey, who apparently tried to seduce his fifteen-year-old landlord—if Byron confided to her about this incident (as he did, apparently, about much of his sexual history).

more simply delights in ruining the innocent and supporting the vicious.[1]

Third, Polidori makes his vampire a traveller; as the *Monthly Review* put it, in Polidori's tale, "the natives of England are now first made subject to the horrible attacks of Vampyres" (247). Byron, of course, was a famous traveller; the poem that made him famous, *Childe Harold's Pilgrimage*, is a sort of travelogue. The curse in *The Giaour* confines the vampire to his native place, like a vampire of folklore, but Augustus Darvell, the hero of the fragment on which Polidori based his tale (Appendix A.2), is a traveller, whose most noticeable character trait is a "shadowy restlessness" (232). Strongmore's mobility allows Polidori to give his readers some new chills by bringing a vampire, for the first time, to England (just as, later, Stoker's Jonathan Harker will help to bring Dracula to London). It also allows Strongmore (again like the Italian marquis) to vanish at the end of the tale, thus providing more chills and making the tale as open-ended as *The Corsair* or *Manfred* (1817), which Byron began in Polidori's company in 1816, and which ends with lines that could conclude *The Vampyre*: "He's gone ... / Whither? I dread to think—but he is gone" (3.4.152-53). Polidori considered a sequel but did not live to write it.

Polidori's fourth and most important innovation is to make the vampire a seducer. The vampires of folklore are sometimes sexual but not seductive; their sexuality is that of rape (Barber 9). The *Edinburgh Monthly Review* noticed the disturbing eroticism of Polidori's modern vampire: "The fostering embraces" of the vampire "could not be more disgusting" (243). This innovation unites the first three. The combination of fear and sympathy made possible by the vampire's human consciousness can evolve into a combination of fear and desire. The elegance that the vampire's high status implies makes him attractive; the power it also implies makes him irresistible. (The most notorious sentence in Polidori's diary suggests his sense of his travelling companion as a seducer, if that is the right word, of irresistible power: "As soon as he reached his room, Lord Byron fell like a thunderbolt upon the chambermaid" [33].) The mobility of the vampire enables him to seek out new victims to seduce.

Rather than seeking out victims, vampires before *The Vampyre* typically prey on their own families and neighbours. Mary

---

1 Gambling also plays a prominent part in *Ernestus Berchtold*. Polidori eventually killed himself over a gambling debt.

Shelley is following the older conception (and perhaps remembering Byron's curse) when she makes Frankenstein describe his monster as "my own vampire, my own spirit let loose from the grave, and forced to destroy all that was dear to me" (1818, 104). Frankenstein's description is accurate; the monster murders only those dear to him: William, Justine, Henry, and Elizabeth. Even Strongmore, as a vampire, is not as promiscuous as his successors. His vampirism, moreover, is not infectious (as the *Edinburgh Monthly Review* seems to have expected, in referring to his "fostering embraces"); his two most prominent victims, Aubrey's sister and his beloved Ianthe, die but do not rise again as vampires.[1] In later writers such as Stoker, as in folklore, infectiousness is an essential aspect of vampirism. It is in part a symbol for a fear of sexually transmitted disease, a fear that was just as reasonable in Stoker's day as in ours. (Stoker himself seems to have contracted syphilis at about the time he was writing *Dracula*; he died of it fifteen years later [Farson 233-41].) Behind the rational fear of disease is an irrational fear of sexuality itself. The bite of the vampire is seen as the fatal kiss that will transform its victim into a new, alien, sexual being. This is the kiss for which Jonathan Harker feels a "wicked, burning desire" (69). In *Dracula*, desire is not only always wicked, it is also always burning, as if it were a disease in itself.

As a seducer, Strongmore *is* promiscuous, and his eroticism is infectious. Aubrey learns that "those females whom he had sought, apparently on account of their virtue, had, since his departure, thrown even the mask aside, and had not scrupled to expose the whole deformity of their vices to the public view" (43). The virtuous Miss Aubrey falls victim to his sexuality as a prelude to being vampirized. Aubrey himself is infected with Strongmore's evil, and through the oath of silence he is forced to swear at Strongmore's death in Greece, he even becomes his unwilling accomplice.

Polidori borrowed his oath of silence from Byron. In practically the only fully dramatized incident in Byron's fragmentary story, the dying Darvell makes his friend promise not to reveal his death. Byron in turn seems to have borrowed the oath from *Fantasmagoriana*. "The Family Portraits" (Appendix A.1.a), the longest story in the collection and the one Mary Shelley recalls

---

1   Coleridge may be hinting at the infectiousness of vampirism when he has Christabel take on Geraldine's serpentine characteristics (583-612). If so, Polidori did not take the hint.

most vividly in her 1831 introduction to *Frankenstein* (355), contains a deathbed revelation of the origins of a family, a revelation that is sealed by an oath of silence and that, when revealed, helps to resolve the story's complicated dynastic plot (201). "The Death-Bride" (A.1.b) contains two such oaths: the villain asks the Italian marquis to swear not to reveal his past misdeeds (224), and the heroine's father asks both the villain and the marquis to swear not to reveal that her twin sister has returned from the dead (211, 213). This device seems to have particularly impressed the Genevan party. The oath in both Byron's fragment and Polidori's tale is designed to facilitate the villain's return from the dead, and in Polidori's tale it has two parts, corresponding to the two oaths in the earlier story: "swear that for a year and a day you will not impart your knowledge of my *crimes* or *death* to any living being" (51; emphasis added).

The significance of these oaths is partly self-referential. Just as the characters promise not to reveal secrets, so the stories in which they appear refuse to provide rational explanations for their supernatural events; they belong to the "unexplained supernatural" school of Horace Walpole and Matthew Gregory Lewis, not to the "explained supernatural" school of Ann Radcliffe. "The Family Portraits" begins with a frame-narrative about a ghost-story session; one of the participants explains the rules: "it is agreed amongst us that no one shall search for any explanation, even though it bears the stamp of truth, as explanations would take away all pleasure from ghost stories" (174).

The precise significance of the oath in Byron's fragment is unclear, since the fragment breaks off immediately after it is sworn. Darvell's friend commits himself to more than silence, however; he also agrees to throw a ring into the Bay of Eleusis and then to visit the temple of Ceres (234-35). Since these locations were associated with the Eleusinian mysteries, the actions are presumably designed to bring about Darvell's return from the dead; the oath would then prevent the friend from interfering with his plans. If these are evil plans (though nothing that Darvell actually does or says in the fragment is particularly evil), then the friend will have been actively involved in them, against his will, like the unwilling vampire in *The Giaour*.

Polidori resorts to the simpler technique of having Strongmore revived by moonlight, and he has the robbers who have killed him, not Aubrey, place the corpse in the moonlight. Thus Aubrey's involvement in Strongmore's plans is only passive; the oath prevents him from stopping them. His enforced passivity both contributes to the terror of the tale and gives it much of its psychological interest.

There are obvious parallels between Lord Strongmore's domination of Aubrey and Lord Byron's domination of Polidori. Aubrey is much more innocent than Polidori himself, however, and the narrative continually indulges in irony at the hero's expense. Aubrey is only just emerging from childhood (characterized by an interest in Gothic fantasy) into adulthood (characterized by an interest in marriage) when he meets Strongmore:

> He was handsome, frank, and rich: for these reasons, upon his entering into the gay circles, many mothers surrounded him, striving which should describe with least truth their languishing or romping favourites: many daughters at the same time, by their brightening countenances when he approached, and by their sparkling eyes, when he opened his lips, soon led him into false notions of his talents and his merit. Attached as he was to the romance of his solitary hours, he was startled at finding, that ... there was no foundation in real life for any of that congeries of pleasing horrors and descriptions contained in the volumes, which had formed the occupation of his midnight vigils. Finding, however, some compensation in his gratified vanity, he was about to relinquish his dreams, when the extraordinary being we have above described, crossed him in his career. (40-41)

Later in the tale, Miss Aubrey appears poised on the same threshold: "If she before, by her infantine caresses, had gained his affection, now that the woman began to appear, she was still more attaching as a companion" (53); it is her turn to meet Strongmore. Ianthe, whom Aubrey loves and loses in the interim, is a "frank infantile being" (46); he may love her partly because she reminds him of his sister or simply of the world of his childhood.

Strongmore belongs to both worlds. He is an experienced traveller who can guide Aubrey through the grand tour, and an experienced man of the world who can warn him about the perils of the marriage market: "know, if not my bride to day, your sister is dishonoured. Women are frail!" (58). Yet he is also a vampire, a creature from Gothic fantasy. Meeting him arrests Aubrey on the threshold, and the oath of silence imprisons him there. He has an adult's knowledge of what is happening but a child's inability to do anything about it. He has the combination of consciousness and helplessness characteristic of the victim of a nightmare—or of the vampire in *The Giaour*.

Kay Stockholder has proposed interpreting literary works as if they were dreams, with their protagonists as the dreamers (5). Such an approach seems peculiarly appropriate to a nightmarish work like *The Vampyre*. If we read the tale in this way, Aubrey is ultimately responsible for everything in it, since it is, after all, his dream (Stockholder 14). Some of the other characters, according to Stockholder, represent his impressions of the people in his life; Miss Aubrey would presumably fit into this category. Others might be composites. Still others—and a vampire would presumably fit into *this* category—are "fantastic figures" which represent "a sudden eruption of glaringly antithetic desires" (Stockholder 18-19). Just as Frankenstein's monster is his creator's double— his own vampire—so Strongmore may be Aubrey's double; there may be a terrible appropriateness in his preying on the women Aubrey loves. Or the "antithetic desires" may be, in Eve Kosofsky Sedgwick's term, homosocial: the desires of Aubrey and Strongmore for each other. Certainly Ianthe and Miss Aubrey are such sketchy characters as to illustrate Sedgwick's contention that "the ultimate function of women [in fictions like this] is to be conduits of homosocial desire between men" (99), and Aubrey does eventually die of a burst blood vessel, as if he were the vampire's real victim.

The tale itself, as Carol A. Senf has argued, hovers between two worlds, or more precisely between two generic affiliations: on the one hand, the realism of the satire on London society; on the other, the "unexplained supernatural" of the Gothic nightmare. The oath threatens to disrupt the generic balance. In realistic terms, Aubrey's worrying about breaking an oath sworn to a being as evil as Strongmore seems implausible. Ingeniously, Polidori provides realistic reasons for his not doing so. First, Aubrey reflects, "even if he were to break his oath, and disclose his suspicions, who would believe him?" (55). Then, frustration at his inability to act and fear of the consequences of his failure to act drive him to madness—a madness that has been carefully anticipated by the delirious fever to which he succumbs in Greece after Ianthe's death and by the depression he suffers on his trip back to England.

Mary Shelley uses the same combination of reasons to make the plot of *Frankenstein* plausible. Victor decides not to reveal his suspicions about the murder of his brother William because he is afraid they will not be credited. "I well knew that if any other had communicated such a relation to me, I should have looked upon it as the ravings of insanity" (1818, 104). Later, he is afraid to tell his father the truth about the murder of his friend Clerval, for the same reason: "I had a feeling that I should be supposed mad, and this for ever chained my tongue, when I would have given the whole world to have confided the fatal secret" (1818, 208). Like Aubrey after the death of Ianthe, he succumbs to a delirious fever after the animation of the monster; like Aubrey on his way back to England, he suffers from depression back in Geneva. After the murder of Clerval, he succumbs, like Aubrey, to a second delirium; after the murder of his bride and the death of his father, he succumbs to a third.

The Modern Œdipus and the Modern Prometheus

Polidori's association of vampirism with silence—like the parallels between Aubrey and Strongmore, Miss Aubrey and Ianthe—suggests that he shared the Romantic interest in incest. If the vampires of folklore prey on their families, modern vampires create new families that are incestuous by definition. It is because she is, in a sense, Dracula's lover that Lucy Westenra is reborn as his daughter. Louis refers to Claudia frankly as "my daughter and my love" (Rice 256). And incest is the great unspeakable in Romantic literature (as it was until recently in modern society).[1] It is the crime that Manfred longs to bury in oblivion but that he "cannot utter" when the spirits ask him what he wants to forget (*Manfred* 1.1.138). It is the crime on which Percy Shelley's tragedy *The Cenci* (1819) turns, and which its victim Beatrice describes as one of "The crimes which mortal tongue dare never name" (4.4.128).

Polidori's novel, *Ernestus Berchtold; or, The Modern Œdipus* (1819), is explicitly concerned with incest, and the reviews commented on the unspeakability of the theme. In a startling anticipation of the Freudian theory that the desire for incest is both universal and universally repressed, the *Edinburgh Monthly Review* accused Polidori of "giv[ing] free utterance to the sentiments which linger about every imagination, but which it is the prime object of all moral training to subdue"; he "only dares to express what better men blush even to feel" (Appendix B.2.a;

---

1 As Sedgwick points out, homosexuality has until recently been equally unspeakable (94-95).

249). Almost as startlingly, the *European Magazine* preferred Polidori's novel not only to Horace Walpole's *The Mysterious Mother*
(1768) but to Sophocles' *Œdipus Tyrannus* (c.425 BC), because
"subjects of this kind are more fitted for narrative than for dramatic representation" (Appendix B.2.b; 255). In a novel, which
can be read in silence, mortal tongue need never name the
subject.

Ernestus Berchtold is less revolutionary than *The Vampyre* but a
more fully realized work of fiction. The novel presents an unusually complete collection of Romantic incest motifs; the *Edinburgh
Monthly Review*, ever hostile, says that "in the simple particular of
revolting combinations [that is, incest], [it] outdo[es] the inspired
ferocity of the noble bard himself" (249) (Byron had dealt with
incest in *The Bride of Abydos* [1813] and *Parisina* [1816] as well
as *Manfred*). Like the tale, the novel was inspired largely by Polidori's travels with Byron. Its cast includes not one but two cari-
catures of Byron: one is a heartless seducer, the other only a
pompous nincompoop. Olivieri, the heartless seducer, is the
more detailed caricature of the two. (The woman he seduces
turns out to be his sister, in a scandalous allusion to Byron's affair
with Augusta Leigh.) That the younger and more innocent hero,
Ernestus, should come under the sway of this libertine provides
another parallel with the case of Aubrey and Strongmore, and
that of Polidori and Byron. Their friendship and rivalry again has
a marked homosocial quality; Ernestus's sister, Julia, for instance,
falls in love with Olivieri partly because of Ernestus's admiration
of him (131), and he seems to take an interest in her partly as a
way of getting at Ernestus (110). By the end of the novel, Olivieri
is less like Byron himself than like a guilt-ridden Byronic hero.
Just as Manfred, for example, asks the Witch of the Alps to "lay
[him] low" with the dead, "in any shape—in any hour— / With
any torture—so it be the last" (2.2.152-54), so Olivieri tells
Ernestus, "I shall be content to die, though on the wheel" (139).
The other Byronic figure, Count Wilhelm, the pompous nincompoop, plays only a tangential role in the plot and makes a much
simpler point. He is essentially a Childe Harold, much given to
"speaking with elegance upon the fallen glories of some sunken
nation" and deprecating the public attention he so assiduously
seeks (117), just as Byron unconvincingly claims, "I have not
loved the world, nor the world me" (*CHP* [1812-18] 3.113-14).

The novel's narrative strategy reflects Polidori's uneasy sense
of himself as an apprentice writer in the company of a figure like
Byron and of two other less famous but still imposing literary

geniuses. Polidori was always trying to interest his companions in his writing, and he was always failing. At a party in Dover, where some of Byron's friends had come to say goodbye before he crossed the Channel, Polidori "delivered [his] play into their hands" and "had to hear it laughed at" (*Diary* 30). In Geneva, when the ghost story project was apparently already under way, he produced this unfortunate drama again: "Shelley etc. came in the evening, talked of my play etc., which all agreed was worth nothing" (*Diary* 123). Fourteen years later, Mary Shelley recalled this evening—or a discouragingly similar one—for Thomas Moore's life of Byron. Byron agreed to read the play out loud, and

> In spite of the jealous watch kept upon every countenance by the author, it was impossible to withstand the smile lurking in the eye of the reader, whose only resource against the outbreak of his own laughter lay in lauding, from time to time, most vehemently, the sublimity of the verses;—particularly some that began "'Tis thus the goîter'd idiot of the Alps,"—and then adding, at the close of every such eulogy, "I assure you when I was in the Drury Lane Committee, much worse things were offered to us." (3:275-76)

Shelley's account of *Ernestus Berchtold* suggests that she did not remember Polidori's plot as well as her own reaction to his desire to join in the ghost story project: "Poor Polidori had some terrible idea ..." (1831, 355).

Most of *Ernestus Berchtold* is made up of the oral confessions of Ernestus, a Swiss patriot and veteran of the Napoleonic wars. We never learn with certainty who his listener is (he may be Ernestus's nephew) or why Ernestus is confiding in him, but we do learn something about his response to what he is hearing, and it is like Byron and the Shelleys' response to Polidori. Ernestus seems to fear that the young man will concentrate on the aesthetic defects in his narrative and ignore its deeper significance: "You may think I rest too much upon these instants of my life; but I dread to narrate my miseries; the recalling to memory anguish and grief racks my heart" (91). (Ernestus' apology is like Frankenstein's apology to Walton: "I fear, my friend, that I shall render myself tedious by dwelling on these preliminary circumstances; but they were days of comparative happiness, and I think of them with pleasure" [1818, 101].) Even if the young man understands what he is trying to say, Ernestus fears that he may simply laugh at it. After enumerating the good things his beloved Louisa has done for him—she has made him famous, saved his life and his honour, and restored his faith in God and his hope of an afterlife—he turns to his listener: "I know not your belief, your principles; you may sneer at the feeling which dictates my ranking the two last with the former ..." (126). *Ximenes* (1819), Polidori's only surviving play, has a religious theme (its original title, *The Modern Abraham*, anticipates the subtitles of *Frankenstein* and *Ernestus Berchtold*); if this was the play his listeners laughed at, Polidori may well have felt they were sneering at his religious beliefs.

Polidori has ingeniously dovetailed these autobiographical details with the novel's central theme. The young man's main function is to foreground Ernestus's difficulties in telling his story, and most of these difficulties have less to do with the attitude of the listener than with the content of the story. After marrying Louisa, Ernestus discovers that she is his sister. Polidori has given his novel the form of a spoken narrative in order to dramatize the unspeakability of incest.

Whenever Ernestus approaches the heart of his story, he is compelled to interrupt himself or to resort to circumlocution. After describing Louisa's pure love for her father, Doni, he adds that he wishes his relations with her had been purely fraternal: "Oh, if that smile had fallen upon myself, as it then fell upon her father, if I had only felt its cheering influence without that burning passion it has excited in this breast; but I must not anticipate my narration" (94). He reflects on his destiny in a passage reminiscent of *Manfred* (1.2.65-71): "My love has left me, a scattered pine amidst this desolate scene, but first it has destroyed all who were bound to me, my love has proved,—but I must preserve my strength,—I have horrors to relate ..." (101). By the time he describes his marriage, the accumulating context gives a sinister connotation to an otherwise conventional reference to the inexpressibility of happiness: "I cannot paint to you the delirious state of mind, in which the next months passed over my head" (148). Within a page, he makes that connotation explicit—or rather, he once again backs off just before making it explicit: "Louisa was mine—Louisa mine! But Heaven had not smiled upon our union—no, no. It was but the anger of a God veiled under the brightest hues. Louisa was my,—but I must relate the whole" (149). As it turns out, he cannot relate the whole. He gives his listener his father's written confession instead: "I cannot tell you more; read that damning tale, and then you may know what I dare, nay dare not rest upon" (151). Doni wrote the confession for the same reason Ernestus hands it on to the young man: he could not bear to confide in his children, and he could not even bear for them to read it until he was dead.

The same prohibition is enforced within the narrative. In addition to Louisa, Ernestus has an acknowledged sister, Julia, and Louisa has a brother, the Byronic Olivieri. Near the beginning of the novel, shortly after Ernestus first meets Louisa, the spirit of their mother appears to Julia, warning her that her brother is in danger, and adding that if she passes the warning on to him, she will share in his danger. (She disobeys this prohibition and becomes the object of Olivieri's attentions.) Her mother is unable to explain precisely what the danger is: "it was a vague threat, that seemed the more terrific, because it could not be decidedly represented to the mind" (91). Near the end of the novel, the mother appears to Ernestus. She warns him against ingratitude to Doni (a form of the filial rebellion that is the Œdipal counterpart to his incestuousness) and then vanishes, "with an expression of sorrow upon her face, as if she were not allowed to continue" (146).

When Ernestus begins to suspect that Olivieri has seduced Julia, he does not dare confide his suspicions to Louisa and Doni. When he tries to talk to Julia, she responds: "Oh! do not ask me, my shame must not be spoken" (117). When the seduced, abandoned, and dying Julia consigns her child to his care and tells him her story, she makes him promise not to tell it to Louisa and Doni, and this death-bed oath of silence is reminiscent of *The Vampyre* (131). (The child may grow up to become the young man to whom Ernestus tells his story.) When, after marrying Ernestus, Louisa first sees a portrait of his mother—the mother she does not remember—she is unable to explain the awe she feels (149). This portrait finally reveals the truth to Doni. The cost of disobeying the prohibition is high: writing his confession kills Doni, and the merest hint of its contents kills Louisa (151). (The motif of a fatal portrait may be adapted from "The Family Portraits.")

Doni's confession reveals that the complicated and disastrous history of his family is the result of a Faustian pact he made in his rash and selfish youth. The Faustian pact is sometimes (as in *Manfred*) associated with incest; partly because of this association and partly for more practical reasons, the pact becomes as unspeakable as incest itself. Doni does not describe his encounter with the evil spirit: "I could not without recording some part of the spells by which I raised this monster, and he has but too fully proved his power for me to be willing to put the least clue into the hands of any one which might bring the curse I have felt upon him" (164-65). His refusal is like Frankenstein's refusal to tell Walton how he made his monster: "'Are you mad, my friend?' said he, 'or whither does your senseless curiosity lead you? Would you also create for yourself and the world a demoniacal enemy?'" (1818, 231). Ernestus links the unspeakability of incest to that of magic when he says that Louisa's name "is now a spell that conjures up horrid thoughts" (97).

Despite the unspeakability of incest, what Ernestus finds most striking and attractive about Louisa is her voice. In one respect, he is atypical as the hero of a Romantic incest narrative: he has not grown up with Louisa, like Manfred and Astarte or Laon and Cythna (Richardson 739). Instead, he meets her as an adult (like Œdipus and Jocasta, or Byron and Augusta) and falls in love at first sight—or rather, at first hearing. He hears her before he ever sees her; she is singing in Italian, "that language which, in its very sound, breathes love" (73). When he meets her again, he is "so moved by her voice" that he can hardly speak (93). The self-deconstructing association of an irresistible voice with the unspeakable is clearly a part of Polidori's design. When the French invaders imprison Ernestus in the Château de Chillon, Louisa sings to him from a boat outside. Her voice manages both to harmonize with his feelings and to change them:

> Gradually stealing upon my ear, I heard a distant voice, which in melancholy notes seemed to sympathize with my sorrows. I listened; it approached; the measured strokes of an oar interrupted the heavenly strain; suddenly breaking into livelier notes it sung of hope; the voice was, they were Italian words, it was my vision's voice. It gradually sunk away into indistinct sounds. I seemed another being, hope breathed upon my heart, and Louisa wore the semblance of that enchanter....
> (99)

She also arranges for his escape. In Milan, he accompanies her on her charitable visits to hospitals. Although she is masked, the sick and dying never fail to recognize her: "they soon distinguished her powerful tones which pierced through the bond of grief around the most withered heart, and poured upon it those precious consolations afforded by her religion" (109). Her voice allows both the sick and Ernestus himself to "assimilat[e] feminine characteristics"—a process which is, according to Alan Richardson (747), the main benefit of Romantic incest. The novel presents hope, especially religious hope, as an essentially feminine virtue.

In Louisa's absence, Ernestus is seduced by a "syren" (111)—that is, a woman whose voice is the seductive opposite of hers—but Louisa saves him from vice as she has saved him from Chillon. Years after her death, her voice still echoes in his ears. When he rereads their favourite books, "every word again sounds upon my ear, as if she spoke it. I turn round and am undeceived, Louisa is not by my side, though her voice seems speaking as when we were innocent" (103). It is another part of Polidori's self-deconstructing design that this uplifting voice should have led Ernestus into guilt.

Louisa's voice is the echo of her mother's. When Ernestus comes to Milan, he hears Louisa's mother described, without realizing that she is his own mother:

> Her presence was commanding, but her voice was persuasive; its tones struck the heart and produced those emotions, which all remember, none can express, the feeling, as if we had been always virtuous, and were worthy of listening to the voice of a being superior to ourselves.... Louisa was her counterpart....
> (104)

Once again the power of the voice is associated with the unspeakable: none of the mother's auditors can express what her voice makes them feel.

The power of the voice is frequently associated with the incestuous in Romantic literature. When Manfred describes his sister Astarte, he lays more emphasis on her voice than on any other feature: "her eyes, / Her hair, her features, all, to the very tone / Even of her voice, they said were like to mine" (2.2.105-07). When the spirits summon up her ghost, he begs her to speak to him: "I would hear yet once before I perish / The voice which was my music" (2.4.134-35). When she answers him, he exclaims: "I live but in the sound—it is thy voice!" (2.4.151). The hero of Percy Shelley's *Alastor* (1815) is more than incestuous: his beloved is a visionary feminine version of himself. The first thing he notices about her is that "Her voice was like the voice of his own soul / Heard in the calm of thought" (153-54).

In *Frankenstein*, the power of the voice is associated not with literal incest or the autoeroticism of *Alastor* but with the friend or lover who is an ideal counterpart to the self. Walton thinks he has found such a friend when he rescues Frankenstein. Frankenstein's voice certainly harmonizes with Walton's dearest aspiration, to discover the Hyperborean zone: "Even the sailors feel the power of his eloquence: when he speaks, they no longer despair; he rouses their energies, and, while they hear his voice, they believe these vast mountains of ice are mole-hills, which will vanish before the resolutions of man" (1818, 235). When she revised her novel, Shelley added a number of references to the effects of this voice on Walton himself. He calls it "a voice whose varied intonations are soul-subduing music" (1831, 319). After he has decided to transcribe Frankenstein's story, he remarks: "Even now, as I commence my task, his full-toned voice swells in my ears" ([1831] 320) like Ernestus remembering Louisa as he rereads their favourite books.

Frankenstein himself feels the power of the voices of his best friend and his fiancée. On his trip to Britain where he will create a female monster, he is wracked with remorse and shrinks from human contact, but there is one exception: "the voice of Henry soothed me," because "in Clerval I saw the image of my former self" (1818, 183). He sees in Clerval an image of his Edenic youth, on which he, like Ernestus, likes to dwell. When Frankenstein's sufferings drive him mad, his cousin and fiancée, Elizabeth, not only recalls his former self but recalls him to himself: "her gentle voice would soothe me when transported by passion, and inspire me with human feelings when sunk in torpor" (1818, 213). After Elizabeth's death, and shortly before his own, he assures Walton: "wherever I am, the soothing voice of my Elizabeth, and the conversation of Clerval, will be ever whispered in my ear" (1818, 234).

In *Frankenstein*, as in *Ernestus Berchtold*, even the most high-minded voice can have disastrous effects. Professor Waldman of the University of Ingolstadt is one of the novel's most genial characters, and he has the sweetest voice Frankenstein has ever heard (1818, 76). But his lecture on the progress of chemistry seals Frankenstein's fate. The 1831 version of the novel includes a graphic description of the effect of his voice on his star pupil. It uses the same musical imagery that Polidori applies to Louisa's voice: "As he went on, I felt as if my soul were grappling with a palpable enemy; one by one the various keys were touched which formed the mechanism of my being: chord after chord was sounded, and soon my mind was filled with one thought, one conception, one purpose" (1831, 329). Like the hero of *Alastor*, Frankenstein is hearing the voice of his own soul.

Waldman's voice links Frankenstein's affections with his scientific work so that—as he confesses—work can take affection's place (1818, 83). Similarly, Louisa's voice links the two concerns of *Ernestus Berchtold* and the novel's two parts, the prologue devoted to the French invasion of Switzerland and the main narrative of magic and incest. Unlike *The Vampyre*, the novel places its Gothic and realistic elements in different compartments, but it is careful not to seal them off from each other. As William Patrick Day has pointed out, it is unusual for Gothic novels to address historical and political issues explicitly (*Circles* 33), and it is most unusual for them to integrate these issues with their central, psychological concerns as closely as *Ernestus Berchtold* does. Louisa first fills Ernestus not with incestuous love but with patriotism:

> I was suddenly struck with the sound of a voice, which I shall never, never forget. In unison with my feelings at that moment, the notes sometimes broke out into the wildest tones of defiance; at others, suddenly sinking, they seemed uncertain and soothing. I dared not look around; I felt as if entranced, and I imagined I heard the voice of these mountains, mocking the invaders, then sinking into despondence. (72-73)

Almost immediately, she accuses him of failing to hear his country's voice: she "asked me, why I was idling amidst these valleys, when my country called me to the post of danger" (73). He promptly leaves home to enlist. As a result, "the fame of Berchtold, Ernestus Berchtold, was echoed by the wild rocks to the voice of every peasant" (122).

Opposed to these patriotic voices are foreign voices, specifically French ones. At first, modified by a characteristically Swiss sound effect, they seem harmless, even seductive: "I burnt with the desire of viewing nearer those actions, which in our solitary village, echoing only a softened sound of their horrors, seemed to wear a certain air of grandeur and glory" (70). When the French have triumphed and captured Ernestus, he hears their voice more clearly: "Upon my name being mentioned the bridge [at Chillon] was lowered, and I soon heard the clash of the chains employed in raising it after me. It seemed to be accompanied by a voice that bade hope to leave me" (97). As we have seen, Louisa's voice of hope rescues him from this voice of Dantean despair.

Two subsidiary symbols help to link the novel's psychology and its politics, Ernestus's incest and his patriotism. The first is his mother's grave. His passionate love of Switzerland is based partly on his obscure sense that his mother has literally become part of the land. He spends much of his childhood decorating her grave with flowers, or lying on it with Julia, discussing the possibility of an afterlife; his patriotism is thus linked with the supernatural (67). When he returns from fighting the French, the grave is the first spot he visits (91).

The second subsidiary symbol is a "ribbond" or scarf that Ernestus asks Louisa to give him and that he wears into battle like a knight wearing his lady's favour—or a child clutching his security blanket (74). He has worn it ever since and shows the young man that it is still "bound round [his] heart" (75). Between these two literal references to the scarf, Ernestus makes it into a metaphor for his fate: "every moment since [receiving it from Louisa] has only served to weave closer round me the meshes of that net, which has shut me out from joy" (74). Soon after he receives Louisa's favour, he receives a parallel favour from his country, when the commander of the Swiss forces hangs a medal round his neck, presumably on a ribbon or scarf. Ernestus emphasizes the parallel: "I stood for a moment still; in one hand I held the medal, with the other I pressed the scarf of my unknown friend closer to my heart" (80). The scarf is associated with the unspeakability of incest when Olivieri, who has joined the Swiss forces as a volunteer, recognizes it but is too tactful to speak of it to Ernestus (81, 90). It is associated with the supernatural when Ernestus grasps it in the night to convince himself that Louisa is more than "an unsubstantial, supernatural vision" (77).

The French invasion of Switzerland in 1798 was a turning point for the first generation of English Romantics. It seemed glaringly hypocritical of the Revolutionaries to invade a country that had been free, peaceful, and at least partly democratic, for five hundred years. (The younger Romantics, who had been spared this disillusionment, retained a sympathy with the ideals of the Revolution, and Byron devoted much of the third canto of *Childe Harold's Pilgrimage*—another product of the summer of 1816—to a meditation on the character of Napoleon, with whom he partially identified. Polidori's critique of French imperialism is dovetailed with his caricature of Byron.) Coleridge's "France: An Ode" (1798) apologizes for his former Revolutionary sympathies in terms of the voice of freedom: "Forgive me, Freedom! O forgive those dreams! / I hear thy voice, I hear thy loud lament, / From bleak Helvetia's icy caverns sent" (64-66). At a later stage in the Napoleonic wars, Wordsworth wrote his "Thought of a Briton on the Subjugation of Switzerland" (1807):

Two Voices are there; one is of the sea,
One of the mountains; each a mighty Voice.
In both from age to age thou didst rejoice,
They were thy chosen music, Liberty! (1-4)

Now that the voice of the mountains has been silenced, it is all the more essential to preserve that of the sea, the voice of British liberty. These English Romantics share the association of the voice and freedom, paradoxically, with Rousseau, the Swiss philosopher who was credited with—or blamed for—inspiring the French Revolution (and who, like Napoleon, plays a major role in the third canto of *Childe Harold's Pilgrimage*). In the final chapter of the *Essay on the Origin of Languages* (1754), Rousseau remarks, "There are some tongues favorable to liberty. They are the sonorous, prosodic, harmonious tongues in which discourse can be understood from a great distance." He is thinking of the need for clarity in the popular assemblies that had governed ancient Athens and that still governed the democratic cantons of Switzerland. He thinks that Italian (the language in which Louisa inspires Ernestus to defend his country) may be such a tongue. French, however, can only be a tongue of tyranny: "any tongue with which one cannot make oneself understood to the people assembled is a slavish tongue. It is impossible for a people to remain free and speak that tongue" (72-73; cf. Derrida 168).

It is not surprising that these writers (or any writers) should choose a linguistic symbol for a major thematic complex. The voice is a peculiarly appropriate symbol for the sorts of affection they are interested in, at once unusually intense and unusually introverted—a passionate love for one's sister, as in *Ernestus Berchtold* or *Manfred*; or for an internal feminine counterpart to oneself, as in *Alastor*; for an external counterpart, as in *Frankenstein*; or for the motherland or ideology that has shaped the self, as in *Ernestus Berchtold*, "France: An Ode," and "Thought of a Briton"—because the voice is the most interior of all modes of expression, the one that retains the most intimate association with the speaker and achieves the greatest intimacy with the hearer. As one speaks, one hears one's voice inside one's head and feels it in one's breath (Derrida 166). The voice of the beloved echoes in the same interior space, enforcing a perfect harmony (Derrida 240). Derrida suggests that the erotic power of the voice has a specifically Œdipal source (235-36), and Louisa's voice is powerful because it is an echo of her mother's.

The taboo against speaking of incest, in these texts, is an attempt to prevent incest, because in these texts incest is consummated in the harmony of voices. According to Derrida, Rousseau thinks "language [and] history ... are born at the same time as the prohibition of incest" (265). Doni's written confession prohibits the incestuous relations between Ernestus and Louisa: it is the *non du père*, and, since it identifies him as their father, it is also the *nom du père*; it certainly has a castrating effect on Ernestus. Frankenstein's written account of the origin of his monster, and of his own horror at what he has done, plays a similar if less prominent role in Shelley's novel (1818, 155).

The myth of Prometheus is a myth of origins: Prometheus created humanity before giving it fire. The modern Prometheus discovers the origin of life, with disastrous consequences. The modern Œdipus, like the Œdipus of myth, discovers only the origin of his own life, but with almost equally disastrous consequences: five deaths in *Ernestus Berchtold*; seven, counting that of the monster, in *Frankenstein*.

Victor Frankenstein, the modern Prometheus, is of course also a modern Œdipus. Shelley's symbolic use of the voice hardly begins to suggest his incestuousness. In the first version of the novel, his fiancée is his cousin; in the second, though they are no longer related by blood, he calls her his "more than sister" (1831, 323). Immediately after the animation of his monster, he has a nightmare in which Elizabeth turns into the corpse of his mother in his arms—a detail that is not surprising, given that his mother, on her death-bed, has told Elizabeth both to take her place and to marry Victor. The animation of the monster is a more-than-incestuous act. Frankenstein insistently speaks of his research in sexual terms, and he explicitly says that he wants to be the monster's only parent. He begets it on himself (Cantor 110-11; Mellor 121-22). The fruit of this monstrous conception acts out the other half of the Œdipus complex for him, since, as a result of its crimes, his father dies of grief (Veeder 151-53).

Ernestus Berchtold, the modern Œdipus, is likewise a modern Prometheus. He and the other Swiss attempt to resist the French Revolutionaries who have usurped the Swiss title of democrats, just as the Titans resisted the usurping Olympians. Polidori's counter-revolutionary Prometheanism may even be more appropriate to the Greek myth than the revolutionary Prometheanism celebrated by Percy Shelley in *Prometheus Unbound* (1820) and criticized by Mary Shelley in *Frankenstein* (cf. Mellor 80-86). The Titans, after all, were the *ancien régime*. Ernestus ends up exiled in the Alps, like Prometheus nailed to the Caucasus, with the vulture of remorse preying on his vitals.

Doni is also a Promethean figure. His confession, which reveals the truth about Ernestus's marriage, corresponds to the secret that Prometheus reveals in order to obtain his release: if Zeus consummates his intended marriage to Thetis (to use the traditional euphemism), he will bring about his own downfall. Ernestus's marriage has already brought about his downfall, but the confession does bring about Doni's release from his sufferings, since writing it kills him.

The confession also corresponds to the gift of fire, which is often interpreted as a gift of forbidden knowledge or thought. At the beginning of *Prometheus Bound* (c.430 BC), Zeus's torturer Kratos (Might) accuses the Titan of stealing "fire, / Spark of all knowledge" (6-7); Prometheus himself claims that he has given humanity fire, "And with it knowledge" (254). *Prometheus Unbound* gives the idea a characteristically Romantic linguistic twist: Prometheus "gave man speech, and speech created thought" (2.4.72). This is sometimes seen as a gift of doubtful value. Byron says that "Prometheus stole from heaven / The fire which we endure," not enjoy (*Childe Harold's Pilgrimage* 4.163; cf. Cantor 123-24). The story of *Ernestus Berchtold* is the story of how Ernestus receives the gift that he must endure—the knowledge of his own origin—and of how he passes this gift on to his unnamed listener. After giving him Doni's manuscript, he urges him: "leave me, depart tomorrow upon your intended journey, if that you stay, who knows but the curse which has attended me through life may yet be acting, and may fall upon you as well as all others whom I have loved" (152). It may already be too late. The young man may leave his uncle with the fatal story of his origins ringing in his ears.

John William Polidori: A Brief Chronology

1795   JWP, oldest son of Gaetano Polidori and Anna
            Maria Pierce Polidori is born (7 September).

1804-09(?) JWP attends Ampleforth College, a school run by
            Benedictine monks north of York.

1811-15   JWP studies medicine at the University of Edin-
            burgh, graduating as the youngest MD in the uni-
            versity's history; his doctoral thesis is on sleep-
            walking.

1816   JWP publishes an essay "On the Punishment of
            Death"; Byron hires him as his personal physician
            (April); they travel through Belgium and Germany
            to Switzerland; they meet Percy Shelley, Mary
            Godwin, and Claire Clairmont in Geneva (27
            May); they agree to write ghost stories: after a
            conversation on the principle of life (15 June),
            Mary Shelley begins *Frankenstein* (16 June?);
            Byron begins the "Fragment" later completed by
            JWP as *The Vampyre* (17 June); JWP begins *Ernes-
            tus Berchtold* (18 June); Byron fires JWP, and he
            walks to Italy (September).

1816-17   JWP is expelled from Milan (30 October); travels
            to Bologna, Florence, and Arezzo, where he visits
            his uncle, the physician Luigi Polidori; to Pisa,
            where he studies with the surgeon Andrea Vaccà;
            to Rome (February); to Venice; returns to England
            (April).

1817-18   JWP attempts unsuccessfully to practice medicine
            in Norwich; suffers a disabling head injury (14
            September), which inspires *An Essay upon the
            Source of Positive Pleasure* (June 1818).

1819   JWP, in London, publishes *Ximenes*, a tragedy, and
            other poems; *The Vampyre* is published, without his
            permission or knowledge, as Byron's (1 April);
            JWP publishes *Ernestus Berchtold*.

1820   JWP gives up literature for the law; considers
            entering the priesthood.

1821   JWP publishes *The Fall of the Angels: A Sacred Poem*; visits Brighton; commits suicide over a gambling debt incurred there (24 August).

A Note on the Texts

The Vampyre was never published in a form with which the author was satisfied. The text's publishing history has been documented by Henry R. Viets. There is no record of the tale until its publication in the *New Monthly Magazine*; given Polidori's surprise at *The Vampyre*'s publication, it is extremely unlikely that he gave it to Henry Colburn, the publisher. It seems reasonable to postulate that John Mitford, whose "Extract of a Letter from Geneva, with Anecdotes of Lord Byron, &c." prefaced the *New Monthly Magazine* issue of *The Vampyre*, could have obtained the manuscript from "the lady" for whom Polidori wrote the tale (Macdonald 178).

While Polidori struggled to establish his rights to *The Vampyre*, the first of a series of book versions appeared, issued by Colburn and Company of Great Marlborough Street. According to Viets, there were six separate book texts of *The Vampyre* issued in London in 1819. Only the second publication mentions Polidori at all, and, even so, he shares the credit with Byron; the title-page reads "The Vampyre; a tale related by Lord Byron to Dr. Polidori." All other book states of the text either attribute the text to Byron, or simply omit an author altogether. A copy of the fifth book issue, housed in the Harvard College Library, is "bound with interleaves and contains corrections by Polidori for a presumed second edition" (Viets 102)—an edition that never appeared. Because Polidori was never given the opportunity to do so during his lifetime, we wish to present the reader with a text that accords, as closely as possible, with Polidori's latest determinable intentions for his published tale. The Harvard College text, then, with Polidori's holograph annotations of substantives and accidentals, is the copy text for this edition.

In editing the text, we have corrected three obvious typographical errors and expanded holograph ampersands and abbreviations such as "tho" to full words. In order to follow Polidori's obvious intentions for his holograph revisions, it has occasionally been necessary to emend. For example, on the first page of the tale, Polidori changed the vampire's "face" to his "finely turned head," but he did not actually cross out the word "face"; we have done so. He changed the vampire's name from "Ruthven" to "Strongmore," but he did not catch all the instances of "Ruthven" in the text; we have emended to "Strongmore" throughout. For a full account of Polidori's revisions and our emendations, we refer the reader to our University of Toronto Press edition (1994).

Polidori's only full-length novel, *Ernestus Berchtold; or, The Modern Œdipus*, was, like *The Vampyre*, published in 1819—but with his knowledge. Only one edition of the novel was published. Consequently, editing the text was straightforward. Longman did a poor job with *Ernestus Berchtold*; we have silently corrected some thirty obvious typographical errors ("sill" for "still," "retainining" for "retaining," etc.). We have also regularized Polidori's use of quotation marks, which vacillates between an eighteenth-century convention which does not separate speech markers like "he said" or "she said" from the actual speech, and the less ambiguous modern style. We have chosen the modern style, which Polidori uses more often. We have not otherwise regularized, standardized, or modernized either text.

THE VAMPYRE: A TALE

IT happened in the midst of the dissipations attendant upon a London winter, that there appeared at the various parties of the leaders of the *ton*[1] a nobleman, more remarkable for his singularities, than for his rank. He apparently gazed upon the mirth around him, as if he could not participate therein. It seemed as if, the light laughter of the fair only attracted his attention, that he might by a look quell it, and throw fear into those breasts where thoughtlessness reigned. Those who felt this sensation of awe, could not explain whence it arose: some attributed it to the glance of that dead grey eye, which, fixing upon the object's face, seemed not to penetrate, and at one look to pierce through to the inward workings of the heart; but to throw upon the cheek a leaden ray that weighed upon the skin it could not pass. Some however thought that it was caused by their fearing the observation of one, who by his colourless cheek, which never gained a warmer tint from the blush of conscious shame or from any powerful emotion, appeared to be above human feelings and sympathies, the fashionable names for frailties and sins. His peculiarities caused him to be invited to every house; all wished to see him, and those who had been accustomed to violent excitement, and now felt the weight of *ennui*, were pleased at having something in their presence capable of engaging their attention. Nay more in spite of the deadly hue of his finely turned head, many of the female hunters after notoriety attempted to win his attentions, and gain, at least, some marks of what they might term affection. Lady Mercer,[2] who had been the mockery of every monster shewn in drawing-rooms since her marriage, threw herself in his way, and did all but put on the dress of a mountebank, to attract his notice:—but in vain:—when she stood before him, though his eyes were apparently fixed upon her's, still it

---

1 The fashion, the vogue (French); by extension, people of fashion.
2 A caricature of Lady Caroline Lamb, who had once visited Byron disguised as a page, and who would later attend a masquerade dressed as Don Juan (Marchand 129, 321). Polidori borrowed the name "Ruthven" (the original name for his vampire) from Clarence de Ruthven, Lord Glenarvon, the villain of Lamb's novel *Glenarvon* (1816), an account of her affair with Byron. "Mercer" may be an equally insolent allusion to Margaret Mercer Elphinstone, who had been kind to Byron during the separation scandal. When he and his sister were snubbed at a party, she came up to him, "gave him a familiar nod, and said, 'You should have married *me*, and then this would not have happened to you!'" (Marchand 230-31).

seemed as if they were unperceived;—even her unappalled impudence was baffled, and she left the field. Yet though the common
adultress could not influence even the guidance of his eyes, it was
not that the sex was indifferent to him: but such was the caution
with which he spoke to the virtuous wife and innocent daughter,
that few knew he ever addressed himself to females. He had,
however, the reputation of a winning tongue; and whether it was
that this even overcame the dread of his singular character, or
that they were moved by his apparent hatred of vice, he was as
often among those females who adorn the sex by their domestic
virtues, as among those who sully it by their vices.

About the same time, there came to London a young gentleman of the name of Aubrey: he was an orphan left with an only
sister in the possession of great wealth, by parents who died
whilst he was yet in childhood. Left also to himself by guardians,
who thought it their duty merely to take care of his fortune, while
they relinquished the more important charge of his mind to the
care of mercenary and negligent subalterns, he cultivated more
his imagination than his judgment. He had, hence, that high
romantic feeling of honour and candour, which daily ruins so
many milliners' apprentices. He believed all to sympathise with
virtue, and thought that vice was thrown in by Providence as by
authors in Romances merely for the picturesque effect of the
scene: he thought that the misery of a cottage merely consisted in
the vesting of clothes, which were as warm, perhaps warmer than
the thin naked draperies of a drawing room, but which were more
pleasing to the painter's eye by their irregular folds and various
coloured patches. He thought, in fine, that the dreams of poets
were the realities of life. He was handsome, frank, and rich: for
these reasons, upon his entering into the gay circles, many
mothers surrounded him, striving which should describe with
least truth their languishing or romping favourites: many daughters at the same time, by their brightening countenances when he
approached, and by their sparkling eyes, when he opened his lips,
soon led him into false notions of his talents and his merit.
Attached as he was to the romance of his solitary hours, he was
startled at finding, that, except in the tallow and wax candles
flickering, not from the presence of a ghost, but from a draught
of air breaking through his golden leathered doors and felted
floors, there was no foundation in real life for any of that con-
geries of pleasing horrors and descriptions contained in the
volumes, which had formed the occupation of his midnight vigils.
Finding, however, some compensation in his gratified vanity, he

was about to relinquish his dreams, when the extraordinary being we have above described, crossed him in his career.

He watched him; the very impossibility of forming an idea of the character of a man entirely absorbed in himself, of one who gave few other signs of his observation of external objects, than the tacit assent to their existence, implied by the avoidance of their contact: at last allowed his imagination to picture some thing that flattered its propensity to extravagant ideas. He soon formed this person into the hero of a romance, and determined to observe the offspring of his fancy, rather than the individual before him. He became acquainted with him, paid him attentions, and so far advanced upon his notice, that his presence was always acknowledged. He gradually learnt that Lord Strongmore's affairs were embarrassed,[1] and soon found, from the notes of preparation in —— Street, that he was about to travel. Desirous of gaining some information respecting this singular character, who, till now, had only whetted his curiosity, he hinted to his guardians, that it was time for him to perform the grand tour, a tour which for many generations had been thought necessary to enable the young to take some important steps in the career of vice, put themselves upon an equality with the aged, and not allow them to appear as if fallen from the skies, whenever scandalous intrigues are mentioned as the subjects of pleasantry or of praise, according to the degree of skill shewn in their conduct. They consented: and Aubrey immediately mentioning his intentions to Lord Strongmore, was surprised to receive from him a proposal that they should travel together. Flattered by such a mark of esteem from him, who, apparently, had nothing in common with other men, he gladly accepted the invitation, and in a few days they had passed the circling waters.

Hitherto, Aubrey had had no opportunity of studying Lord Strongmore's character, and now he found, that, though many more of his actions were exposed to his view, the results offered different conclusions from the apparent motives to his conduct. His companion was profuse in his liberality;—the idle, the

1 There really was a Lord Ruthven; Polidori may have changed the name to Strongmore in order to make the tale less libellous as well as less obviously Byronic and more his own. The new name has connotations of phallic potency and size. Byron's affairs were so embarrassed at the time of his leaving England in 1816 that he had had to sell his books; he had to leave London early on the morning of 23 April in order to avoid the bailiffs (Marchand 230, 233-34).

vagabond, and the beggar, received from his hand more than enough to relieve their immediate wants. But Aubrey could not avoid remarking, that it was not upon the virtuous, reduced to indigence by the misfortunes attendant even upon virtue, that he bestowed his alms. These were sent from the door with hardly suppressed sneers; but when the profligate came to ask something, not to relieve his wants, but to allow him to wallow in his lust, or to sink him still deeper in his iniquity, he was sent away with rich charity. This was, however, attributed by him to the greater importunity of the vicious, which generally prevails over the retiring bashfulness of the virtuous indigent. There was one circumstance about the charity of his Lordship, which was however still more deeply impressed upon his mind: all those upon whom it was bestowed, inevitably found that there was a curse upon it, for they were all either led to the scaffold, or sunk to the lowest and the most abject misery. At Brussels and other towns through which they passed, Aubrey was surprized at the apparent eagerness, with which his companion sought for the centres of all fashionable vice; there he entered into all the spirit of the faro table.[1] He betted, and always gambled with success, except when the known sharper was his antagonist, and then he lost even more than he gained; but it was always with the same unchanging face, with which he generally watched the society around. It was not, however, so when he encountered the rash youthful novice, or the luckless father of a numerous family; then his very wish seemed fortune's law—his apparent abstractedness of mind was laid aside, and his eyes sparkled with vivid fire. In every town, he left the formerly affluent youth, torn from the circle he adorned, cursing, in the solitude of a dungeon, the fate that had drawn him within the reach of this fiend; whilst many a father sat frantic, amidst the speaking looks of mute hungry children, without a single florin of his late immense wealth, wherewith to buy even sufficient to satisfy their present craving. Yet he took no money from the gambling table; but immediately lost, to the ruiner of many, the last gilder he had just snatched from the convulsive grasp of the innocent. This might but be the result of a

---

1   Byron himself was not a great gambler, but he would express enthusiasm for gambling in a journal entry of 1821-22 (*Byron's Letters and Journals* 9:23). Faro is one of the oldest and simplest of card games. It is named after a picture of a pharaoh on a French deck of cards. It was a favourite of aristocrats in late-eighteenth- and early-nineteenth-century Europe.

certain degree of knowledge, which was not, however, capable of combating the cunning of the more experienced. Aubrey often wished to represent this to his friend, and beg him to resign that charity and pleasure which proved the ruin of all, and did not tend to his own profit;—but he delayed it—for each day he hoped his friend would give him some opportunity of speaking frankly and openly to him; this, however, never occurred. Lord Strongmore in his carriage,[1] and amidst the various wild and rich scenes of nature, was always the same: his eye spoke less than his lip; and though Aubrey was near the object of his curiosity, he obtained no greater gratification from it than the constant excitement of vainly wishing to break that mystery, which to his exalted imagination began to assume the appearance of something supernatural.

They soon arrived at Rome, and Aubrey for a time lost sight of his companion; he left him in daily attendance upon the morning circle of an Italian countess, whilst he went in search of the memorials of another almost deserted city. Whilst he was thus engaged, letters arrived from England, which he opened with eager impatience; the first was from his sister, breathing nothing but affection; the others were from his guardians, these astonished him; if it had before entered into his imagination, that, there was an evil power resident in his companion, these seemed to give him almost sufficient reason for the belief. His guardians insisted upon his immediately leaving his friend, and urged, that such a character was to be dreaded, for the possession of irresistible powers of seduction, rendered his licentious habits too dangerous to society. It had been discovered, that his contempt for the adultress had not originated in hatred of her character; but that he had required, to enhance his gratification, that his victim, the partner of his guilt, should be hurled from the pinnacle of unsullied virtue, down to the lowest abyss of infamy and degradation: in fine, that all those females whom he had sought, apparently on account of their virtue, had, since his departure, thrown even the mask aside, and had not scrupled to expose the whole deformity of their vices to the public view.

Aubrey determined upon leaving one, whose character had not yet shown a single bright point on which to rest the eye. He resolved to invent some plausible pretext for abandoning him

---

1 In 1816, despite his financial embarrassments, Byron travelled in an enormous and expensive replica of Napoleon's carriage (Marchand 232). He still had not paid for it when he died, eight years later.

altogether, purposing, in the mean while, to watch him more closely, and to let no slight circumstances pass by unnoticed. He entered into the same circle, and soon perceived, that his Lordship was endeavouring to work upon the inexperience of the daughter of the lady whose house he chiefly frequented. In Italy, it is seldom that an unmarried female is met with in society; he was therefore obliged to carry on his plans in secret; but Aubrey's eye followed him in all his windings, and soon discovered that an assignation had been made, which would most likely end in the ruin of an innocent, though thoughtless girl. Losing no time, he entered the apartment of Lord Strongmore, and abruptly asked him his intentions with respect to the lady, informing him at the same time that he was aware of his being about to meet her that very night. Lord Strongmore answered, that his intentions were such as he supposed all would have upon such an occasion; and upon being pressed whether he intended to marry her, merely laughed. Aubrey retired; and, immediately writing a note, to say, that from that moment he must decline accompanying his Lordship in the remainder of their purposed tour, he ordered his servant to seek other apartments, and calling upon the mother of the lady, informed her of all he knew, not only with regard to her daughter, but also with regard to the character of his Lordship. The meeting was prevented. Lord Strongmore next day merely sent his servant to notify his complete assent to a separation;[1] but did not hint any suspicion of his plans having been foiled by Aubrey's interposition.

Having left Rome, Aubrey directed his steps towards Greece, and crossing the Peninsula, soon found himself at Athens. He there fixed his residence in the house of a Greek; and was soon occupied in tracing the faded records of ancient glory upon monuments that apparently, ashamed of chronicling the deeds of freemen only before slaves,[2] had hidden themselves beneath the sheltering soil or many coloured lichen. Under the same roof as himself, existed a being, so beautiful and delicate, that she might have formed the model for a painter, wishing to portray on canvass the promised hope of the faithful in Mahomet's paradise,[3] save that her eyes spoke too much mind for any one to

---

1 Possibly an allusion to Byron's recent separation.
2 The contrast between the ancient glory and the modern degradation of the Greeks was commonplace. Byron had exploited it both in *Childe Harold's Pilgrimage* (2.10, 74-76) and in *The Giaour* (103-41).
3 The houris: see Qur'an 44.51-59, 55.56.

think she could belong to those beings who had no souls. As she danced upon the plain, or tripped along the mountain's side, one would have thought the gazelle a poor type of her beauties; for who would have exchanged her eye, apparently the eye of animated nature, for that sleepy luxurious look of the animal suited but to the taste of an epicure.[1] The light step of Ianthe[2] often accompanied Aubrey in his search after antiquities, and often would the unconscious girl, engaged in the pursuit of a Kashmere butterfly,[3] show the whole beauty of her form, floating as it were upon the wind, to the eager gaze of him, who forgot, in the contemplation of her sylph-like figure, the letters he had just decyphered upon an almost effaced tablet. Often would her tresses falling, as she flitted around, exhibit in the sun's ray such delicately brilliant and swiftly fading hues, as might well excuse the forgetfulness of the antiquary, who let escape from his mind the very object he had before thought of vital importance to the proper interpretation of a passage in Pausanias.[4] But why attempt to describe charms which all feel, but none can appreciate?—It was innocence, youth, and beauty, unaffected by crowded drawing-rooms and stifling balls. Whilst he drew those remains of which he wished to preserve a memorial for his future hours, she would stand by, and watch the magic effects of his pencil, in tracing the scenes of her native place; she would then describe to him the circling dance upon the open plain, would paint to him in all the glowing colours of youthful memory, the marriage pomp she remembered viewing in her infancy; and then, turning to subjects that had evidently made a greater impression upon her mind, would tell him all the supernatural tales of her nurse. Her earnestness and apparent belief of what she narrated, excited

---

1 Cf. Byron, *The Giaour* (473-92) and Byron's note to 490. As Byron points out, Islam (despite Western misconceptions) does not teach that women have no souls.

2 The first two cantos of *Childe Harold's Pilgrimage* are dedicated to "Ianthe," the eleven-year-old Lady Charlotte Harley, daughter of Byron's lover Lady Oxford. He describes her eye as "wild as the Gazelle's" (Ded. 28). The name means "Flower of the Narcissus" (*The Complete Poetical Works* 2:272-73).

3 Cf. *The Giaour* (388-99).

4 The author (fl. AD 143-76) of *Description of Greece*, an encyclopaedic work covering Greek history, topography, daily life, customs and rites, legends and folklore, and especially works of art, so that antiquarians used it as a guide to ruins.

the interest even of Aubrey; and often as she told him the tale of
the living vampyre, who had passed years amidst his friends, and
dearest ties, forced every year, by feeding upon the life of a lovely
female to prolong his existence for the ensuing months, his blood
would run cold, whilst he attempted to laugh her out of such idle
and horrible fantasies. But Ianthe cited to him the names of old
men, who had at last detected one living among themselves, after
several of their near relatives and children had been found
marked with the stamp of the fiend's appetite. When she found
him incredulous, she begged of him to believe her, for it had been
remarked, that those who had dared to question their existence,
always had some proof given, which obliged them, with grief and
heartbreaking, to confess its truth. She detailed to him the traditional appearance of these monsters, and his horror was
increased, upon hearing a pretty accurate description of Lord
Strongmore. He, however, still persisted in persuading her, that
there could be no truth in her fears, though at the same time he
wondered at the many coincidences which had all tended to
excite a belief in the supernatural power of Lord Strongmore.

Aubrey began to attach himself more and more to Ianthe; her
innocence, so contrasted with all the affected virtues of the
women amongst whom he had sought for his vision of romance,
won his heart; and while he ridiculed the idea of a young man of
English habits, marrying an uneducated Greek girl, still he found
himself more and more attached to the almost fairy form before
him. He would tear himself at times from her, and, forming a
plan for some antiquarian research, he would depart, determined
not to return until his object was attained; but he always found it
impossible to fix his attention upon the ruins around him, whilst
in his mind he retained an image that seemed alone the rightful
possessor of his thoughts. Ianthe was unconscious of his love, and
was ever the same frank infantile being he had first known. She
always seemed to part from him with reluctance; but it was
because she had no longer any one with whom she could visit her
favourite haunts, to whom she could point out the beauties of the
spots so dear to her infantile memory, whilst he was occupied in
sketching or uncovering some fragment which had yet escaped
the destructive hand of time. She had appealed to her parents on
the subject of Vampyres, and they both, with several present,
affirmed their existence, pale with horror at the very name. Soon
after, Aubrey determined to proceed upon one of his excursions,
which was to detain him for a few hours; when his hosts heard the
name of the place, they all at once begged of him not to return at

night, as he must necessarily pass through a wood, where no Greek would ever remain, after the day had closed, upon any consideration. They described it as the resort of the vampyres in their nocturnal orgies, and denounced the most heavy evils as impending upon him who dared to cross their path. Aubrey made light of their representations, and tried to laugh them out of the idea; but when he saw them shudder at his daring thus to mock a superior, infernal power, the very name of which apparently made their blood freeze, he was silent.

Next morning Aubrey set off upon his excursion unattended; he was surprised to observe the melancholy face of his host, and was concerned to find that his words, mocking the belief of these horrible fiends, had inspired them with such terror. When he was about to depart, Ianthe came to the side of his horse, and earnestly begged of him to return, ere night allowed the power of these beings to be put in action;—he promised. He was, however, so occupied in his research, that he did not perceive that day-light would soon end, and that in the horizon there was one of those specks which, in the warmer climates, so rapidly gather into a tremendous mass, and pour all their rage upon the devoted country.—He at last, however, mounted his horse, determined to make up by speed for his delay: but it was too late. Twilight, in these southern climates, is almost unknown; immediately the sun sets, night begins: and ere he had advanced far, the power of the storm was above—its echoing thunders had scarcely an interval of rest—its thick heavy rain forced its way through the canopying foliage, whilst the blue forked lightning seemed to fall and radiate at his very feet. Suddenly his horse took fright, and he was carried with dreadful rapidity through the entangled forest. The animal at last, through fatigue, fell, and he found, by the glare of lightning, that he was in the neighbourhood of a hovel which hardly lifted itself up from the masses of dead leaves and brushwood surrounding it. Dismounting, he approached, hoping to find some one to guide him to the town, or at least trusting to obtain shelter from the pelting of the storm. When near the door, the thunders, for a moment silent, allowed him to hear the dreadful shrieks of a woman mingling with the stifled, exultant mockery of a laugh, continued in one almost unbroken sound;—he was startled: but, roused by the thunder which again rolled over his head, he, with a sudden effort, forced open the door of the hut. He found himself in utter darkness: the sound, however, guided him. He was apparently unperceived; for, though he called, still the sounds continued, and no notice was taken of him. He found himself in contact with some one, whom he immediately seized; when a voice cried, "Again baffled!" to which a loud laugh succeeded; and he felt himself grappled by one whose strength seemed superhuman: determined to sell his life as dearly as he could, he struggled; but it was in vain: he was lifted from his feet and hurled with enormous force against the ground.—His enemy threw himself upon him, and kneeling upon his breast, had placed his hands upon his throat—when the glare of many torches penetrating through the hole that gave light in the day, disturbed him.—He instantly rose, leaving his prey, he rushed through the door, and in a moment the crashing of the branches, as he broke through the wood, was no longer heard. The storm was now still; and Aubrey, incapable of moving, was soon heard by those without. They entered; the light of their torches fell upon nothing but the mud walls, and the thatch loaded on every individual straw with heavy flakes of soot, though at this moment it was apparently untenanted. There was one spot slippery with blood but it was hardly visible on the black floor. No other trace was seen of human presence having disturbed its solitude for many years. At the desire of Aubrey they searched for her who had attracted him by her cries; he was again left in darkness; but what was his horror, when the light of the torches once more burst upon him, to perceive the airy form of his fair conductress brought in a lifeless corpse. He shut his eyes, hoping that it was but a vision arising from his disturbed imagination; but he again saw the same form, when he unclosed them, stretched by his side. There was no colour upon her cheek, not even upon her lip; yet there was a stillness about her face that seemed almost as attaching as the life that once dwelt there:—upon her neck and breast was blood, and upon her throat were the marks of teeth having opened the vein of the neck:—to this the men pointed, crying, simultaneously struck with horror, "A Vampyre! a Vampyre!"

A litter was quickly formed, and Aubrey was laid by the side of her who had lately been to him the object of so many bright and fairy visions, now fallen with the flower of life that had died within her. He knew not what his thoughts were—his mind was benumbed and seemed to shun reflection, and take refuge in vacancy—he held almost unconsciously in his hand a naked dagger of a particular construction, which had been found in the hut. They were soon met by different parties who had been engaged in the search of her whom a mother had missed. Their lamentable cries, as they approached the city, forewarned the parents of some dreadful catastrophe.—To describe their grief would be impossible; but when they ascertained the cause of their child's death, they looked at Aubrey, and pointed to the corpse. They were inconsolable; both died broken-hearted.

Aubrey being put to bed was seized with a most violent fever, and was often delirious; in these intervals he would call upon Lord Strongmore and upon Ianthe—by some unaccountable combination he seemed to beg of his former companion to spare the being he loved. At other times he would imprecate maledictions upon his head, and curse him as her destroyer. Lord Strongmore chanced at this time to arrive at Athens, and, from whatever motive, upon hearing of the state of Aubrey, immediately placed himself in the same house, and became his constant attendant. When the latter recovered from his delirium, he was horrified and startled at the sight of him whose image he had now combined with that of a Vampyre; but Lord Strongmore, by his kind words, implying almost repentance for the fault that had caused their separation, and still more by the attention, anxiety, and care which he showed, soon reconciled him to his presence. His lordship seemed quite changed; he no longer appeared that apathetic being who had so astonished Aubrey; but as soon as his convalescence began to be rapid, he again gradually retired into the same state of mind, and Aubrey perceived no difference from the former man, except that at times he was surprised to meet his gaze fixed intently upon him, with a smile of malicious exultation playing upon his lips: he knew not why, but this smile haunted him. During the last stage of the invalid's recovery, Lord Strongmore was apparently engaged in watching the tideless waves raised by the cooling breeze, or in marking the progress of those orbs, circling, like our world, the moveless sun;—indeed, he appeared to wish to avoid the eyes of all.

Aubrey's mind, by this shock, was much weakened, and that elasticity of spirit which had once so distinguished him now seemed to have fled for ever. He was now as much a lover of solitude and silence as Lord Strongmore; but much as he wished for solitude, his mind could not find it in the neighbourhood of Athens; if he sought it amidst the ruins he had formerly frequented, Ianthe's form stood by his side—if he sought it in the woods, her light step would sound wandering amidst the underwood, in quest of the modest violet; and often she would suddenly turning round, show, to his wild imagination, her pale face and wounded throat, while a meek smile played upon her lips. He determined to fly scenes, every feature of which created such bitter associations in his mind. He proposed to Lord Strongmore, to whom he held himself bound by the tender care he had taken of him during his illness, that they should visit those parts of Greece neither had yet seen. They travelled in every direction, and sought every spot to which a recollection could be attached: but though they thus hastened from place to place, yet they seemed not to heed what they gazed upon. They heard much of robbers,[1] but they gradually began to slight these reports, which they imagined were only the invention of individuals, whose interest it was to excite the generosity of those, whom they defended from pretended dangers. In consequence of thus neglecting the advice of the inhabitants, they travelled on one occasion with only a few guards, more to serve as guides than as a defence. Upon entering, however, a narrow defile, at the bottom of which was the bed of a torrent, with large masses of rock brought down from the neighbouring precipices, they had reason to repent their negligence; for scarcely were the whole of the party engaged in the narrow pass, when they were startled by the echoed report of several guns, and by the whistling of bullets close to their heads. In an instant their guards had left them, and, placing themselves behind rocks, had begun to fire in the direction whence the report came. Lord Strongmore and Aubrey, imitating their example, retired for a moment behind the sheltering turn of the defile: but ashamed of being thus detained by a foe, who with insulting shouts bade them advance, and being exposed to unresisting slaughter, if any of the robbers should climb above and take them in the rear, they determined at once to rush forward in search of the enemy. Hardly had they lost the shelter of the rock, when Lord Strongmore received a shot in the shoulder, which brought him to the ground. Aubrey hastened to his assistance; and, no longer heeding the contest or his own peril, was soon surprised by seeing the robbers' faces around him—his guards having, upon Lord Strongmore's being wounded, immediately thrown up their arms and surrendered.

By promises of great reward, Aubrey soon induced them to convey his wounded friend to a neighbouring cabin; and having agreed upon a ransom, he was no more disturbed by their presence—they being content merely to guard the entrance until their comrade should return with the promised sum, for which he had an order. Lord Strongmore's strength rapidly decreased; in two days mortification ensued, and death seemed advancing with hasty

1 Byron had had a narrow escape from robbers on an excursion from Athens to Cape Colonna in December 1810 (*BLJ* 2:30-31).

steps. His conduct and appearance had not changed; he seemed as
unconscious of pain as he had been of the objects about him: but
towards the close of the last evening, his mind became apparently
uneasy, and his eye often fixed upon Aubrey, who was induced to
offer his assistance with more than usual earnestness—"Assist me!
you may save me—you may do more than that—I mean not my
life, I heed the death of my existence as little as that of the passing
day; but you may save my honour, your friend's honour."—"How?
tell me how? I would do any thing," replied Aubrey.—"I need but
little—my life ebbs apace—I cannot explain the whole—but if you
would conceal all you know of me, my honour were free from stain
in the world's mouth—and if my death were unknown for some
time in England—I—I—but life."—"It shall not be known."—
"Swear!" cried the dying man, raising himself with exultant violence, "Swear by all your soul reveres, by all your nature dreads,
swear that for a year and a day you will not impart your knowledge
of my crimes or death to any living being, in any way, whatever may
happen, or whatever you may see."—His eyes seemed bursting
from their sockets: "I swear!" said Aubrey; he sunk laughing upon
his pillow, and breathed no more.[1]

Aubrey retired to rest, but did not sleep; the many circumstances attending his acquaintance with this man arose upon his
mind, and, he knew not why, when he remembered his oath a
cold shivering came over him, as if from the presentiment of
something horrible awaiting him. Rising early in the morning, he
was about to enter the hovel, in which he had left the corpse,
when a robber met him, and informed him that it was no longer
there, having been conveyed by himself and comrades, upon his
retiring, to the pinnacle of a neighbouring mount, according to a
promise they had given his lordship, that it should be exposed to
the first cold ray of the moon that rose after his death.[2] Aubrey

---

1   The incident of the oath and death is the closest point of contact
    between Polidori's tale and Byron's fragment (Appendix A.2). Byron's
    oath, in turn, is based on the many similar oaths in *Fantasmagoriana*
    (Appendix A.1.a-b). Behind them all, perhaps, is the oath of silence in
    Hamlet (1.5.146-95). Polidori has heightened Byron's rhetoric; his oath,
    like Shakespeare's, is at once highly emotional and highly ritualized.

2   This simple technique of resuscitation replaces the elaborate ring cere-
    mony in Byron's fragment. Polidori seems to have made up the idea that
    a dead vampire could be revived by moonlight. As a doctor, he was
    probably aware that it reversed the old Galenic notion that moonlight
    accelerated the decomposition of dead bodies (Ariès 360).

was astonished, but taking several of the men, he determined to go and bury it upon the spot where it lay. When however he reached the summit he found no trace of the corpse, nor could he discover any remnant of the clothes, though the robbers assured him that they pointed out the identical rock on which they had laid the body. For a time his mind was bewildered in conjectures, but he at last returned, convinced that they had secretly buried his friend's remains for the sake of the dress in which he died.

Weary of a country in which he had met with such terrible misfortunes, and in which all apparently conspired to heighten that superstitious melancholy which had seized upon his mind, he resolved to leave it, and he soon arrived at Smyrna. While waiting for a vessel to convey him to Otranto,[1] or to Naples, he occupied himself in arranging those effects he had with him belonging to Lord Strongmore. Amongst other things there was a case containing several weapons of offence, more or less adapted to ensure the death of the victim. There were several daggers and ataghans.[2] Whilst turning these over, and examining their curious forms, what was his surprise at finding a sheath apparently ornamented in the same style as the dagger discovered in the fatal hut—he shuddered—hastening to gain further proof, he found the weapon, and his horror may be imagined, when he discovered that it fitted, though peculiarly shaped, the sheath he held in his hand. His eyes seemed to need no further certainty— they seemed gazing to be bound to the dagger; yet still he wished not to believe his sight; but the particular form, the varying tints upon the haft and sheath were alike, and left no room for doubt; there were also drops of blood on each.

He left Smyrna, and on his way home, at Rome, he inquired concerning the lady he had attempted to snatch from Lord Strongmore's seductive arts. Her parents were in distress, their fortune ruined, and she had not been heard of since the departure of his lordship. Aubrey's mind became almost broken under so many repeated horrors; he was afraid that this lady had fallen a victim to the destroyer of Ianthe. He became morose and silent; and his only thought seemed to be how to urge the speed of the

1 A port in southern Italy, the setting of *The Castle of Otranto* (1764), by Horace Walpole, the first Gothic novel.
2 In a note to *The Giaour* (355), Byron describes an ataghan as "a long dagger worn with pistols in the belt, in a metal scabbard, generally of silver; and, among the wealthier, gilt, or of gold" (*CPW* 3:418).

postilions, as if he were hastening to save the life of some one he held dear. He arrived at Calais; a breeze, which seemed obedient to his will, soon wafted him to the English shores. He hastened to the mansion of his fathers, and there, for a moment, he appeared to lose, in the embraces and caresses of his sister, all memory of the past. If she before, by her infantine caresses, had gained his affection, now that the woman began to appear, she was still more attaching as a companion.

Miss Aubrey had not that winning grace which gains the gaze and applause of the drawing-room assemblies. There was none of that ephemeral brilliancy which can only exist in the heated atmosphere of a crowded apartment. Her blue eye was never lit up by the levity of the mind beneath. There was a melancholy charm about it which did not seem to arise from misfortune, but from some feeling within, that appeared to indicate a soul conscious of a brighter realm. Her step was not that light footing, which strays where'er a butterfly or a colour may attract—it was sedate and pensive. When alone, her face was never brightened by the smile of joy; but when her brother breathed to her his affection, and would in her presence forget those griefs she knew destroyed his rest, who would have exchanged her smile for that of the voluptuary? It seemed as if those eyes,—that face were then playing in the light of their own native sphere. She was yet only eighteen, and had not yet been presented to the world, her guardians having thought proper to delay her presentation at court until her brother's return from the continent, when he might be her protector. It was now, therefore, resolved that the next drawing-room,[1] which was fast approaching, should be the epoch of her entry into the "busy scene."[2] Aubrey would rather have remained in the mansion of his fathers, to feed upon the melancholy which overpowered him. He could not feel interest about the frivolities of fashionable strangers, when his mind had been so torn by the events he had witnessed; but he determined to sacrifice his own comfort to the protection of his sister. They

---

1 "A levee held in a drawing room; a formal reception by a king, queen, or person of rank; that at which ladies are 'presented' at court" (*OED*).

2 This is not a very distinctive phrase—the quotation marks may mark it as a cliché rather than a quotation—but it does occur in the same context (a young woman's début in society after her brother's return from a journey) in Frances Sheridan's *Memoirs of Miss Sidney Bidulph* (1761): "It was just on his return to England that the busy scene of his sister's life opened" (9).

therefore soon arrived in town, and prepared for the day, which
had been announced as the one on which a drawing-room was to
be held.

The crowd was excessive—a drawing-room had not been held
for a long time, and all who were anxious to bask in the smile of
royalty, hastened thither. Aubrey was there with his sister. While
he was standing in a corner by himself, heedless of all around
him, engaged in the recollection that the first time he had seen
Lord Strongmore was in this very place—he felt himself suddenly
seized by the arm, and a voice he recognized too well, sounded in
his ear—"Remember your oath."[1] He had hardly courage to turn,
fearful of seeing a spectre, that would blast him, when he perceived, at a little distance, the same figure which had attracted his
notice on this spot upon his first entry into society. He gazed till
his limbs almost refusing to bear their weight, he was obliged to
take the arm of a friend, and forcing a passage through the
crowd, to throw himself into his carriage, and be driven home.
He paced the room with hurried steps, and fixed his hands upon
his head, as if he were afraid his thoughts were bursting from his
brain. Lord Strongmore again before him—circumstances
started up in dreadful array—the dagger—his oath.—He roused
himself, he could not believe it possible—the dead rise again!—
He thought his imagination had conjured up the image his mind
was resting upon. It was impossible that it could be real—he
determined, therefore, to go again into society; for though he
attempted to ask concerning Lord Strongmore, the name hung
upon his lips, and he could not succeed in gaining information.
He went a few nights after with his sister to the assembly of a near
relation. Leaving her under the protection of a matron, he retired
into a recess, and there gave himself up to his own devouring
thoughts. Perceiving, at last, that many were retiring, he roused
himself, and entering another room, found his sister surrounded
by several gentlemen, apparently in earnest conversation; he
attempted to pass and get near her, when one, whom he
requested to move, turned round, and revealed to him those features he most abhorred. He sprang forward, seized his sister's

---

1 Another not-very-distinctive phrase, but Polidori may have remembered
  it from Sir Walter Scott's *Guy Mannering* (1815), which he and Byron
  had both read, and in which, as in his tale, there is a reference to an
  oath of silence (384). Polidori may also be thinking of a phrase from
  Lamb's *Glenarvon* (1816): "Lady Margaret reminded him of his vow;
  and a fearful silence ensued" (15; chap. 4).

arm, and, with a hurried step, forced her towards the street: at the door he found himself impeded by the crowd of servants, who were waiting for their lords; and while he was engaged in passing them, he again heard that voice whisper close to him—"Remember your oath!"—He did not dare to turn, but, hurrying his sister, he soon reached home.

Aubrey became almost distracted. If before his mind had been absorbed by one subject, how much more completely was it engrossed now, that the certainty of the monster's living again pressed upon his thoughts. His sister's attentions were now unheeded, and it was in vain that she intreated him to explain to her what had caused his abrupt conduct. He only uttered a few words, and those terrified her. The more he thought, the more he was bewildered. His oath startled him;—was he then to allow this monster to roam, bearing ruin upon his breath, amidst all he held dear, and not avert its progress? His very sister might have been touched by him. But even if he were to break his oath, and disclose his suspicions, who would believe him? He thought of employing his own hand to free the world from such a wretch; but death, he remembered, had been already mocked. For days he remained in this state; shut up in his room, he saw no one, and eat[1] only when his sister came, who, her eyes streaming with tears, besought him, for her sake, to support nature. At last, no longer capable of bearing stillness and solitude, he left his house, roamed from street to street, anxious to fly that image which haunted him. His dress became neglected, and he wandered, as often exposed to the noon-day sun as to the mid-night damps. He was no longer to be recognized; at first he returned with the evening to his home; but at last he laid him down to rest wherever fatigue overtook him. His sister, anxious for his safety, employed people to follow him; but they were soon distanced by him, who fled from a pursuer swifter than any—from thought. His conduct, however, suddenly changed. Struck with the idea that he left by his absence the whole of his friends, with a fiend amongst them, of whose presence they were unconscious, he determined to enter again into society, and watch him closely, anxious to forewarn, in spite of his oath, all whom Lord Strongmore should approach with intimacy. But when he entered into a room, his haggard and suspicious looks were so striking, his inward shudderings so visible, that his sister was at last obliged to

---

1 Then the standard past tense of the verb: "ate."

beg of him to abstain from seeking, for her sake, a society, which affected him so strongly. When, however, remonstrance proved unavailing, the guardians thought proper to interpose, and, fearing that his mind was becoming alienated, they thought it high time to resume again that trust, which had been before imposed upon them by Aubrey's parents.

Desirous of saving him from the injuries and sufferings he had daily encountered in his wanderings, and of preventing him from exposing to the general eye those marks of what they considered folly, they engaged a physician to reside in the house, and take constant care of him. He hardly appeared to notice it, so completely was his mind absorbed by one terrible subject. His incoherence became at last so great, that he was confined to his chamber. There he would often lie for days, incapable of being roused. He had become emaciated, his eyes had attained a glassy lustre;—the only sign of affection and recollection remaining displayed itself upon the entry of his sister; then he would sometimes start, and, seizing her hands, with looks that severely afflicted her, he would desire her not to touch him. "Oh, do not touch him—if your love for me is aught, do not go near him!" When, however, she inquired to whom he referred, his only answer was, "True! true!" and again he sank into a state, whence not even she could rouse him. This lasted many months: gradually, however, as the year was passing, his incoherences became less frequent, and his mind threw off a portion of its gloom, whilst his guardians observed, that several times in the day he would count upon his fingers a definite number, and then smile.

The time had nearly elapsed, when, upon the last day of the year, one of his guardians entering his room, began to converse with his physician upon the melancholy circumstance of Aubrey's being in so awful a situation, when his sister was going next day to be married. Instantly Aubrey's attention was attracted; he asked anxiously to whom. Glad of this mark of returning intellect, of which they feared he had been deprived, they mentioned the name of the Earl of Marsden. Thinking this was a young Earl whom he had met with in society, Aubrey seemed pleased, and astonished them still more by expressing his intention to be present at the nuptials, and by desiring to see his sister. They answered not, but in a few minutes his sister was with him. He was apparently again capable of being affected by the influence of her lovely smile; for he pressed her to his breast, and kissed her cheek, wet with tears, flowing at the thought of her brother's being once more alive to the feelings of affection. He began to speak with all his ~~wonted~~ warmth, and to congratulate her upon her marriage with a person so distinguished for rank and every accomplishment; but he suddenly perceived a locket upon her breast; having opened it, what was his surprise at beholding the features of the monster who had so long influenced his life. He seized the portrait in a paroxysm of rage, and trampled it under foot. Upon her asking him, why he thus destroyed the resemblance of her future husband, he looked as if he did not understand her—then seizing her hands, and gazing on her with a frantic expression of countenance, he bade her swear that she would never wed this monster, for he—But he could not continue—it seemed as if that voice again bade him remember his oath—he turned suddenly round, thinking Lord Strongmore was near him but he saw no one. In the meantime the guardians and physician, who had heard the whole, and thought this was but a return of his disorder, entered, and forcing him from Miss Aubrey, desired her to leave him. He fell upon his knees to them, he implored, he begged of them to delay but for one day. They, attributing this to the insanity, they imagined had taken possession of his mind, endeavoured to pacify him, and retired.

Lord Strongmore had called the morning after the drawing-room, and had been refused with every one else. When he heard of Aubrey's ill health, he readily understood himself to be the cause of it; but, when he learned that he was deemed insane, his exultation and pleasure could hardly be concealed from those, among whom he had gained this information. He hastened to the house of his former companion, and, by constant attendance, and the pretence of great affection for her brother and interest in his fate, he gradually won the ear of Miss Aubrey. Who could resist his power? His tongue had dangers and toils to recount[1]—could speak of himself as of an individual having no sympathy with any being on the crowded earth, save with her, to whom he addressed himself;—could tell how, since he knew her, his existence had begun to seem worthy of preservation, if it were merely that he might listen to her soothing accents.—In fine, he knew so well how to use the serpent's art,[2] or such was the will of fate, that he gained her affections. The title of the elder branch falling at length to him, he obtained an important embassy, which served

---

1 A reminiscence of Othello's courtship of Desdemona (1.3.128-70), also recalled in *Glenarvon* (34; chap. 9).
2 Cf. Genesis 3.

as an excuse (in spite of her brother's deranged state), for hastening the marriage, which was to take place the very day before
his departure for the continent.

Aubrey, when he was left by the physician and his guardians,
attempted to bribe the servants, but in vain. He asked for pen
and paper; it was given him; he wrote a letter to his sister, con-
juring her, as she valued her own happiness, her own honour,
and the honour of those now in the grave, who once held her in
their arms as their hope and the hope of their house, to delay but
for a few hours that marriage, on which he denounced the most
heavy curses. The servants promised they would deliver it; but
giving it to the physician, he thought it better not to harass any
more the mind of Miss Aubrey by, what he considered, the
ravings of a maniac. Night passed on without rest to the busy
inmates of the house; and Aubrey heard, with a horror that may
more easily be conceived than described, the notes of busy
preparation. Morning came, and the sound of carriages broke
upon his ear. Aubrey grew almost frantic. The curiosity of the
servants at last overcame their vigilance, they gradually stole
away, leaving him in the custody of an helpless old woman. He
seized the opportunity, with one bound was out of the room, and
in a moment found himself in the apartment where all were
nearly assembled. Lord Strongmore was the first to perceive
him: he immediately approached, and, taking his arm by force,
hurried him from the room, speechless with rage. When on the
staircase, Lord Strongmore whispered in his ear—"Remember
your oath, and know, if not my bride to day, your sister is dishonoured. Women are frail!"[1] So saying, he pushed him towards
his attendants, who, roused by the old woman, had come in
search of him. Aubrey could no longer support himself; his rage
not finding vent, had broken a blood-vessel,[2] and he was conveyed to bed. This was not mentioned to his sister, who was not
present when he entered, as the physician was afraid of agitating
her. The marriage was solemnized, and the bride and bride-
groom left London.

Aubrey's weakness increased; the effusion of blood produced
symptoms of the near approach of death. He desired his sister's

---

1   In *Glenarvon*, Viviani/Glenarvon remarks that the heroine, Calantha, "is
    a woman, and as such, she must be frail" (69; chap. 21).
2   Haidée also dies of a broken blood-vessel in Byron, *Don Juan* 4.59-69
    (1821).

guardians might be called, and, when the midnight hour had struck, he related composedly the substance of what the reader has perused—and died immediately after.

The guardians hastened to protect Miss Aubrey; but when they arrived, it was too late. Lord Strongmore had disappeared, and Aubrey's sister had glutted the thirst of a VAMPYRE![1]

---

1   Strongmore's escape left room for a sequel, and in November 1819 Polidori reported to his sister: "I have just written to Longman to see if they would undertake to buy a second part of the *Vampyre* from me—as I must have something to engage my mind & I now find nothing to do" (Macdonald 173). Nothing came of the plan.

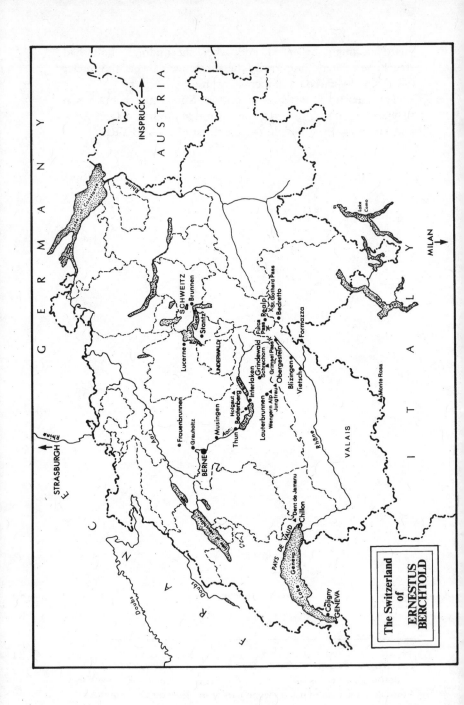

The Switzerland
of
**ERNESTUS
BERCHTOLD**

ERNESTUS BERCHTOLD;

OR, THE MODERN ŒDIPUS

JOHN WILLIAM POLIDORI, M.D.

"The gods are just—
But how can finite measure infinite?
Reason! alas, it does not know itself!
Yet man, vain man, would with this short-lin'd plummet
Fathom the vast abyss of heavenly justice.
Whatever is, is in its causes just,
Since all things are by fate, but purblind man
Sees but a part o' the chain, the nearest links
His eyes not carrying to that equal beam
That poises all above."

DRYDEN'S ŒDIPUS[1]

Leila—each thought was only thine!—
My good, my guilt, my weal, my woe,
My hope on high—my all below.
Then deem it evil—what thou wilt—
But say, oh say, *hers* was not guilt.—

THE GIAOUR[2]

---

1 John Dryden and Nathaniel Lee, *Oedipus* 3.1.239-48. Polidori mistakenly has "basis" for "chain" in 246.
2 Byron, *The Giaour* 1181-83, 1143-44.

INTRODUCTION

THE tale here presented to the public is the one I began at Coligny, when Frankenstein was planned, and when a noble author having determined to descend from his lofty range, gave up a few hours to a tale of terror, and wrote the fragment published at the end of Mazeppa.[1] Though I cannot boast of the horrible imagination of the one, or the elegant classical style of the latter, still I hope the reader will not throw mine away, because it is not equal to these. Whether the use I have made of supernatural agency, and the colouring I have given to the mind of Ernestus Berchtold, are original or not, I leave to the more erudite in novels and romances to declare. I am not conscious of having seen any where a prototype of either; yet I fear that whatever is original, is not always pleasing. Nor is this my only apprehension. A tale that rests upon improbabilities, must generally disgust a rational mind; I am therefore afraid that, though I have thrown the superior agency into the back ground as much as was in my power, still, that many readers will think the same moral, and the same colouring, might have been given to characters acting under the ordinary agencies of life; I believe it, but I had agreed to write a supernatural tale, and that does not allow of a completely every-day narrative.

THE AUTHOR.

---

1 "The tale which lately appeared, and to which his lordship's name was wrongfully attached, was founded upon the ground-work upon which this fragment was to have been continued. Two friends were to travel from England into Greece; while there, one of them should die, but before his death, should obtain from his friend an oath of secrecy with regard to his decease. Some short time after, the remaining traveller returning to his native country, should be startled at perceiving his former companion moving about in society, and should be horrified at finding that he made love to his former friend's sister. Upon this foundation I built the Vampyre, at the request of a lady, who denied the possibility of such a ground-work forming the outline of a tale which should bear the slightest appearance of probability. In the course of three mornings, I produced that tale, and left it with her. From thence it appears to have fallen into the hands of some person, who sent it to the Editor in such a way, as to leave it so doubtful from his words, whether it was his lordship's or not, that I found some difficulty in vindicating it to myself. These circumstances were stated in a letter sent to the Morning Chronicle three days after the publication of the tale, but in consequence of the publishers representing to me that they were compromised as well as myself, and that immediately they were certain it was mine, that they themselves would wish to make the *amende honorable* to the public, I allowed them to recall the letter which had lain some days at that paper's office." (J.W.P.) [For Byron's fragment, see Appendix A.2.]

PART FIRST

UPON the left side of the lake of Thun lies the small village of Beatenberg, which, under the care of a simple pastor contains no individual above the rank of a peasant: it was in this village that I was born./Misfortune seemed to be anxious at my very birth to stamp me for its own.—Just at the termination of the short war between Austria and Prussia, of the year 1778,[1] my mother arrived at this village in company with a gentleman severely wounded, as he said, in the slight skirmishes, which had alone formed the military display of this campaign. There was a mystery about them, which they seemed to wish should not be unravelled. The worthy pastor,[2] therefore, whom I have since called father, did not make any inquiries of his guests, though it appeared to him very singular, that the most difficult and steep roads should have been preferred for the route of an invalid towards his home. The tender care of my mother towards this gentleman was exemplary; it seemed as if that courage and firmness, which was wanting in his breast, had taken refuge in her's. They were not Swiss, for the language they spoke was unknown to Berchtold the parish priest. They apparently understood German and French; but they said so very little, and that with such evident embarrassment, that nothing could be learnt from their conversation. There being no inn at the solitary Beatenberg, the pastor, with his usual kindness, on hearing of the arrival of strangers at the close of the evening, had immediately waited on them to offer his services and house. They were to have been his guests, only for the night; but the fatigue of the journey again

---

1   The two empires had been rivals since the accession of Maria Theresa and Frederick II (both 1740). In 1778, Joseph II, Maria Theresa's son and co-regent, initiated hostilities in the hope of winning Bavaria from Prussia to offset the loss of Lower Silesia in the War of the Austrian Succession. The results were inconclusive, and a peace treaty was signed in 1779.

2   The elder Berchtold seems to be modelled on a priest Polidori met on his journey from Geneva to Milan in September 1816: "At Brieg I sent for the curate, a good old man of sixty. We conversed together in Latin for two hours; not at all troublesome in enquiries, but kind in answering them." Eventually, he "Left me in sight of Brieg, telling me he hoped to see me again in heaven" (*Diary* 160-61). In the meantime, the curate had told Polidori a number of stories about the French invasion, most of which made their way into *Ernestus Berchtold.*

forced open the wound in the gentleman's side; determined, however, to proceed, he attempted to walk to the litter prepared for him; the exertion proved too great, he fell into my mother's arms, and almost instantly expired.

My mother was distracted; already far advanced in pregnancy, she fell upon the body, no longer capable of that firmness and resolution, which she had shown, when her companion's safety depended upon it. She listened to no one; but frantic, she sat by the dead body, alternately shedding tears, and bursting into a loud laugh. Berchtold urged those soothing doctrines of which he was minister, but in vain; he spoke in vain of another world, of future hope; none could like him, soothe the pillow of the dying peasant, but here were miseries no hope could assuage. She at last fell exhausted upon the ground, she was conveyed to bed, and in a few hours I and a sister saw the light. But this did not allay her grief, she sunk into a silence that nothing could induce her to break; her eyes were fixed, and she at last died without a struggle. She was buried by him, whom Berchtold imagined, in spite of the disparity of his years, to have been her husband; and over their grave were placed those simple crosses, which you must have seen in the neighbouring church-yards. The pastor could not place any inscription upon their tomb, for he had been so engaged in attendance upon my mother, that he had not noticed the departure of her only servant, who took with him every thing of value belonging to his former mistress. He knew not what to do, there was no clue in his hands by which he could restore us to our family; for there was nothing to be found, except some linen and a locket, with my mother's portrait.

Berchtold was a man whose humble endeavours had always been engaged in the attempt to fulfill those duties his profession imposed upon him. In these mountainous districts, the office of a parish priest is extremely arduous; he is often called up in the middle of the night, while the snow is falling, to go many miles over the frozen glaciers, to administer to the dying peasant the sacraments of the church. Berchtold never allowed the most distant hamlet to want religious comfort; he was old, yet often has he crossed to the foot of the Holgaut, merely to help the unfortunate in their attempt at resignation, under domestic calamity. He was not, therefore, likely to cast us from him; he immediately had us conveyed to the cottage of a married sister, and caused us to be brought up as luxuriously as an Alpine village allowed.

I remember little of my early years, it seems, that I have vague visions of an age, when were spent whole days in gathering flowers, to adorn my sister's head and breast, from the precipitous bank that descends to the lake, when, at night, I was lulled half trembling, to sleep by the tales of my foster-mother concerning ogres and spirits from the dead. But all this is indistinct. When about six years of age, I was removed to the house of Berchtold. He called me son, and if the tenderest care and the greatest sacrifices could entitle him to the name of father, which I gave him, it was not wrongfully bestowed. One of the first circumstances which I can remember, is that one day, while sitting with him upon a bank, near the church-yard, gazing on the scene around, and watching the white sails which gleamed upon the lake beneath our feet; I threw my arms around his neck, and asked him, "Why they called me orphan?" He told me that my father and mother were dead. Retreating from him, I started, and trembling, asked him if he were then dead? He did not at first understand me; but upon my calling him by the name of father, he remembered that I had never heard the history of my birth. He took me to his breast, and weeping, told me, that I was indeed an orphan, that I was not his child. He then took me to the church-yard, and pointing to the raised sod, he told me my parents were there. I did not clearly understand him. I had then no idea of death; my mother, for so I called his sister, had told me tales of the dead,[1] but these terrified without being understood. All the graves, save those of my parents, were adorned with flowers; upon my remarking this to him, he told me that they having died strangers there, none were bound to love them. I was hurt to see those flowers, which though faded, showed the attention of some living being, refused to my mother's tomb; it sunk deeply on my mind. And for years after, I felt a vague pleasure in strewing their graves with the fresh flowers that formerly were employed in adorning my sister's head. Often have I laid myself down looking upon their grassy covering, as if I expected that some of those tales of my mother would be realised with regard to myself, and that I should see them rising from their grave. My sister soon joined me in these meditations, and almost the first infantile communications which passed between us, rested upon another world. She would sit by me, and often the worthy pastor surprised us, after the sun had set, calling to our memory those tales we had heard when with our foster mother.

---

1   The title of Utterson's translation of *Fantasmagoriana*; see Appendix B.2.

We did not mingle with the other children of the village, for we delighted too much in each other's company; we spent hours together in talking about what had in a most unaccountable manner taken possession of our minds, or else we gamboled round Berchtold. He, debarred by his religion from the enjoyment of a domestic circle of his own children, had formed so strong an attachment to us, that his greatest delight was, when not engaged in his parochial duties, to join us in our games and infantile occupations. With all the simplicity of old age, he would lie down and allow us to play with his white locks, or tell us stories, which, though of a different nature from those of his sister, did not interest us the less. He was a good classical scholar, and was well versed in the history of his own country. From these sources he drew his tales, and at an early age he inspired me with an ardent love for independence and liberty, at the same time that he instilled into my heart, a burning thirst for the means of asserting a superiority over my equals. The anecdotes of Themistocles, Alcibiades and others, upon whom the fates of their country had depended, rested on my mind.[1] Berchtold described to me the fallen glories of Rome, of that nation which once held sway over the known world. In short there was a material defect in my education, which is not uncommon, my imagination was stimulated, while my judgment was not called forth,[2] and I was taught to admire public instead of private virtues. I rested upon those situations which one in the million attains, and in which the passions of others are to be guided, while I was not shown how to conduct myself, when my own inclinations and feelings might attempt to lead me astray in the common occurrences of life. With a strongly susceptible mind I imbibed deeply these first impressions, and throughout life this defect in my education has followed me. As I advanced in age, I gradually became acquainted with the Latin and Greek historians. Berchtold rashly, though innocently, took advantage of my thirst for relations of battles and deeds of renown, to induce me to learn. I consequently had Plutarch and Livy in my hands, long

---

1 Themistocles (c.524-c.460 BC) was the great Athenian commander of the Persian War; Alcibiades (c.450-404 BC), of the Peloponnesian War; but they were both accused of personal misconduct.

2 These two faculties are often contrasted in eighteenth-century literature: see Joseph Addison (1672-1719), *Spectator* 35 (10 April 1711); and Sir Richard Steele (1672-1729), *Spectator* 136 (6 August 1711) and 167 (11 September 1711).

before I read any book tending to give man the power of regulating his passions.[1]

I joined the villagers only in those military exercises, which are constantly performed after the day's labour in every hamlet. Sometimes I would go with the chamois hunter,[2] and reaching the higher ridges of the Alps, whose snowy summits were visible from the lake, I forced myself to follow him in his venturous pursuit. But it for a long time required a strong exertion of my mind to induce me to venture amidst the vast solitudes of eternal snows. I always felt an inward shuddering and awe at the sight of my native wildnesses. Even now I cannot bear to listen to those, who, amongst our magnificent scenes, which man has not yet overcome, and which mock his power, can talk of pleasure, and dwell upon the beauty of the scenery. I cannot feel this. I seem always to crouch beneath some invisible being whose power is infinite,[3] and which I am conscious I cannot resist. It seems that I hear him laughing audibly at our vain attempts to encroach upon his dominion. It appears to me as if the avalanche were but the weapon of his impatience, while he insidiously steals upon those habitations he has covered with his snows, by the silent, gradual approach of the glaciers. Let mankind labour for ages upon these ribs of the world, and their work shall not be seen. The pyramids might rise unnoticed upon the rocks before my view, undistinguished from the fragment that falls unperceived with the passing torrent. I cannot bear that human strength should be unable to stamp its hand upon these towering memorials of convulsions we could not influence, could not hope to controul. This morbid feeling may have been excited by my foster mother constantly pointing to the Jungfrau, whose white peak forms so prominent a feature in the view from her house, while she related the peasant's tale of those mischievous spirits who dance upon its glittering icy coat, decked by the moon's ray.[4] I gained, however, health and vigour from these excursions, and I became at last one of the most noted for activity in all the canton.

---

1 Plutarch (AD 46?-120?), author of *Parallel Lives*; Titus Livius (59 BC-AD 17), author of *Roman History*.
2 Cf. W. Wordsworth, *Descriptive Sketches* (1793) 366-71; and Byron, *Manfred* (1817) 2.1.11-12.
3 Cf. P.B. Shelley, "Mont Blanc" (1816) 96-97; and *Manfred* 1.1.60-75.
4 Cf. *Manfred* 2.3.1-4. The Jungfrau was not ascended until 1811, so that to the young Ernestus it would still be beyond human reach.

I rapidly arrived at my twentieth year. My kind friend the pastor could not be induced to part with me. I was the only prop of his old age, I latterly, always accompanied him in his visits amongst the mountains, often joined him in his prayer over the dying, and frequently have I supported him at the brink of that grave, over which he was calling down the mercy of God, and which was soon to be his own refuge. My sister increased in beauty, and each day added some new charm to her person, and some additional accomplishment to her mind. I often represented to my father that I was of an age when I should begin to do something, and attempt to take the burthen of myself and my sister off his hands. He would agree with me in my arguments, but when the moment came, he was always so overpowered with sorrow, that I could not induce myself to leave him for the few remaining days he had to live.

I seldom visited Thun or Interlaken; I did not feel pleasure in the society of men. I there found them engaged in all the petty interests, which pervade human breasts in the narrow sphere of a miserable provincial town. I found they could not sympathise with one whom they looked upon as a wild romantic mountaineer. About this time the French revolution began to exalt my imagination even more than the history of nations gone by, and I burnt with the desire of viewing nearer those actions, which in our solitary village, echoing only a softened sound of their horrors, seemed to wear a certain air of grandeur and glory. I ardently wished to join those soldiers who had driven back the foreign invaders from their native plains. I little thought then how soon I was to be engaged in resisting these very men, amidst my own native mountains.

When the discussions between Berne and the French concerning the Pays de Vaud[1] arrested the attention of all, anxious to

---

1   The Vaud had been a subject territory of the canton of Berne for more than 200 years, so that news of the French Revolution was received more favourably there than elsewhere in Switzerland. On 28 December 1797, the French Directory promised its protection to any Vaudois who rose against Berne; the Vaudois revolution began on 2 January 1798. Its demands were moderate, but Berne refused to discuss them. On 23 January, the French General Ménard invited the Vaudois to proclaim their independence from Berne; that night, they did so. On the twenty-fifth, Ménard sent an ultimatum to the Bernese, telling them to withdraw from the territory; the envoy bearing the ultimatum was attacked, and Ménard invaded. He reached Lausanne on the twenty-ninth and was enthusiastically received. Enthusiasm waned, however, with the imposition of French war taxes and conscription, and some Vaudois fought for Berne until its fall in March (Godet 7:61-63).

be amongst men in action, and tired of my total want of employment, I again begged my friend to let me depart to the capital; but still, at his prayer, I remained with him. I laid myself down upon the snow, shining as it then was in the first rays of spring, and abandoned myself to visions of battle and renown. My spirits gradually left me, there was a craving for exertion about me, which I found it impossible to overcome. I seized my gun, and going amidst the eternal glaciers and rocks, I sought by forcing myself to exert my body, to lose this feeling of vacuity. But I often lost sight of the chamois, engaged in the thought of my country, and bounded from rock to rock, no longer occupied with what I imagined was before me. My sister would endeavour to sooth me by her caresses. I told her of my visions with regard to my country's cause, and at moments excited even in her breast the sparks of enthusiasm. But she generally echoed Berchtold's sentiments with regard to the indecision and incapacity of the government.

Tired one evening of listening to Berchtold, who attempted to repress my ardour, by representing to me that the country was betrayed, and that, in consequence of the tardiness and imbecility of the rulers of Switzerland, in spite of the courage and daring of its peasantry, it was doomed to become an easy prey to France,[1] I left him determined again to seek refuge in the chase. I accordingly set out the next morning, intending to remain several days amongst the mountains; but I grew listless, and at the close of the second day, I still found myself upon the Wengern Alp. I issued forth from the chalet where I had taken some refreshment, and soon lost myself in

---

1 The governments of the cantons might be blamed for not preventing internal unrest by instituting reforms (Bonjour 219; Zschokke 169), but, even if they had done so, they would probably have been helpless against the great powers, which were then dividing Europe among themselves, and which were not committed to preserving Swiss neutrality. As Talleyrand would write in August 1798, "Switzerland today must be either Austrian or French" (Palmer 2:413). To make matters more difficult, Austria was Switzerland's traditional enemy, while France was an old ally (Bonjour 213-14). *The History of the Invasion of Switzerland* (1803), by J.H.D. Zschokke, is mainly concerned with the democratic cantons in the East; Polidori read it and applied some of Zschokke's remarks, not always appropriately, to the aristocratic canton of Berne. Zschokke does comment on the military advantages that the eastern cantons lost through delays, or tardiness (263), and he accuses the government of Uri of "imbecility" for refusing to join forces with the other cantons (249).

reflection. I now looked with pleasure upon the Jungfrau's white head, glistening on the blue canopy of heaven. All the horrors of the Grindewald at my feet, the high summit of the Schrechorn, with the echoing thunders of the numerous avalanches, no longer appalled me. It seemed as if they now put on their terrors against a presumptuous foe, in defence of their children. There was no cloud upon the dark blue sky,—there was no mist upon the rocks; and though the snow still covered the whole surface of the mountains around, still there was a genial warmth and splendour in the sun's reflected ray, that vivified and strengthened. There was no sound, save that of the distant cataract, and falling avalanche. I stood a long time leaning upon my musket, to look upon this scene. How could avarice hope to find a resting place in the minds of those nursed amidst such objects?[1] How could slavery expect to find its votaries resident amidst such fortresses? The tyrant could not dare to add these horrors of nature to those already revelling in his breast. A slave who shrinks before the frown of a despot, could not stand erect amidst these awful monuments of a power that mocks at human prowess. Upon this occasion, it seemed as if the sun threw its proudest ray upon these rocks; they had seen, might hope to see, men worthy of gazing upon that nature which, lifting unappalled its head amidst the thundering clouds, had snatched their weapon from their grasp, and had thrown it at its feet, while, with its snowy head, it struck in defiance the arching canopy of heaven. I was thus engaged in thought, which but served to increase my indignation at the conduct of men, who sacrificed to personal interest the safety of their country, when I was suddenly struck with the sound of a voice, which I shall never, never forget. In unison with my feelings at that moment, the notes sometimes broke out into the wildest tones of defiance;[2] at others, suddenly sinking, they seemed uncertain and

---

1 In 1816, Polidori wrote to his radical friend William Taylor (1756-
  1836): "I do not know whether you were in Switzerland to me it is not
  interesting magnificent scenery with petty souls every thing around me
  should elevate the souls of the natives liberty such as it is has debased
  them an attention to petty trifles with a neglect of noble ends.... Indeed
  every part of the dwelling places of mankind that I have yet seen seem
  to contain men not modified by the situation except in clothing all one
  mass of insensible brutifi[e]d matter" (Macdonald 79). Zschokke,
  however, claims that: "Ambition and avarice found no aliment in those
  peaceful valleys ..." (16).
2 Zschokke stresses the way that "patriotic songs accompanied with military music" inspired the Swiss to resist (250 and n.).

soothing. I dared not look around; I felt as if entranced, and I imagined I heard the voice of these mountains, mocking the invaders, then sinking into despondence. Gradually the voice approached,—I could distinguish words.—I heard footsteps. I suddenly turned round, and beheld a figure; I cannot describe it to you. Arrayed in a dress foreign to these mountains, her white drapery, breathed on by the wanton breeze, now betrayed the delicate form of her limbs,—now hid them from my sight. Her dark eye seemed exultingly to gaze upon my native rocks, while the wild notes of defiance played upon her lips. She suddenly saw me, and was silent. She looked around, as if for some one; and I then perceived, at a little distance, a man worn down more by grief than by age. I approached, and re-assured her. She blushed, and in that language which, in its very sound, breathes love, told me that she did not understand me. I could not answer; but, gazing on her, I seemed to be fascinated by her words. The old man approached, and we soon entered into conversation. I spoke Italian fluently; her surprize and pleasure cannot be painted, when she heard me address her father in her native language. I walked by her side, and I was often so lost in thought, that I was obliged to answer, by an unmeaning yes or no, the questions of the old man. Our conversation at last turned upon Switzerland; he seemed to be perfectly conversant with its situation. She entered with enthusiasm into its cause, and asked me, why I was idling amidst these valleys, when my country called me to the post of danger.[1] These simple words from her lips caused an emotion in my breast that drew the blood to my cheeks. She thought of me. I at once promised to join my countrymen tomorrow. She then told me, that orders had arrived at the neighbouring towns for an instant levy to join the army of d'Erlach, which it was expected would be immediately brought into action.[2]

I was yet walking by her side, when we arrived at Lauterbrunnen. At the gate of a small cottage, after having asked me to

---

1 Zschokke reports that when the women of Schwyz "met with a coward who sought to withdraw himself by flight from the danger of his country, they stopped him, and forced him to return to the frontier, and take his place in the ranks of the army" (296).
2 Karl-Ludwig d'Erlach (1746-98) was a member of an old and patrician Bernese family. He had been an officer of the Swiss Guard in Paris, the colonel of a regiment of dragoons, and a member of the Bernese Council of Two Hundred. He was commander-in-chief of the Bernese forces when he was killed at Ober Wichtrach on 5 March 1798 (Godet 3:7).

take some refreshment, which I declined, they bade me farewell.
There was a carriage waiting at the door. The thought rushed
upon my mind that I might never see her again. I know not by
what impulse, but, ignorant of the forms of the world, I summoned courage, at the moment of parting, to ask of her a ribbond
with which she was playing;[1] that, as I said, I might wear it in
remembrance of her who had made me decide upon joining the
patriots. Blushing, she looked at her father, who smiled consent,
and she bound round my arm the scarf which she had worn
during the morning. I have often heard that song again; I have
often seen that form; and many are the years I have worn that
scarf:—they have been years of misery and grief. Memory has no
moment to look back to between the present and that happy day.
Yet, for such another moment of enthusiasm I would undergo all
my miseries afresh. I revert to it as the Arab, in the midst of the
rising sands, turns to his visions of the green speck upon the
desert's sandy ocean; amidst dangers, that is his hope; in anguish,
that is his refuge. That moment seemed to bestow upon me the
happiness which my fancy had so long pictured in the future. But
every moment since has only served to weave closer round me the
meshes of that net, which has shut me out from joy. I then,
however, felt as if time no longer weighed upon me; and I was
grieved, when arriving at my father's door, I found that the joys
of hours had passed as those of a minute.

I found my sister in tears; Berchtold, with his grey locks hiding
the hands covering his face. Hearing my footsteps, my aged father
rose, and taking me in his arms, with tears in his eyes, he told me,
that he could no longer take upon himself to hinder me from
joining my countrymen in the sacred cause of independence. He
bade me take leave of my sister, and, while my courage remained,
to surmount the pang of bidding her farewell. He told me, that
he had caused my sister to prepare every thing for a parting,
which he feared was to be our last. He embraced me, and rushed
out of the house. My sister's eyes, wet with tears, now turned
upon me, anxious to show the same resolution as my father had
displayed, she hastened my departure. She gave me my gun and
powder flask,—bound round my waist more than half the savings
of Berchtold; and kissing me, bade me farewell. Bewildered by
the rapidity of my different emotions, I hurried to the side of the

---

1 According to Zschokke, the patriotic women of Schwyz "adopted as a
   mark of distinction a knot of white ribbon round the head" (295-96).

lake, looked once more up the steep mountain, on the ascent of
which Beatenberg raised its white cottages, and, turning the point
of land which encroached upon the lake, I was soon wafted, in
company with many others, towards the town of Thun. I did not
heed the white sails hurrying along the blue rippling waves. I
could not gaze upon the rich cultivated scenery of the lake.[1] My
mind was straying midst those wild glaciers, that once had been
my horror,—which to-day had shewn me the unknown. Why does
fate cause the approaches of misery to be decked with all the
show of promised happiness? From this moment begins my
eventful history; till now I had only been in the hands of the foul
fiends that have tormented me, as plastic clay, which they formed
in that manner, best fitted to contain the miseries they were
preparing to pour upon it.[2] You may think I have rested too much
upon my early years, which passed without action; but those
years saw deposited in my breast the seeds which have brought
me to the state of apathy and misery you witness. That vision has
proved to me the harbinger of more woes than it promised pleasures, and that scarf, which you see is yet bound round my heart,
has felt it beat more violently through anguish, than it did even
through hope, at the moment it first encircled my arm. My life till
now had passed in dreams. I had not known the rude blast of
worldly interests; I had been unconscious of the activity of the
bad passions, and had only viewed man in the shape of my foster-
father, breaking by his presence the shackles of grief that
restrained the energies of his children, as the sun destroys the icy
bonds that bind the vital powers of the spring. In the cause of
charity and virtue, I had seen employed those powers and that
activity which, exerted in a less degree, have often excited the
admiration of the multitude, and concealed follies, nay, crimes,
from even the philosopher in that halo of fame they bring around
them. The earliest impressions, I received, were those from my
foster-mother's tales, and they have not left me even at present;
how much less, when but entering on manhood. I had so often

---

1 Polidori had been greatly impressed by it in 1816. "The views the most
   beautiful I ever saw; through pines over precipices, torrents ... and the
   best-cultivated fields I ever saw. The lake sometimes some hundred precipitous feet below my feet; at other times quite close to its edge; boats
   coming from the fair; picturesque towered villages; fine Alps on the
   other side, the Jungfrau and others far off. The bottom of the lake is
   especially magnificent" (*Diary* 156).
2 Cf. Homer, *Iliad* 24.527-33.

gazed upon my mother's picture, which my sister wore round her neck from her earliest infancy, that, while sitting by her tomb, it seemed as if her image had haunted me in my sleep, for I frequently found myself arguing as if I had had actual proof of the existence of beings superior to ourselves.

The evening had closed before I arrived at Thun. The town was crowded with the peasantry of the neighbouring mountains; there were fires throughout the streets, around which stood the aged and the boy, the mother and the virgin. They were all come to offer their arms in defence of their country.[1] I approached the town-house; the door was crowded with petitioners, who were attempting to induce the sentinel to give them precedence in the enrolment of their names. I stood for some time watching the earnestness with which the aged laid hold of their very weakness and uselessness, as a reason why they should be preferred in the cause of death; while the young, elate with the hopes of youth, showing their sinewy limbs, appealed to their expectations of victory from their strength, as a reason why they should first be put upon the lists for battle. Their arms were more various than their ages; an iron wedge, sharpened and fastened to the end of a stick, served some as the substitute for a hatchet; burnt stakes and the chamois hunter's rifle mingled with the scythe rounded into a sabre, and the sickle straightened to a sword.[2] While thus silently gazing upon the scene, a magistrate, a friend of Berchtold, going to his post, recognized me, and approaching, led me through a private entrance into the council chamber. My proffered services were immediately accepted, and I was directly ordered to put myself at the head of those villagers, who could be found in the town belonging to Berchtold's parish, avoiding, however, as much as possible the burthening myself with the infirm and women. I received orders to reach Berne in the shortest possible time, and to depart with the earliest dawn. I went out into the streets, a great part of the peasants had retired under the arcades which are on each side of the streets of Thun; they there formed one promiscuous mass, in which it was impossible to dis-

---

1 Adapted from Zschokke: "Every where were seen, not only men in the vigour of life, but old men, children, and even women, without regard to the weakness of sex or age, who prepared to offer their arms for the service of their country" (207-08).

2 Cf. Joel 3.10. Zschokke comments repeatedly on the crude weapons the Swiss were forced to use: "stakes, forks, clubs, and halberds" (265; cf. 295).

tinguish between man and woman. All was silent, save the dead sound of heavy footsteps and the hoarse voice of individuals like myself, treading amidst these sleepers, and calling out the name of that place, whose inhabitants they sought. The night was damp and dark, there was no light in the heavens, and often as I went, I stumbled over the body of some unseen person, who, uttering a note of impatience, again turned himself to sleep. Imitating the example of the others, I called out the name of Beatenberg at every step, and soon mustered almost the whole population of Berchtold's parish. I had a painful task, the old pointed to their children, and with tears in their aged eyes, asked me if I intended to hinder them from setting the example to their children, of dying for their native soil. The women, pointing to their lovers, would take no refusal; they seemed determined to witness their conduct on the day of battle, and see if they were worthy of the love they claimed. I spoke separately to the young men, and advised them to steal from their companions and meet me at a certain hour about a mile from the town.

They retired to rest, and I laid myself down in the street to sleep; I was soon lost to all external objects, and I again saw hovering at my side, her, who had seemed in the morning but a vision. She smiled upon me, again urged me by those words;— but suddenly it seemed as if the earth parted between us, and a huge chasm opened at my feet; we seemed to stretch our hands towards each other; I threw myself into the gulph, and awoke.[1] Finding it but a dream, I again attempted to compose myself to sleep, but in vain; her image still stood before me, and the moment I rested upon it, the idea of my orphan state and her apparent affluence startled me. I had not asked her name. I knew nothing of her; her form, her face, her voice, and her words already began to appear to my memory as the recollections of an unsubstantial, supernatural vision; but at this moment my hand fell upon the scarf, which I had now bound round my chest. The touch roused me from my painful reveries, and hope pervaded my breast. I started from the ground convinced that she did exist, I fell upon my knees, and uttered aloud a prayer to the Divinity to make me worthy of her. Hardly had the words passed my lips, when a loud hoarse laugh sounded on my ear. It was but a drunk-

---

1   Cf. Lorenzo's nightmare, in the first chapter of *The Monk* (1796), by M.G. Lewis, who visited Byron and his party, and told them ghost stories, in August 1816. See Appendix A.4.

ard laughing at some wild imagination of his own; but it made me shudder. I left the town; a heavy thick rain was falling, there was no wind, nothing seemed stirring, the shape of the distant mountains could be perceived by the white mass they presented on the dark canopy of night, every thing else was of one dead hue. I leant myself against the trunk of an old tree, and the dawn had, unperceived by me, risen in the east, when I found myself roused by the salutations of many of my comrades.

I had in vain attempted to dissuade the old and the women from joining us; they were all with us at the appointed hour. I again as fruitlessly endeavoured to show them the embarrassment they would prove to our march; they would not listen, and I gave orders for the men to proceed. In consequence of the exercise the peasants had been accustomed to in their native villages, I found no difficulty in forming them into something like a regular body. Towards night, as I had purposely pressed the march throughout the day, I was glad to perceive that the number of the old and infirm had much diminished. Next morning I again proceeded; it was with great difficulty that I could restrain myself and comrades from stopping to assist the women and old men who fell by the roadside through actual weakness and fatigue. Their cries imploring assistance from lovers, from sons, were heart-rending; I shut my ears and dared not listen. The nearer I approached Berne, the more deserted I found the country, all had flocked to the town or to the posts of danger. At last, with a body of two hundred men, not even yet entirely deserted by the women, I entered the capital. I read dismay and horror upon every face, even the peasantry, which here, as at Thun, crowded the streets, were silent; there were no signs of enthusiasm, but the glance of suspicion fell from every eye. Just as we were approaching the great place, we met a party of soldiers with their bayonets wet with blood. They seemed with hasty steps to be hurrying from a spot that brought something horrible to their mind. They did not speak, but we soon learnt that they were the murderers of Stetter and Ryhiner.[1] They washed the blood of their countrymen from their weapons in the blood of their

---

1   Karl-Ludwig Stettler (b.1741) and Karl Ryhiner (b.1744) were murdered on 4 March 1798. Stettler was colonel of the Sternenberg regiment at the time of the occupation of Fribourg. Far from being a traitor, he had ridden to Berne to exhort the council to resist. He was on his way to rejoin his troops when the assassinations took place (Godet 5:628, 6:362).

invaders, and at last bathed them with their own. Posterity may then spare their names the brand of infamy, for a momentary fit of rage against those they imagined traitors to their country.

We were ordered immediately upon our arrival to reinforce the army at Frauenbrunnen,[1] and were joined upon our departure by other militias, and by the venerable Steiguer,[2] who had just thrown up the insignia of civil office in the determination of dying for his country. We arrived at a critical moment, the French having an advantage in cavalry and artillery, which the Swiss could not resist, were upon the point of surrounding the small army, the only impediment in their road to Berne. Steiguer immediately perceived the danger; ordering us to follow, he rushed forwards, and attacked the troops which, having already passed the right flank of General d'Erlach, were upon the point of gaining the road on his rear. The combat was obstinate, our chief attack was upon the artillery, with which the enemy was attempting to cross the road. Our women did not shrink, they rushed forward, threw themselves upon the wheels of the guns, and allowed themselves to be hewn to pieces ere they would quit their hold.[3]

The army under d'Erlach had in the meantime began its retreat to Grauholtz.[4] We found ourselves surrounded and en-

1   The Bernese forces had been defeated by the French at Fraubrunnen
    shortly before their final defeat at Grauholz.
2   Niklaus Friedrich von Steiger (1729-99) had been elected *avoyer* or
    Schultheiss (chief magistrate) of Berne in 1787 and held the post until
    1798. He led the anti-French and counter-revolutionary party in
    Switzerland. After the fall of Berne and the proclamation of the Helvetic
    Republic, he fled to Bavaria, where he continued to work for the over-
    throw of the Republic until his death the following year.
3   This recalls one of the war stories Polidori had heard from the old
    curate of Brieg: "One maid in the ranks, when her comrades were
    obliged to retreat, seeing a cannon yet unfired, went with a rope-end
    and fired it, killing thirty [?] French. She was taken; a pardon was
    offered. She said, 'I do not acknowledge any pardon; my action is not
    pardonable; a thief [one?] pardons, not a just man.' They killed her with
    swords" (*Diary* 161-62). The association of female heroism with artillery
    also recalls an anecdote in Zschokke: "Women and girls employed them-
    selves in dragging the cannon taken at Lucerne from Brunner, and they
    conveyed them over rocks by frightful roads as far as Rothenthurm"
    (295).
4   The defeat of the Bernese forces at Grauholz, on 5 March 1798, made
    the fall of the Swiss Confederacy inevitable. D'Erlach, the Bernese com-
    mander, had about 1,000 troops; Balthasar de Schauenbourg (1748-
    1831), the French commander, about 20,000 (Godet 3:537).

gaged amidst the very carriages of our enemy's guns, which we had taken. By great exertions at last we formed ourselves again into a compact body, and suddenly, as if by one impulse, falling upon our knees, we offered a prayer to the God of battle.[1] The enemy thinking we were about to throw down our arms, checked themselves for a moment; we arose; the officers placed themselves at the head of the column, which set up a loud shout, ran upon the foe, and bearing all opposition down, soon reached Urteren, where we made a momentary stand, and then reached Grauholtz.

The troops were immediately employed in raising an abbatis[2] in front. While the men were thus engaged, Erlach and Steiguer met; at the instigation of the latter, the general came forward, and thanked my troop for the intrepidity it had shown during the whole combat. I was particularly noticed by them, and received from the aged general a medal he wore round his neck, as a token of his country's gratitude. "I have seen," he said, "the sun rise to-day upon freemen; I shall not see it set upon my countrymen.[3] Our country is lost; it cannot thank its sons; let me, therefore, who have directed its last efforts for freedom, acknowledge the few hours' respite you have obtained to its fate, by presenting you with this mark of honour, which I obtained from a free nation." The loud roar of cannon burst upon our ears; he left me. I stood for a moment still; in one hand I held the medal, with the other I pressed the scarf of my unknown friend closer to my heart. Again we fought, but again their numbers enabled them to turn our flank, and, in spite of the strength of our position, we were obliged to retreat. One more struggle at the gates of Berne, and all was lost. The slaughter was horrible. Determined to sell my life as dear as I could, I rushed into the thickest of the fight; but my peasants followed me; they snatched me from danger, and bore me struggling through the town. I reproached them with having deprived me of an honourable death; one approached with aged steps; looking me in the face, he merely mentioned the

---

1 Cf. 1 Samuel 1.1, 1.3, 1.11, and 4.4, Isaias 37.16, and many other Old Testament passages. Zschokke describes the Swiss tradition of praying on the battlefield (70).

2 An obstacle or fortification made of trees with their branches sharpened and bent towards the enemy.

3 Polidori has improved on d'Erlach's remark to his aide-de-camp, on the morning of the battle: "My friend, I see the sun rising, but never more shall I see him set" (Mallet du Pan 205).

name of Berchtold. I understood him; and, leaving Berne, we turned our steps towards Thun.

Unfortunately, the slaughter by the enemy's sword was not the only horror that attended the dispersion of our troops. The peasants and soldiers never, in their legendary tales, having heard of a defeat accompanied by a retreat, on their native soil, imputed the whole to the treachery of their officers.[1] The French had from the very beginning spread papers to this purport amongst them. As we proceeded, we therefore found the bodies of many of their officers hacked to pieces by the infuriate stragglers. Upon our arrival at Musingen, we found General d'Erlach in the hands of some of these men, who had determined to convey him to Berne. With him was his wife, who had accompanied him in his flight, and a young officer, whom I had remarked earnestly engaged in looking at my scarf, at the moment I was receiving the general's thanks at Grauholtz. I remonstrated with the soldiers, but in vain. I gradually, however, contrived to approach the general, and, when I thought myself sufficiently near to shield him, drawing my sword, I called upon the Beatenbergers to assist me, and instantly attacked them. The young officer, possessing himself in the struggle of a sword, was soon by my side. The peasants joined us; we drove the soldiers through the village; but in the meanwhile some stragglers issued from the houses, and striking the defenceless old man with their hatchets, left him for dead in the arms of his wife. When I returned, I found him apparently reviving through her care; it was only for a moment, he could not speak; it appeared, however, as if he recognised me, for he pressed my hand, and turned his closing eyes, first on his wife, then towards me. Thinking he recommended her to my care, I promised that I would protect her to the utmost of my power; his eye glistened, and he expired.

At this moment I again heard the cries of the soldiers. As there was an unfrequented path over the mountains from this place towards Hoestetten, whence the young officer might easily get to Lucerne, I advised him to pursue it, and get immediately out of the canton of Berne. We parted. Gathering my peasants together, I directly set off with Madame Erlach in the cart towards Thun. She did not shriek or weep, she seemed stupified by the greatness

---

1 In his account of the defeat at Grauholz, Zschokke quotes a description of "the Bernese troops, who, in their rage against their officers, swore terribly, talked at random, and only agreed with one another in saying that they were sold and betrayed" (173).

of her loss, and, when arrived at the city, she without difficulty allowed herself to be taken from the body, and to be conveyed in a boat to Berchtold's, whence she retired in a short time to complete solitude, where she saw no one, and soon after died.

I cannot paint to you the joy of Berchtold when he once more held me within his arms. My sister's tears flowed now as profusely as at our parting, but from a different cause. I had only been away a few days, yet the crowded events that took place in that short period made it appear as many weeks. The first spot I sought with my sister was my mother's grave. There I sat with her silently engaged in thought; after some time we began to converse, and as I had nothing hidden from her, I soon told the whole of my history from the morning of that day on which I had seen the unknown. She seemed disturbed, and upon my pressing her to explain to me what passed in her breast, she advised me to beware, for that it was probably one of the spirits of the Jungfrau's eternal frosts that had accosted me. I laughed at what I deemed her folly; but I soon perceived that there was something more on her mind than she was willing to confess. In vain I besought her to disclose it to me; she told me she durst not, and asked me as a favour not to speak to her any more on this subject. Alarmed, I knew not why, I looked at her with earnest attention. She could no longer bear it, but throwing herself into my arms, informed me that while I was away she had seen our mother, who had appeared to her, arrayed in mourning, announcing, that I was in the greatest danger, and that she must guard me, but that unless she wished to share my peril, she must conceal it from me. "Ernestus," my sister said, "I cannot obey, let your fate be mine, and I am content." Saying this, she again pressed me to her bosom, and wept. I was moved, I sat down by her side; bound in each other's arms, we gazed upon the green sod in silence, unwilling to disturb those thoughts which we knew must be the same in the breasts of both.

Anxious to learn some tidings concerning the fate of my native country, I went every day to Thun. My indignation was excited by the recital of the cruelties and extortions of the French, and, when they dared to attempt disarming the inhabitants, determined not to submit to so base an insult, I was proscribed, and sought refuge amongst those mountains which had been the scenes of my prowess in the chase. I went and sat whole days by the rocks in the Wengern Alp, where I first saw that form which has since engrossed the whole of my thoughts. I made enquiries at Lauterbrunnen concerning the two strangers, but ineffectually; they had

merely been there as other travellers, to view the sublime scenery
of the mountains, and had not been heard of since. I remained a
whole month amidst these rocks, only going to Beatenberg at
night, when Berchtold and my sister would receive me, and sup-
plying me with provisions for the ensuing days, tell me of all the
insults that added to the shame of Switzerland. But at last they
showed me the proclamation of Schwarenberg against the six
eastern cantons.[1] I immediately announced my determination to
join them. Berchtold said nothing; my sister followed me out of the
house, and begged to be permitted to accompany me. I refused,
and upon her reminding me of her dream, told her, that, as it
promised she should share my peril, it would prove impossible for
me to go into any real danger without her, that therefore she need
not follow me, or, if the fates decreed it, we should meet at that
moment without any endeavours on our part to assist their fiat. I
painted to her the horrors of the exterminating warfare that was
carried on, and asserted that it was most likely not the peril of the
sword in which she was to partake. In short, I forced her to
promise me not to follow, by representing to her the misery Berchtold would undergo, if at once deprived of both of his adopted children. I led her back to the door, and left her in his arms.

It is useless for me to give you an account of this campaign. It
is recorded in history with even all the unsuccessful struggles for
liberty, as one of those gleamings of that noble spirit in men,
which, though generally hidden under the pressure of vice and
corruption, at times bursts forth like the volcano's fire.[2] I was

1 After the proclamation of the Helvetic Republic in April 1798, five
  cantons rebelled: Uri, Schwyz, Unterwalden, Zug, and Glarus. (Polidori
  may be counting Obwalden and Nidwalden, the two halves of Unterwalden, as separate cantons.) The Helvetic government issued a proclamation telling the inhabitants of these cantons that they had been
  misled by their leaders and assuring them that the new constitution
  would not threaten their political or religious freedom and would not
  lead to an increase in taxes. Schauenbourg backed this up with a proclamation of his own, threatening to hold the priests of the five cantons
  personally responsible for the politics of their parishioners and setting
  up a blockade to starve the rebels into submission. But the rebels were
  defiant, and the French troops under Schauenbourg had to put them
  down by force (Godet 5:786, 6:118; Palmer 2:417; Zschokke 229-32).
2 Polidori recalls Zschokke's peroration: "No monument has been raised
  to perpetuate the memory of their valour, and bear their names to posterity; but ... the remembrance of their deeds shall not perish. They will
  be recorded in the annals of history after the heroic actions of the age of
  William Tell, and will add new lustre to the Swiss name" (337).

*indulgente
clemente*   *exceptur
Scambiano*

taken prisoner, and could find no means of escaping, till the
French, towards the end of June, after the restoration of
Rapinat,[1] became more lenient in their treatment of their prisoners, and less careful in their watch over them. I once more joined
the Underwalders, and was again witness to the defeat of my
countrymen.[2] I met the young officer I had saved from slaughter
at Musingen. His name was Olivieri. We had no time for intercourse, always in action or on the march, we only saw one
another in the field, where we often joined and tried to vie with
each other in acts of daring and courage. We became at last noted
in the army, and though only volunteers, we each soon found
ourselves at the head of about ninety men, who always were ready
to obey our commands.

In the midst of our struggles in the Underwald, intelligence
reached us of an insurrection having taken place in the upper
Valais;[3] it was deemed necessary by the leaders of our army to
send them assistance, and thus cause a diversion in our favour.
They proposed that one hundred men should be given to each of
us, and that with this force we should be sent to aid the Valisians
in their attempt. It was a hazardous undertaking, we had to cross
upon the flanks of the enemy, and should be obliged, it was supposed, to pass through the Grimsel, which was in the possession
of the French. When it was proposed, no one was found to volunteer; no Underwalder would leave his home in the hour of
danger. I had however remarked a number of Schweitzers, who
had joined us singly, having left their dwellings, though not coun-

---

1 Jean-Jacques Rapinat (c. 1750-1818), one of the French commissioners
   with the Helvetic army.

2 The Underwalders rose up against the Helvetic constitution in the fall of
   1798, after the other democratic cantons had been forced to accept it.
   As Polidori noted in his diary, "They were for freedom, and fought as
   the cause deserved" (161).

3 Until its incorporation into the Helvetic Republic, Valais had been an
   autonomous prince-bishopric. The lower Valaisans, who had been
   subject to the upper Valaisans for 300 years, accepted the Republic; the
   upper Valaisans rebelled in early May, however, in defence of their
   Catholic religion. They were defeated and Sion was burned on 17 May.
   They rebelled again in 1799, over conscription, and were put down with
   a massacre. The Valaisans did not revolt until after the eastern cantons
   had capitulated, and they were suppressed before the Underwalders
   revolted again in the fall. Polidori has manipulated the dates to make
   sporadic episodes of resistance look like a continuous and coordinated
   rebellion.

tenanced by their countrymen who were ranged on the other side,[1] to partake in the dangers of the patriotic Underwalders. To these men we applied, and in a short time, two hundred men were selected. We kept almost upon the summit of the high ridge that joins the Furca from the Lake of Lucerne, and crossing the glaciers by rocks, that even in the chase of the chamois would have startled me, we arrived at Realp, and soon crossed into the Valais. At Obergesteln we learnt that some French troops had that very night crossed from the Grimsel, while the whole body of peasants were engaged in the lower part of the valley, amidst the fastnesses attempting to stop that force which was advancing by the bridge of Hochflue. They had committed great outrages, and had caused those, who were able, to fly behind the glaciers of the Rhone.

Our undertaking now seemed desperate. The number of the French in the rear of our allies was greater than ours, and the end of the Valais through which we were to advance was flat and open, without any shelter, surrounded by steep mountains. Olivieri was however before me, we had each one hundred chosen men, and he seemed resolved on advancing. Not knowing how to procure intelligence of the enemy, I immediately offered to advance by myself and reconnoitre. As I well knew every part of this valley, I was certainly the fittest person in our body for such an undertaking; but my companion would not hear of ceding the post of danger to me; we were obliged to draw lots, and it fell upon him, and he departed.

In the mean time the women, hearing of our arrival, came from their fastnesses, and joined us. They seized upon every thing which offered the semblance of a weapon, and resolved to follow us. As my companion did not return as soon as I expected, fearful of a surprise, I determined to advance, and, if possible, gain some of the passes before the enemy knew of our arrival. I, however, previously sent forward a young woman, to see if she could obtain any intelligence of Olivieri. I then ordered the men to follow in silence, and marching all the evening, we at last, towards night, reached the village of Blizingen, where the valley straightens, and becomes more inclosed and rocky. The river here runs through a deeply-cut channel, more resembling a ravine than a common bed. As I knew there was but one path, and that very

---

1 Schwyz had capitulated and accepted the Helvetic constitution on 4 May (Zschokke 318-32).

steep and dangerous, I ordered my men to rest upon their arms, while I went along the river's channel to learn something concerning the enemy, who I thought could not have advanced much farther. At last, being arrived opposite the village of Vietsch, I heard a great noise, and saw many lights; making no doubt but that these proceeded from the point where the enemy was stationed, I returned. I found my men asleep; arousing them I ascended at their head the steep sides of the mountain, and making them march parallel with the path, but much higher, I brought them above the village, and hid them in a wood of pines that stretches along the steep. I now no longer feared the superior numbers of the enemy, the ascent was so precipitous that we could not be attacked, except to great disadvantage, while we could either join the Valisians, or fall upon the foe with every prospect of victory.

I determined once more to go and discover their exact position, giving the word that if I thought it a fit moment for an attack, I would fire my gun, and then sound my hunting horn, so that no mistake could occur from the firing of any drunken soldiers or guard. Wrapt up in my mantle I descended from the wood, and found the men lying securely asleep in the road between the houses. They were certainly all there; anxious to know something concerning my companion, I resolved, in spite of the risk, to awaken some straggler, and learn from him if any prisoner was amongst them. I accordingly approached one who, stretched along the edge of a precipice over the river, was sunk in a sleep that seemed that of the innocent. Putting my pistol to his breast, I awoke him. Alarmed, he was upon the point of calling out, when I threatened him with instant death. To my inquiries he answered, that a person had been surprized by some stragglers in the course of the day, and he added that he was then lying bound in a cottage in the very centre of the village, destined to be in the morning a butt for their muskets. It did not appear that his having been found armed had excited suspicion, as he was taken for a common peasant. Determined to save Olivieri, I knew not what to do with this sleeper, to shoot him would alarm the enemy, they might immediately dispatch my friend, and yet I could not leave this man to raise his comrades. I pushed him down the precipice, and directly entered the village. All were asleep, I found the cottage, there was a light in the window. I stole close to it, wrapping myself up in my mantle. I looked in; you may imagine my alarm when I saw two soldiers awake in conversation, while my friend, upon his back, was bound to a bench fastened to the floor. There were several soldiers at my feet, with their arms by their sides, a sudden thought struck me, I seized one of their guns and firing it, I instantly retreated to the other side of the cottage, where I had remarked a window close to the fatal bench. As I expected, the two soldiers went out to inquire about the report which they had heard; I took advantage of the few moments, leapt into the room by the window, roused Olivieri, who gazed upon me expecting death; I made a sign for silence, cut his bonds, and was again out of the cottage with my companion, when I heard the door open to admit the two soldiers. We hastened up the ascent, and when, amidst the rocks I fired my own fowling piece, and blew a national air upon my horn. Before the enemy, alarmed by the two soldiers, who missed their prisoner, could form, we were amongst them, and morn had hardly dawned before we had cut to pieces the whole of this detachment. I could have induced the men to give quarter, but the women were outrageous, they followed our soldiers, and dispatched the wounded, whom their more merciful companions had spared, while they excited the Schweitzers to slaughter even those who threw up their arms; none were saved.[1] The Valisians who were making head against this body, hearing the report of so many guns, did not know what to believe; they however approached, and when they heard the Swiss war cry of liberty, they immediately joined us. Their joy cannot be expressed by words; Olivieri and myself had in the mean time met, and his thanks were profuse; but what was my sorrow to find that the young woman had been seized and bayoneted in cold blood, because she would not acknowledge the right of the French to a superiority over her nation; she had pretended not to know my companion, and thus avoided betraying us, by not being confronted with him.

We had gained a victory, but it only served to delay the subjection of this noble peasantry; they were obliged to come at last to a capitulation. We could not be included in it; the French asserted that the Schweitzers were deserters. We therefore determined to attempt once more a passage over the most unfrequented Alps. To avoid the Grimsel, where the French might pass

---

1 Polidori recalls Zschokke's account of the courage and ferocity of the Swiss rebels: "they paid no regard to their wounds, but remained in their posts, suffering themselves to be cut in pieces, without ever asking quarter, as they never gave it" (336). The French sustained more than ten times as many casualties as the Swiss in the course of the campaign.

to interrupt our passage, we crossed at once into the valley of Formazza. Hidden in the day amidst the woods, or upon the tops of precipices, my few companions, for our numbers had been greatly diminished, journeyed in the night by a circuitous route into the Vadi Bedretto, and thence over the St. Gothard by the path we had come, towards the valley of Stantz. We had there expected to find our former companions yet struggling for life, if not for victory. We entered the valley, there was no living creature to be found, there was a silence unbroken by any sound of human labour, the hoarse ravens fluttered above us, as if they thought we also came to spread their banquet.[1] We could find no one to guide us, no one even to tell us of our misfortune. Our imaginations pictured sufficient. The villages were burnt, the cattle lay slaughtered on the field, it seemed as if death, with one sweep of his scythe, had cut off the life of all. Creeping along the sides of the mountains, we approached Stantz, we expected to find the destroyers there; but when we were in sight, there was no town appearing. We found but sixteen straggling houses yet standing, all the rest were burnt; these also bore the Frenchmen's mark, they were billetted. We looked at one another in silence. The birds of prey were not disturbed by our presence, they continued feeding on the dead. While walking amidst these ruins, I at last heard the sound of a voice, it was the cry of sorrow. A mother had found words to call on heaven for strength to bear her individual grief, heedless of her country's death. I saw her amidst these ruins, her hands were tearing up the soil to give the last refuge her country could afford to her child,—a grave. She did not at first perceive me, when she did, her hand worked doubly quick, while, with her eyes fixed upon the corpse, her hurried lips uttered, "hold your hand, hold your hand for a moment, I shall soon be ready to follow." I dug her son's grave, and left her striking the sod as if she repented of having resigned the body to the earth.

We assembled our few remaining companions, Olivieri and myself addressed them, we advised them to separate and seek

---

1 Schauenbourg crushed the revolt in Unterwalden, devastated the canton, and burned Stans (the capital of Nidwalden) on 9 September (Godet 5:786, 6:749). As Zschokke's English translator remarks, "even the cattle were slaughtered." The desperate courage of Ernestus and his followers may be based on the translator's anecdote of "two hundred men of Schwitz, who came to succour their allies, [but,] finding they arrived only to be spectators of their ruin, rushed upon the ranks of the French, and were cut off to a man" (343).

singly a refuge in their homes. While yet speaking one of them brought before us a man, who seemed to have risen from the grave. His grey locks, thinly scattered on his head, were entangled, his eyes were sunk so deep within their sockets, that their lustre seemed the last glimmering of life before it sinks. He had sought death from the foes, and they, in mockery, had bade him live. They had fastened him to a table in the open air, with several days' provision within his reach, and had placed before his sight the corpses of his aged wife, his children, and grandchildren, all marked with the wanton infliction of their barbarous cruelty, not even excelled by the voracity of the vulture or beasts of prey.[1] This wretched being told us that the Schweitzers had troops placed the whole length of the other side of the lake, to hinder the fugitives from this valley escaping.[2] Upon this intelligence our men became dejected; the thoughts of dying ingloriously by the hands of their treacherous countrymen, weighed upon their mind. They spoke some time amongst themselves, and then begged of us not to desert them, assuring us that if we enabled them to reach the upper part of Schweitz unbroken, they then could disperse to their families without danger. We could not refuse them. We ordered them to go along the shore, and see if they could find any boats; they soon got together more than enough to convey us over. But they had been observed by an individual, who had immediately put off in his skiff and crossed to the other side. This rendered greater caution necessary, as he would undoubtedly inform the enemy of our neighbourhood. We offered to take the old man with us; he refused; determined, not even in ruin, to desert those spots which had seen his birth, and infancy, and manhood, he returned to the bodies of his children, threw himself upon them, apparently resolved to breathe his last

---

1 This incident is based on another of the war stories Polidori heard from the curate of Brieg: "The cruelty of the French was dreadful; they stuck their prisoners in a variety of ways like sheep. One old man of eighty, who had never left his house but whom they found eating, they strangled, and then put meat and bottles by him as if he had died apoplectic" (*Diary* 161).

2 From another of the curate's war stories: "The hundred men who came from the higher part of Scwhytz attempting to go to their relief, were through their own countrymen forced to cut their way and march by night; and, when in retreating they came to the other shore of Lucerne Lake, they had again to cut through their own countrymen to arrive at their homes" (*Diary* 162).

sigh in defending these mangled remnants from further insult: all that we could do was to lay a fresh stock of provisions by his side.

Hoping to find the enemy unprepared, upon some point or other, we immediately entered our boats. They however watched us, and at the moment of our landing, appeared before us in a body so numerous, that it seemed impossible to escape. We formed our men in the very water into a wedge, and taking a gun and bayonet ourselves, we led them against the foes, determined either to cut our way through, or to fall upon the field of battle. After repeated charges we at last succeeded, but our numbers were reduced to fifty, and several were wounded. We mustered upon the very spot where the liberty of Switzerland had been sworn to by the three patriots; it was the valley of Brunnen.[1] Fortunately the Schweitzers did not pursue us. Travelling night and day, we at last gained the higher parts of the canton, whence my companions came. We separated, and it was a proud moment when they brought their wives and children to thank us as the preservers of their husbands and fathers. Olivieri and myself were now alone amongst the mountains, as a reward was set upon our heads, and as we here depended entirely upon the fidelity of many who had shunned our cause, we determined to depart and seek some other refuge. My friend knew not where to go, being ignorant, as he said, where his family was; he having left it privately, while travelling, to join the Swiss. He however determined to go into the Austrian dominions, and there seek for information. We parted with mutual protestations of friendship, and a promise from him of letting me know by means of Berchtold, when he had found safety. We had had little communication; I therefore scarcely knew more than that Olivieri was not his family name, and that he was an Italian. I had often remarked his eyes to be fixed upon my scarf, but his delicacy preventing him from speaking upon a subject, he perceived I was not willing to converse on, was the cause of our parting without further communication. He was indeed the brother of that object, which had never deserted my thoughts, which, sleeping and waking, my lips had often called upon. No night passed, though dangers surrounded me on every side, without her image rising to cheer for a moment my wearied heart; but the dreams always ended unhappily. It

---

1 The Everlasting League of Schwyz, Unterwalden and Uri, sworn at Brunnen on 1 August 1291, is traditionally seen as the origin of the Swiss Confederation.

seemed as if the fates were determined to embitter even those moments, in which I was engaged in a noble cause, thus to prepare my mind for those pangs which follow guilt. You may think I rest too much upon these instants of my life; but I dread to narrate my miseries; the recalling to memory anguish and grief racks my heart; but I have begun, and you shall hear the whole.

Knowing the country well, and being acquainted with every pass, I found no difficulty in reaching the neighbourhood of Beatenberg, and I was soon locked in my sister's arms. Berchtold and Julia's anxiety about me had been great, they had heard by report of my being in action, and had seen in the papers the immense reward offered for my person. Seeing me safe they could not contain their joy; but morning came, and I was obliged to depart into the mountains, for who could be trusted? Treachery and avarice had proved at last the master passions in many breasts, though they had at first worn the mask of the noblest virtues. Promising to be back at night, I flew to the Wengern Alp, and there again visited the spot, which now began to appear sacred to my mind. At night I returned to the pastor's cottage; I only found my sister there, he was gone to Thun. Leaving the house, Julia led me to our mother's grave, and again begged of me to be cautious, for constantly while I had been absent the same admonition had been given. It did not seem to her to relate to a personal danger; it was a vague threat, that seemed the more terrific, because it could not be decidedly represented to the mind. She then begged of me to relate the dangers I had undergone; I gave her a minute account of the whole.

Amongst other things which she mentioned to me, was the arrival of a stranger, who had taken up his abode at Interlaken, and who excited the wonder of his neighbours by the account his servants gave of his riches, and by their intimation of his having communication with an evil spirit. The source of his riches was unknown. Many were the tales related concerning him, and if but half were true, she said, he must certainly be possessed of a wonderful power. He was old and apparently wretched. His only daughter accompanied him, her beauty was as much the subject of conversation, as the riches of her father. These were the only rumours my sister had heard, for they had only arrived a few days before. I wish that I had never known more. I did not laugh at the idea of the supernatural part of the report. We were both too strongly imbued with the tales of our foster-mother not to attach some credit to them. My sister's dreams, in which our mother visited her, my own which always portended misfortune, had enforced upon our minds the belief of the interference of superior beings.

For several nights I returned, but Berchtold was yet, as we imagined, at Thun. My sister and myself left entirely to ourselves, again talked over the feats of Olivieri, and she often asked me to repeat them, seeming with pleasure to rest upon every circumstance regarding him. Foolishly, I also took a pleasure in relating them, for though we had been constantly rivals, there was a frankness, a heedless daring about him, that excited admiration, at the same time, that the warmth of his expressions called forth a reciprocal feeling of love. I knew not then how to discover the sting protruding from the rich scales of the snake. We conversed upon our mother, and my enquiries were numerous about her person, her voice. I cannot explain it, but I wished even from Julia's dreams to aid the representation I had formed from her portrait of a being, who seemed even after life, to feel an interest in my fate. In the locket, there was a melancholy look about her dark blue eyes, that was rendered heavenly, by the soft smile playing upon her open lip. I had gazed upon it so often, that I had her image before me, even when far from home, but it was only distinct in the face, which appeared to be gazing on heaven, with the consciousness of having obtained a prayer for me. Since my sister's dreams, it seemed as if I knew a mother's care, and I often sighed, to think, that though thus thoughtful of me even in heaven, she did not think me worthy of enjoying her smile.

One morning I left my sister, and retired to the wild borders of the Brientz lake.[1] The sun rose, and with its glittering ray painted on the water, the reflected images of the wild rocks upon the other side. There is a point which juts into the lake, and on it are the ruins of an old church; I did not feel inclined to exert myself to reach a more distant spot, but I laid myself down by an arching gateway, round which the ivy clustered, as if by its tenacious grasp, it would hold together the monuments of another age, upon which the breath of time was acting with a destructive power, unheeded by man. I seemed to feel this breath of time acting upon me as upon these works of man, the wild joys of youth seemed sunk into the melancholy uniform feeling attendant upon age, when all joy is passed, all hope extinguished by the consciousness of the presence of death. I gazed upon the

---

1   Polidori passed this spot on his travels and described it as "wilder, but not so beautiful as the Lake of Thun" (*Diary* 157).

mists as they rolled slowly along the hills, veiling successively the various beauties of the banks, and watched the cloud's shadow, depriving the lake of its glittering sheen. I rested upon their passing powers, but did not notice, that the glow of the bright sun invariably returned upon the spots, before darkened by a shadow. The peasants' barge, and the light skiff, passed rapidly before me, but unheeded they passed in silence, for it appeared, as if, even they sympathized in my grief. It was mid-day, I rose to shelter myself from the sun's ray, and sought that side of the point towards Interlaken. There was a small light skiff upon the water, and in it was a female figure. It was at some distance, it gradually approached; my heart fluttered, my breathing became difficult, my eyes were fixed upon a form I seemed to recognise. Her face was not lit up, as I had seen it, by all the fire of her indignant eye; carried along by her small latin sail,[1] she approached. Her eye was gazing upon the rippling wave, cut by her prow, it seemed as if joy did not dwell there, her eye-lash veiled its splendour, while her black locks curling on the breeze, floated playfully around. Her breast at times would heave as if the sorrow in her bosom was loath to grieve her, but she seemed unwilling it should go, for she rested upon it. I stood intently gazing, it seemed as if my least motion would have at once destroyed an illusion. The current brought her heedless close to the shore, and the boat struck the bank; she looked around and saw me. It was plain she recognised me, for her eyes fixed upon her scarf. To paint to you, the varying expressions of that eye, and the varied colour of that cheek, is impossible. With slow hesitating steps she approached, our eyes did not dare to meet, and I stood by her for some moments in silence; at last with a trembling voice, she asked me if my name were not Ernestus Berchtold? "If you own that name, fly instantly, you have been betrayed, and the blood-suckers are already, at Interlaken upon their way to Berchtold, do not go there to-night." I could hardly acknowledge my name, I was so moved by her voice; she offered to convey me to the other side of the lake, if I thought myself safer there. Unconscious of what I was doing, I entered her boat, and taking the oars, tried by violent exertions to rouse myself; we did not speak; when upon the other side, I landed. Farewell fell from her lips, and it seemed as if the echoes mocking me, repeated farewell. I stood still, watching her

---

1   A lateen sail, a triangular sail suspended from a yard-arm that is
    attached to the mast at an angle of forty-five degrees.

as entering the current of the Aar, she was gradually borne down towards Interlaken; even when she had passed the bridge, I gazed, and seemed to see a white speck, that I imagined was her.

I turned away, and towards evening found myself upon the same spot on which I had first seen her. Again, she had appeared. At first, she had guided me into the path of honour, this day she ensured my safety. Was she then a vision? I asked myself. Was it my guardian angel, who invested that form? I did not think of pursuing my route to any place of greater safety, it seemed as if this spot where my protector had appeared, was secure, I laid me down beneath the rock, that had witnessed her presence, and offering up a prayer to heaven, I gave way to all the visions my imagination offered. She had recognised me, she knew my name, my rank, and still felt an interest in my safety. If you have ever known, what it is to be in love, you may judge what my feelings were, if not, my words are useless, I hardly slept the whole night.

Next day I roamed restless over the Alpine heights around, I did not heed the horrors or the beauties of these solitudes. The cataract fell by my side, and yet I heard it not, wherever the valley wound, thither I followed; but as evening threw its stillness over nature, ere the light canopy of heaven was darkened, I found myself upon the covered bridge of Interlaken, I had forgotten my danger. The open spaces between the beams supporting the roof, enabled me to see the different houses which skirt the river's side. Mine eyes however gazed upon that one, in which I had heard, the new inhabitants of this neighbourhood had taken up their abode. I had imagined my unknown was the beautiful daughter I had heard of from my sister; and I had not long been upon my station, when I saw her come forth, supporting upon her arm the feeble steps of the old man I had seen with her upon the Wengern Alp. Her eyes, fixed upon his languid face, seemed anxiously to be watching the features of her invalid father. There was a bush not far from the door beneath the wide-spreading canopy of a lofty elm; she placed him there, and I saw reflected on her face, the smile which beamed upon the old man's, as he gazed upon the setting sun. I watched her slightest action, her every glance, it seemed as if her words soothed the pains of sickness, and lightened the languor attendant upon an invalid's inactivity. Oh, if that smile had fallen upon myself, as it then fell upon her father, if I had only felt its cheering influence without that burning passion it has excited in this breast; but I must not anticipate my narration. The sun sunk behind the mountains, she carefully shielded her sire from the damp. I watched her retiring steps, heard the door close after her, and at last turned away.

Intending to depart again to some retired spot, I was advancing, when I perceived that there was some one at the end of the bridge apparently watching me, and then retiring as if to look up the road. Alarmed, I seized my hunting knife and approached him: seeing me advance, he came towards me, it was the servant of Berchtold. He had seen me from a neighbouring height, and anxious, as he said, for my safety, had immediately followed me, and finding me on the bridge, had several times spoken to me without my paying the least attention; perceiving at last how I was engaged in contemplating the beautiful object before me, he had contented himself with guarding the entrance to the bridge. I enquired about the French soldiers, he turned pale, but at that moment I hardly noticed it; he told me that they had been watching Berchtold's house during the whole of the night, apparently aware of my being in the habit of going there every evening. He informed me that there were only two remaining, whom he had supplied so abundantly with wine, that if I chose to venture towards the cottage, he would inform Berchtold and my sister where they could meet me, while he engaged the attention of my pursuers. How easily I was deceived; I have since known the value of men's professions; then I was young and confident in virtue. Berchtold and my sister met me, but there were other soldiers in the neighbourhood; those the servant led to a pass by which I must descend on my return. It was but another instance of that venal boasted honour which so much stains the Swiss patriotic history.[1]

In the mean time I learnt from Berchtold that he had walked to Berne, hoping to cause my sentence of outlawry to be cancelled; that the French employers had lulled him with hope until he had been rash enough to acknowledge my being in this neighbourhood; when they would listen to him no longer, but sent the

---

1 In his text to R. Bridgens' *Sketches Illustrative of the Manners and Costumes of France, Switzerland, and Italy* (1821), Polidori makes some disparaging remarks about the Pope's Swiss Guard: "There has always been an idea of Swiss fidelity, and hence royal guards and noble porters have been chosen from that nation. But, if royalty could learn from experience, they would never have employed them except against the poor; for, hang out a few bags of gold on the waving inimical banner, and they will cluster round it as bees swarming round the pan-enchanted bough" (text to plate 31).

soldiers I have mentioned. Even Ochs, who had formerly been his school-fellow, had laughed when he reproached him for so vile a breach of confidence.[1] I spoke with my sister apart, and informed her of my discovery, she was surprised, and seemed downcast; but Berchtold, who had gone to listen, and reported all silent, joining us, we could not proceed in our conversation. I embraced them, and had begun to descend the steep, when I heard myself challenged; having my gun with me, I fired, and the challenger fell; but one leapt upon my back, it was my own servant, and I was surrounded. I struck upon every side, but it was in vain: determined, however, to be revenged, I threw myself upon the ground with the traitor; as we turned, I succeeded in getting him undermost, and plunged my hunting-knife up to the hilt in his chest. He groaned and died. I surrendered.

I was hurried to Interlaken, put into a boat, and before the dawn of day, was locked in the prisons of Thun. I expected to be immediately taken out and shot. I was not, however, disturbed till night, when I was awakened from a sound sleep, and, guarded by a company of soldiers, was ordered to be conveyed to the castle of Chillon, upon the lake of Geneva.[2] Entering into conversation with the soldier who marched by my side, I heard from him that Berchtold and my sister had in vain applied for admission to my dungeon, upon hearing of my misfortune; that the reason I was removed at this late hour arose from the magistrate's fearing a

1 Peter Ochs (1752-1821) was the head of the pro-French party in Switzerland. He was actually born in France, though of a Swiss family. He went to Basel in 1769 and obtained a doctorate in jurisprudence there in 1776. In 1797, he helped Napoleon to draft a constitution for the Helvetic Republic, based on the French constitution of 1795. After the establishment of the republic, he became president of the Senate, and then of the Directory. He was deposed by Frédéric-César de la Harpe (1754-1838) in 1799 (Godet 5:176-77).

2 There may have been a Roman post on the little island at the east end of Lake Geneva; the current fortress dates from the eleventh century. François Bonivard (c.1494-1570), the hero of Byron's poem, was imprisoned there from 1530 to 1536. It was still in use as a political prison in 1798 (Godet 2:508-09; Palmer 2:403). Polidori, who took a personal pride in *The Prisoner of Chillon*—as in all the poems Byron produced during their time together (Macdonald 272 n.25)—did not fail to visit the fortress on his travels: "Crossed to Chillon. Saw Bonivard's prison for six years; whence a Frenchman had broken, and, passing through a window, swam to a boat. Instruments of torture,—the pulley" (*Diary* 153).

rescue by the people, who once or twice in the day had seemed, by their tumultuous meeting, inclined to force the prison of him whom they called their only remaining patriot. From him I first learnt that my name was in every mouth; that there were romantic tales printed about me, and spread over all the country in spite of the police which endeavoured to suppress them. I did not feel any vain exultation at this; I was too near death; but I certainly experienced some satisfaction in the thought, that for Louisa,—that—that was her name. For years locked up within my breast, it has not passed my lips. I have not dared to utter that name, not even whisper it to my own ear; but it has been deeply engraven here. It is now a spell that conjures up horrid thoughts; once it did not.

But I must command myself. I had not visited this part of Switzerland yet, though beautiful, and perhaps richer than any I had seen, it passed unobserved before my eyes. The simple villagers, hearing my name, came round the inns at which we stopped, and looked upon me in silence. Mothers brought their children to me to kiss, as if my kiss could call down a blessing, or inspire heroism. I crossed the Dent de Jamanu, and soon saw the castle once the prison of Bonniva, now destined to be my own.

The draw-bridge was up, and the sentinels were parading as if they esteemed the castle of importance. Upon my name being mentioned the bridge was lowered, and I soon heard the clash of the chains employed in raising it after me. It seemed to be accompanied by a voice that bade hope to leave me.[1] The rude stare of the soldiers, and the bustling scene of the officers, running to and fro, did not tend to relieve the sorrow that weighed upon me. I had dared danger in the chase upon the Alps; death in battle; yet here the thoughts of leaving all, oppressed me. I did not think of the pain of parting with existence; but Berchtold, my sister, the vision of the Wengern Alp, all seemed to press upon my imagination with eyes, that, by their look, seemed to denote a breaking heart. My head fell upon my breast, while, with folded arms, I walked along the vaulted passage. I was searched, all was taken from me, my knife, the little money I had. The rude jailor already had his hand upon the scarf, retaining it with a firm grasp, I looked at him, and seeing his daughter close by his side,—"if that child," I said, "should be far—far from thee, and thou couldst not

---

1 Cf. the inscription over the door of Dante's hell: "ABANDON EVERY HOPE, YOU WHO ENTER" (*Inferno* 3.9).

hope to see her but in heaven, couldst thou part with the only relic of her memory?" He looked upon his child, and let go his hold.

I was taken into a room where several officers were deliberating concerning me. I had stood before them some time, when one asked me my name. "Ernestus Berchtold" was my answer. "It is the traitor;" fell from the lips of one. I looked upon him; he could not stand my glance, but sunk into silence. They were considering whether they should lead me to instant execution, or whether I should be confined till the pleasure of the government at Berne should be known, as it was thought that they might wish to make a more public exhibition of the punishment of him they so gratuitously called a traitor. I was respited by one voice, and was instantly ordered to my dungeon.

To descend into the prison, which is below the level of the water, it is necessary to go down a narrow circular staircase. While descending it, we were stopped by that child upon whom I had rested my appeal to the jailor; to pass her we were obliged to go singly; when I came close to her, I felt something pressed into my hand, while at the same time she made a sign with her finger for silence. I put her present into my breast and followed her father, who was before me, while the others were at my back. I entered a long vault, its floor was the solid rock, and its high roof was supported by seven thick massy pillars. The waves of the lake dashed sullenly against the walls above my head, and the feeble light that pierced the high windows only showed me the damp black sides of this prison. There were the steps of a prisoner marked during a long imprisonment upon the very rock;[1] I still heard the noise of bolts, but did not heed it, till I arrived at a narrow cell, partitioned off from the greater dungeon, which I had not perceived in the general obscurity. Into this narrow space I was forced to enter. It was not sufficiently long for me to lie down at full length, and the barred grating, which, far above my reach, was intended in mockery to represent a window, received no reflected light from the dark floor of Bonniva's prison. I heard the doors fastened one after another.

Beneath the slowly sounding wave I was cut off from humanity; the monotonous dashing against the castle's base alone broke

---

1   A reminiscence of the "Sonnet on Chillon," which Byron prefixed to *The Prisoner of Chillon* (1816), and in which Bonivard's "very steps have left a trace / Worn, as if [the] cold pavement were a sod ..." (*CPW* 4:3).

the dread silence; it seemed like the loud note of the moments in nature's last hour. My spirits fled, and I leant against the stones to which I was chained, with hands clasped, and my eyes painfully straining, as if they sought at least to see the real horrors of my dwelling. Fatigued by my long journey over the steep Jamanu, I sought to sit and sleep, but the damp floor for a long time kept my racking mind awake to all the torments of thought, while it hoped for a momentary oblivion of woe.

At last I sunk into repose, and it was not until late the next morning that I awoke, but I awoke refreshed; I had seen the constant attendant upon my dreams, and I soon lost myself in thought upon her various appearances. The waves above me seemed silenced to a calm, and the sun's powerful meridian ray reflected upon the various sides of the greater vault, penetrated, though in a feeble glimmer, my solitary cell. Gradually stealing upon my ear, I heard a distant voice, which in melancholy notes seemed to sympathize with my sorrows. I listened; it approached; the measured strokes of an oar interrupted the heavenly strain; suddenly breaking into livelier notes it sung of hope; the voice was, they were Italian words, it was my vision's voice. It gradually sunk away into indistinct sounds. I seemed another being, hope breathed upon my heart, and Louisa wore the semblance of that enchanter; oh that I had died, that she had left me to myself to die! it was not the will of heaven. Again I heard the splashing sound of the oar, and again that voice sounded on my ear; it was no longer the thrilling notes of an air, but in slow recitative it bade me hope, it told me that a boat should be stationed at two or three stone throws distance from the castle, ready at all times to receive me if I could manage to get out, and that in the mean time endeavours were making at Berne, to gain a repeal of the sentence passed upon me. Again the song of hope sounded in my cell, losing itself gradually in the distance, it at last left me with nothing human within hearing.

I now remembered the child's present; feeling in my breast, it proved to be a file and a knife; I instantly began to work at the wall, dividing me from the great dungeon; while thus busily employed I heard the bolts of the vault withdrawn; my jailor entered, he spoke not, but threw me my pittance of bread, and laid down my pitcher of water. Hardly was he gone, when I resumed my work, the dampness of my cell aided me. The mortar was soft, and the wall built of small stones; when therefore I had scraped the mortar away from the crevices, I did not find any difficulty in forcing them out. One by one I tore away many, and I

ERNESTUS BERCHTOLD   99

had already almost pierced the wall, when, fearful of penetrating entirely through, lest the jailor might next day detect my attempt, I managed to replace most of the rubbish in its situation, and to push the rest into a corner. I now began with my file to cut the chain that surrounded my waist. The jailor came next morning, and told me, that at the dawn of the ensuing day I was to be conveyed to Berne. This gave me additional strength, the hopes of liberty, of seeing Louisa, spurred me on, and in a few moments I was free from my chains. With what impatience I waited for the night. It came; I forced a passage through the wall, and I found myself in the great vault without a manacle. The moon's ray seemed with a smile to seek the ground on which I trod, for its cold beams pierced the grated apertures above, and illumined some dreary spots. I was not yet free, the window was high above my reach; but I did not despair, taking the whole length of the dungeon to give me power, I leapt, and caught with my hands at one of the bars. I raised myself, and resting my knee upon the shelving sill, I immediately began to employ my file, and the rusty bars soon gave way to my arm.

I paused a moment, the cool fresh air of the night, no longer poisoned by the noxious vapours of the subterranean dungeon, played amidst my hair; I seemed to inhale life. The moon's ray, decked with one glittering streak of light the whole breadth of the wide lake; it seemed the path of hope. Not far distant was a barge; in three or four hours my murderers would be at my prison door. The ground was covered with snow even to the water's edge; I leapt into the lake, and being a good swimmer I reached the boat numbed by the cold, I had hardly the strength to raise myself into it. There was no one to be found; there were some coarse provisions, a peasant's habit, and a letter; it had no direction, "if safe," it said, "proceed to Milan, you will hear of us there. Your sister is well, Berchtold ill, but do not go to him, he knows we are attempting to save you, and he shall immediately be informed of your escape. The daughter of Olivieri's father." It was now that I learnt that Olivieri was the brother of Louisa Doni. It was now explained why he so attentively examined my scarf.

I could not resolve on leaving Switzerland without seeing Berchtold, there was a western breeze, I hoisted the latin sail, and in a few minutes I was free from immediate danger, and on my way towards Beatenberg. It was necessary that I should keep amongst the mountains, and I only dared approach the most solitary chalets. They were generally deserted, and it was with difficulty that I procured sufficient to support nature during the three days I was upon my way. Arriving at Œschi, I took a boat from the side of the lake, and crossing, was soon at the foot of the steep, on which stands Beatenberg. The stillness of the night was broken by the sound of voices chaunting, which, stealing down the mountain, sunk upon the wave. Alarmed I knew not why, I rushed up the path; before the church porch, around the great cross that stood upon the green sward, knelt Berchtold's parishioners arrayed in white. Though the red glare of the pine torch fell upon their faces, it did not allow me to distinguish any one. Breathless I stood incapable of motion. The chaunt ended, the minister of peace arose, it was not Berchtold; "he's dead," I cried, and rushed forward; alarmed, the peasants rose, they recognized me and were silent; my sister took my hand and bade me pray for him who had died. Incapable of any longer bearing the anxiety attendant upon my fate, I knew not what I did, I knelt, I heard the solemn chaunt sing Berchtold's requiem, and could not join it. The earth closed over him, and the minister led me to my former home.

I was inconsolable, they talked to me of ensuring my safety; I was deaf to their remonstrances, and only listened to grief; my sister was left alone with me. She wept with me, and ere it was dawn, had persuaded me to depart. She told me that Louisa had been with her, had made her promise to join her, in case of Berchtold's death, so that I need not be under any anxiety on her account. She informed me that Louisa had walked with her over my haunts, had enquired after every minutest circumstance about me. My sister said, she thought she loved me. I could listen to no more, embracing her, I issued forth, visited my mother's and Berchtold's grave, and soon lost sight of Beatenberg.

Louisa loved me! it was too true, if that love had fallen upon any one else it would have proved a blessing. On me; you see my withered lineaments, my sunken eye, my feeble step, think you, a common curse could thus blast the bloom of life? Berchtold was but the first victim to my love. My love has left me, a scattered pine amidst this desolate scene,[1] but first it has destroyed all who were bound to me, my love has proved,—but I must preserve my strength,—I have horrors to relate,—going through the Simplon, then a road only passable by mules or on foot,[2] I soon arrived at Milan.

---

1 Cf. *Manfred* 1.2.65-71.
2 On his trip to Switzerland, Polidori had been impressed by Napoleon's achievements as a road builder (*Diary* 82, 86). The Simplon Pass is described by W. Wordsworth in *The Prelude* (1805) 6.488-572.

I was in safety, the city was in possession of the Austrians.[1] I had hardly rested at the inn, at which I took up my abode and was making enquiries, in hopes of discovering the Donis, when Olivieri entered. We flew into one another's arms, he answered none of my enquiries, but leading me to his carriage, we arrived through the corso[2] at a palace close to the gates. We got out, I knew not whither he was leading me, the doors of the saloon were thrown open, and I found myself in the presence of his father, his sister. The old man advanced, and taking my hand, which hung by my side, he thanked me for having twice saved the life of his son. I knew not what to say; conscious I owed my life to Louisa's interference, I could not find words to thank her. The father at last led me towards his daughter, and bade her attempt to thank me. Her eyes turned upon me, suffused with blushes she had some words upon her lips, when I forced myself to stop her. "Do not mock me, what do I owe to you? my life is nothing, when compared to that thirst of honour, you inspired in my breast." Again, she blushed and was silent. At that moment, another carriage arrived, it was my sister attended by two faithful domestics of my friend; locked in my arms, she was at last taken thence to be clasped in those of my preserver.

. After taking some refreshment, the father led me into another room, he there told me that Berchtold's last request was, that he should supply his place, and take my sister and myself to him, as his children. As he spoke, he showed me at the same time, the last lines which my foster-father had written a few moments before he died. They contained our history as far as he was acquainted with it; in them he bade me trust always in God, and recommended me to bow under that dispensation, which had made me an outcast on my native soil, and not to murmur at the will of him, who had deprived me of the feeble support a Swiss pastor could afford against the pressure of events, since he had raised me up a protector, so much more powerful in the father of him whose life I had saved. Doni took me by the hand, and perceiving the tear trembling in my eye, he begged of me to let him supply the place of Berchtold. He called me son; Louisa's father could not call me so in vain, I fell upon his neck, but could not speak.

---

1   The Cisalpine Republic, proclaimed in June 1797 after Napoleon's first invasion of Italy, had been occupied by the Austrians and Russians in March 1799.
2   A broad street where races and processions were held.

PART SECOND

YOU have visited our alpine scenes and have undoubtedly been witness to the approach of one of those dreadful visitations of angry nature, which sometimes occur in the pent-up valleys. The black speck gathers upon the mountain's brow; amidst the silence and dead stillness of the air, it seems as if all were resting, in hopes of gaining strength to resist the desolating fury of the powers let loose against them. Only the lowing of the cattle, which, with its hollow lengthened sound, seems to give unheeded notice of the dread storm's approach, echoes upon the air, awed by the very stillness. Yet the sun shines brilliantly on the scene, doubled in the unrippled surface of the lake that seems proudly to bear the beauteous image, as if it were conscious how soon that smiling scene would be changed.—So passed the years, in which day succeeded day in unperceived succession, in which I lived under the same roof, partook innocently of the same joys and sorrows as Louisa. There was yet a weight upon my heart I could not explain; my dreams always terminated unhappily, and sleep, that refuge common to all misery, was to me like the waking hours of others. Immediately after our arrival, my sister was visited with a threatening appeal from our mother, who bade her depart with me once more to our native wilds, and never return. We could not understand the decrees of fate, lulled by the peace and apparent happiness around us, we were unconscious of what was in future,—we remained,—and I am what you see—a spectre amongst the living.

Encouraged by Louisa, I again returned to my studies. All the morning engaged in the library of my benefactor, I followed them under his direction, chiefly reading the modern poets and historians, with whom I had little acquaintance. Louisa would often come, and, sitting by my side, read the same passages, and discuss the merits of a particular image, often directing my taste, and pointing out many beauties I had not before perceived, even in my favourite authors. You see those volumes; they are those we read together; they now form my whole library, but you cannot know the pleasure there is contained in a single one of those pages. I read them, and every word again sounds upon my ear, as if she spoke it. I turn round and am undeceived, Louisa is not by my side, though her voice seems speaking as when we were innocent.

In the evening we assembled in the saloon of the palace. Doni was distinguished from his countrymen by a state of affluence, which was apparently boundless, but which was the more extraordinary in this respect, that it did not excite the envy of his neighbours. His riches indeed seemed less for his own use than for that of his friends. He was of a noble family, but being the off-spring of a younger branch, he had been early inured to hard-ships. Disdaining the mean idle life he was obliged to lead, in subservience to the will of a proud relation, he had left Milan at an early age, and had travelled into the East. He never, however, spoke of his journey, and always seemed anxious to direct the conversation into another channel, whenever it turned upon sub-jects in any manner connected with it. He had returned rich, no one knew whence; but there were whisperings abroad, that he had not gained his riches by commerce; though no one could trace where his riches lay; yet as his gold was poured forth with so liberal a hand, his wealth was deemed almost infinite. He had been strikingly handsome, and was extremely intelligent; but grief had weighed down his energies, and sorrow had broken his faculties. After his return he had married. Beauty was the mere casket, the riches were within; his wife was described as having possessed a mind, that without laying aside all that appealing del-icacy and weakness, which binds woman to man; had all those powers and accomplishments, which unfortunately in her sex have generally been the panders to vice; but which, with her, were the handmaids to virtue. Her presence was commanding, but her voice was persuasive; its tones struck the heart and produced those emotions, which all remember, none can express, the feeling, as if we had been always virtuous, and were worthy of lis-tening to the voice of a being superior to ourselves. The poor fol-lowed her steps, not with their usual boisterous cry for charity, but in silence; they seemed to watch the glance of her eye, as if the sympathy which shone there, had made them even forget their ragged miseries. Louisa was her counterpart, when I heard any one describing what her mother had been, it seemed that I could read the whole upon her daughter's face, and methought I could often perceive the speaker reading on the same page. Doni had loved her; nay more, had adored her, but she had married him by the persuasion of her parents, while her heart was engaged to another far away; he had returned, they saw one another, and fled together; Doni pursued them, fired at the car-riage which was escaping and blood fell upon the road;—they did not stop. Doni then entirely lost all command of himself, he fell in the road, calling for mercy and relief from that curse, which had already begun to blast him. He had never recovered the shock; had retired from all those gaieties in which he had been once engaged, and devoted himself to the education of his children. For their sake he had, however, again entered into society, but in a very different style from his former magnificence. These are the circumstances which I heard of his history, from those friends with whom I spoke in the course of the two first years of my stay at Milan; besides this, I also found the reports of his supernatural powers to be believed: and whenever I enquired concerning them, the speaker always looked round the room, before he ventured to speak, and would then only answer in whispers.

I have mentioned our evening assembly in the saloon of the palace; thither all distinguished by rank or science came—all visitors were alike welcome. There, no ceremony, which is but the vain-pointing of selfishness to its sacrifices, incommoded those, who, invited by the society they found there, chose to take a chair in this circle. Louisa's father always held the reins of conversation in his own hands, and instead of letting it fall upon the common place subjects of fashion, he turned the minds of his company to disquisitions that gave to each an opportunity of showing his information or judgement. At times, the existence and powers of the Deity were canvassed,—at times, the reality of beings intermediate between God and man; their qualities, and the facts related concerning them, came under consideration. Other evenings heard discussions upon the nature of virtue, whether it really were definite and felt, as is beauty, in every breast, or whether it were not merely an object of policy and self-convenience. The father and son generally took opposite sides, and under one or the other, each individual of the company enlisted himself, accordingly as it happened that he were either in a humour to be pleased with the general dispensation of providence throughout the day to himself, or was smarting under what he conceived to be an undeserved infliction of the evil spirit.

Olivieri made it a point to bewilder every one. He was a little older than myself; his head, though not perfect, had much beauty; a fine forehead, black hair, a dark, though small eye, united to a Grecian contour, formed, if not a pleasing, a striking physiognomy. I soon found that he had read much. His body also had been exercised; though not graceful, he was active, and hardly any excelled him in a certain quickness of adaptation, both of mind and body, to any thing required. His opinions were paradoxical and singular. In religion he outwardly professed Catholicism, and strongly opposed those scribbling philosophers, who by sarcasm, attempt to overturn the religion of ages, though at the same time he allowed the absurdity and falsehood of the prevailing doctrines. This did not appear to arise from a spirit of opposition, but, if the motives he gave were true, from a chain of thought that did honour to his heart, not head. He asserted that Catholicism was the only religion affording to the poor and to the sick of heart, a balm for their evils. Calvinism, deism and atheism,[1] were by him called the professions of the northern nations, cold as their native rocks. Professions to which enthusiasm, and the feeling of a certain refuge, so heart-soothing in Catholicism, were unknown. He maintained that it was not for individuals, who had the advantage of education and imagination, to shelter them from the overwhelming force of mental miseries, and unlooked for misfortunes, to attempt under a real, though vain pretence of the love of truth, to deprive the poor and uneducated millions forming the mass of mankind, of the consolation always offered by this religion, which instead of shunning the poor, gladly seeks their miserable hovel, in the hope of administering present comfort and future hope. Indeed he was inconsistent in his principles. He had not mingled much in general life, but while at Padua, where he had been sent to study, he had sought the acquaintance of all. From the knowledge of man he had there acquired, whether it were that he had constantly met with mean and weak companions, or that conscious of his own bad qualities, he had thence estimated the value of man's professions, he always seemed to view the human character in a darker hue than was warranted by truth, and to have formed his mind into a general contempt for mankind as a mass, and a determination, if ever an occasion offered, of rising at their expence, considering them but as tools to work with. His manners were at first always engaging, and rather pleasing, but this seemed irksome to him, and he gave way to an imperious, assuming air in conversation, which soon disgusted his friends. His ideas of a life after death seemed strangely childish, he did not believe in an immortality, yet he had so strong a love of fame, that there was no reputation he did not covet. He sometimes formed visions of a throne raised upon the blood of his countrymen spilt in civil war; at times, of the fame of a benefactor to debtors and galley slaves. He sought at the same time for the applause of the philosophers

---

1 Calvinism is the predestinarian form of Protestantism founded by John Calvin of Geneva (1509-64). Deism was the rational religion embraced by many eighteenth-century French *philosophes*.

and the drunkard, the divine, and the libertine. Things, of which, even at the moment of action he was ashamed, were often done by him in the view of proving himself capable of excelling even in vice. It was hard to say, whether he owed a certain frankness and easiness of attachment, to his weakness, or to seeds sown in his breast by nature. But whether it were from his incapability of constantly acting up to his system, or to the overpowering force of nature, it was strange to hear him express himself a follower of a doctrine that has proved the leech of human blood, and at the same time refuse to tread upon a worm. The evil was, his riches induced the young to pander for him, the old to flatter him, on account of his specious talents and handsome appearance. He was a student, a gambler, and a libertine.[1]

This man became my companion, his father often pointed me out to him, as the model for his conduct, and when he had to reproach him for the losses at the Ridotto,[2] or when Olivieri sought an excuse in the plea of youth, for the ruin his libertinism had brought on many families, he would speak of me as an example of strength, resisting all the temptations of vice. I was a reed when the storm came, Olivieri had watched me at the meetings in the saloon, I was generally a mere listener, but my curiosity was alive, though silent; my mind had an insatiable thirst for knowledge. I was a catholic, Berchtold had educated me in doctrines, without teaching me the foundation upon which they were built; he thought it impiety to question them. The conversation to which I was now present, seemed to rest upon the entire conviction, that all I believed was false. Yet this was not satisfactory. I heard arguments adduced in support of one assertion which seemed irresistible; but what was my surprise, on another evening to hear the same person adduce more than plausibilities in favour of the contrary hypothesis. I at last was bewildered, I was unwilling to believe

---

1 Olivieri's lack of physical gracefulness is probably a covert reference to Byron's lameness. His "quickness of adaptation" corresponds to what Byron called "mobility": see *Don Juan* (1819-24) 16.97-99 and Byron's note (*CPW* 5:769). For Olivieri's approval of Catholicism, cf. *BLJ* 9:123. For his opposition to the sarcasm of scribbling philosophers, cf. *Childe Harold's Pilgrimage* 3.107. For his scorn for the northern nations, cf. *The Curse of Minerva* (1811) 138 and *Don Juan* 1.64. For his disbelief in immortality, cf. *Childe Harold's Pilgrimage* 2.7. For his ambition of rising in a civil war, cf. "Epistle to a Friend" (1811) 51-54 (*CPW* 1:346), and an 1820 letter to his sister (*BLJ* 7:14).
2 Florio defines a ridotto as "a home or retiring place. Also a gaming house ..." (*OED*).

the human mind incapable of truth, the more I examined, the more difficulty I found in the attainment of it. I heard the deist and the atheist contend; following but one of the chains of argument, I was convinced; looking at them together, I saw the lustre of truth equally on both; I knew not which to choose. I was a sceptic in fact, not in name. Night after night upon my sleepless couch, I called upon the God, whose existence I doubted, to visit me, as if God heeded the belief of an individual, as if the happiness of an infinite being like him depended on a man's faith in his existence.[1] Olivieri perceived the state of my mind, I asked his assistance, he laughed at my attempt at knowledge, and bewildered me still more; I was restless, and seemed at length to be deprived of all motive for action. No superior being to smile upon our efforts, to whom we may show our gratitude, and whose approbation we may obtain; no virtue, but artificial trammels set up under its name, to lure the unwary into the toils of the wittiest knave. I wished I had never left those mountains, amidst which, I had thought, I felt the breath of a superior being, though he was clothed by my imagination in terrors. Nothing above man, and that man the sport of chance, of his own caprice. Yet within my breast it seemed as if aspirings dwelt which seemed to have been born with me. Were they but a mockery? I grew melancholy, whole days confined to my room, I meditated till my brain became a wilderness of various thoughts so entangled I knew not how to extricate myself.

My sister, fearing I was ill, would often sit by me, would bring Louisa, and they would together listen to my doubts. Julia seemed to be as much affected by them as myself, she listened with avidity, and echoed my own ideas. Not so Louisa, she talked of revelation, of a beneficent Deity, who had for a while left man in ignorance, to prove to him his own weakness, but had at last revealed himself, and announced a better state. While she spoke, she seemed like the first vision of the Wengern Alp destined again to save me, and set me free from these bewilderings, the first step towards vice. She soothed my mind, her lips quelled doubt into the peaceful certainty attendant upon Christianity. I no more paid any attention to the conversation of the evening, but set myself down by Louisa, and listened to her, while she was engaged in some work, which, though it employs the hands, leaves the mind at liberty. I sat by her, asking for some errand,

---

1 Ernestus's doubts and confusion recall Calantha's, on her first entry in society (Lamb 58-59; chap. 17). For a disapproving response to such doubts, see Appendix B.2.c.

some office, in doing which I might do her bidding; she was evidently gratified by my attentions, she would blush at my approach and smile; she would make room for me by her side. Oftentimes I gazed in silence upon her, and often our eyes met. Her breath at moments played upon my cheek, and sometimes her hand by accident touched mine. She would bid me read poetry to her, and often love was the subject of the poet's lay; my voice trembled, I dared not look upon her, for fear she should perceive the emotion upon my face. I loved her, but it was not a common love. I did not rest upon the hope of gaining her, she appeared a being superior to myself, of whom I was unworthy, yet it seemed, as if her smile were necessary to induce me to exert myself, and was a reward sufficient for the greatest deeds. She would sing to me, she would walk with me in the garden; but you must imagine, I cannot paint the charm, the magic, in her conversation. I have not described her person, for I could not, her mind was more heavenly than her eye, its expressions more delicately varying than the bloom on her cheek; there was meekness attendant upon power, softness upon strength.

If she had not left me for a moment, I might have been spared much guilt; but the sickness of a near relation was a call she could not resist. I had often followed her, when masked, she attended upon the sick in the hospitals. It is an Italian custom: often have I, disguised in the covering gown of the Misericordia, stood by her, whom it was impossible not to recognize.[1] The dying called for her, though they knew her not; they soon distinguished her powerful tones which pierced through the bond of grief around the most withered heart, and poured upon it those precious consolations afforded by her religion. Her manner, her voice, her gestures, seemed at such moments to be those of a being who was conscious of the truth of what it announced; not from the testimony of man, but from having witnessed the presence of the very Deity. The loud groan, the stifled sigh, were silenced in her presence; pain seemed to have no power; conscience no sting. She left me to visit her relation.

---

1 During his month in Milan (October 1816), Polidori visited the hospital regularly (*Diary* 181-82). At this time, hospitals were for the poor; the well-off were treated at home. The Misericordia was a benevolent society founded in Florence in 1244. The uniform worn by its members on duty covered the whole body and head; there were holes for the eyes. Polidori apparently saw members of the society at an execution in Rome in 1817 (*Sketches*, text to plate 30).

For some days I felt lost; I knew not to whom to apply; my sister seemed always occupied; she spoke with me; but I was sorry to find she had imbibed those doctrines so easily eradicated, as I thought, from my own mind. I observed Olivieri paid her particular attention, and often conversed with her. He at last perceived how restless I was; he seized the opportunity, determined to gain an object, which I did not think him capable of attempting. During my stay at Milan, I had hardly ever been out in the evening, for, as it is not customary for unmarried females to go into society, I should have lost the pleasure of sitting by Louisa. Now I had no inducement to remain at home. Olivieri persuaded me to accompany him to the theatre of La Scala.[1] I was induced by the splendour of the scenery, the beautiful dancers, the exquisite singing, to return. I was led into the boxes of our friends, and behind the scenes. I found my companion was every where well received. The dancers and actresses crowded around him: their conversation was lively and various. Gradually, the freedom in their discourse, which had at first disgusted me, grew indifferent; then pleasing by the wit sometimes shown even upon such subjects. One of these women, to whom Olivieri introduced me, was a mistress in her art, and well understood the artifices by which the young and unwary are misled: she was beautiful, and though her eye was never free from a certain look of confidence, the characteristic of this class, she could soften its expression, and cause it, in the presence of him she intended to inveigle, to send forth such glances as it was impossible to resist. By Olivieri's desire she attached herself to me, and I gradually took pleasure in her company; I saw her neglect the attentions of the first nobles in Milan to gain mine; in the midst of the rapturous applause of the whole theatre, she would turn her eye upon me to see if I approved; she seemed to sacrifice herself for me. When the opera was over, she would take my arm and lead me to the saloon of the theatre, where all were engaged in gambling. Sitting at a window, she drew me into conversation, gradually she approached the table; we at first stood merely as spectators; at last she tempted me to try my fortune: I consented, laid down my stake, it was soon increased to an enormous amount, for I was successful: I

---

1   The famous theatre was built by Maria Theresa in 1776. Polidori, like
    Ernestus, went there regularly and got into trouble there. On 28
    October, he caused a disturbance by asking an Austrian guardsman,
    who was standing in front of him, to remove his hat; he was expelled
    from the city (Macdonald 120-24).

threw it into her lap, and we parted. For several nights I was equally fortunate; but at length I lost. I was so profusely supplied with money by the kind friend who called me son, that I did not at first heed my losses. I had given all I gained to the syren, who still urged me on: I lost every franc I had. She then supplied me; I was ashamed to take it of her, though it was what I myself had gained; but I hoped my luck would change; I lost the whole. She then began to exert her more baneful powers, she led me from folly to vice, in search of what she assured me was an antidote to memory; I joined the libertine and the desperate. I was ashamed of letting Doni know that he, whom he had pointed out as a model of virtue to his son, had sunk into the lowest debauchery. Louisa's image often—often was before me; but how dare I name her in conjunction with my vices. She had thrice been a ministering angel, guiding my steps, but then I was innocent. I dared not now rest upon the thought; and often I threw myself deeper into the sinks of vice, in hopes that such reflections would not pursue me thither.

The syren, instigated by Olivieri, led me into every excess; while he plied me again with insinuations against religion, and sneers upon my credulous conscience that pictured a future state. I was now glad to seek refuge in unbelief; and I strove to lose myself in those thoughts which I had before fled, and from which I had been saved by my protecting angel. He also excited me to gamble, lent me money himself when I had none, and gathered round me every incentive to vice. He had been mortified at his father's holding me up as a pattern of strength against temptation; he was revenged, he exposed my weakness. I had hardly resisted the first approaches of vice, and had, in a short time, sunk below the lowest frequenters of its haunts.

One night I was desperate, every thing of value that I had was gone. Olivieri himself had been unsuccessful; and I knew not where to seek for the money I wanted to satisfy my creditors. I rushed out from the house, and found myself in the Piazza del Duomo. My brain was hot, my hair dishevelled; I rushed along, not knowing what I was about. I knew not where to apply. To destroy at once Doni's opinion of my virtue by telling him my situation, seemed worse than my present feeling. I stood still holding my head with my hand; I lifted my eyes from the ground on which they had been fixed. It was night, there was no light save from the glimmering stars and the newly risen moon, upon the dark canopy of heaven. The white façade of the Duomo raised its huge mass in contrast with the night; shining even upon its dark veil, it seemed to awe the mind by its indistinct mass, which, weighing on the earth, forced itself upon the eye when all else was lost in the shading darkness. All was still and sunk to rest; I alone seemed waking midst sleep; in anguish, midst repose. I stood, I know not why, for some time gazing upon the marble statues and forms which gained a certain charm from the moon's silvering light. The mats, spread like a curtain before the doors, being raised by the dying breeze, struck with a measured impulse the wall: unconsciously I entered. Save where the light of the moon fell upon the heavy columns, vesting them with the faint hues of the coloured glass that adorned the windows, it was all darkness that seemed sensible to the touch. I walked towards the high altar. There is a subterranean chapel dedicated to St. Borromeo, which receives its light through the flooring of the dome.[1] The silver lamps, hung over the shrine, sent up a column of light to the very roof. I descended the stairs, and found myself within the chapel. The lamps were almost failing, and the silver walls darkened by the torch of the devotees absorbed the little light they emitted. I approached the shrine; the dried corpse of the saint, arrayed in his pontificals, seemed, by its repose, to invite me to seek peace where he possessed it. His eye, which once might also have known anguish, was now sunk in the socket, and presented but a mass of blackened mould in the corner of its former throne. I gazed upon it until I thought I saw it move; methought there was a smile upon its lips, as if it mocked my thoughts of peace. I repose with him, a benefactor to the poor, a saint! A laugh was almost playing upon my lips, when the words, half stifled with emotion, "intercede my patron, intercede for Berchtold," sounded on my ear.—I turned; a female figure, I had not observed, was kneeling near the wall in earnest prayer. I approached, "who prays for Berchtold? your prayer is mocked." Alarmed, she raised her head; it was—you know whom I would say—it was Louisa. She looked upon my face convulsed with the violence of my emotions, upon my dishevelled hair. "Is it you? Ernestus," she said, rising, "are you come to pray; heaven has

---

1   The incorrupt corpse of St. Carlo Borromeo (1538-84), cardinal-arch-bishop of Milan, lies in a chapel under the altar of the cathedral. Polidori visited the chapel and described it as "very rich in silver, crystal, and jewels. The body is vested in pontificals, and quite dry. The orbits seem only filled with a little heap of black dirt, and the skull etc. is black" (*Diary* 182). Byron, for some reason, found the body "very agreeable" (*BLJ* 5:125).

then heard even me, and has not left you. Break not my heart." I could not utter more. She took my arm, we passed through the long nave; I dared not look around, methought some other form would burst upon my eyes in spite of the circling darkness, and blast me. A carriage was waiting at a little distance; she had left the gay dance to pray for me. I had handed her into her carriage, and was going; "Berchtold," she said, "will you leave me?" She wished me, the wretch, to be still near her. I jumped into the carriage, and blessed the darkness that hid my face; we spoke no more. Every one had retired at Doni's. She took my hand when leaving me, and pressing it in her's, whilst she gazed upon my face; she bade me think—she would have said more; a tear fell from her unwilling eye, and she hastily turned away.

I returned to my room, I had not entered it for many days. Louisa knew my guilt; sleep would not refresh me, my thoughts revelled in a maddening breast. Whither could I turn for refuge from their power? Religion I had cast from me, as a foul fiend's mock; Louisa! rest upon purity, I dared not; then my native mountains rushed upon my sight, I seemed bounding along the crags, Berchtold smiled upon my innocence, I laughed aloud— innocence? it was but the want of temptation. I threw myself upon my bed, and though not asleep, I became so stupified by the very excess of pain, that even the phantoms of conscience no longer passed with distinctness before me. The night seemed to hang suspended over my head, as if in pity it would hide me from the day, so slow was its progress; morning at last returned, but with it were the same thoughts as had visited me during the night.

It was hardly day before I heard some one at my door, I opened it, it was Doni. I turned away my head ashamed to look upon him, he did not reproach me, telling me that he knew my present way of life needed a more abundant supply of money, than he had given me, he bade me to apply to him for any sum I wanted. I could not speak, I had expected he would have attempted to show me my vices in all their native horror; he pressed his offer upon me; ashamed to tell him the whole amount of my folly, I at last named a sum not half sufficient to satisfy my creditors, but I thought it would stop the mouths of the most clamorous, and that in the mean time, by economizing my allowance, I might clear the rest. He asked me repeatedly, if it was the entire sum I owed; I answered yes; he left me, and in a few minutes returned, with gold to the amount required; "take it" he said, "it is no loss to me, but your wonted happiness I see is fled, that grieves me. Believe one who is older than yourself, Vice is not the path of happiness." I was silent. I intended immediately to pay my debts as far as I could, and at once to free myself from the life of a gambler, and a libertine.

My sister came to see me in my room, for I was ashamed of appearing at the breakfast table. I observed that the colour in her cheeks was gone, that she no longer was the open-hearted girl I remembered; attributing this however to the effect of my own follies upon her mind, I said nothing. She remained with me some time, but I no longer felt that pleasure I had always known in her company upon former occasions. We seemed both afraid of touching upon any thing relating to ourselves, and both evidently with minds deeply occupied about other important objects, talked of the most trivial circumstances.

When night came, I issued forth, determined to pay my debts, as far as was in my power; I entered the saloon of the theatre; there were only the banker and the punters arrived; they had arranged every thing for the faro table, and immediately they saw me, they began talking of the various successes of the last night. They told me how Olivieri had regained every thing at the very close of the evening. One or two gradually stepped in; amongst them was my friend, he was in high spirits; I took him aside, and told him that I was weary of this kind of life, and was determined to pay every one as far as I had it in my power. He would not let me finish, he laughed at my intentions, and told me, that as our good luck was now returned, it would be a folly to throw it away, that as I acknowledged myself incapable of paying the whole, it would be as well to owe a greater as a lesser sum.

His companions soon perceived the subject of our conversation, and joined us. They all ridiculed my intention, and I was persuaded to venture once more. I at first lost, but suddenly the rouleaus[1] poured upon me; one more stake, and I had regained even all my enormous losses; it was soon too late to retire, I almost lost all I had that morning received from Doni. It was now quite useless to think of retreating, I fell again into my former life, with more than double energy. I was at times surprised to find that great sums were paid to several of my creditors, I could not learn by whom; I imagined it was by Olivieri's father; this did not stop me. My vicissitudes were great, but I could never entirely extricate myself, so that I was always either lured by hope or urged by despair.

---

1   Rolls of coins, wrapped in paper.

I need not describe to you the progress of my other vices; debauched women, men of whom one is ashamed, and wine, are generally the attendants upon gambling. I could not seek the house of Doni, nor of virtue; I threw myself into every haunt of desperate characters like myself, and learnt to boast alike of the smile of the prostitute, or of the tear of the debauched virgin; when losing, I stupified my mind with wine, and was glad to fall from my chair, provided memory failed with my senses. Noted cheats, and men proscribed from society for their low dissoluteness, often seized upon my arm on the Corso, as if I were one of their equals, and I dared not repel their familiarity, for I was in their power. Once Louisa saw me in this situation, she never again rode out on the Corso; I had the maddened impudence to bow to her. I at last became mad, and once, was induced to aid in depriving a young novice of all his wealth, by means of false dice. I could not however stand by and see his horrible despair, he had beggared a wife and two lovely babes. I had just then been lucky, I confessed my participation to him, and gave him the whole amount of his loss; it became known, and I was laughed at; but for once I could withstand ridicule.

At the Doni palace in the mean time, the same outward appearance was preserved; there were still the same evening assemblies, but they were less frequented, for Olivieri was almost always with me. He was apparently afraid I should escape him; he was constantly stifling all thoughts that arose in my breast, tending towards a return to virtue. He never left me but when I was deeply engaged in play or debauch; then he constantly went I knew not whither. I have since found it out, and that discovery has not been the least of those pangs my guilt has brought upon me. I entered so little into society, that I heard nothing of what was passing there. I was, however, one day standing on the Corso with Olivieri, speaking to some ladies who had drawn up their carriage close to a shop, when the conversation turning upon the number of foreigners, who were moving about in consequence of the peace which had just been concluded,[1] a lady turning, asked me if I had seen the stranger who excited so much the curiosity of all circles. Upon my saying I had not, she began expatiating upon his singular character, rested upon his powers of fascination, and told me that all the ladies were in love with him. I did

---

1   The Treaty of Lunéville, 9 February 1801. Napoleon had invaded Italy a
    second time and defeated the Austrians at Marengo in June 1800.

not pay much attention to this, thinking it but the foolish prattle of a young girl. She however continued; she wondered that I had not seen him, as he was a constant attendant upon Louisa, she having engrossed the whole of his attention, much to the mortification of all Milan.

Now I was roused. I let go Olivieri's arm, and wandered about alone. I dared not hope that Louisa could resist one whom all seemed to admire. The whole weight of my guilt fell heavily upon my recollection, and one after another all my vices presented themselves, arrayed against me. I did not return that day to any of my usual haunts. Towards evening, I found myself, fatigued with wandering, at the gate of the Doni palace. I know not what inspired me, it seemed as if I wished to gain the certainty of my fate. My steps, which till now had been slow and measured, suddenly quickened. I found myself at the entrance of the saloon; all was silent; the red purple glare of sunset pierced the windows. I stood for a moment still; a sigh burst upon my ear—I entered—Louisa was sitting looking upon the setting sun. It was her sigh. She did not turn: "Is it you, my father?" I did not speak, she turned her head, her face was pale, but a blush mantled her cheek at the sight of me; her eyes were sunk and dim, but they brightened at my presence. She spoke my name, she rose, and with faultering steps attempted to reach a door leading to her apartments. I murmured audibly, but with a stifled voice: "She flies me, she flies, she hates me!" She turned. "Oh no: I do not, Ernestus, do not believe it." She fell upon the floor; I approached, knelt by her side, but dared not touch her. I attempted it, my hand retreated; there seemed to be pollution in my touch; I dared not. The cool air played upon her face, and the chill of the marble floor gradually recovered her; she opened her eyes; I was now near her; I could see the marks of a suffering mind upon her face; her cheek now had no colour, save that reflected from the red light of the illumined west. Her tresses were disordered and neglected; her eyes sunk deep in their socket, how changed from the vision of the Wengern Alp! Her subdued voice could hardly articulate, when she again assured me with earnestness that she did not hate me, that she forgave me. Tears flowed down my cheeks, and I did not try to stop them. She looked upon me: "It is too late," she said, smiling with the smile of a broken heart; "it is too late, Berchtold; I wish that I could weep, but my eyes are dried up." The sounds of approaching footsteps were heard; she rose with difficulty; trembling, I offered my arm, she took it. I thought she would have spurned it. I could hardly support my own weight. I saw her to her door, and threw myself upon the staircase near it; but I soon heard strange voices in the saloon; the thought of its being his voice, who, I had heard, was my rival, at once made me start. I rose, retired for a moment to my room, and then entered.

The apartment was now lit up. The company were in greater numbers than I had ever seen before. My rival, I said to myself, is then so attractive. No one observed my entry; they all seemed engaged around one man. It was my rival; I never saw so singular a figure. His bust and head were handsome, and bore the signs of strength. His black hair was in ringlets; his face was pale with a blueish tint that diminished even the colour of a naturally pale eye. His hands were joined with their palms turned towards the ground; his eyelids almost covered his eyes, which turned upon the floor, while his head erect, bore in its general expression the marks of contempt. He was speaking with elegance upon the fallen glories of some sunken nation; when he had ended, and the conversation had became more general, he raised his eyes, and affecting surprize, he seemed ashamed of having attracted so much notice, though he did not blush, for the hue of his features seemed invariable. He retreated to a corner of the room, left vacant by the pressure of the company towards the spot he had just occupied. He there bent down his head, as if abstracted in thought; but looking under his eye-brows, he was evidently engaged in remarking the effect he had made upon the company. He again gradually got a circle round him, and again was apparently carried away by the great powers of his mind, and held forth upon some subject, and then once more retreated. I was tired of watching such acting, and looked round for my sister. She was at that moment entering; she immediately addressed Doni, who seemed alarmed, and went out. I approached—Louisa was ill and could not appear. Julia looked upon me as if she knew it had been my presence which had thus affected her friend; I could not bear that look: "Do not reproach me, I feel all the shame of my crimes." "I reproach you!" she answered, "You mock me, I! it is not for one like me to do it." She turned away, I did not understand her; I asked her why she rested upon one like her. "Oh! do not ask me, my shame must not be spoken." The noble stranger approached, and broke off our conversation by asking after Louisa. I could not stand by him, but joined some of my former acquaintances; for though my heart was breaking, I dared not leave the room, determined to watch minutely every action of him I fancied my rival.

I entered into conversation, and forced myself to enquire about this stranger, who thus engaged the attention of all. There was a certain affectation of mystery about him, which induced all to seek him, in hopes of penetrating the veil he threw round his actions. I met with one who had known him intimately in his own country. From whom I learnt several traits of his character; it appeared that this German was much distinguished amongst his countrymen for his talents,—that he was generally esteemed a hater of all the vanities of the world, but that he passed many hours at his toilette; that he was deemed broken-hearted from having been crossed in love; but that he was incapable of feeling that passion, being wrapt in selfishness, that made him sacrifice every thing around him to the whim of the moment: that he was deemed irresistible, and that no woman upon whom he fixed his eye could withstand the fascination of his tongue, but that he had never dared to tempt any woman, who was not of the most abandoned character; that even they were never addressed with boldness, but were always made to compromise themselves by some folly with him in public, before he would give them the least marked sign of attention; that in fine he was a confirmed coward with women. In society he was playing off a strange coquetry with the whole world, affecting to be modest and diffident, whilst he protruded himself into notice. He was, however, rich, handsome, and noble by birth, I was an orphan dependent upon charity. He was every where received with great attention, no where with greater than in Doni's palace.

Perceiving that Louisa's father did not return, I became alarmed, and anxious to gain some information, I sought for him. He was walking with hasty steps before her door. Upon seeing me, he was turning away, but moved by my broken voice, he stopped, looked upon me, and addressed me, "You saved my son, Berchtold, but my daughter, my beloved daughter dies; it is, however, useless to speak to you, leave me, go to your room, Louisa's better." Every thing seemed confused to me, I could not believe that I was the cause of Louisa's illness, I could not believe that she could love such an outcast as myself. I was several times in the course of the night by her door, listening for some sound that should assure me of her existence. I fell asleep at last upon the sofa in my room, and I saw her in my dream as when she first appeared before me, glowing in health, buoyant with spirits; suddenly I thought she ran towards me, but ere she reached me, she faded like a flower, and fell to the ground. I awoke, all was still, but my heart beat violently. It seemed as if this were the fulfilment of my former dreams, my vices were the evils, the warning voice of my mother commanded my sister to fly, for they were doomed to be the death of all I loved.

Morning came, my first enquiries were concerning Louisa; she was very ill, and in a state of great weakness. Doni was not yet risen, and was apparently quite overcome. During the whole day, I was not one moment at rest; I wandered from one room to another, and sent every instant to enquire concerning my protector's daughter. I stood by the door watching all who came from her room, and begged them to tell me every change they observed. Towards evening a packet was put into my hands; it contained receipts from every one of my creditors. There was no explanatory paper. Imagining it to be the gift of Doni, I determined to thank him; I went to his room; I found him lying upon his couch very much fatigued and exhausted; he was courting repose, but it was in vain; anxiety was painted upon his face, and grief seemed to stamp him with its chilling furrows. My first question was concerning his daughter. I then showed him the packet, and had begun to thank him, when he interrupted me. "Young man, thank not one, who wished that you should first have paid the price of your vices before he freed you from your embarrassments. I had resisted my daughter's entreaties, till last night, she offered to give up her allowance, every thing, to free you; I refused, but I could not long do so, to a child I thought dying." I was thunderstruck, the packet fell from my hand; I thought I should have fallen through shame; but he spoke again, "Would that your apparent shame were the least security against your follies, but I believe you to be incurable." He motioned me away; I fell at his feet, and called Heaven to witness that I would never again partake of vicious pleasures. He raised me from the ground, pressed me to his bosom, and with a blessing told me, that if I kept this promise, he might yet be happy; he bade me leave him to his hopes, again embraced me, and I left him.

For the first time during the last many weary months, I felt something like repose in my mind. It seemed as if the vow I had made to heaven might be relied on, and as if I again might know the consolation of a conscience at rest. That night I slept quietly and soundly, for Louisa was announced to be much better, and my heart felt a little repose. It was but to give me strength to bear worse than I had yet endured.

Next morning Louisa saw me, she was upon the bed of sickness, but she had partly recovered the shock my abrupt entry had caused her. I shall never forget the moment I entered. I had expected she would have received me with marks of horror; she smiled; oh, no! she did not hate me. I sate by her, she allowed me to take her thin cold hand within my own; it chilled my heart with its touch. There was a clear whiteness that overspread her face, where it was not tinged by the hectic flush,[1] her eye shone with a glassy brilliancy that seemed not mortal, it was the glance of death mocking my senses through a beauteous vizor, for there were the seeds of death sown deep in her broken heart. She spoke but little, what she did utter, however, were words of kindness, and they were all her weakness allowed her to say. She often turned her brilliant eyes upon me, and the soft smile upon her lip, I thought was excited by the gentle whisperings of hope, that I was snatched for ever from vice. The latter part of the morning was passed near her in a silence that was not mute, for there is a language which, though not addressed to the ear, still speaks the thought within. Her physician came and advised me to retire. I bade her farewell; an anxious look accompanied the words, "where are you going?" but when I intimated my determination of staying at home, I cannot describe to you the joy expressed upon her face as she repeated my farewell.

I had been so little at home, that I knew nothing of what had lately happened. I was, therefore, much surprised, when, upon desiring a servant, towards night, to see if Doni was in his apartment, he refused, saying he had not courage. Upon making enquiries, I found that their master's supernatural powers had been much talked of lately amongst the servants; for during the latter days, unusual noises had been heard in his room, and every morning, all his things had been found in a strange confusion while he was apparently so exhausted, that it was evident he had had no rest during the night. Thinking all this very explicable from the state of anxiety in which he had been kept, I tried to convince the servant, but he appeared firm in his belief, and refused to carry my message.

Louisa seemed rapidly to recover strength. As we were in the very middle of summer it was thought proper by her physicians that she should be removed to a cooler situation than the neighbourhood of a great city. We accordingly retired to the banks of the Lago Maggiore. The palace close to the lake was refreshed by the cooling breeze that passed over the water's vast expanse, and the playful fountains that sported with their noisy showers in the

---

1 A symptom of tuberculosis.

apartments towards the land, promised to shield the invalid from the noxious effects of an Italian sun; while the magnificent scenery of the varying basin before our view, seemed to promise relaxation to the mind. We arrived late at night, and immediately retired to our beds. I arose betimes, and issuing forth ascended the numerous terraces, which, one above another, seemed like the work of some enchanter. When viewed from the water's edge, garden seemed to be hanging above garden, as if man had acquired the power of piling nature's gifts even into the air. I did not heed this, for my native mountains were in sight; I did not gaze upon the rich islands, which seemed like fairy dwellings springing from the lake; I gazed upon Monte Rosa, which, high above the neighbouring hills, asserted the glory of its alpine birth. Though all around seemed burnt by the sun's ray, it mocked his power and bore its unvarying white vest, in defiance of his frown, upon its aged limbs. While yet engaged looking upon its high summit, with all the crowded images of infancy offered by my memory, my sister passed me. She seemed lately to have lost all her spirits, she did not appear to be attracted by the beautiful scene near us, or the sublimity of the alpine ridge beyond. She was gazing upon the ground, I joined her, she started, and with a trembling voice asked me, "Why I was come?" I answered her; at that moment I saw Olivieri turn the corner of the alley and approach; but immediately he saw me he retired, and I at the same time perceived that my sister was violently agitated. I looked at her, and begged of her to tell me what I was to imagine; she hastily replied, "Nothing, nothing;" and her colour, which had deserted her at the sight of Olivieri, returned with greater rapidity than it had fled the moment before. I insisted upon an explanation; she said she was unwell, weak, and made other excuses of the same nature. I now remembered her agitation a few evenings before, when we were interrupted by the Count Wilhelm. I threatened, if she would not satisfy me, to seek an explanation from Olivieri. She fell upon her knees before me, begged me not, assured me that it concerned a third person. I was moved, I had the weakness to promise that I would seek no farther.

I had not seen my friend till this moment, since the payment of my debts; he had never been home, and I had not sought him. He had not accompanied us, and I had not been aware that he was expected. I re-entered the house, hoping to find him; but no one had seen him, and he did not appear at breakfast.

Louisa made her appearance at that meal. You may imagine

my pleasure at again seeing her out of her sick chamber. She made room for me by her side. I accompanied her into the orange-walk near the house, and I sat near her for two hours while she enjoyed the beauty of the scene. She looked at the Alps, then at me, it seemed as if the recollection of our first meeting passed through the minds of both. Involuntarily I opened the bosom of my vest and showed her the scarf, which I had constantly worn since that day. She smiled. "I did not think of this at that time," she said, "I did not know your name, but when the fame of Berchtold, Ernestus Berchtold, was echoed by the wild rocks to the voice of every peasant, I sighed and wished he might be the chamois hunter of the Wengern Alp. It was I sent the saviour of my brother's life to battle. I sent the hero to aid in the rescue of his country; it was in vain, yet I was conscious of a feeling of pride whenever I thought of it." She spoke of my former life, and passed in silence over that part, when every moment had been spent in shame. I cannot describe my sensations to you. The feeling of how little I deserved such praise, mingling with the pleasure of hearing it from Louisa's lips, embittered what else would have been the proudest moment of my life. Her father joined us, and seemed pleased at seeing us together; he seated himself upon the other side of his daughter, and we spent the whole morning together in conversation, till the sun becoming too powerful, Louisa was obliged to retire for shelter and repose, and we separated.

Day passed after day, and Louisa's health seemed rapidly to recover; but my sister evidently became more and more restless. She generally avoided, and very seldom sought our society. I knew not what to understand; determined however to force her to an explanation, I one evening, finding her alone, induced her to walk out with me. We wandered, without perceiving it, into the garden. She seemed determined upon silence. Wrapt in thought, the sun's red disk fast sinking in the west, the birds' evening carol, the varied light of the heavens reflected from the soft silky clouds over the purpling surface of the lake, the cooling breeze which played upon her feverish cheek, were all unnoticed. Yet she was wont, in all that feeling of nature's charms which accompanies youth, to gaze upon that orb, and figuring it as the image of that Providence she adored, think the birds sang hymns of thanks to him for all he gave. But now she passed, and all was unheeded. There was a seat upon the river's side, which, shaded by the plants that crept entangled round the branches of a noble chestnut, formed a bower, whence all the beauties of the rich nature round could be viewed. I attempted in vain to enter upon the subject of what was causing this apparent misery in her breast; she was abstracted, and answered merely by monosyllables. I at last ceased to press her, and we both sunk into silence.

The spreading clematis of the bower hid us completely from the path near us, while its open leaves allowed us to see distinctly all that passed in the avenue. There was a wall of cypress which ran along one side of the gravel walk, fully exposed at this moment to the sun's rays. I saw at last approaching from the bottom, the Count our protector; he seemed in earnest conversation with some one, but I could perceive no one near him; yet his lips and hands certainly moved as if he spoke. As he gradually approached, I could even distinguish sounds. I motioned Julia to observe him; she did so and soon pointed to the hedge. I could not at first see to what she directed my attention; but at last I perceived the outline of a figure, through the shape of whose body the very leaves were visible; something in the manner that I have seen in the summer, a current of heated air, accurately defined by the wavering outline of the things between which and our sight it stands, only that this was even more sensible to vision. I could not distinguish its voice, but I at last caught some of the words of Doni. I had hardly time to make these observations, when the Count seemed to start, and the figured vapour went.

We did not move; we for some time seemed rooted to our seats; at last Doni disappeared amidst the trees, and we looked at each other. It was then true what we heard at the lake of Thun, our protector had communication with a spirit. My sister seized the subject of conversation with avidity. We related to one another several slight circumstances, which had come to our knowledge, many incidents which we could not explain. The reluctance of the servants to approach the chambers of the Count all pressed upon our minds. The immense wealth, which seemed inexhaustible, must, it appeared to us, be connected with this untenanting spirit. We resolved not to mention the circumstance we had just witnessed to any one. But it was not effaced from our own memory. We returned to the house and saw our protector there as usual, but his face was, or I imagined it to be, pale; his eyes wandered, and then seemed to fix their angry glance at times upon us; but whether this were imagination or reality, I could not decide. I went to bed, but not to sleep, the thoughts of having seen an unembodied being, the tales of my foster-mother, of power, of wealth, arising from the communication with beings of another world, arose before me. Obtaining such a power, it seemed as if I might learn the things hidden in the earth's deepest recesses, the ocean's depth; I even thought, that by such a power, I might tear away the veil which the first Cause has thrown over itself. Nor did these visions disappear with the morning's light, they were as distinct in the sun's brightness, as in the night's obscurity. I arose determined to speak on the subject with the Count. He met me with an affectionate embrace; I took his hand, had the words upon my lips, when, meeting his eye, I saw expressed therein such anxious fear, such meaning, that the words fell into inarticulate sounds; instantly his eye was as usual; nothing but brilliancy was there. We went together to fetch Louisa from her apartment, and descended to the breakfast table.

Louisa seemed to take a great pleasure in my society, and sought in every way to bring me near her; she seemed afraid of trusting me to myself in my first steps towards retracing the paths of virtue. She again resumed the subject which had formed the topic of conversation, before her fatal departure to visit her sick relation. She painted to me the charms of a religion, which taught us to look up to the infinite power above us, not as to an object of terror and fear, but of love and hope. Her mind, without losing the least of that delicacy which is the magic charm that spreads its influence round the footsteps of woman, was energetic and clear. Her simplicity was not misled by the winding, intricate sophisms of the deist and unbeliever; her belief was built upon persuasion, which, though it had at first depended upon faith, had not scorned the bulwarks of reason. The earnestness with which she spoke, did not make her appear bold or presuming; for the mild look of her dark eye seemed looking to heaven to beg for inspiration from him, whose cause her lips were pleading. She would often lead me towards the chapel, and without affectation, would kneel down by my side motioning me to imitate her, and bending devoutly before her maker, would pray for me. I did not think of myself; but gazing upon that veiled eye, which did not seem to think itself worthy of looking towards the throne of God, while petitioning for strength against mortal weakness, a prayer would involuntarily rise from my heart for her. I did not feel the time long when near her, though it was even spent in prayer; to have communication with the Almighty in union with her, seemed to be an additional bond amongst those numberless ties which bound me to her. From the first moment that I had seen her, she seemed to visit this earth as my protecting angel; now it appeared as if such a being had led me to the throne of him of whose commands she was the bearer. I did not notice the lapse of months; and autumn had already vested the scene around with its checquered hues, ere this happiness was interrupted; I had even forgotten all my imaginations concerning the being attendant upon Doni. It seemed as if misfortune could no longer visit me; such is human foresight.

I have already mentioned to you the singularity of my sister's conduct; it grew more and more remarkable. She never came down in the morning, but, confined to her room, she spent the hours in solitude: when she did appear, it was but to retire to a corner, where, enveloping herself in her shawl, she apparently brooded over some thoughts that destroyed her peace. Her appearance was completely changed; her auburn hair, which once floated in ringlets of soft varying light upon her shoulders, was now entangled and neglected; her cheeks, on which was wont to play a hue more delicate than that of the white rose, were pale and sickly; her eyes no longer shone with sparkling lustre, they were now heavy and inflamed from the want of sleep. I often saw the silent tears fall from her eye; but it was in vain to question her; she wept bitterly at every enquiry I made, and seemed agitated to the most violent excess whenever Olivieri's name was mentioned. I was bewildered by the enquiries of Doni and Louisa, who constantly expressed their anxiety concerning her.

We were assembled together at the breakfast table as usual one morning, and were conversing about Julia, who had made her appearance the evening before at the supper table, which she had not done for a long time, when a servant came to tell us that her maid had applied several times in the course of the last hour for admission to her room, but that she could obtain no answer. Louisa offered to see if she could obtain admission; in vain, we went together; all, all was silent. We burst open the door, there was no one, every thing seemed in disorder, the bed had not been slept in the last night; upon the floor there were many pieces of paper torn into fragments; and upon the table there was a note addressed to myself. I took it trembling, I was afraid she had committed some desperate act. I could not open it, but gave it into Doni's hand; he read it:

My shame can be no longer hidden; I fly then to hide myself; curse not your sister, my own feelings are sufficiently bitter to satisfy even the injured honour of Berchtold.—Your degraded Julia.

I sunk upon the bed; Olivieri immediately presented himself to my mind as the seducer of my sister. I could not speak, and my friends were silent, they looked upon me with pity. I dared not inform them of my suspicions, they would bring the old man's grey hairs to their grave, and would cut off the feeble thread of life in Louisa. She bore up against the shock; and while the tear trembled in her eye, she sat down by me, and strove to sooth, not console me, for that she knew was impossible.

Servants were sent in every direction. I searched all the neighbourhood. I determined instantly to go to Milan, and make enquiries directly from Olivieri, concerning the fate of my sister. I made a plausible excuse for my departure, and soon reached the Corso, Doni's palace. The servants had not seen him for some time. I forced myself to seek him in the places which had been my former resort. My late companions hailed my approach; but I turned from them in disgust. Olivieri had no where been heard of lately. Distracted by my suspicions, which now seemed to wear the semblance of certainty, after several days spent in the vain search, I returned to the Lake.

We soon fixed ourselves again at Milan. It was now impossible to keep his son's absence a secret from Doni. He learnt it, but did not seem to imagine any connection between the flight of my sister and his son's conduct. Perceiving this, I did not intimate to him my horrible doubts, but left him in entire ignorance. In the mean time I made the most minute enquiries concerning both; but could learn nothing.

Louisa's health in the mean time gradually recovered; but she never lost the hectic flush upon her cheek; she gained strength, but the seeds of death were hidden, not destroyed. During her gradual recovery, I was always with her; and if you can picture the happy hours of one sitting by a being he loves—adores, at the same time, that his imagination paints her to him as a spirit of heaven, you may imagine my happiness, when sitting by Louisa, whose smile, whose glance told me she loved. She had gained me fame; had saved my life, my honour; had restored to me the hopes of a future state, the belief in a kind God. I know not your belief, your principles; you may sneer at the feeling which dictates my ranking the two last with the former; but, young man! believe one who has experienced the whole of fate's wanton inflictions;— he who can still rest upon futurity, confident in the goodness of his maker, may find a refuge in the greatest misery; he who cannot, may indeed despair, he has but the present, and that may indeed be dreadful.

Louisa's image was always with me. I loved her, but so did every one; I could not for that reason hope to gain her. I was an orphan, how often has the thought of that sunk my buoyant hope, which still would revive. I had no rank. Count Wilhelm had again renewed his addresses. It seemed dishonourable in me to continue any longer near her, endeavouring to gain her affections; it seemed as if the debt of gratitude I owed to Doni forbade my attempting to gain his daughter. The count had rank and wealth. I could not hope that her father should prefer me, degraded by vice, my birth perhaps tainted with dishonour, to one whose name was a spell upon all Europe. I had determined to leave Milan, and to plead the necessity of further enquiries for my sister. Doni approved of my intentions, and in a few days I was to set off. I had been preparing for my departure, and had been talking to the servant about the trifles necessary for a solitary journey; it was not yet the hour for the company to assemble, and lost in sorrow I was slowly approaching the saloon, when those notes which had sung hope to me in prison, sounded on the air. They were falling upon the breeze broken, and in a melancholy tone; though the air was lively, it seemed as if Louisa sought to sing of hope, while her heart could not echo back the strain. I had not heard the song since I sunk into vice. The sound was silenced, I entered; Louisa was leaning upon her harp, her head was fallen upon her hand. There was no light, and the lowering clouds hid the little daylight that might have been afforded by the setting sun. I could just distinguish her form, almost lost in the obscurity; suddenly she moved, struck her harp in wild notes, and sung the words of a broken heart. I could not hear more; Louisa's name fell from my lips; "Sing not so, Louisa; if you have not happiness, who shall possess it?" She sunk upon a chair, and I approached. "You leave me to morrow," she said, "I shall no longer have any one to cheer me, any one, whom I can"—She stopped and hesitated. I stood breathless by her side. "I shall, I will return." "You will find me a corpse, I feel no power of life within me, it seems as if my soul still clung to life that it might converse with you, when you are gone." I took her hand; I bade her, if she loved me, not to speak in words that pierced my heart. "Love you," she answered, "you cannot know what I feel towards you, I am myself ashamed that any can divide my heart with God, but you—" I fell upon my knees. "I will not go, I cannot, Louisa has confessed her love, she loves the orphan Berchtold, if that words could express the least part of what I feel, I would speak. I love you, let my silence speak the rest." I felt her feeble hand press mine, she had fainted, her weak health had not given her strength to listen. We had not heard the storm which had burst over our heads, I had not seen the flashes of heaven's anger, which had unobserved spread its lurid light around us. I lifted her in my arms, carried her to her chamber, and delivered her to her maid. She recovered.

I was alone; the thunders echoed still in the distance, and the horizon was lit by the forked lightning. But in my breast the convulsions were not subsiding. At the first moment it seemed as if happiness indeed were mine; but Doni's image came quickly across my mind, and all I owed him seemed to be imaged as so many reproaches for my having stolen the affections of my benefactor's daughter. The company assembled, but I could not join them. The tumult in my breast was too powerful to allow me to participate in the light frivolity of a drawing room. I retired to my chamber, and was soon lost in meditation upon that fatality, which made the very circumstance on which I had rested as the bourne of all my hopes, a cause of anguish and reproach. I determined to see the Count immediately after the company had retired. No malefactor, who is listening in expectation of hearing the lengthened toll, warning him of the executioner's approach, ever counted the moments with greater anxiety than mine. The clock struck, and each brazen sound seemed to vibrate through my body, as if it bore grief upon its sound. At last the carriages began to depart, and I entered the apartment of my friend. I had never dared to call him father, it seemed to my mind too sacred a title to be profaned by me; he was Louisa's father.

I had been some time in his apartment before he entered. He came, his face was full of anxiety. "My daughter," he said, "I fear is going to relapse, something has agitated her strongly, and she will not tell even her father what it is. Berchtold," he continued, "you have never before seen a father in the agony that I endure, my daughter's life sinks visibly before me, and I cannot discover the cause. You have therefore no conception of the pain it brings." I knew not what to say. "Olivieri too is I know not where, perchance in the haunt of the lowest vice, perhaps acting again the hero, as when with you. You are not my child, yet you now form my only comfort, my only hope." I could not hear more;—he praise me! who had, like the snake stinging the child enchanted by the beauty of its scales, robbed him of his treasure, insidiously won his daughter's love; I interrupted him. "I am a wretch, not worthy of your affection, your daughter loves me, I have dared to tell her she was my only hope; spurn me from you, I expect it; but do not blame her." I fell upon my knees, "Do not blame her for loving such a wretch as me, she pitied me and my daring devotion changed pity into love." My head was hid within my hands, I expected to be cursed by him I looked up to as a father. He raised me from the ground. "Ernestus, this is nobly spoken, I will not reproach you with your former vices, Louisa shall be security to me, that you will always prove what you now show yourself." I was amazed; I embraced him, but could not speak. Louisa was to be mine,—my guide, my wife. At that moment happiness seemed to be descending from heaven to be our handmaid, while in fact despair and horror were preparing their flight from the lowest abyss to wait upon our nuptials.

Next morning I was admitted to Louisa's chamber; I told her that her father had consented to our union. A gleam of joy crossed her pale face, she said she was happy, but those words were in a broken and weak voice. I heeded it not, so great was my joy, I sat with her, she listened to my plans of happiness, and smiled; it seemed as if she were conscious of their being but to be imagined. I was at last called away by my own servant, who putting a letter in my hand, told me that he had found it thrown in at the door. It was my sister's hand writing; fearful of agitating Louisa, I hastily put it into my bosom, and making an excuse left her. When in my chamber, I opened the note. The lines were few:

A mother appeals for her child to your charity, she has but a short time to live, but her child has not a broken heart. Julia.

Berchtold had been written, but a tear had effaced the characters. There was the name of an obscure street in the most retired part of Milan.

I immediately repaired thither, and soon found myself in an abode of misery I cannot describe. It was upon the highest story, the roof in several parts let in the hot ray of the sun, and the window was not glazed, but stuffed with dirty rags. It could not be called a shelter, for the floor bore on its black soft texture the marks of every cloud that had passed over it. In one corner there was a bedstead, over which was spread a blanket, that seemed not to have been removed for many years, it was so black and thick with dirt. A broken dish, and rags, which I but too well recognised as the remnants of my sister's dress, were the only things upon the floor. I heard a difficult breathing, which proceeded from the bed. I approached, and found my sister. She was pale and squalid, her hair, entangled and loose, covered her face and bosom, and her clasped hands hung from the bed. She was apparently asleep, and her child was grasping her breast with its little hand, trying in vain to obtain sustenance from its fevered mother. I stood for some time gazing upon her; finding she slept soundly, I descended the creaking stairs, and sending some person of the house for clothes and food, I waited till they returned and carried them up with me. The noise I made awakened her, she shrunk from me; "I did not call you for myself, but this child's cry pierced my heart,—do, do not therefore curse me, if I have even brought you to witness your sister's infamy. I could not die and leave my child sinking unaided upon my putrid corpse."[1] I spoke kindly to her, she looked upon me, and said, "Ernestus," with an incredulous voice, and burst into tears. I soothed her, spoke to her of her child, induced her to take a little nourishment, and saw her feed her little babe. She looked at its eager eye and face while feeding, at moments hugged it to her bosom, while a stifled laugh escaped her; she did not seem to notice me, and I spoke not. At last she fell exhausted upon the bed. I gave her the clothes I had brought, she did not heed me.

I hastened to Doni, related what I had seen; he ordered every thing to be got ready at the palace, and procuring a litter he accompanied me to the abode of my wretched Julia. At sight of him, she hid her face, and would not speak. I had her conveyed to the litter with her child, and we arrived at the palace. The physician of the family being sent for, announced to us, that from the state of exhaustion, into which she had fallen, there were but a few hours remaining of her life. I watched by her all night, she did not speak; I took Louisa for my model, and spoke to her of those hopes which had seemed on her lips to have the power of soothing sickness, and to still the fears of death. She was moved by what I said, for her cold hand pressed mine. I put questions to her with regard to her seducer; she was silent; but a convulsive motion seemed to seize her whole features. I urged her no more. She seemed to revive a little in the morning; auguring well from it, I began to speak to her of her child, talked to her of its health, said it should be named Ernestus, and promised that I would be its father. She raised her fallen head, and looking with tears in her eyes, blessed me, but hardly had the words fallen from her lips, when shuddering, she said, "my blessing! that, that's a curse." I took her to my breast, she shrunk from me, "you know not whom you embrace." "It is my sister, whom I hold in my arms," I cried,

---

1 A reversal of the predicament of Agnes and her dead baby in Lewis, *The Monk*, chap. 11.

she burst into loud sobs, and fell again, upon her pillow. "You shall hear," she replied, "what a sister!" She prepared to relate to me the whole of her late history; I advised her to repose awhile first. "Well, well, I shall have the less time to feel the blush of shame, and to hear your reproaches, 'tis better so." She fell asleep after uttering these words, but she was restless, her face was convulsed, and the twitching of her arms began to give the signs of the rapid approach of death.

I seized this moment of apparent rest to enquire for Louisa. She was much better; we had kept our discovery of Julia a secret, fearful of agitating her too much; I determined therefore to see her, lest, making some enquiry concerning me, she might hear how I was engaged. I entered her room, and staid with her for some time; she spoke of her love, and added, that all that she thought wanting was the presence of her brother and Julia. I could not answer, but rose, and again went to my unconscious sister. She was disturbed in her sleep, and was calling upon Louisa's name; she seemed to reproach her for not seeing her; but then she appeared to meditate and said; "true, true, I am an outcast." She awoke, looked wildly around, met my eye. She was lost some time in thought, and then addressed me; "I know what you are waiting for but ere I unfold the whole of my shame, give me your solemn promise that you will grant your sister her last dying request." I gave it her.[1] "You will then never mention to either of my former friends what I narrate, and you will let me die, certain that you will never injure him that ruined me, for still, still I love him." I assured her, that I would leave it to heaven to punish him,[2] for I was conscious it was Olivieri, Louisa's brother. It was him, the account that I had given of his bravery in the Swiss war, the description I had made of his daring feats had gained an entire possession of her imagination. When, therefore, she met him at Milan, his beauty, his specious manner and apparent knowledge had completed her fascination. I myself, when bewildered by doubts, had sapped the foundation of her religious principles; and Olivieri, who was not blind to her partiality, had fanned the spark of scepticism, till he had destroyed all belief in virtue and a future state. I lost myself at the gambling table; and my conduct was but an additional proof in her mind, that the

---

1 Perhaps a reminiscence of the oath of silence in *The Vampyre* (51).
2 An echo of the Ghost's injunction to Hamlet not to punish his mother: "Leave her to heaven" (1.5.86).

present was all that belonged to man. Before we left Milan, the seducer accomplished his criminal purpose. Though however, she had become a convert to his theories, she could not divest herself of all feeling of shame, much less could she entirely drive from her heart those doctrines which Berchtold had instilled at that age when the first impressions become part of our very nature; they hung around her, and haunted her day and night; she had sought for courage to apply to Louisa or myself in her difficulties, but had not dared.

Her mind being in this state, she described the effect upon it, at sight of that being almost lost amidst the ambient air in conversation with Doni, as wonderful. Her mind had immediately recovered its elasticity, for she hoped, if she could obtain communication with such a being, to be able to find some certainty amidst the horrid doubts that revelled in her mind, and to procure the means of hiding her shame, or daring to face the day, by means of its power. Determined to learn the spell which could raise a transparent, all-pervading being, she resolved to watch, without remission, the conduct of the Count; she learnt nothing for some time. He apparently differed in no habit from the others around. But the impression in her mind was not effaced: at last it appeared to her that upon certain days, the Count never touched animal food, and she found by observation that this happened on every combination of seven in the days of the month.[1] Upon enquiry amongst the servants, she found that upon the morning of those days, the room of Doni was always in the greatest confusion, and she herself remarked, that upon the evening preceding, he seemed always more anxious, and the day after more fatigued than usual.

Julia resolved to watch the Count upon the next seventh night; she found that it was possible to look into his room through the wainscot of a closet for wood that opened into the passage leading to his apartment. The night came, meat had been avoided, all were gone to their rooms, only the footsteps of the domestics arranging every thing for rest, sounded on her ear; she described herself, as having listened apparently for hours, though only minutes elapsed, while these sounds continued. At last, all was silent; she said, that not even the vine leaves overspreading her casement were heard to rustle; for every breeze was hushed,

---

1 This calendrical magic may be a reminiscence of the instructions
   Darvell gives his friend in Byron's fragment: see Appendix A.2 (234-35).

all was so quiet, that the ear seemed to feel as it were the silence. She was awed, her heart beat quick, she held her breath; at that moment she thought a slow step sounded along the corridor; alarmed she knew not why, she seized her lamp, and was upon the point of rushing out, when the door slowly opened, and a figure clad in a white robe entered; its dark black eye was fixed; its grey locks seemed as if no breath of air could move their weight; no sign of life, save the moving feet belonged to it, for the face was pale, the lips blueish. It approached with an unvarying step; it was Doni! its hand took her's within its cold grasp, its eye shone, as if a tear had passed over it, its lips quivered as if it wished to speak, or thought it spoke. She stood still, motionless; while it approached, it seemed as if she had strength for any thing, but when it turned to go, the lamp fell from her hand, and she fell upon the floor. It was morn, ere her wildered senses returned, it was too late. Doni never noticed in any way the event of that night. She was bewildered, she knew not what to think, it seemed from his unchanged conduct towards her, that he was unconscious of the event. Yet she asserted that she could not have mistaken the features of him who had visited her in that awful manner; her imagination laboured, her judgment laid down the balance and became as dead. Her phantasy painted to her mind pictures of splendour and of power, more brilliant than those of the Arab tale-teller, or God creating Bramin.[1] But more than all, it represented to her the means of ensuring Olivieri's love, which she could no longer flatter herself she possessed; he had not seen her, but for a moment, since she had left Milan dishonoured, and then it was but to laugh at her fears, which she was but too conscious were not in vain.

Day followed day towards the seventh. At times she caught Doni's eye fixed upon her, as if it sought to read her mind; but she thought this might be imagination, yet it seemed to her as if her intentions were divined, and that from some cause or other, they could not be opposed, else why this silence? The fatal night came. Julia, determined to brave every thing, went down that evening, which she had not lately done, to supper. Her agitation was great, but she forced herself to conceal it. She was conscious the Count's eyes were fixed upon her's, yet she dared not to look up and meet

---

1   The Arab tale-teller is presumably Scheherazade. In *An Essay upon the Source of Positive Pleasure* (1818), Polidori refers to "the Hindoo with three hundred millions of Gods" (39).

his. She rose to depart, he came to her to say good night, his voice failed him, his hand shook. She retired to her room; she determined, frightened by the awful silence of her protector, to give up her intention. She threw herself upon her bed, but sleep abandoned her, or if it for a moment came, it presented such brilliant visions to her eye, that nothing mortal was to be compared to it. She seemed to have spirits instead of pages to attend her, genii instead of servants. It seemed as if at their bidding the very earth would heave and show within its entrails, all its richest treasures. Olivieri appeared joined with her in this state of power. She roused herself. The clock with its solemn peal seemed trembling to intrude upon the solemn night. One might have thought nature were dead, for not even the owl shrieked, and the darkness and nocturnal sleep that weighed on the earth, seemed no longer the type of the eternal rest of the world, but its fulfilment, all appeared sunk into such undisturbed repose. Julia alone seemed living, she looked in the creation like the Arab in the sandy plain, animate amidst inanimation, organized amidst unorganized matter. Even she must have appeared as if she were some spirit of another more restless sphere, for her hurrying glance, the fearful resolution breathing in her face, must have made her bear the stamp of something more than mortality. She seized her lamp, started, then advanced, and laughed with that laugh which plays upon the lips, when the heart ceases to beat through violence of feeling.

At last she reached the gallery of her protector's room; she opened with a trembling hand, the door of the adjoining closet, and entered. The dread silence still continued, it was only broken by the loud breathing of her heaving bosom. She sat down upon the pile of wood in the corner of the closet. She could not find courage to pursue her undertaking; at last a deep groan made her start; terrified she leant against the wall; as she gradually recovered herself, she raised her eyes, and looked through a crevice that opened to her sight the Count's room.[1] I could not learn

---

1 This is the only incident in the novel that corresponds to the account of Polidori's idea for a story given by Mary Shelley in her 1831 introduction to *Frankenstein*: "Poor Polidori had some terrible idea about a skull-headed lady, who was so punished for peeping through a key-hole— what to see I forget—something very shocking and wrong of course; but when she was reduced to a worse condition than the renowned Tom of Coventry, he did not know what to do with her, and was obliged to despatch her to the tomb of the Capulets, the only place for which she was fitted" (355).

what she saw, she however informed me that she discovered the means of raising a superior being; but that startled at his appearance, she had sunk to the ground. She found herself, when recovered, upon her bed, but no one was near her. She determined to put her power into effect the ensuing night. She would not join the family at breakfast, but remained in her room all day. She did attempt to raise a spirit, but what was her horror, when the walls of her apartment echoed but scoffs and mockings, they seemed to say that she needed not a greater price than the gratification of her passions, and that they would not give her more; that she was theirs already, and that to command them could only be obtained by one not already damned. Unappalled she repeated her call, but it was in vain, all sunk to quiet. Desperate, for her shame could no longer be hidden, she formed at once the resolution of leaving the house and seeking her seducer. She got out, and entering a boat, managed by skulking along the banks of the lake throughout the day, to arrive in the night at Sesto Calende;[1] she thence easily obtained a conveyance, and reached Milan.

She had sought refuge at a small inn, and sending to Olivieri, he came to her, but it was only to make fully known to her the horrors of her situation. It appears he treated her with brutality, though she did not say so. He staid with her but a few minutes, and left her for ever. He offered her no assistance, seemed even to have implied that if unwilling to return to her brother, she might live by exposing her shame to all, and boldly seeking whom she might inveigle. He left her with only the small sum remaining from what she had taken with her, and immediately left Milan to go she knew not where. She had thence retired to the room where I had found her, and had there managed to support life, and was delivered of her child. Her money however failed her, and, at last, her poor neighbours, tired of assisting her who could no longer pay them, having refused to aid her any more, she had struggled with the pains of hunger for two days in solitude, hoping for relief from death. But her milk had failed, and her child's voice had pierced its mother's heart; she could not resist such an appeal; she arose, wrote the few lines to me, and staggering, in the morning while all were at rest, to the gate of the palace, had thrown them under the gate. From thence she had hardly found strength sufficient to reach her miserable couch, when fatigued, she sunk into a kind of stupor from which my approach had roused her.

---

1 A town at the southernmost tip of Lago Maggiore.

This is the substance of what my sister told me. Her narration was broken, and many were the pauses she was forced to make to recover strength. Her feeble breath hardly seemed sufficient to allow her to end her tale. Night came, and she was delirious. She screamed for Olivieri, called on him to come and see her die. She held my hands, and looking on me asked me my name, denied it could be me, for I could not be more kind than Olivieri; but why rest upon such a scene? She died in the morning without a return of reason, but still calling, in the last moment, upon her lover.

My sister was dead. Her tale had unfolded to me the causes whence her misconduct arose. I was the source of all, my colouring of Olivieri's good qualities, my exposing to her the sources of doubt in those doctrines our sainted foster-father had taught us, my example in the career of vice were the causes of her fault—her death. It was yet but the second victim to my fate; there were two others wanting; I sat by the dead body reflecting upon the horrible fatality that had caused my virtues and my vices to prove alike mortal to the two beings who for many years had been the only companions I possessed in nature, the only sympathizers in my joys and sorrows. If the pangs of conscience could be depicted, I would, for your sake, young man, paint in its truest colours, the horror I then felt, the pangs I now feel; but the attempt would be vain. I had loved my sister with all that affection two isolated beings naturally feel towards each other. She had been to me as the weaker part of myself, which always needed protection and defence. To me she had been the holder of all my secrets, the partaker of all my sorrows; when an outcast, she had received me; when a wretch, she had not spurned me.

No one was with me when she died. The servant of Louisa found me many hours after her decease, extended upon her corpse. She came from her mistress to seek me. I rose; I knew not how to conceal the anguish of my mind. Louisa soon discovered it, and obtained from me the knowledge of my sister's illness and death. She did not enquire further; she perceived I was not willing she should know the rest, and was silent. I was astonished to see how firmly she bore the shock, she exerted herself to find some means of allaying my grief, but she did not know that it was conscience that worked within. I left her, and her pretended strength was gone. She had forced herself to assume an apparent calm to assuage my grief, but could not command her own.

My sister was interred privately. Doni and myself, were the only mourners, and a tablet, with merely the name of Julia Berchtold, marked the spot where my sister lay. Her child was put to nurse. I gave him his mother's and my own name, that I might still have a bond between us. Every day I went to see the little orphan, and taking him from the fearful nurse, I gazed upon his infantile face, while a bitter tear fell from the eye of him who had been the cause of his birth being loaded with infamy and shame. While I looked upon him he would smile, but that smile brought to my mind my sister's; it was a melancholy playing of the lips, that seemed to mock at the pleasure that excited it; the eye was not lit up with the same feeling, but still appeared absorbed in its continued grief.

PART THIRD

I HAD already undergone more than falls to the lot of most men in this valley of miseries; but I was not allowed repose; from this moment my heart was torn piece-meal, by fiends each more horrible than the other. Not many days had elapsed since Julia's death, when Olivieri's father received an anonymous warning to prepare himself for the worst news. The letter was dated Strasburgh. Next day he read in another letter, that his son, under an assumed name, had been taken with several others of a band of robbers, who had for a long time infested the banks of the Rhine. Doni had now become aged and infirm, he was not capable of undergoing the fatigues of a long journey, yet it was hardly possible to hinder him from setting off, to attempt saving his only son. He blessed me when I insisted upon performing that office. "You have twice saved his life in the field of honour, may you be as successful in snatching him from the death of infamy." He gave me unlimited power, and rushed into his daughter's apartment to seek there for the comfort all else seemed to deny him.

I departed, travelled night and day, I saw Switzerland again, but did not even notice it, my mind was anxious, was alarmed; it seemed as if heaven wished by repeated inflictions of its bitterest curses, to humble to the dust the family circle of my protector. I was so rash, that for a moment I dared to question Providence. So weak is all mortal knowledge; misery is but the fruit of vice, virtue never feels the world's infamy; there is a heavenly beam of certainty in the merciful justice of their God that enables the just to look upon all the inflictions of this life, but as the most lenient atonement due to a tender, though offended father, for those weaknesses belonging even to our nature.

I arrived at Strasburgh; its fretted spire, rising high above the houses, upon the far extended plain, for a long time marked the bourne to which I was tending, while the winding road that forms the approach, seemed to mock my endeavours to reach it. Justice had been summary, there had not even been a regular trial, but a court martial had been summoned, and instantly had condemned the prisoners to death. A respite had however been granted for a few days, in consequence of the hopes entertained of inducing some individual to betray the secret retreats of their comrades. I immediately proceeded to the prison and asked admission. Application being made to the governor, and it being evident that I was not one of the gang, I obtained it. I entered;

bolt after bolt slowly sounded as they were forced from their rusty clasps, and I found myself in a low gallery, the damp was slowly falling in measured drops from the arched vault above, and the coldness of the chilly air made me shiver. The jailor bore a torch before me; its red light at last rested upon the strong fastenings to a narrow door. I gave him money, and seizing the torch, entered.

Upon a little straw, covering a few loose stones in a corner, lay a form, which seemed reckless of all. The light of the torch did not cause it to move, its hands were upon its face, clenched; its whole posture was strained, as if by the convulsive stiffening of its limbs it would harden itself against the inflictions of the mind. I could not speak; thrice I strove to utter the name of Olivieri, and thrice it stuck in my throat. "Speak, I can listen to my fate," Olivieri at last said in a hurried voice, "Death they say silences all voices, if it can silence that which echoes through the chambers of my breast, scaring oblivion and repose, I shall be content to die, though on the wheel, waiting, when all my limbs are crushed, for that repose the iron bar may give." He did not move, but seemed to mutter this, addressing himself as much as me. "Olivieri," at last fell trembling from my lips. He with one exertion stood erect; his eyeballs straining in their sockets, seemed to seek the horrid certainty they knew would blast them. Berchtold appeared before him. He threw himself upon the straw, and with a hand clenching with furious grasp his long black hair, he seemed to force his head upon the ground, fearing his eyes should again turn upon me. I sate upon the stones at his side, laid my hand upon him, bade him be comforted. He shrunk as if my touch froze him. I told him of my hopes of obtaining his release, of the wealth I could employ in bribing his judges. He looked up; "You talk to me of mercy; Julia was seduced by me." "I know it," I replied, "it is your father, who acts by me, I am but my benefactor's agent. For him I am to attempt to save his son." "His son?" he echoed in a faltering voice, "true, I was his son." I in vain asked him for information on which to proceed; he would give me none. I left him.

I applied to the court which had passed his sentence. I saw the members who had composed it in private. They gave me an account of the desperate gang to which he had belonged, and painted in horrid colours the devastations they had committed in the French territory. It appeared that Olivieri had put himself at the head of these outlaws, and had with the most daring rashness and carelessness of life, always eluded the numbers that often seemed to surround him. I made those who appeared favourable to my pleading great presents, under the pretence of enabling them to aid the furtherance of my objects. Amongst the others, the governor seemed to have the most influence. I gave him immense sums, which he promised to expend for the prisoner's advantage. The next day was appointed for the execution. I had not seen Olivieri again, I was anxious not to encourage too much his hopes of life, while all seemed uncertain. I called early in the morning, upon the governor; I saw him. He raised my expectations very high, he said, that if I could but find the slightest pretence for a respite, that it was determined to grant it. "If I were to judge by your riches, he and yourself must be of higher rank than you pretend." I had concealed both our names. "Now, if you can but show that some one of influence is interested in his fate, we will admit of an appeal." Rashly I was induced to utter the names of Olivieri Doni, and Ernestus Berchtold. I was surprised at seeing the man before me turn of a most deadly pale. His limbs seemed to fail him, but he in an instant recovered himself; his voice alone betrayed an emotion I could not understand. He assured me that he would instantly occupy himself about it, and I left him. An hour afterwards I received a note from him saying, that I should prepare a carriage and post horses upon the bridge, and as the clock struck the first hour of the morning, that I should present myself at the prison door, where I should meet my friend. That this had been thought the best means of allowing his escape. Passports were enclosed, which would allow us to pass the bridge, and we should then be in safety. I immediately prepared every thing, anxious for the arrival of the moment when I was again to save the brother of Louisa.

Towards evening, restless, I issued out. I wandered up and down that part of the main street, which, covered by arcades, brought to my recollection the towns of my native country. Memory was rapidly crowded with the images of infancy, while the evening tints, and the stillness of nature soon enabled me to abstract myself entirely from the surrounding objects. I at last found myself in the cathedral. There was no one there, even devotion seemed for a while to have laid aside its pomp to enjoy the balmy freshness of an April evening. I had at last advanced into the most obscure part of the aisle; when turning round, a light figure dressed in the singular vestment of the neighbouring peasantry, caught my eye. Her step was hurried, and her head moved anxiously as if seeming to shun observation. Thinking that my presence might be painful, I was retiring, when she beckoned to me. I stood still, and she was immediately by my side. She hastily addressed me. "You are a friend of Olivieri Doni's, you perceive from my knowing his name, that I am in his confidence. He once professed love to me, he has probably done so to many more, who are now like me ashamed of their name; but even if I told it you, it would be useless. Hoping to be of service, and anxious to hear of him who still possesses my affection, though he has broken the peace of her, who loves him; but I deserve it, for I am guilty, he cannot love guilt; I am so lowered, that I was not ashamed to gain my object, by seeking one of the prison guard. I have just left him intoxicated. From him I learnt, while he was blabbing all, that he was called upon to perform a service this night in the course of his duty, that he disliked. I gained from him that he was to belong to a party, who were to lurk in one of the streets and seize my lover and yourself, at the moment you thought yourselves secure of freedom, for that the police were anxious to take you, who, they suspected belonged to the same gang, and therefore had resolved to arrest you, while engaged in aiding the escape of your friend, which alone will ensure your condemnation." I was astonished, could I then be so shamefully betrayed? I immediately remembered the sudden emotion of him, who had promised so much, when he heard our names, and it flashed upon my mind, that I had a faint recollection of his name as being that of an officer in the French troops opposed to us in the Underwald, who having been placed in a post of importance, had been surprized by Olivieri and myself, and had been, in consequence of his precipitate flight, broken and disgraced. It was now nearly dark, I could not think of deserting Olivieri without still attempting his rescue. The girl's information might be false. I spoke with her, she appeared sincere; I offered her money, she refused it; my case was desperate, I determined to confide in her, I got her to lead me to the neighbourhood of the prison, and show me all the turnings and secret cuts through the different streets. I soon gained a perfect idea of the plan of this part of the town, and I began to hope in consequence of the intricacy and number of turnings in this neighbourhood that I might elude the ambush, if I could at any point break through the guards. I did not entirely open my plan to my guide, but asked her if she knew of any certain place of refuge, whither I could retreat in case of need. She led me and showed me her apartment, it was miserable, but there was an air of neatness about it that seemed, in contradiction with the poverty, visible in every article. "If you can arrive here without being observed, you are safe."

To avoid suspicion, I immediately left her and returned to my hotel, which was close to the river. The hour approached, I armed myself with a sabre and a pair of pistols, and hiding under my large Italian cloak another sword and pair of fire arms, I sauntered negligently out of the inn door, and calling my servant, I told him in a loud voice to take care the horses were ready, as I intended to set off the moment I had fixed on. This I did to blind any one, who might be watching my motions. Then turning down some of the most abrupt windings, I first went whither I had learnt the different parties were to be placed. By means of keeping close to a shaded part of the walls of the streets, which being lit by a single reverberating lamp[1] suspended in the middle between the houses, were rather dark, I could approach very near them without being perceived. I discovered one point which I thought weaker than the rest, for the number of the men seemed smaller, the silence being greater. I then returned, entered the main street leading to the prison, and soon found myself at its gate, without meeting any one. The high narrow windowed walls, were suddenly illuminated by the moon bursting in all its splendour from behind a cloud, and high above my reach I perceived some one watching me, he retreated and I heard the gates open. I could not perceive who was there, for the hollow opening was in the dark shadow thrown over it by a salient buttress. My heart beat violently. It might not be Olivieri, a person was pushed out, I heard the words, "I am free," spoken in a voice that denoted the despair within. I approached, it was Olivieri. Throwing off my mantle, I stood before him; he did not notice me, though the moon's ray was full upon us. I roused him, thrust the sword and pistols into his hand, and bade him follow me. "We are not safe, we must baffle the traitors yet," said I, "be firm, we have escaped greater perils than these, follow me." His broken voice, merely answered, "To death."

I hastened towards the point I thought the weakest. A shrill whistle sounded at our back, and we found ourselves surrounded. The first who approached, were dead at our feet. They retreated before us, we had broken their circle and were already free towards the street down which it was necessary to turn. "Now to the right," I cried to my companion. A shot struck him and he fell; I rushed to the spot hoping that he might rise. I struck on every side determined not to leave him in their hands, their

---

1 A lamp with a reflector.

numbers increased, but at the same time I heard a trampling of feet at my back; desperate, I rushed forward; a female shriek struck my ear, and at the same time I found myself joined by about twenty men. Their blows told, we caused the town-guard to retreat, I could not again find Olivieri's body. I rushed along the streets, and was soon at the young woman's door. I heard voices; alarmed, I listened, they were evidently from their conversation trying to console some one. I knocked, a female voice immediately exclaimed, "'Tis he," and the door was opened. I entered, Olivieri was extended upon a couch, attempting to write a few lines; he had just finished. Around him were many men in a strange uncouth garb. They were his former companions, who having received the same intelligence from the girl as myself, had resolved to attempt a rescue, and had stolen singly into the town. Olivieri gave me what he had written, it was to his father; his pale face was turned towards me, his feeble arm could hardly support its own weight. "Berchtold, I have not deserved the risking yourself for me; can, can you forgive me dying." "I do," was my answer, and I held his extended hand. He threw himself upon his bed, and in a stifled voice, "There is another, whose forgiveness I do not ask, but tell, oh! tell her, it was her shame that has damned me, that made me desperate, damned me." "She's dead, she too would have forgiven you; she died speaking of you, but not cursing you." His limbs were instantly relaxed, and moved no more.

We were now aroused by the entry of another robber, the soldiers were approaching, I begged of them not to leave the body of my Louisa's brother to their insults; they lifted it from the couch, and placed it in a recess so artfully contrived, that it bid defiance to the most accurate search, and they promised me they would return and bury it. We took the young woman with us, and separating, we singly hastened to a spot by the river's side, where we hoped to find boats. Ten only reached it, we entered a small wherry. The town was in such confusion that the necessary orders had not been sent to the different boundaries. We let the boat float down the stream, and soon found ourselves beyond the fortifications. We landed on the German side, and presently reached one of the dwellings of the freebooters. I now learnt that it was this same girl, who had written the anonymous letter to her lover's father. I offered her a considerable sum of money, again offered to secure her an independence, she refused it all, and insisted upon remaining with those men amongst whom she had first known Olivieri. I remained with them a considerable time, anxious to see the body of my former friend secure against any insult, and before I left them, aided by the daring of these men, who managed to enter the town and take the body from its secret hiding place, I had the satisfaction of consigning him to the earth. I gave them all the loose money remaining with me, secure upon my letters of credit of having more than enough to convey me whither I liked.

I reached Inspruck,[1] not deeming myself safe in any part of the French territory, I determined to remain here, and I wrote to Doni merely mentioning that I had been unsuccessful, and telling him where I had stopped. I thought it best not to tell him more for fear of my letter being intercepted, and hoping that when I saw him I should be able to break the fatal news to him. My last hope was vain, for all the papers and public prints contained a full account of the daring attempt I had made to save a robber from the ignominious sentence of the law. Our real names were also mentioned, and at the same time that many rested upon the courage, they pretended had been shown in this attempt, many took advantage of the connection of our names with a gang of robbers to throw discredit upon our former conduct in the cause of Switzerland. It was soon known through my banker, at Inspruck, that I was the notorious Ernestus Berchtold, and I was surrounded by people, who were glad to seek some refuge from their ennui, in gazing upon one, whose name seemed to have something like romance attached to it.

Count Doni arrived, Louisa too, though weak and feeble, still in better health than when I had last seen her, accompanied him. She had been forced to exert herself to support her father under his anxiety for his son, and then under the severe blow of seeing his own name in all the prints, known to all as the father of Olivieri, "a captain of banditti." The spring had given her the requisite strength, and I was glad, after so long an absence, to see her once more sitting by my side with renovated life. I could not take my eyes from her, and I rested upon her face so long, that I gradually forced myself to hope that her hectic flush was but her natural colour. We were constantly together, and tried in each other's presence to forget the griefs that weighed upon us both. I had given the last lines of my former friend to his father. He had read them in his own room, and though when we next met I remarked that his eye turned upon me wet with tears, as he evi-

---

1 Polidori's spelling for Innsbruck, a city in western Austria.

dently did not intimate the least inclination to expose to me what his son had written, I did not seek to learn the substance of Olivieri's note; though I was anxious to learn whether he had disclosed his conduct towards Julia. We never after mentioned his name, and we tried to keep the thoughts of his melancholy fate out of our minds, by resting upon our hopes of Louisa's welfare.

Count Wilhelm, whom I have before mentioned, found us on his way to his native country; hearing of our being at the same hotel, he sent in his name to my friend. Day after day he remained at Inspruck. The whole of the evening was spent with us in our apartment, and he seemed to seek more and more the means of showing attentions to Louisa. At first I was not disturbed by them, but at last I became fretful and irritable, for it appeared as if Louisa took a pleasure in his conversation. I had heard so much of his power of attaching women, that it seemed impossible for her to resist him. Every thing he did, though the most simple action, was perverted in my mind, to a covert sneer at my poverty and insignificance. I often answered him abruptly, and even insulted him. Louisa's meek eye turned upon me, but it seemed to have lost its influence. I one night found him by her side, he seemed to be earnestly pleading, he had hold of her hand, and she smiled. Stung to the quick by so slight a circumstance, I turned furiously away and retreated to my chamber. Had Berchtold taught me to command my passions, had he but shown me as models for my conduct, men, in the privacy of life, I might have escaped much. It is vain to rest upon it. I had thought that Louisa's influence over my mind, would have hindered me ever again losing myself, hurried away by any passion. But here Louisa's form arose in all the hideousness of jealousy's distorting mirror! I was mad. My clenched fist struck the table, I could not command myself. I remained some time in this state, when turning my eyes towards my bureau, I perceived an almanack; I seized it in mockery; I counted up the days since she had told me she loved me. I was suddenly struck, it was the 28th day of the month, it was a combination of seven. It seemed as if by one exertion I might free myself from doubt, and be at once lost in the horrible certainty, or be for ever blest in the knowledge of Louisa's heart.

I did not reflect; the hour struck; I seized my lamp, and rushing out was already close to the apartment of Doni, when wavering on the wick the flame suddenly sunk and expired. Yet nothing around was dark, it seemed as if I was surrounded by a mist formed by a dazzling light, too dazzling to allow me to view the objects round. I was a moment startled, but undismayed I strove to rush forward, my feet were bound to the floor. I strove but in vain to move. Gradually the light cleared, and gradually the features of that face, which I had so often gazed upon in my imagination, my mother's, appeared distinctly before me. Her form was majestic, but in her eye there was a softness, which was not even destroyed by the severity of her feeling. "Ernestus," were her words, "heaven has decreed at my prayer, that this crime shall be spared to you, you shall not act ungratefully."—She seemed to vanish with an expression of sorrow upon her face, as if she were not allowed to continue, and felt the horror that burst upon me in consequence of the ignorance in which I was left. My senses forsook me, and the dawn of day had already pierced the thick clouds before I recovered.

I did not return to my room, I went into the open air, my thoughts were hurried; baffled, I was not subdued; jealousy still was not banished, I did not rest upon my mother's apparition, so strongly had the idea of Louisa's infidelity taken hold of me. While walking amidst the intricate windings of a public garden, I heard voices near me. One was Count Wilhelm, I heard him boasting of the favours of some lady, whom another thought loved him, and he suddenly presented himself before me; I grossly insulted him. He took a pleasure in torturing me with his pretended concern at my mistress's kindness to another. I struck him, we fought and he fell severely wounded. I stood by him and he was amply revenged. He told me that he had seen me entering the preceding evening, that being at that moment engaged in speaking about me, and Louisa having expressed her wish that I might be received into the Austrian service,[1] he was offering his interest to forward my views, and that knowing how easily I was irritated, he had purposely taken her hand. He advised me to fly, I was obliged to do so for I was no longer safe where I was.

Louisa was then innocent. I cursed that fate which seemed to hang about me, always shielding me from death. I had fought in battle, but never yet had received the slightest wound: I had escaped from prison while the axe was falling. My rashness seemed to be incapable of hurting me; for there was a shield around me, that snatched me from peril. I was preserved from worse than death. Even this last act could not divide me from

---

1 Joining the Austrians would give Ernestus an opportunity to renew his struggle against the French.

Louisa. She loved me indeed. Alarmed at seeing my antagonist brought in wounded, she did not shriek; she did not give herself up to loud and weak lamentations; but conscious, that probably my life depended upon the event of his wound, she sacrificed herself entirely to the care of the invalid. With unremitting attention she watched by his bedside. But when he was declared free from danger, then the cold hand of strengthened disease made itself felt. She was obliged again to return to her sick chamber. But first she begged her father to inform me of the favourable result. I returned. Doni met me on the stairs,—embraced me; but no joy was visible on his face. He announced to me the dangerous state in which Louisa lay, but did not reproach me; she had forbidden it. I was introduced into her room. Consumption was ruining her system; she was faint and weak; her continued cough and the marked colour on her cheek, but too well denoted the power it had acquired. I could not even ask her how she felt; but the tears fell down my cheek on the moist hand that held mine. She allowed me to stay with her. Talked to me of that power, whose pleasure it was to strengthen the weak and console the wretched, she said that he had soothed the agony of death's visible approach, and until she saw me, that she had found relief in the thought of the short time we should be separated. But now she saw my grief, she was sorry I should be left alone, even for those few moments, without a being, to whom I was attached; that she again wished for life, if amidst all its miseries she could but hope for the power of consoling me through these inflictions. In fine, she did not speak of herself, but of me—of the wretch who had gradually broken the weak threads which bound her pure soul to life. Count Wilhelm perfectly recovered, left us. I had seen him, and as the only atonement in my power, had acknowledged my folly, and had begged he would pardon it, though it had been so severely felt by him. He returned a vague answer, and I saw him no more.

Doni's interest was great; his wealth insured him friends, active in bringing back to their neighbourhood one whose riches fell in beneficent showers upon all. By their influence, he soon obtained a pardon for my resistance to the civil authorities in behalf of Olivieri, and I was granted permission to return to any part of the French territory. As the cold Alpine air seemed to hasten the rapid steps of his daughter's decline, he determined upon having her conveyed again to the borders of the Lago Maggiore, which had seemed last year to have possessed such renovating powers. We departed, and soon found ourselves fixed in our abode. Nature wore the same aspect as the year before. Palanza, with its white walls and glittering columns shone as brilliantly in the sun's ray; the smile of heaven seemed to play upon the fairy islets of the Boromei, and the rich woods of Belgirato reflected in the blue surface of the water, seemed to put the beauty of this in competition with the sublimity of the wild rocks of the upper part of this long lake. But Louisa's health had faded. She could hardly hope, if the disease continued its hasty steps to see these scenes again. But still that fairy enchanter, hope, acted upon me, and as each day she gained some slight addition to her strength, I pictured to myself years of happiness united with her I had long so ardently loved. She would not undeceive me, but left me the illusion. She was again able to enjoy the freshness of the air, and to walk out, amidst the varying scenery around. I supported her, and felt the light pressure of her feeble form resting upon my arm. She would stop, and draw some reflections on the bounty of God, even while in pain, from the various pictures before her; always attempting to turn my mind towards those thoughts, which she well knew could alone give me consolation, and a resting place in this vale of miseries.[1] But still she seemed to recover strength. I entreated her to hope, and not to give way to such desponding thoughts. Her father, who was deceived as well as myself, begged of her to console herself; talked to her when alone of me, and spoke of his hopes of seeing us united, of her forming the only prop to his old age, and that I, how could he say it? was alone worthy in his estimation of receiving from a father's hand so great a treasure.

Unwilling to grieve her father, she yielded to my importunities, promised to be mine, if upon a certain day her acquired strength had not given signs of decay. You may imagine with what anxiety, with what hopes I watched each intervening moment. Every cold breeze made me shudder; every cloud that veiled the sun's ray caused me pain. I counted her breathings: whenever she moved, watched the firmness of her step. The day arrived. She was not weaker, but had seemed to find renewed energy in the thought of being mine. She was mine. I cannot paint to you the delirious state of mind, in which the next months passed over my head. I had a right to protect. I was something to that being; but I will not rest upon these feverish moments, you may imagine

---

1 Perhaps a variation on the cliché "vale of tears," itself perhaps a variation on Shakespeare, *Othello* 3.3.266.

them; Louisa was mine—Louisa mine! But heaven had not smiled upon our union—no, no. It was but the anger of a God veiled under the brightest hues. Louisa was my,—but I must relate the whole. Her health, as the winter approached declined again, and we returned to Milan. We lived with her father.

To engage my wife's attention, I resolved upon fitting up a part of the palace anew for our private use. Every thing was ordered, when it occurred to her that the best ornament we could add would be the portrait of her father. I had recovered from my sister our mother's locket, and shewing it to Louisa, we determined upon having it copied and hung opposite the Count's. To give Doni, as we thought an agreeable surprize, we determined upon having them privately executed, and placed in their situation without his cognizance. I sought for a painter, and spent whole mornings with him at his eazel, directing him how to paint my mother. I described to him, as well as I could, her appearance to me at Inspruck, and pretending that I had seen her in a dream, I insisted upon his representing her in such a situation. He executed it, and by the magic effect of his pencil, excited a most extraordinary impression of awe in my breast, whenever I turned my eyes upon the picture. She seemed starting from the canvass; the outline of her figure was lost in the blaze of light, and her face, meek amidst splendour, severe, though with features naturally mild, seemed speaking those words I had heard. I took Louisa to see it; she felt the same awe as myself, though she could not assign a reason for it, but she continued gazing, till I perceived her eyes wet with tears.

The pictures were privately introduced into the house. We had succeeded in keeping them secret from Doni. In a few days was Louisa's birth day, we resolved therefore to make him our guest upon that occasion in our new apartment. We invited several of our most intimate friends. Every thing passed in gaiety. At last, all the company were gone, and we remained alone. We then, taking him each by one hand, led him into what we intended should be our private sitting room, telling him he should then see our best friends, the one in heaven, the other on earth. The door was opened; directly before him was his own portrait; he seemed surprized and pleased; he turned round; I had hardly announced to him that the one he then saw was my mother's, when he fell. Alarmed we raised him. "Your mother! did you say, your mother?" He threw himself upon the floor, and called upon God to free him from the consciousness of horror like to his. We knelt by him close together; he saw us, raised his aged hands, and with a fluttering voice bade us, if we dreaded heaven's most dreadful curse, to separate. But again he fell to the ground, crying, "It is too late, too late, the crime is consummated." We raised him, he turned hastily away, for he was opposite the portrait, and besought us to take him thence. We led him to his chamber; he motioned us to leave him.

We retired in silence, we knew not what to understand; was it merely the greater effect of that portrait's power which had been exerted over us. We could not hope it, we were lost in conjectures. Louisa's health was so much broken that I was alarmed for the effects it might have upon her, and, therefore, strove to turn her mind from the subject; but in vain. She did not sleep the whole night, the anxiety concerning her father would not allow her to seek forgetfulness even for a moment. The effect may be imagined upon so weak a constitution. Her father refused to see us for several days, and each day I saw the mind acting upon my wife's health with alarming rapidity. When this reached the ears of her father, he could no longer resist our importunities, he saw us; but the sight of his haggard and wild countenance did not restore Louisa. He had evidently been engaged in writing. We pressed him to explain his conduct. He replied, I knew not what I wished to learn. "It will blast you, as it has done your friend. You must learn it, but it shall be when I am in the grave, and before him who has thus punished my crime; then, then, I may intercede for you, if I myself am sufficiently purified by suffering. He may hear a father's, though it be a criminal's, prayer." His words seemed almost incoherent, he at times called me son, but then with hurried impatience he corrected himself; he asked me whence I got that portrait, I put the locket into his hands. "'Twas mine, I gave it," he hurried, pressed it to his breast, and bade us leave him. We did; he saw us daily, but in silence; he seemed absorbed in one thought, and to that he could not give utterance. He took little, too little, nourishment; but always occupied in writing; he seemed but to find strength for that; when we saw him, he was hardly capable of motion. His task was at last finished. We had been with him as usual, when we were suddenly recalled. He was dying; he bade us kneel down by his side, he blessed us. He took the papers from his table, and putting them into my hands, he bade me read them when he was in the grave, and know the horrors that awaited me; he commanded us to trust in God's mercy, and he sunk, blessing us, upon his couch, breathed no more.

I bore my Louisa from this scene, she was from this moment confined to her bed. I saw the Count laid in the vault of his ancestors, and then returned to my wife's chamber, whence I never issued till I had no longer a wife. It was evident that all art was unavailing. It was the undermining of a constitution, not by a common bodily disease, but by the griefs of a heart that had never lately found a moment's respite from the most bitter inflictions. Yet, even at this moment, she seemed to forget herself, in her attempts to console me. She alone broke the silence around; I sat in mute despair; I saw Louisa before me, and I was to be left isolated, scathed by divine anger, without consolation. She held my hand, spoke to me of another world; for a moment her words would even subdue my grief, and let me feel as if that hope were enough. At last, seeing the silent sorrow that was preying confined within my breast, she sought to rouse me, bade me read those papers; I did in a luckless moment; only hinted at the horrible mystery unfolded there, and saw the last convulsive throe I was destined to witness in any bound to me by love. I cannot tell you more; read that damning tale, and then you may know what I dare, nay, dare not rest upon. My history is quickly ended. I was dragged from the now lifeless Louisa; but I stole from my guards in the night, gained an entrance into the room, where death showed, as if boasting his beauteous victim, dressed in pomp. The wax tapers seemed to burn dimly, as if in unison with the solemn scene; the black walls, the felted ground, the corpse stretched out, arrayed in white, the stillness visible upon that beauteous face, stilled even the tumult in my breast. She did not seem dead but asleep, I had held her in my arms, upon my breast, looking as she then looked, I gazed upon her for moments, it seemed as if I believed the still appearance wronged my senses. I was about to press her to my heart, my lips were approaching hers, but I started; there were two flies already revelling on those lips, and she could not chase them. I hurried away, I could not remain any longer there. I followed her bier also, and I saw my dearest, my last bond to this earth deposited there, where peace seemed to invite me too. Religion, Louisa's words, however, had not lost all influence, I resisted that will, which would have led me to immolate myself a victim to the manes of those my love had slain. The hopes of a futurity, of Louisa in heaven, upheld me.

I retired first to Beatenberg, there in the former house of Berchtold, I spent some time: it was too near the first scenes of memory. I left them and came hither; here, amidst these rocks, bound to me by no memory of the past, I spend the few hours allotted me by heaven, in penance; here each day, my prayer is offered up, that in mercy I might be taken to Louisa. My life has been a life of anguish, of vice, of crime; but still amidst these there have been moments, there has been a being, which, if life could be renewed, would cause me to dare all again, once more to go through those few moments. Often in my dreams I see that form, but now, if when in this mortal life her beauty could not be described, how can I now, that her form, her face, are decked with the smile of him, who glories in the glory of his children. When she now appears in my dreams, there is no longer that hideous chasm opening between us; she is always decked as if for another bridal day, and I awake confident in that day's approach without guilt.

But leave me, depart to-morrow upon your intended journey, if that you stay, who knows but the curse which has attended me through life may yet be acting, and may fall upon you as well as all others whom I have loved. These papers will explain to you what I have withheld, the life of Doni. If that you return this way, you may find me dead. Drop not a tear over my grave, I shall be with Louisa. Farewell, but depart knowing that there exists a consolation, which man cannot take from you, which misfortune cannot destroy, the belief in a future state, in the mercy of a redeeming God. It is there I find refuge.

THE LIFE OF COUNT FILIBERTO DONI

The family to which I belong is one of the most noble in Lombardy; but I, being the son of the younger branch, did not enjoy many of those advantages which belong to high rank. I was sent at a very early age to a college of Jesuits, and soon distinguished myself so much, that all the allurements the society was in the habit of holding out to young men of promise, were employed to attach me to this community. I had, however, been educated amongst the mountains; and having been nursed by an old retainer of the family, I had conceived so high an idea of the importance and consequence attached to nobility, that I could not resolve upon putting on a dress, which bound me to forego all those advantages and pleasures, the early associations excited by my nurse, had taught me to believe, belonged to the entry of a nobleman into that very world, my venerable master endeavoured, in vain, to persuade me, was every thing horrible. In the mountains, a son of even the lateral descendants from the Lord, is always looked up to with so much respect and veneration by the poor inhabitants of these districts, that it is no wonder if I was deceived. When the religious began to flatter and distinguish me above my companions, as I was not conscious of any exertion in the acquisition of that mental superiority about which they talked, I attributed their attentions to the respect they felt for one of such exalted rank, as I imagined myself born to, having been left also for the whole of the time with the men, without having paid a single visit to my family, the distant memory of what I had seen at home, appeared to me in contrast with the plain life of my superiors, as something magnificent and passing comparison. My parents, hearing of the talents of their son, were anxious for his entry into an order, whose influence they well knew could be profitable in the greatest degree, not only to the individual, but to the whole of his family. When, therefore, they found that their son was determined not to bind himself by any bond which should hinder him from enjoying, what his imagination had pictured; they thought the best plan in such a case was to allow me to view nearer, that misery which attends nobility devoid of riches. I was accordingly sent for home.

I arrived—I was astonished at not being led to one of those numerous palaces I met on my way to my father's, in the streets of Milan. My guide and myself came at last into the Corso; I began to reconcile myself, seeing the end of the city before me nothing but palaces on both sides; when suddenly, we turned down a narrow street, and I came to the gate of an obscure house. I did not speak, but my feelings were hurt. I ascended a narrow staircase, and I found myself in the presence of my mother. She was lying on a couch covered with leather, dressed in all the dirty tawdry of one who glories in the past; she was playing with a dog with one hand, while the other was stretched over an earthenware brazier. A dirty servant, slip shod, with hair which had apparently never been touched by a comb, led me into the room, and announced me. My mother did not even move, she was too busily engaged by her puppy to notice me. At last, tired of seeing only the same jumps, turning round in the act of stretching her weary limbs, she saw my figure; imagining it to be that of her son, she addressed herself to me. "Ah, Filiberto, so you are really come home to load your parents with your expences, when you might have become a jesuit with every prospect of power. Well, we shall see how your father will bear it. For my part I will not sacrifice any more first representations for your follies. I had already engaged a box at the Scala, with the money I had spared from our very food; when your father, hearing of it, went and sold the tickets because you were expected." These were the first words, I remember, my mother spoke to me. I cannot describe to you the various feelings they excited in my breast. I could not believe this to be my mother. I did not answer her; but engaged in thought, I sat down, and soon lost sight of the white cold walls and brick floor, in the bitterness of my imaginations. My father entered, throwing off his huge great coat, which, placed upon his shoulders, covered both his body and the clay vessel containing the heated charcoal; he embraced me, and seemed really pleased to see me.

I spent a miserable day, for it was the very one on which a new opera was to be brought out, and all the usual companions of my mother, having, by intrigue and what not, secured places, she was left alone without even her *cavalier servente*,[1] in the company of her husband and son: this was insupportable, and she did nothing the whole evening but vent her bad temper upon me, sneering at my foolish ideas of rank. My father, who seemed accustomed to these scenes, quietly took his seat in a retired part of the room, and with his great coat confining the warm air arising from his *scaldino*[2] around his body, soon fell asleep. The servant came in after the Caffè, and spinning at my mother's side, for a time diverted her attention from me, by joining with the complete appearance of an equal in all that mean criticism of their neighbours, which is esteemed the more witty according to its ill-nature. I was at last glad to go to bed. You may imagine what was the bed room of the son, when the receiving room of the *Padrona*[3] was such as I have described.

As I passed by a door upon the staircase, I saw two heads put out to look at me; they were my sisters; I cannot describe to you the sensation I felt, when I found no one had thought it necessary to bring them to see their brother, or even to mention them to him. I found them dressed in the most coarse clothes, and I had hardly been there a few minutes, before they began recounting to me the hardships and privations they had lately undergone in consequence of the anxiety of my mother to secure a box at the opera for this night. It is useless to paint more scenes of this nature; my mother was vain, and spent even what should have been given to feeding her children, in the most distant imitation

---

1   The escort (and all-but-openly acknowledged lover) of a married woman. See Polidori, *Diary* 206 and *BLJ* 6:226.
2   A small earthenware brazier.
3   "The master's wife, the lady of the house" (Italian).

of the rich, to whom she had the honour of being allied, and who condescended to laugh at her for her pains. My father loved quiet above all things; his income was small, very incompetent to supply the foolish vanity of my mother, he was therefore always in debt, and even obliged to be a mean hanger on upon the elder branch of the family.

Next day I went with my father to visit the head of our family, and I there saw what my imagination had represented to me. The numerous servants seemed bustling about, as if their wills were too rapid for their limbs. The rich liveries, which were almost reflected in the burnished floors of marble and precious woods, the porphyry columns, the fresco paintings, and the silken coverings to even the footstools astonished me. I followed in silence the officious servant, who seemed amazed at my astonishment at that splendour, in which he had always bustled, though but the son of a cowherd. We were conducted into the boudoir of our relation. He was at his toilette, every thing breathed effeminacy, all was luxurious, the delicately coloured curtains let in the enfeebled light of the noon day. When I entered I could hardly distinguish the objects around, for coming from rooms illuminated by all the powers of the sun, my eyes could not feel the weaker impressions of this veiled obscurity. My relation struck with the astonishment I displayed at such magnificence, amused himself with calling forth signs of wonder from me. I was invited to stay with him, and I accordingly went from my mother's, who was glad to get rid of the inconvenience arising from the addition I caused to be made to the daily expences, at the same time that she was proud of having to talk about the notice I had excited at the Palazzo Doni. My relation conducted me every where. I was introduced by him to the casino of the nobles, and was always in his box at the theatre of La Scala. He advised me to attach myself to an old countess, whose *cavalier servente* was just dead. I did so, and soon had the honour of carrying her shawl, and whispering in her ear even to the exclusion of her superannuated husband, at all the places of public resort.

I was now initiated into all the magic enjoyments of wealth and splendour. Without any riches or merit of my own, I enjoyed all the luxuries, which were not a little heightened by the visits I paid my father's house, where I saw poverty in its most appalling state, accompanied by pretensions to rank. I was intoxicated. The Countess had several daughters, these I seldom saw, though they were approaching rapidly to womanhood. It however happened, that soon after I had obtained a footing in her house, that a birth-day of her eldest child occurred. She resolved upon celebrating it by a little ball, chiefly composed of the immediate connections of the family. I was admitted by virtue of my office. I had never before been in a ball-room. The splendid chandeliers, the gay dresses, and the beautiful women, surrounding me on every side, raised a scene before me, which even my most vivid fancy had never imagined.

I could not dance, I was therefore a mere spectator; but I was not idle, I had never been accustomed to see unmarried females, for they are not admitted into the society to which I belonged. There appeared a charm about them I could not define; they fixed my attention, and as each moved in the light dance, with all the agility and grace attendant upon youth, while their retreating looks seemed to denote a fear that they excited observation; I attempted in vain to discover what fascinated me. My heart beat violently, it seemed as if I had never before witnessed beauty. Towards the end of the evening, a party of foreigners entered; they had come to reside in Milan; with them was a young lady. She entered into the dances. She had not the light airy step of her companions, she had not the same brilliancy of eye, but there was something so powerful in her meek glance, in her measured graceful step, that enchained the senses. From that moment I could gaze upon no one else. She alone seemed to be moving, she alone seemed to be the object worthy of attention. I was yet gazing upon her, when the Countess called me to join her party at tre sette.[1] I accompanied her, but it was in vain for me to attempt fixing my mind upon the cards before me. I saw nothing but that figure which had been that moment before my sight. I made blunders that called forth impatient exclamations from my partners, and I was at last allowed to rise upon the plea of a head-ache. I instantly entered the other room, but she was gone.

She had however left her image in my breast. For several days I did not see her again, but at last she began to appear in public, for being a foreigner, her parents did not confine her as is customary amongst Italians. I often left the Countess in the Theatre, and placing myself in the pit, near the box in which she was, watched her slightest motion. There was a melancholy look about her that seemed to indicate an acquaintance with grief, that was extraordinary in so young a person. Her dark blue eye was seldom unveiled; her long modest eyelashes generally hid their

---

1   A card game for four players.

splendour, and her silence, and her uninterested glance, added a charm to her figure I cannot describe. Her goodness and charity were spoken of by all, her beauty was not envied or denied by her own, while her gentle manners and winning smile, seemed to gain the heart of all the other sex. I accompanied the Countess to her house. I sat by her, but could not speak with her. It seemed as if the emotion in my breast, stifled the words I was about to utter. She however noticed me, and her parents in repeating their compliments to the lady I accompanied, included me in a general invitation to the house.

As it was not the custom for ladies of rank to rise until a late hour, I had a great part of the day upon my own hands. I used generally to lounge about, and sometimes go to the Ambrosian Library,[1] in quest of something to engage my attention. One morning I was there as usual, and I found the Ernachs there. Matilda was with them, they were just then occupied in viewing the manuscript of Virgil, with Petrarch's annotations.[2] When the Cicerone pointed out the last note of this latter poet, in which he speaks of his love to Laura, I could not help remarking, a momentary emotion which passed across the face of Matilda. Her mother also observed it, and immediately taking her arm, accompanied her into the room containing pictures of several of the greatest masters. I followed them, and entered into conversation by pointing out the heads of the Milanese Raphael,[3] which one cannot examine without feeling a stillness come over our senses foreign to our nature. There is so much beauty and heavenly quiet about them, that they indeed resemble representations of a poet's dream. Before we parted, I was accepted as the guide to the curiosities, which they had not yet seen, and my office was to begin the next day.

It is useless to describe to you the gradual steps of love. I at last neglected the attentions due to the Countess, while sitting by the side of Matilda. At last, no longer capable of enduring the feelings within my bosom, I confessed my love to the object I adored. She was not angry, nor did she seem surprised; but in a

---

1 The Bibliotheca Ambrosiana, founded in 1609, is one of the world's greatest libraries; it was also one of the first to be open to the public.
2 Polidori had been greatly impressed by this literary relic (*Diary* 182). A cicerone is a tour guide.
3 *The Marriage of the Virgin* (1504). Polidori saw it in 1816 and commented: "The Milanese Raphael has some heads expressing such mild heavenly meekness as is scarcely imagined" (*Diary* 182).

voice that betrayed inward agitation, she begged of me to lay aside all hopes of gaining her hand, and conjured me not to mention it to her father. I was confused and abashed. I retired and returned to the palace, where I confined myself to my chamber. Not having appeared for several days in society, and enquiries being made concerning me, I was soon sought for by my kind relation. He seemed so anxious about the ill health, which he imagined was the cause of my absence from those gaieties in which I always seemed to delight, that I was induced to lay open to him the whole of my heart. He tried to administer consolation, but could not succeed; my vanity was mortified, and reflecting upon my poverty, I had imagined that I was despised for some richer rival. He seemed to know Matilda better, told me he could not believe it, but I dwelt so much upon the subject, that he saw it was useless to oppose my opinion any longer. He attempted to induce me to accompany him into society, but I refused, and for some days remained alone in my chamber.

Sick with all the splendour around, which seemed to mock me, I determined in spite of the expected reproaches of my mother, to return to my father's house, where by long confinement I fell ill. My kind relation hearing of this came to me, and tried to represent to me the folly of my conduct; but disappointed love and mortified vanity, did not allow me to listen. Seeing me thus haunted by the idea of riches, he generously offered to advance me a considerable sum, and to give me letters to a friend at Alexandria, where I might he thought employ my capital to the greatest advantage in commercial speculations. I thanked him, and accepted his kind offer. I soon left Milan, determined never to return till those riches were mine, which should enable me to assert a rank equal to any in my native city. I arrived at Alexandria, and was soon engaged in mercantile speculations, with an eagerness that caused all my transactions to appear more like the ventures of a desperate gambler than the secure projects of a merchant. I found several Europeans established in this city, chiefly engaged in the commerce of grain.

Amongst the rest, there was one who seemed to form a particular attachment to me; he was several years older than myself, and was noted amongst us for a certain avoidance of pleasure which did not appear natural to his years. He was always engaged, when not occupied in his business, either in reading or in a solitary ramble through the burnt neighbourhood of this ruined town.[1] I was the only person he sought; he seemed to place his confidence in me, and made many enquiries, at first vaguely, concerning those I had known at Milan. Happening to name the Ernachs, his face immediately became anxious, and his questions evidently bore a stamp of interest they had not before shown. This excited my attention and caused me to make more particular enquiries concerning him. Little was known; he was a German, and it was thought he had been disappointed in love. He perceived the attention I began to show him, and one evening when we were alone, he told me that he had at first been induced to seek my society, from a letter he had received from Matilda. "You must have perceived the interest, with which I listened to your account of the family of the Ernachs; know that I love Matilda, that I have reason to believe my affection is returned, but that owing to my poverty, I have never dared to confess even to her the feelings of love I bear within my breast. We were together from earliest infancy, all our pleasures were in common, and though, when I grew to manhood, I no longer dared to use the familiarity of my earlier years with her, who began to vest the charms of woman, still we partook in the pleasures of each other's occupations. Many things we studied together. I read the lighter authors of literature to her while she was engaged in those occupations attendant, in our country, upon every female member of a family. I at last opened Petrarch, and read those sonnets in which love is so delicately pourtrayed. You cannot conceive my emotions, when I perceived that she felt them as I did myself, and that she often raised her modest eyes, while a blush mantled her cheek, to gaze upon me, while my trembling voice seemed not to be reading the sentiments of another, but speaking the feelings of my own breast. We seemed, indeed, not to want to comment upon what we were both sensible expressed only those truths which echoed in the breasts of both.[2] When, however, I retired, I always upbraided myself for thus exposing, though indirectly, that love, of which I had no reason to think her parents would approve, for I had no profession, and was not born to

---

1 Alexandria had declined more or less steadily since classical times; by the 1770s, the date of Doni's visit, it was a fishing port with a population of only 6,000.
2 An innocent version of Francesca's account of how she and Paolo were seduced by a book (Dante, *Inferno* 5.121-38).

riches. When, however, I saw her, and she again asked for the author whose delicate pencil only traced the most fading hues of love, I again read. We were thus engaged, when we were interrupted by her mother, who had stood unperceived some time watching the emotions but too visible in our countenances. She did not then speak, but taking another opportunity, when I was alone with her, she gently intimated, that I had not acted honourably in thus engaging the attention of Matilda to such poetry, as was but too powerful a seducer of the mind. I was but too conscious of it. I acknowledged my error, and promised to take no further occasion of thus acting upon her daughter's susceptible heart. She placed entire confidence in me, and was not deceived. I applied to my father, who, at my desire, sent me hither to push my fortune, and I have succeeded as well as I expected."

How shall I convey to you an idea of what passed in my mind? Before me stood the unconscious cause of my being rejected by Matilda. He had told me, he loved her, that she loved him. I was silent when he ended, I could not rouse myself to speak to him; he, thinking that his narration had tired me, made an apology, to which I could only answer by monosyllables; he retired and left me to my own thoughts. It was evident Matilda preferred another. My feelings may be imagined,—cannot be described. It seemed as if some demon actuated me, I fell upon my knees, and dared even to call God to witness my vow of obtaining the object of my affections, in spite of all obstacles. It seemed as if I felt more at peace after having thus resolved upon not yielding even to him she loved, the possession I ambitioned.

I sought Huldebrand, for so was my rival called, determined to worm into his confidence, and gain the whole of his secret. I told him not to impute my abstraction on the former evening to any thing but my mind being engaged in thought upon a circumstance, which I noticed at Milan, and which was now fully explained. I then mentioned to him the emotion I had noticed in Matilda's countenance, while listening to the memorial of Petrarch with regard to the duration of his love. This immediately secured his attention, and I soon learnt many circumstances with regard to their early years; and I became convinced, that there was really no engagement between them.

In the mean time my speculations, which had been begun rashly, had for the greater part turned out badly, and I found myself with a capital considerably diminished. Huldebrand who could not remain ignorant of my losses proposed to me, as I seemed ignorant of the best means of securing a profitable commerce, to join him. I did so; but growing tired of the slow advantages to be obtained by the regular channels, I at last induced him to join me in a speculation that seemed to promise a certain and at the same time immense profit. We ventured, and lost all we risked. My loss did not grieve me much, for it had reduced my Matilda's favoured lover to the same want as myself. He was not however dismayed, nor did he reproach me, but immediately exerting himself to recover all that remained of our property, he proposed, that we should join some Armenians, who were about to leave Alexandria and penetrate into the interior of Asia, in hopes of finding some opportunity of bettering our small fortunes. I consented, and we accompanied them.

We entered Persia, and travelled even into India. We soon found our capitals rapidly increasing, for, imitating the Armenians, we bought upon several occasions precious stones, which we resold almost immediately greatly to our advantage. It is, in no way necessary for me to give an account of these countries, towards the understanding the fatality that attended my life. I travelled through them careless about the scenery or inhabitants; the whole of my attention was engaged in my endeavours to acquire wealth. Matilda stood constantly before me as the bride of Huldebrand, and my father's house always appeared in contrast with the palace of the head of our family. I soon entered into the spirit of the traffic I was engaged in, and restrained as I was by Huldebrand's steadiness, we rapidly indeed accumulated an immense sum, which we carried always with us in precious stones.

I had been particularly struck by the venerable appearance of one of our companions, he was aged, his head was white with the numbered years that had passed since his birth. This was the more remarkable from the contrast it offered with the jet black hair and beards of his countrymen. He was never engaged in their occupations, he never seemed to be concerned in any mercantile transaction, yet he seemed to be careless of his money, which he gave profusely to all. He seemed to delight in the society of strangers, and therefore sought ours; but Huldebrand not speaking his language did not gain the same hold of his affections as myself, he indeed treated me completely as his son, and often directed me in the conduct of our concerns; his advice was always advantageous.

This stranger seemed to look upon me as his pupil, and he gradually turned my mind to the objects around me. But he did not improve my heart by the opening of my mind. He was himself extremely rich; when therefore he held forth upon the happiness of contented poverty, I thought he was but a mere visionary, imagining the Arabian delights of a sandy desert, while shaded by the canopying foliage of a grove, and surrounded by all the riches of a cultivated country. I looked around, and I saw the genius and the ideot both equally subservient to the will of the wealthy. I saw virtue trodden under foot, and vice, that monster in rags in the cottage, adored as a goddess in the temples of the gaudy palace. Wherever I went, it seemed as if gold, in the bustling of the whole of life, had the same effect as a few aspers[1] thrown amidst the obstreperous crowd that immediately leaves off its hideous yell in haste to scramble for the miserable gain. Riches were a thirst upon me. I could not believe that Matilda or Ernach, her father, could resist the splendour of wealth. But Huldebrand was with me, half our common property was his. He loved,—was beloved. Whenever I looked upon him, my heart did not beat quicker; it seemed for a moment to pause, as if his sight blasted its vital action, but it beat again with redoubled violence, when Matilda's image rose upon my mind, and my former vow was again repeated.

Though my appetite for riches was not sated, it was gratified; our speculations had been constantly doubling our capital, and we had already left the banks of the Euphrates, turning our steps towards Europe, when we gradually entered the vast desert that spreads its subtle sands from the Red Sea, almost to the Mediterranean. Having all our wealth about us in jewels and gold, we were anxious about our safety. Every night the cry of the watchful sentinel bidding us be upon the alert, while it called to the roaming Arab to depart, sounded on my waking ears, and often I arose in painful anxiety, to gaze upon the far spread horizon, lost sometimes in the misty light of the bright moon. I envied the sound sleep of the poor camel-driver, who lay extended by the animal entrusted to his care, as heedless of my wealth, as the brute about the fate of his burden. At last the ground seemed to acquire firmness to the foot, and the camel already began to browze upon the solitary stunted plants that here and there spread their parched growth to the no longer beneficent ray of an eastern sun. I thought myself secure, night came, and I was standing by my open tent, for I could not rest; I was gazing upon a long line which bounded the horizon, with a thin dark streak,

---

1 Small silver coins that circulated in the Levant from the twelfth to the seventeenth century.

indicating the palm boundary to our toilsome pilgrimages; there were slight clouds flitting before the moon, and as their shadows fled over the vast expanse, my heart beat quicker, for each, as it approached from the horizon, seemed to my hurried imagination, as the dark shadow formed by an Arab troop; one followed the other, always bearing deceit with it. At last from the long line of palms, a black speck seemed to move with great rapidity; I could trace no cloud upon the heavens, which could throw its dark shadow upon this track; I breathless called a sentinel, the alarm was given, but we were surrounded; I went about like a madman, encouraged the men to fight,—fought. The circle was gradually straightened round us; the men fell by the distant arrows at first, but the work of death was not slower, when the sword clashed against sword, and the robber's foot trod upon his antagonist's. I struggled, my riches were lost; while yet struggling amidst our very tents, I heard the old Armenian cry for help, he was combating with a young Arabian, who had thrown him to the ground. I rushed forward, bade the robber defend himself; we fought, I succeeded in disarming him, and was upon the point of thrusting my sword through his body, when he begged of me to spare his life, promising that both the Armenian and myself should be safe. I saw all resistance was at an end, I gave him back his weapon, and approached the old man who was wounded. He took my hand, thanked me for my attempt to save him, but he thought his wound was mortal; he bade me at the same time console myself for the loss of my accumulated wealth, saying that he would, ere he died, make me ample amends.

Our lives, at the intercession of the Arab I had spared, who proved to be a man of rank amongst the robbers, were granted us. He conveyed the Armenian to his own tent, and I anxiously placed myself by the old man's side, watching, with the agitation of a desperate gambler, every various expression of his countenance; it was my last stake. Huldebrand I knew was not killed, but had been given, as part of the booty, to one of the robbers, in hopes of his ransoming himself, but he was ruined like myself, had lost every thing; I was however, if not deceived, to obtain riches as abundantly as before. Matilda might then be mine; I made no further enquiries about him who had partaken the vicissitudes of commerce and of life with me, who had been almost beggared by my rashness, and whose steadiness had enabled me to recover every thing, and to gain wealth. I sat by the old man; every sound that fell from his lips, seemed the announcement of his bequest, but he was silent on that subject.

Five days elapsed, at last the sixth was passing, and his strength was evidently rapidly failing, his breath became hurried, and his eyes began to take that lustre, which seems to be the last exertion of the departing soul; he then spoke, "I wished," he said, "that my life had been spared but a short time longer, I could then have bestowed wealth upon you, without the conditions that may now startle you. Know, but how dare I tell it? you may look upon me with horror, and while I am wishing to bless you, may turn away from me. I have a power that is supposed to bring the curse of the Almighty upon it; I can,—I have the power of raising a spirit from the vast abyss,[1] and make him lay at my feet, the infinite wealth enclosed within the earth's recesses. But if you would listen to one aged, who has borne this blasting power from early youth, you would refuse the dangerous gift. For there is a condition necessarily bound to that power, which will undoubtedly quell your ardent longing even for riches." It was in vain that he addressed me thus, Matilda and wealth connected rose to my imagination. I pressed him to explain himself. He did. He told me that either I could only call for a certain sum at a time, and that at each time, some human domestic infliction, worse than the preceding, would fall upon me, or that, I at once, could gain unlimited power, and constant domestic prosperity, on the condition of giving myself up for ever to the will of a malignant being.[2] He had chosen the first, had called but once for the exertion of the demon's power, but his happiness had been withered by that once. I did not hesitate, I laughed in my own mind at domestic happiness, I had lived only in Italy, and in the East, I begged of him to disclose his secret; he did. I bound myself to the first condition.

I impatiently rose, I left the old man upon his dying couch, and retreated to my own tent. I raised the spirit, his hideous form might have appalled a stronger heart than mine. I trembled, but his mocking laugh subdued my fears, and bending my knee, I acknowledged him as my superior through life. I cannot describe the scene, I could not without recording some part of the spells by which I raised this monster, and he has but too fully proved his power for me to be willing to put the least clue into the hands

---

1 A reminiscence of Glendower's boast: "I can call spirits from the vasty deep" (Shakespeare, *1 Henry IV* 3.1.50).

2 These Mephistophelean conditions may have been suggested by M.G. Lewis, who translated parts of *Faust* orally on his visit to Geneva in 1816; the translation also helped to inspire *Manfred* (*BLJ* 7:113).

of any one which might bring the curse I have felt upon him. Besides riches, I gained other powers, but these are not connected with yours and my Louisa's fate, I shall not speak of them.

I returned to the sick man's tent, the Armenian was dead. I did not feel sorry, how could I at that moment; I was exultant, my wealth was so enormous, I did not see a possibility of spending it. The next day the robbers buried my benefactor in the burning sands. I proposed a ransom for myself to the Arab, he insisted upon my accepting my freedom. I did, and we eat together; no longer fearing treachery, I made him a present to an enormous amount.[1] He was surprized, but did not make even the smallest enquiry.

I roamed about the encampment, for I was desirous of seeing these robbers in their native barren plain. While wandering about their black tents, I heard a voice of pain issuing from one of the most miserable. It was Huldebrand, he was calling, in the delirium of a fever, for a drop of water to allay his thirst. The well was close to me. The tent was open, no one was near, he was extended upon the sandy floor, with hardly any clothes to defend him from its hot touch. I, even I, could not resist this appeal, I seized a vessel lying by his side, and drew it from the well full. I was turning towards him, when suddenly his tones altered, he seemed to press his breast, while in the softest words he addressed some one. I approached, he was imagining Matilda stood by him. The words sounded on my ear,—"I know, Matilda, that you love me." The pitcher fell upon the sand, and the water was drank up by the burning dust, and I turned away with a raging heart, from the dying Huldebrand.

I instantly determined upon leaving the spot. The noble Arab escorted me to the utmost boundary of the desert, and I was safe from danger. I hired camels and horses, and proceeded to Aleppo,[2] spreading every where that I was a merchant, who had been very successful in my speculations. This was easy to me, for I could refer to people with whom I had had transactions, and my name was known. I hastened to Italy, and soon reached Milan, I entered with all the pomp of riches; I will not describe my entry,

---

1 Byron explains the laws of Arab hospitality in a note to *The Giaour* (343): "To partake of food—to break bread and salt with your host— insures the safety of the guest, even though an enemy; his person from that moment is sacred" (*CPW* 3:417).

2 A Syrian city (one of the most ancient in the world) famous to English readers from Shakespeare, *Othello* 5.2.352.

it was foolishly splendid, nor will I attempt to paint to you the daily display I made of some new folly; they were produced by the intoxication of a madman. Matilda, for she held no less a powerful influence over me than my avarice, was the object of the whole. I found her health much decayed, she had not heard of Huldebrand for more than two years. Yet there was perhaps a greater charm in that pale cheek and languid eye, than I had found in the delicate colouring of the one, or the splendour of the other. If I could gain her love now, it would, indeed, be an ample compensation for her former rejection. I began by spreading the report of her lover's death, though I was not certain of the fact, yet I thought, at any rate, that he could not re-appear so soon as not to allow me time to accomplish my end. I then went to her father's, and in the course of the conversation announced it.

Matilda was inconsolable, but she took pleasure in my society, for I could talk to her of Huldebrand, I related indifferent particulars concerning him, the eagerness with which she listened reached my heart; I determined, however, to endure even these pangs, rather than lose the opportunities afforded me of sitting by her side. As in the course of narration, I introduced the relation of actions in which I had been his benefactor, she blessed me for it. I felt like a baffled demon. I gradually began to talk of myself. I sounded the father and mother with regard to a marriage; obtained their full consent and approbation. They gradually broke it to their daughter. She wondered at my seeking for a widowed heart; insisted upon my taking some months to consider of it, while she herself fulfilled the term of mourning she thought due to her lover's memory. I was anxious, and fearful of Huldebrand's appearance. I pressed my suit with earnestness; my relations, her father, her mother, used all the arts of persuasion to induce her to anticipate the day. She did, and we were married.

It now seemed as if I could dare the world. I had Matilda, had wealth, the only objects my mind had ever rested upon were mine. I had two children, Louisa and Olivieri. You cannot imagine the splendour in which I lived. Where could the mortal be found who had greater supposed sources of happiness than mine? yet I was miserable; Matilda was mine, my wife, but her affections still rested upon the image of my rival. I doated upon her; it seemed as if the price of guilt I had paid bound her the more to me, as if she were to form the only happiness I was to know, and she did not love me. She differed entirely from my countrywomen; she enjoyed her domestic circle, she was modest; and while she stood amongst the abandoned wantons, who formed the only society around her, she stood erect, as if she were sent by Heaven to show deluded men the beauties of the virtues they despised.

I had not enjoyed the society of my wife more than three years, when my momentary happiness was blasted. Matilda came home one day, as I imagined, from the Corso, flurried and violently agitated. She threw herself upon the sofa, and lost in thought, she did not perceive that I was near her. She drew from her breast a note: I could see over her shoulder; it struck me that it was Huldebrand's hand-writing. She seemed to look upon it as if she could not believe her eyes. She viewed it, her hands fell, and the movement of the eyelids over the fixed eyes seemed to denote the belief in a deceit of the senses. Her breath was still, her cheek pale, she did not move. I unavoidably discovered myself; she turned, looked at me, and the tears bursting from her eyes, rolled down her cheeks, as she rushed out of the room. I dared not follow her. Huldebrand might be stalking in my very house, might be close to me, his words of reproach might be already in the air, prepared to damn me with their sound. I should be proved in the world's face, a liar, a wretch without a spark of generosity, of gratitude, in Matilda's face—I hid myself in my chamber, for the consciousness of my guilt caused me at first to wish for concealment. But the thought of my rival roused me; was it not possible to remove him? I rushed out of my room, and was upon the point of going through the great gate, when I perceived a figure descending the staircase, wrapt closely in a large mantle. It was a woman—it was Matilda. Her hurried step and anxious glances thrown around caused me to watch her. She went out into the street, I followed her; there was an obstacle near the theatre, she cleared it, but I lost her in the crowd of carriages. In vain I tried every opening leading to the theatre, I could not recover a trace of her. At last I was obliged to lean exhausted against the wall, and Ernach, her father, coming from the theatre, discovered me. Perceiving my agitation at sight of him, he insisted upon escorting me home. He attempted to lead me to explain to him the cause of my trembling limbs, which weighed upon his arm. He did not know that he sought to know my shame; I insisted upon his leaving me, and I at last fell exhausted upon a chair in my saloon.

I know not how long I had remained in this situation by myself; I at last heard Matilda's light step ascending the staircase. I did not move, my eyes remained still gazing on the ground when she entered. At sight of me she started, but she commanded herself—approached me with a faultering step. I attempted to clasp her to my bosom, as if—I know not what passed in my mind. She retreated. "You have a right to know where I have been in this clandestine manner." I hid my face with my hands, I was conscious she had been to see Huldebrand. She had been with him, she would say no more. I threw myself at her feet, she turned away. "I can no longer even esteem you," were the last words she said, when she left me.

She went out several times in the course of next day; once I attempted to follow her. She perceived me at the door: "Filiberto," she said, "seek not to pursue my steps, I am but active in the cause of virtue. Retire and leave me. You must be aware of what hangs over your head. Would that heaven may grant I could avert it from my husband, my children's father." I was left in a state of mind that bordered upon phrenzy. I rushed out of the house, and turning my steps another way, I did not return towards my home till night. When I did return, I found every thing in the greatest confusion. There was a carriage with posthorses at the gate. The moment I approached, my valet came to me to tell me of my shame. Matilda had been seen leaving Milan, with a gentleman in her company. I jumped into the carriage, and followed upon the road they were reported to have taken.

I did not speak during the whole time; I did not listen, though my servant, having entered with me, was telling me more of the circumstances. Night and day I travelled in pursuit. I seemed to be gaining on them. I at last overtook them just as I was entering a village in Savoy. They were upon the point of leaving it. I sprung out of my carriage, and with the speed of a demoniac I ran after them. In my furious haste, I fell. I did not attempt to rise, but instantly fired; my wife's shriek was heard: they, however, drove on. When my carriage with fresh horses overtook me, my servant tried to raise me, I had dislocated my ancle.[1] Blood, my servant told me, could be traced upon the road, as if it had fallen from

---

1   The records of the ghost-story project of 1816 begin with an injury to
     Polidori's ankle. On 15 June, Polidori jumped off the balcony of the
     Villa Diodati to help Mary Shelley up the hill to the house, but the
     ground was wet and he slipped. The conversation on the principle of life
     that, according to Shelley, inspired the nightmare that in turn inspired
     Frankenstein took place that evening, so presumably she began her novel
     the next day, the sixteenth. Byron began his fragment on the seven-
     teenth, and Polidori, with his leg worse than ever, began *Ernestus Berch-
     told* on the eighteenth (Macdonald 83-88).

my wife's carriage. I could but look upon myself as Matilda's murderer, the shriek was her's. My emotions and feelings were so violent and various it would be impossible to portray them. The demon's power was upon me, and his curse proved a bitter one.

I was conveyed home, where I was for a long time delirious; I became calm but not less miserable. My attendants then gave me a letter, which had been found upon my wife's dressing table, after my departure in chase of her. She was innocent, she had not fled with Huldebrand, but with her father. Huldebrand had upon that condition agreed to conceal my crime, my shame. She had left her home, her children; had sacrificed her own to shield my name from infamy. I did not at this intelligence relapse into the violent ravings I had undergone. I sunk into a state of apathy, whence nothing could rouse me. I refused even to see my children, and hardly ever leaving my chamber, I spent the night and day with short intervals to self-reproach in combating inflictions of the mind more dreadful than any corporeal penance of the holy anchorite.[1]

Many years had thus passed, I had not once seen my children, not even heard of them, for I would speak with no one. I at last saw them by accident. You know Olivieri's violent character. He had constantly enquired after me, always baffled by the servants in his wish of seeing me; he at last seized his opportunity, but Louisa had watched him, and they both appeared in my sight struggling with one another; for she was trying to hinder his disturbing me. If Matilda herself had stood before me she could not have affected me more; for Louisa, though her features are different, her eye dark, has the expression that gave such power to her mother's looks, playing upon her face. She at last, no longer capable of resisting her brother, threw herself at my feet, and earnestly begged me not to be offended with her dear Olivieri. I took her to my arms. From that moment I was aroused. I could not leave my daughter, but gave up all my time to the education of my children; but I brought another curse upon my head, for I neglected Olivieri; except in his literary studies I did not assist him, his mind was allowed to be biassed by any one who chose to trouble themselves with acting upon him. Louisa on the contrary was my constant companion, she rewarded my care. You know her, if ever a wretch like me might have hope, it must be in the prayers such a being can offer up for me to the throne of heaven.

---

1 Anchorites were Catholic hermits, who often practised extreme forms of penance.

After some time I proposed journeying through the different countries of Europe, to show my children the different peculiarities of nations. We had already entered Switzerland when my son left me. I had been accustomed to his often quitting me for days together, and hardly noticed his departure. Louisa and myself proceeded to the different spots remarkable for their beauty or sublimity. On the Wengern Alp we saw you. We soon after heard daily of the feats of Ernestus Berchtold and Olivieri. I don't know why, but the thought of the chamois hunter we had seen being this Ernestus, first struck my daughter, and I soon joined in the belief. A letter from Olivieri appointed Interlaken as the place of meeting; we went there. Events in which you were concerned brought us again to Milan.

The immense riches I had obtained from the spirit under my command, though much diminished, were yet more than sufficient to maintain us in sufficient splendour, not to fear any thing like a competition. But Olivieri and yourself were gamblers. Louisa forced me again to risk an infliction equally severe as the last, for your sake. I could not resist her prayers for you. I again called the spirit from his immortal haunts, and Olivieri's infamy was the consequence. Your debts had proved so enormous, that in my attempt at saving him from an ignominious death, I was again obliged, though I knew the horrible powers of the demon, to call upon him. I did so. He announced to me that I had exhausted my spells, and that after this infliction, as nothing round me would remain, on which he could breathe his pestilential breath, he would no longer obey my summons. I called upon him to take back his gold, he laughed and left me. I had no suspicion of Olivieri's seduction of your sister; when therefore his letter was put into my hands, you may imagine how your noble conduct affected me. I did not speak of it, for what could a father say? Must I even acknowledge it to you, I sometimes rested upon it with a feeling of consolation, for I hoped, that crime of my son's might be the infliction upon his father, meant by the demon as passing all others. Louisa I thought might then be spared, and you two might at least be happy.

But you married; I dreamt of happiness, on Louisa's birth-day accompanied you to your room, and the demon's threat I found had indeed been fulfilled. Your mother's portrait was Matilda's. Olivieri had seduced, you married a daughter of Matilda, of Matilda's husband, and I was the murderer of her father.

THE END.

Appendix A: Ghost Stories

[Appendix A.1 includes English translations of the two stories from *Fantasmagoriana* that seem to have made the biggest impression on the Geneva circle. A.2 is Byron's abandoned ghost story, the basis for *The Vampyre*. The title and date of A.3 suggest that it may be P.B. Shelley's response to the ghost-story project, although there is no external evidence for this. When M.G. Lewis (1775-1818) visited Geneva in August 1816, he told five ghost stories to Byron, Polidori, and P.B. Shelley, who recorded them in his lover's journal (A.4); whether or not they helped to inspire Polidori or M.W. Shelley, they are among the ghost stories of the Villa Diodati.]

1. From *Tales of the Dead* (1813, reprinted by permission of Terry Hale)

a. "The Family Portraits"[1]

> No longer shall you gaze on't; lest your fancy
> May think anon, it moves.——
> The fixture of her eye has motion in't.
>   WINTERS TALE[2]

NIGHT had insensibly superseded day, when Ferdinand's carriage continued its slow course through the forest; the postilion uttering a thousand complaints on the badness of the roads, and

---

1 This is the story remembered by Mary Shelley in 1831 as "the tale of the sinful founder of his race, whose miserable doom it was to bestow the kiss of death on all the younger sons of his fated house, just when they reached the age of promise. His gigantic, shadowy form, clothed like the ghost in Hamlet, in complete armour, but with the beaver up, was seen at midnight, by the moon's fitful beams, to advance slowly along the gloomy avenue. The shape was lost beneath the shadow of the castle walls; but soon a gate swung back, a step was heard, the door of the chamber opened, and he advanced to the couch of the blooming youths, cradled in healthy sleep. Eternal sorrow sat upon his face as he bent down and kissed the forehead of the boys, who from that hour withered like flowers snapt upon the stalk" (355).

2 Shakespeare, *The Winter's Tale* 5.3.60-61, 67.

Ferdinand employing the leisure which the tedious progress of his carriage allowed, with reflections to which the purpose of his journey gave rise.

As was usual with young men of rank, he had visited several universities; and after having travelled over the principal parts of Europe, he was now retuning to his native country to take possession of the property of his father, who had died in his absence.

Ferdinand was an only son, and the last branch of the ancient family of Meltheim: it was on this account that his mother was the more anxious that he should form a brilliant alliance, to which both his birth and fortune entitled him; she frequently repeated that Clotilde of Hainthal was of all others the person she should be most rejoiced to have as a daughter-in-law, and who should give to the world an heir to the name and estates of Meltheim. In the first instance, she merely named her amongst other distinguished females whom she recommended to her son's attention: but after a short period she spoke of none but her: and at length declared, rather positively, that all her happiness depended on the completion of this alliance, and hoped her son would approve her choice.

Ferdinand, however, never thought of this union but with regret; and the urgent remonstrances which his mother ceased not to make on the subject, only contributed to render Clotilde, who was an entire stranger to him, less amiable in his eyes: he determined at last to take a journey to the capital, whither Mr. Hainthal and his daughter were attracted by the carnival. He wished at least to know the lady, ere he consented to listen to his mother's entreaties; and secretly flattered himself that he should find some more cogent reasons for opposing this union than mere caprice, which was the appellation the old lady gave to his repugnance.

Whilst travelling alone in his carriage, as night approached, the solitary forest, his imagination drew a picture of his early life, which happy recollections rendered still happier. It seemed, that the future presented no charms for him to equal the past; and the greater pleasure he took in retracing what no longer existed, the less wish he felt to bestow a thought on that futurity to which, contrary to his inclinations, he seemed destined. Thus, notwithstanding the slowness with which his carriage proceeded over the rugged ground, he found that he was too rapidly approaching the termination of his journey.

The postilion at length began to console himself; for one half of the journey was accomplished, and the remainder presented only good roads: Ferdinand, however, gave orders to his groom to stop at the approaching village, determining to pass the night there.

The road through the village which led to the inn was bordered by gardens, and the sound of different musical instruments led Ferdinand to suppose that the villagers were celebrating some rural *fête*. He already anticipated the pleasure of joining them, and hoped that this recreation would dissipate his melancholy thoughts. But on listening more attentively, he remarked that the music did not resemble that usually heard at inns; and the great light he perceived at the window of a pretty house from whence came the sounds that had arrested his attention, did not permit him to doubt that a more select party than are accustomed to reside in the country at that unfavourable season, were amusing themselves in performing a concert.

The carriage now stopped at the door of a small inn of mean appearance. Ferdinand, who counted on much inconvenience and few comforts, asked who was the lord of the village. They informed him that he occupied a *château* situated in an adjoining hamlet. Our traveller said no more, but was obliged to content himself with the best apartment the landlord could give him. To divert his thoughts, he determined to walk in the village, and directed his steps towards the spot where he had heard the music; to this the harmonious sounds readily guided him: he approached softly, and found himself close to the house where the concert was performing. A young girl, sitting at the door, was playing with a little dog, who began to bark. Ferdinand, drawn from his reverie by this singular accompaniment, begged the little girl to inform him who lived in that house. "It is my father," she replied, smiling; "come in, sir." And saying this, she slowly went up the steps.

Ferdinand hesitated for an instant whether to accept this unceremonious invitation. But the master of the house came down, saying to him in a friendly tone: "Our music, sir, has probably been the only attraction to this spot; no matter, it is the pastor's abode, and to it you are heartily welcome. My neighbours and I," continued he, whilst leading Ferdinand in, "meet alternately at each other's houses once a week, to form a little concert; and to-day it is my turn. Will you take a part in the performance, or only listen to it? Sit down in this apartment. Are you accustomed to hear better music than that performed simply by amateurs? or do you prefer an assemblage where they pass their time in conversation? If you like the latter, go into the adjoining *hope; pleased*

room, where you will find my wife surrounded by a young circle:
here is our musical party, there is their *conversazioni.*" Saying this,
he opened the door, made a gentle inclination of the head to Ferdinand, and seated himself before his desk. Our traveller would
fain have made apologies; but the performers in an instant
resumed the piece he had interrupted. At the same time the
pastor's wife, a young and pretty woman, entreated Ferdinand, in
the most gracious manner possible, entirely to follow his own
inclinations, whether they led him to remain with the musicians,
or to join the circle assembled in the other apartment. Ferdinand,
after uttering some commonplace terms of politeness, followed
her into the adjoining room.

The chairs formed a semicircle round the sofa, and were occupied by several women and by some men. They all rose on Ferdinand's entering, and appeared a little disconcerted at the interruption. In the middle of the circle was a low chair, on which sat,
with her back to the door, a young and sprightly female, who,
seeing every one rise, changed her position, and at sight of a
stranger blushed and appeared embarrassed. Ferdinand entreated
the company not to interrupt the conversation. They accordingly
reseated themselves, and the mistress of the house invited the new
guest to take a seat on the sofa by two elderly ladies, and drew her
chair near him. "The music," she said to him, "drew you amongst
us, and yet in this apartment we have none; I hear it nevertheless
with pleasure myself: but I cannot participate in my husband's
enthusiasm for simple quartets and symphonies; several of my
friends are of the same way of thinking with me, which is the
reason that, while our husbands are occupied with their favourite
science, we here enjoy social converse, which sometimes, however,
becomes too loud for our *virtuoso* neighbours. Today, I give a long-
promised tea-drinking. Every one is to relate a story of ghosts, or
something of a similar nature. You see that my auditors are more
numerous than the band of musicians."

"Permit me, madam," replied Ferdinand, "to add to the
number of your auditors; although I have not much talent in
explaining the marvellous." *obstacle*

"That will not be any hinderance to you here," answered a very
pretty brunette; "for it is agreed amongst us that no one shall
search for any explanation, even though it bears the stamp of truth,
as explanations would take away all pleasure from ghost stories."

"I shall benefit by your instructions," answered Ferdinand:
"but without doubt I interrupt a very interesting recital;—dare I
entreat—?"

implore / supplicate   que dis done qc

The young lady with flaxen hair, who rose from the little seat, blushed anew; but the mistress of the house drew her by the arm, and laughing, conducted her to the middle of the circle. "Come, child," said she, "don't make any grimace; reseat yourself, and relate your story. This gentleman will also give us his."

"Do you promise to give us one, sir?" said the young lady to Ferdinand. He replied by a low bow. She then reseated herself in the place destined for the narrator, and thus began:

"One of my youthful friends, named Juliana, passed every summer with her family at her father's estate. The *château* was situated in a romantic country; high mountains formed a circle in the distance; forests of oaks and fine groves surrounded it. It was an ancient edifice, and had descended through a long line of ancestry to Juliana's father; for which reason, instead of making any alterations, he was only anxious to preserve it in the same state they had left it to him.

"Among the number of antiquities most prized by him was the family picture gallery; a vaulted room, dark, high, and of gothic architecture, where hung the portraits of his forefathers, as large as the natural size, covering the walls, which were blackened by age. Conformable to an immemorial custom, they ate in this room and Juliana has often told me, that she could not overcome, especially at supper-time, a degree of fear and repugnance; and that she had frequently feigned indisposition, to avoid entering this formidable apartment. Among the portraits there was one of a female, who, it would seem, did not belong to the family; for Juliana's father could neither tell whom it represented, nor how it had become ranged amongst his ancestry: but as to all appearance it had retained its station for ages, my friend's father was unwilling to remove it.

"Juliana never looked at this portrait without an involuntary shuddering and she has told me, that from her earliest infancy she has felt this secret terror, without being able to define the cause. Her father treated this sentiment as puerile, and compelled her sometimes to remain alone in that room. But as Juliana grew up, the terror this singular portrait occasioned, increased; and she frequently supplicated her father, with tears in her eyes, not to leave her alone in that apartment—'That portrait,' she would say, 'regards me not gloomily or terribly, but with looks full of a mild melancholy. It appears anxious to draw me to it, and as if the lips were about to open and speak to me.—That picture will certainly cause my death.'

"Juliana's father at length relinquished all hope of conquering his daughter's fears. One night at supper, the terror she felt had thrown her into convulsions, for she fancied she saw the picture move its lips; and the physician enjoined her father in future to remove from her view all similar causes of fear. In consequence, the terrifying portrait was removed from the gallery, and it was placed over the door of an uninhabited room in the attic story.

"Juliana, after this removal, passed two years without experiencing any alarms. Her complexion resumed its brilliancy, which surprised every one; for her continual fears had rendered her pale and wan: but the portrait and the fears it produced had alike disappeared, and Juliana—"

"Well," cried the mistress of the house, smiling, when she perceived that the narrator appeared to hesitate, "confess it, my dear child; Juliana found an admirer of her beauty;—was it not so?"

"'Tis even so," resumed the young lady, blushing deeply; "she was affianced: and her intended husband coming to see her the day previous to that fixed on for her marriage, she conducted him over the *château*, and from the attic rooms was shewing him the beautiful prospect which extended to the distant mountains. On a sudden she found herself, without being aware of it, in the room where the unfortunate portrait was placed. And it was natural that a stranger, surprised at seeing it there alone, should ask who it represented. To look at it, recognise it, utter a piercing shriek, and run towards the door, were but the work of an instant with poor Juliana. But whether in effect owing to the violence with which she opened the door the picture was shaken, or whether the moment was arrived in which its baneful influence was to be exercised over Juliana, I know not; but at the moment this unfortunate girl was striving to get out of the room and avoid her destiny, the portrait fell; and Juliana, thrown down by her fears, and overpowered by the heavy weight of the picture, never rose more."—

A long silence followed this recital, which was only interrupted by the exclamations of surprise and interest excited for the unfortunate Juliana. Ferdinand alone appeared untouched by the general emotions. At length, one of the ladies sitting near him broke the silence by saying, "This story is literally true; I knew the family where the fatal portrait caused the death of a charming young girl: I have also seen the picture; it has, as the young lady truly observed, an indescribable air of sadness which penetrates the heart, so that I could not bear to look on it long; and yet, as you say, its look is so full of tender melancholy, and has such infinite attractions, that it appears that the eyes move and have life."

"In general," resumed the mistress of the house, at the same time shuddering, "I don't like portraits, and I would not have any in the rooms I occupy. They say that they become pale when the original expires; and the more faithful the likeness, the more they remind me of those waxen figures I cannot look at without aversion."

"That is the reason," replied the young person who had related the history, "that I prefer those portraits where the individual is represented occupied in some employment, as then the figure is entirely independent of those who look at it; whereas in a simple portrait the eyes are inanimately fixed on every thing that passes. Such portraits appear to me as contrary to the laws of illusion as painted statues."

"I participate in your opinion," replied Ferdinand; "for the remembrance of a terrible impression produced on my mind when young, by a portrait of that sort, will never be effaced."

"O! pray relate it to us," said the young lady with flaxen hair, who had not as yet quitted the low chair; "you are obliged according to promise to take my place." She instantly arose, and jokingly forced Ferdinand to change seats with her.

"This history," said he, "will resemble a little too much the one you have just related; permit me therefore—"

"That does not signify," resumed the mistress of the house, "one is never weary with recitals of this kind; and the greater repugnance I feel in looking at these horrible portraits, the greater is the pleasure I take in listening to histories of their eyes or feet being seen to move."

"But seriously," replied Ferdinand, who would fain have retracted his promise, "my history is too horrible for so fine an evening. I confess to you that I cannot think of it without shuddering, although several years have elapsed since it happened."

"So much the better, so much the better!" cried nearly all present; "how you excite our curiosity! And its having happened to yourself will afford double pleasure, as we cannot entertain any doubt of the fact."

"It did not happen personally to me," answered Ferdinand, who reflected that he had gone too far, "but to one of my friends, on whose word I have as firm a reliance as if I had been myself a witness to it."

They reiterated their entreaties; and Ferdinand began in these words:—"One day, when I was arguing with the friend of whom I am about to make mention, on apparitions and omens, he told me the following story;—

"'I had been invited,' said he, 'by one of my college companions, to pass my vacations with him at an estate of his father's. The spring was that year unusually late, owing to a long and severe winter, and appeared in consequence more gay and agreeable, which gave additional charms to our projected pleasures. We arrived at his father's in the pleasant month of April, animated by all the gaiety the season inspired.

"'As my companion and I were accustomed to live together at the university, he had recommended to his family, in his letters, so to arrange matters that we might live together at his father's also: we in consequence occupied two adjoining rooms, from whence we enjoyed a view of the garden and a fine country, bounded in the distance by forests and vineyards. In a few days I found myself so completely at home in the house, and so familiarised with its inhabitants, that nobody, whether of the family or among the domesticks, made any difference between my friend and myself. His younger brothers, who were absent from me in the day, often passed the night in my room, or in that of their elder brother. Their sister, a charming girl about twelve years of age, lovely and blooming as a newly blown rose, gave me the appellation of brother, and fancied that under this title she was privileged to shew me all her favourite haunts in the garden, to gratify my wishes at table, and to furnish my apartment with all that was requisite. Her cares and attention will never be effaced from my recollection; they will long outlive the scenes of horror that *château* never ceases to recall to my recollection. From the first of my arrival, I had remarked a huge portrait affixed to the wall of an antechamber through which I was obliged to pass to go to my room; but, too much occupied by the new objects which on all sides attracted my attention, I had not particularly examined it. Meanwhile, I could not avoid observing that, though the two younger brothers of my friend were so much attached to me, that they would never permit me to go at night into my room without them, yet they always evinced an unaccountable dread in crossing the hall where this picture hung. They clung to me, and embraced me that I might take them in my arms; and whichever I was compelled to take by the hand, invariably covered his face, in order that he might not see the least trace of the portrait.

"'Being aware that the generality of children are afraid of colossal figures, or even of those of a natural height, I endeavoured to give my two young friends courage. However, on more attentively considering the portrait which caused them so much dread, I could not avoid feeling a degree of fear myself. The picture represented a knight in the costume of a very remote period; a full grey mantle descended from his shoulders to his knees; one of his feet placed in the foreground, appeared as if it was starting from the canvass; his countenance had an expression which petrified me with fear. I had never before seen any thing at all like it in nature. It was a frightful mixture of the stillness of death, with the remains of a violent and baneful passion, which not even death itself was able to overcome. One would have thought the artist had copied the terrible features of one risen from the grave, in order to paint this terrific portrait. I was seized with a terror little less than the children, whenever I wished to contemplate this picture. Its aspect was disagreeable to my friend, but did not cause him any terror: his sister was the only one who could look at this hideous figure with a smiling countenance; and said to me with a compassionate air, when I discovered my aversion to it, "That man is not wicked, but he is certainly very unhappy." My friend told me that the picture represented the founder of his race, and that his father attached uncommon value to it; it had, in all probability, hung there from time immemorial, and it would not be possible to remove it from this chamber without destroying the regularity of its appearance.

"'Meanwhile, the term of our vacation was speedily drawing to its close, and time insensibly wore away in the pleasures of the country. The old count, who remarked our reluctance to quit him, his amiable family, his *château*, and the fine country that surrounded it, applied himself with kind and unremitting care, to make the day preceding our departure a continual succession of rustic diversions: each succeeded the other without the slightest appearance of art; they seemed of necessity to follow each other. The delight that illumined the eyes of my friend's sister when she perceived her father's satisfaction; the joy that was painted in Emily's countenance (which was the name of this charming girl) when she surprised even her father by her arrangements, which outstripped his projects, led me to discover the entire confidence that existed between the father and daughter, and the active part Emily had taken in directing the order which reigned in that day's festivities.

"'Night arrived; the company in the gardens dispersed; but my amiable companions never quitted my side. The two young boys skipped gaily before us, chasing the may-bug, and shaking the shrubs to make them come out. The dew arose, and aided by the light of the moon formed silver spangles on the flowers and grass. Emily hung on my arm; and an affectionate sister conducted me, as if to take leave, to all the groves and places I had been accustomed to visit with her, or with the family. On arriving at the door of the *château*, I was obliged to repeat the promise I had made to her father, of passing some weeks in the autumn with him. "That season," said she, "is equally beautiful with the spring!" With what pleasure did I promise to decline all other engagements for this. Emily retired to her apartment, and, according to custom, I went up to mine, accompanied by my two little boys: they ran gaily up the stairs; and in crossing the range of apartments but faintly lighted, to my no small surprise their boisterous mirth was not interrupted by the terrible portrait.

"'For my own part, my head and heart were full of the intended journey, and of the agreeable manner in which my time had passed at the count's *château*. The images of those happy days crowded on my recollection; my imagination, at that time possessing all the vivacity of youth, was so much agitated, that I could not enjoy the sleep which already overpowered my friend. Emily's image, so interesting by her sprightly grace, by her pure affection for me, was present to my mind like an amiable phantom shining in beauty. I placed myself at the window, to take another look at the country I had so frequently ranged with her, and traced our steps again probably for the last time. I remembered each spot illumined by the pale light the moon afforded. The nightingale was singing in the groves where we had delighted to repose; the little river on which while gaily singing we often sailed, rolled murmuringly her silver waves.

"'Absorbed in a profound reverie, I mentally exclaimed: With the flowers of spring, this soft pure peaceful affection will probably fade; and as frequently the after seasons blight the blossoms and destroy the promised fruit, so possibly may the approaching autumn envelop in cold reserve that heart which, at the present moment, appears only to expand with mine!

"'Saddened by these reflections, I withdrew from the window, and overcome by a painful agitation I traversed the adjoining rooms; and on a sudden found myself before the portrait of my friend's ancestor. The moon's beams darted on it in the most singular manner possible, insomuch as to give the appearance of a horrible moving spectre; and the reflection of the light gave to it the appearance of a real substance about to quit the darkness by which it was surrounded. The inanimation of its features appeared to give place to the most profound melancholy; the sad and glazed look of the eyes appeared the only hinderance to its uttering its grief.

"'My knees tremblingly knocked against each other, and with an unsteady step I regained my chamber: the window still remained open; I reseated myself at it, in order that the freshness of the night air, and the aspect of the beautiful surrounding country, might dissipate the terror I had experienced. My wandering eyes fixed on a long vista of ancient linden trees, which extended from my window to the ruins of an old tower, which had often been the scene of our pleasures and rural *fêtes*. The remembrance of the hideous portrait had vanished; when on a sudden there appeared to me a thick fog issuing from the ruined tower, which advancing through the vista of lindens came towards me.

"'I regarded this cloud with an anxious curiosity: it approached; but again it was concealed by the thickly spreading branches of the trees.

"'On a sudden I perceived, in a spot of the avenue less dark than the rest, the same figure represented in the formidable picture, enveloped in the grey mantle I so well knew. It advanced towards the *château*, as if hesitating: no noise was heard of its footsteps on the pavement; it passed before my window without looking up, and gained a back door which led to the apartments in the colonnade of the *château*.

"'Seized with trembling apprehension, I darted towards my bed, and saw with pleasure that the two children were fast asleep on either side. The noise I made awoke them; they started, but in an instant were asleep again. The agitation I had endured took from me the power of sleep, and I turned to awake one of the children to talk with me: but no powers can depict the horrors I endured when I saw the frightful figure at the side of the child's bed.

"'I was petrified with horror, and dared neither move nor shut my eyes. I beheld the spectre stoop towards the child and softly kiss his forehead: he then went round the bed, and kissed the forehead of the other boy.

"'I lost all recollection at that moment; and the following morning, when the children awoke me with their caresses, I was willing to consider the whole as a dream.

"'Meanwhile, the moment for our departure was at hand. We once again breakfasted all together in a grove of lilacs and flowers. "I advise you to take a little more care of yourself," said the old count in the midst of other conversation; "for I last night saw you walking rather late in the garden, in a dress ill suited to the damp air; and I was fearful such imprudence would expose you to cold and fever. Young people are apt to fancy they are invulnerable; but I repeat to you, Take advice from a friend."

""""In truth," I answered, "I believe readily that I have been attacked by a violent fever, for never before was I so harassed by terrifying visions: I can now conceive how dreams afford to a heated imagination subjects for the most extraordinary stories of apparitions."

""""What would you tell me?" demanded the count in a manner not wholly devoid of agitation. I related to him all that I had seen the preceding night; and to my great surprise he appeared to me in no way astonished, but extremely affected.

""""You say," added he in a trembling voice, "that the phantom kissed the two children's foreheads?" I answered him, that it was even so. He then exclaimed, in accents of the deepest despair, "Oh heavens! they must then both die!""""—

Till now the company had listened without the slightest noise or interruption to Ferdinand: but as he pronounced the last words, the greater part of his audience trembled; and the young lady who had previously occupied the chair on which he sat, uttered a piercing shriek.

"Imagine," continued Ferdinand, "how astonished my friend must have been at this unexpected exclamation. The vision of the night had caused him excess of agitation; but the melancholy voice of the count pierced his heart, and seemed to annihilate his being, by the terrifying conviction of the existence of the spiritual world, and the secret horrors with which this idea was accompanied. It was not then a dream, a chimera, the fruit of an overheated imagination! but a mysterious and infallible messenger, which, dispatched from the world of spirits, had passed close to him, had placed itself by his couch, and by its fatal kiss had dropt the germ of death in the bosom of the two children.

"He vainly entreated the count to explain this extraordinary event. Equally fruitless were his son's endeavours to obtain from the count the development of this mystery, which apparently concerned the whole family. 'You are as yet too young,' replied the count: 'too soon, alas! for your peace of mind, will you be informed of these terrible circumstances which you now think mysterious.'

"Just as they came to announce to my friend that all was ready, he recollected that during the recital the count had sent away Emily and her two younger brothers. Deeply agitated, he took leave of the count and the two young children who came towards him, and who would scarcely permit themselves to be separated from him. Emily, who had placed herself at a window, made a sign of adieu. Three days afterwards the young count received news of the death of his two younger brothers. They were both taken off in the same night.

"You see," continued Ferdinand, in a gayer tone, in order to counteract the impression of sadness and melancholy his story had produced on the company; "You see my history is very far from affording any natural explication of the wonders it contains; explanations which only tend to shock one's reason: it does not even make you entirely acquainted with the mysterious person, which one has a right to expect in all marvellous recitals. But I could learn nothing more; and the old count dying without revealing the mystery to his son, I see no other means of terminating the history of the portrait, which is undoubtedly by no means devoid of interest, than by inventing according to one's fancy a *dénouement* which shall explain all."

"That does not appear at all necessary to me," said a young man: "this history, like the one that preceded it, is in reality finished, and gives all the satisfaction one has any right to expect from recitals of this species."

"I should not agree with you," replied Ferdinand, "if I was capable of explaining the mysterious connection between the portrait and the death of the two children in the same night, or the terror of Juliana at sight of the other portrait, and her death, consequently caused by it. I am, however, not the less obliged to you for the entire satisfaction you evince."

"But," resumed the young man, "what benefit would your imagination receive, if the connections of which you speak were known to you?"

"Very great benefit, without doubt," replied Ferdinand; "for imagination requires the completion of the objects it represents, as much as the judgment requires correctness and accuracy in its ideas."

The mistress of the house, not being partial to these metaphysical disputes, took part with Ferdinand: "We ladies," said she, "are always curious; therefore don't wonder that we complain when a story has no termination. It appears to me like seeing the last scene of Mozart's Don Juan without having witnessed the preceding ones;[1] and I am sure no one would be the

---

1 In the last scene of Mozart's *Don Giovanni* (1787), the statue of a man Don Giovanni has killed comes to take him to hell. Earlier in the opera, he has insultingly invited it to dinner.

better satisfied, although the last scene should possess infinite merit."

The young man remained silent, perhaps less through conviction than politeness. Several persons were preparing to retire; and Ferdinand, who had vainly searched with all his eyes for the young lady with flaxen hair, was already at the door, when an elderly gentleman, whom he remembered to have seen in the music-room, asked him whether the friend concerning whom he had related the story was not called Count Meltheim?

"That is his name," answered Ferdinand a little drily, "how did you guess it?—are you acquainted with his family?"

"You have advanced nothing but the simple truth," resumed the unknown. "Where is the count at this moment?"

"He is on his travels," replied Ferdinand. "But I am astonished—"

"Do you correspond with him?" demanded the unknown.

"I do," answered Ferdinand. "But I don't understand—"

"Well then," continued the old man, "tell him that Emily still continues to think of him, and that he must return as speedily as possible, if he takes any interest in a secret that very particularly concerns her family."

On this the old man stepped into his carriage, and had vanished from Ferdinand's sight ere he had recovered from his surprise. He looked around him in vain for some one who might inform him of the name of the unknown: every one was gone; and he was on the point of risking being considered indiscreet, by asking for information of the pastor who had so courteously treated him, when they fastened the door of the house, and he was compelled to return in sadness to his inn, and leave his researches till the morning.

The frightful scenes of the night preceding Ferdinand's departure from the *château* of his friend's father, had tended to weaken the remembrance of Emily; and the distraction which his journey so immediately after had produced, had not contributed to recall it with any force: but all at once the recollection of Emily darted across his mind with fresh vigour, aided by the recital of the previous evening and the old man's conversation: it presented itself even with greater vivacity and strength than at the period of its birth. Ferdinand now fancied that he could trace Emily in the pretty girl with flaxen hair. The more he reflected on her figure, her eyes, the sound of her voice, the grace with which she moved; the more striking the resemblance appeared to him. The piercing shriek that had escaped her, when he mentioned the old count's explication of the phantom's appearance; her sudden disappearance at the termination of the recital; her connection with Ferdinand's family, (for the young lady, in her history of Juliana, had recounted the fatal accident which actually befell Ferdinand's sister,) all gave a degree of certainty to his suppositions.

He passed the night in forming projects and plans, in resolving doubts and difficulties; and Ferdinand impatiently waited for the day which was to enlighten him. He went to the pastor's, whom he found in the midst of his quires of music; and by giving a natural turn to the conversation, he seized the opportunity of enquiring concerning the persons with whom he had passed the preceding evening.

He unfortunately, however, could not get satisfactory answers to his questions concerning the young lady with flaxen hair, and the mysterious old gentleman; for the pastor had been so absorbed in his music, that he had not paid attention to many persons who had visited him: and though Ferdinand in the most minute manner possible described their dress and other particulars, it was impossible to make the pastor comprehend the individuals whose names he was so anxious to learn. "It is unfortunate," said the pastor, "that my wife should be out; she would have given you all the information you desire. But according to your description, it strikes me the young person with flaxen hair must be Mademoiselle de Hainthal;—but—"

"Mademoiselle de Hainthal!" reiterated Ferdinand, somewhat abruptly.

"I think so," replied the clergyman. "Are you acquainted with the young lady?"

"I know her family," answered Ferdinand; "but from her features bearing so strong a resemblance to the family, I thought it might have been the young countess of Wartbourg, who was so much like her brother."

"That is very possible," said the pastor. "You knew then the unfortunate count Wartbourg?"

"Unfortunate!" exclaimed Ferdinand, greatly surprised.

"You don't then know any thing," continued the pastor, "of the deplorable event that has recently taken place at the *château* of Wartbourg? The young count, who had probably in his travels seen some beautifully laid-out gardens, was anxious to embellish the lovely country which surrounds his *château*; and as the ruins of an old tower seemed to be an obstacle to his plans, he ordered them to be pulled down. His gardener in vain represented to him, that seen from one of the wings of the *château* they presented, at the termination of a majestic and ancient avenue of linden trees, a magnificent *coup d'oeil*,[1] and that they would also give a more romantic appearance to the new parts they were about to form. An old servant, grown grey in the service of his forefathers, supplicated him with tears in his eyes to spare the venerable remains of past ages. They even told him of an ancient tradition, preserved in the neighbourhood, which declared, that the existence of the house of Wartbourg was by supernatural means linked with the preservation of that tower.

"The count, who was a well-informed man, paid no attention to these sayings; indeed they possibly made him the more firmly adhere to his resolution. The workmen were put to their task: the walls, which were constructed of huge masses of rock, for a long while resisted the united efforts of tools and gunpowder; the architect of this place appeared to have built it for eternity.

"At length perseverance and labour brought it down. A piece of the rock separating from the rest, precipitated itself into an opening which had been concealed for ages by rubbish and loose sticks, and fell into a deep cavern. An immense subterranean vault was discovered by the rays of the setting sun, supported by enormous pillars:—but ere they proceeded in their researches, they went to inform the young count of the discovery they had made.

"He came; and being curious to see this dark abode, descended into it with two servants. The first thing they discovered were chains covered with rust, which being fixed in the rock, plainly shewed the use formerly made of the cavern. On another side was a corpse, dressed in female attire of centuries past, which had surprisingly resisted the ravages of time: close to it was extended a human skeleton almost destroyed.

"The two servants related that the young count, on seeing the body, cried in an accent of extreme horror, 'Great God! it is she then whose portrait killed my intended wife.' Saying which, he fell senseless by the body. The shake which his fall occasioned reduced the skeleton to dust.

"They bore the count to his *château*, where the care of the physicians restored him to life; but he did not recover his senses. It is probable that this tragical event was caused by the confined and unwholesome air of the cavern. A very few days after, the count died in a state of total derangement.

---

1 Literally, "glance" (French); here, apparently, "view."

"It is singular enough, that the termination of his life should coincide with the destruction of the ruined tower, and there no longer exists any male branch of that family. The deeds relative to the succession, ratified and sealed by the emperor Otho,[1] are still amongst the archives of his house. Their contents have as yet only been transmitted verbally from father to son, as an hereditary secret, which will now, however, be made known. It is also true, that the affianced bride of the count was killed by the portrait's falling on her."

"I yesterday heard that fatal history recited by the lady with flaxen hair," replied Ferdinand.

"It is very possible that young person is the countess Emily," replied the pastor; "for she was the bosom-friend of the unfortunate bride."

"Does not then the countess Emily live at the castle of Wartbourg?" asked Ferdinand.

"Since her brother's death," answered the clergyman, "she has lived with a relation of her mother's at the *château* of Libinfelt, a short distance from hence. For as they yet know not with certainty to whom the castle of Wartbourg will belong, she prudently lives retired."

Ferdinand had learnt sufficient to make him abandon the projected journey to the capital. He thanked the pastor for the instructions he had given him, and was conducted to the *château* where Emily now resided.

It was still broad day when he arrived. The whole journey he was thinking of the amiable figure which he had recognised too late the preceding evening. He recalled to his idea her every word, the sound of her voice, her actions; and what his memory failed to represent, his imagination depicted with all the vivacity of youth, and all the fire of rekindled affection. He already addressed secret reproaches to Emily for not recognising him; as if he had himself remembered her; and in order to ascertain whether his features were entirely effaced from the recollection of her whom he adored, he caused himself to be announced as a stranger, who was anxious to see her on family matters.

While waiting impatiently in the room into which they had conducted him, he discovered among the portraits with which it was decorated, that of the young lady whose features had the

---

1   Otho or Otto I, the Great (912-73), traditionally regarded as the
    founder of the Holy Roman empire.

over-night charmed him anew: he was contemplating it with rapture when the door opened and Emily entered. She instantly recognised Ferdinand; and in the sweetest accents accosted him as the friend of her youth.

Surprise rendered Ferdinand incapable of answering suitably to so gracious a reception: it was not the charming person with flaxen hair; it was not a figure corresponding with his imagination, which at this moment presented itself to his view.

But it was Emily, shining in every possible beauty, far beyond what Ferdinand had expected: he recollected notwithstanding each feature which had already charmed him, but now clothed in every perfection which nature bestows on her most favoured objects. Ferdinand was lost in thought for some moments: he dared not make mention of his love, and still less did he dare speak of the portrait, and the other wonders of the castle of Wartbourg. Emily spoke only of the happiness she had experienced in her earlier days, and slightly mentioned her brother's death. As the evening advanced, the young female with flaxen hair came in with the old stranger. Emily presented them both to Ferdinand, as the baron of Hainthal and his daughter Clotilde. They remembered instantly the stranger whom they had seen the preceding evening. Clotilde rallied him on his wish to be *incognito*; and he found himself on a sudden, by a short train of natural events, in the company of the person whom his mother intended for his wife; the object of his affection whom he had just discovered; and the interesting stranger who had promised him an explanation relative to the mysterious portraits.

Their society was soon augmented by the mistress of the *château* in whom Ferdinand recognised one of those who sat by his side the preceding evening. In consideration for Emily, they omitted all the subjects most interesting to Ferdinand; but after supper the baron drew nearer to him.

"I doubt not," said he to him, "that you are anxious to have some light thrown on events, of which, according to your recital last night, you were a spectator. I knew you from the first; and I knew also, that the story you related as of a friend, was your own history. I cannot, however, inform you of more than I know: but that will perhaps be sufficient to save Emily, for whom I feel the affection of a daughter, from chagrin and uneasiness; and from your recital of last evening, I perceive you take a lively interest concerning her."

"Preserve Emily from uneasiness," replied Ferdinand with warmth; "explain yourself: what is there I ought to do?"

"We cannot," answered the baron, "converse here with propriety; to-morrow morning I will come and see you in your apartment."

Ferdinand asked him for an audience that night; but the baron was inflexible. "It is not my wish," said he, "to work upon your imagination by any marvellous recital, but to converse with you on the very important concerns of two distinguished families. For which reason, I think the freshness of morning will be better suited to lessen the horror that my recital must cause you: therefore, if not inconvenient to you, I wish you to attend me at an early hour in the morning: I am fond of rising with the sun; and yet I have never found the time till mid-day too long for arranging my affairs," added he, smiling, and turning half round towards the rest of the party, as if speaking on indifferent topics.

Ferdinand passed a night of agitation, thinking of the conference he was to have with the baron; who was at his window at dawn of day. "You know," said the baron, "that I married the old count of Wartbourg's sister; which alliance was less the cause, than the consequence, of our intimate friendship. We reciprocally communicated our most secret thoughts, and the one never undertook any thing without the other taking an equal interest with himself in his projects. The count had, however, one secret from me, of which I should never have come at the knowledge but for an accident.

"On a sudden, a report was spread abroad, that the phantom of the Nun's rock had been seen, which was the name given by the peasantry to the old ruined tower which you knew. Persons of sense only laughed at the report: I was anxious the following night to unmask this spectre, and I already anticipated my triumph: but to my no small surprise, the count endeavoured to dissuade me from the attempt; and the more I persisted, the more serious his arguments became; and at length he conjured me in the name of friendship to relinquish the design.

"His gravity of manner excited my attention; I asked him several questions; I even regarded his fears in the light of disease, and urged him to take suitable remedies: but he answered me with an air of chagrin, 'Brother, you know my sincerity towards you; but this is a secret sacred to my family. My son can alone be informed of it, and that only on my death-bed. Therefore ask me no more questions.'

"I held my peace; but I secretly collected all the traditions known amongst the peasantry. The most generally believed one was, that the phantom of the Nun's rock was seen when any one of the count's family were about to die; and in effect, in a few days after the count's youngest son expired. The count seemed to apprehend it: he gave the strictest possible charge to the nurse to take care of him; and under pretext of feeling indisposed himself, sent for two physicians to the castle: but these extreme precautions were precisely the cause of the child's death; for the nurse passing over the stones near the ruins, in her extreme care took the child in her arms to carry him, and her foot slipping, she fell, and in her fall wounded the child so much, that he expired on the spot. She said she fancied that she saw the child extended, bleeding in the midst of the stones; that her fright had made her fall with her face on the earth; and that when she came to herself, the child was absolutely lying weltering in his blood, precisely on the same spot where she had seen his ghost.

"I will not tire you with a relation of all the sayings uttered by an illiterate woman to explain the cause of the vision, for under similar accidents invention far outstrips reality. I could not expect to gain much more satisfactory information from the family records; for the principal documents were preserved in an iron chest, the key of which was never out of the possession of the owner of the castle. I however discovered, by the genealogical register and other similar papers, that this family had never had collateral male branches; but further than this, my researches could not discover.

"At length, on my friend's death-bed I obtained some information, which, however, was far from being satisfactory. You remember, that while the son was on his travels, the father was attacked by the complaint which carried him off so suddenly. The evening previous to his decease, he sent for me express, dismissed all those who were with him, and turning towards me, said: 'I am aware that my end is fast approaching, and I am the first of my family that has been carried off without communicating to his son the secret on which the safety of our house depends. Swear to me to reveal it only to my son, and I shall die contented.'

"In the names of friendship and honour, I promised what he exacted of me, and he thus began:

"'The origin of my race, as you know, is not to be traced. Ditmar, the first of my ancestry mentioned in the written records, accompanied the emperor Otho to Italy. His history is also very obscure. He had an enemy called count Bruno, whose only son he killed in revenge, according to ancient tradition, and then kept the father confined till his death in that tower, whose ruins, situated in the Nun's rock, still defy the hand of time. That

portrait which hangs alone in the state-chamber, is Ditmar's; and
if the traditions of the family are to be believed, it was painted by
the Dead. In fact, it is almost impossible to believe that any
human being could have contemplated sufficiently long to paint
the portrait, the outline of features so hideous. My forefathers
have frequently tried to plaster over this redoubtable figure; but
in the night, the colours came through the plaster, and re-
appeared as distinctly as before; and often in the night, this
Ditmar has been seen wandering abroad dressed in the garb represented in the picture; and by kissing the descendants of the
family, has doomed them to death. Three of my children have
received this fatal kiss. It is said, a monk imposed on him this
penance in expiation of his crimes. But he cannot destroy all the
children of his race: for so long as the ruins of the old tower shall
remain, and whilst one stone shall remain on another, so long
shall the count de Wartbourg's family exist; and so long shall the
spirit of Ditmar wander on earth, and devote to death the
branches of his house, without being able to annihilate the trunk.
His race will never be extinct; and his punishment will only cease
when the ruins of the tower are entirely dispersed. He brought
up, with a truly paternal care, the daughter of his enemy, and
wedded her to a rich and powerful knight; but notwithstanding
this, the monk never remitted his penance. Ditmar, however,
foreseeing that one day or other his race would perish, was certainly anxious ere then, to prepare for an event on which his
deliverance depended; and accordingly made a relative disposition of his hereditary property, in case of his family becoming
extinct. The act which contained his will, was ratified by the
emperor Otho: as yet it has not been opened, and nobody knows
its contents. It is kept in the secret archives of our house.'

"The speaking thus much was a great effort to my friend. He
required a little rest, but was shortly after incapable of articulat-
ing a single word. I performed the commission with which he
charged me to his son."

"And he did, notwithstanding—" replied Ferdinand.

"Even so," answered the baron: "but judge more favourably of
your excellent friend. I have often seen him alone in the great
state-chamber, with his eyes fixed on this horrible portrait: he
would then go into the other rooms, where the portraits of his
ancestors were ranged for several successive generations; and
after contemplating them with visible internal emotion, would
return to that of the founder of his house. Broken sentences, and
frequent soliloquies, which I overheard by accident, did not leave

me a shadow of doubt, but that he was the first of his race who had magnanimity of soul sufficient to resolve on liberating the spirit of Ditmar from its penance, and of sacrificing himself to release his house from the malediction that hung over it. Possibly he was strengthened in his resolutions by the grief he experienced for the death of his dearly beloved."

"Oh!" cried Ferdinand deeply affected, "how like my friend!"

"He had, however, in the ardour of his enthusiasm, forgotten to guard his sister's sensibility," said the baron.

"How so?" demanded Ferdinand.

"It is in consequence of this," answered the baron, "that I now address myself to you, and reveal to you the secret. I have told you that Ditmar demonstrated a paternal affection to the daughter of his enemy, had given her a handsome portion, and had married her to a valiant knight. Learn then, that this knight was Adalbert de Meltheim, from whom the counts of this name descended in a direct line."

"Is it possible?" exclaimed Ferdinand, "the author of my race!"

"The same," answered the baron; "and according to appearances, Ditmar designed that the family of Meltheim should succeed him on the extinction of his own. Haste, then, in order to establish your probable right to the—"

"Never—" said Ferdinand "—so long as Emily—"

"This is no more than I expected from you," replied the baron; "but remember, that in Ditmar's time the girls were not thought of in deeds of this kind. Your inconsiderate generosity would be prejudicial to Emily. For the next of kin who lay claim to the fief, do not probably possess very gallant ideas.

"As a relation, though only on the female side, I have taken the necessary measures; and I think it right you should be present at the castle of Wartbourg when the seals are broken, that you may be immediately recognised as the only immediate descendant of Adalbert, and that you may take instant possession of the inheritance."

"And Emily?" demanded Ferdinand.

"As for what is to be done for her," replied the baron, "I leave to you; and feel certain of her being provided for suitably, since her destiny will be in the bands of a man whose birth equals her own, who knows how to appreciate the rank in which she is placed, and who will evince his claims to merit and esteem."

"Have I a right, then," said Ferdinand, "to flatter myself with the hope that Emily will permit me to surrender her the property to which she is actually entitled?"

"Consult Emily on the subject," said the baron.—And here finished the conference.

Ferdinand, delighted, ran to Emily. She answered with the same frankness he had manifested; and they were neither of them slow to confess their mutual passion.

Several days passed in this amiable delirium. The inhabitants of the *château* participated in the joy of the young lovers; and Ferdinand at length wrote to his mother, to announce the choice he had made.

They were occupied in preparations for removing to the castle of Wartbourg, when a letter arrived, which at once destroyed Ferdinand's happiness. His mother refused to consent to his marriage with Emily: her husband having, she said, on his death-bed, insisted on his wedding the baron of Hainthal's daughter, and that she should refuse her consent to any other marriage. He had discovered a family secret, which forced him peremptorily to press this point, on which depended his son's welfare, and the happiness of his family; she had given her promise, and was obliged to maintain it, although much afflicted at being compelled to act contrary to her son's inclinations.

In vain did Ferdinand conjure his mother to change her determination; he declared to her that he would be the last of his race, rather than renounce Emily. She was not displeased with his entreaties, but remained inflexible.

The baron plainly perceived, from Ferdinand's uneasiness and agitation, that his happiness had fled; and as he possessed his entire confidence, he soon became acquainted with the cause of his grief. He wrote in consequence to the countess Meltheim, and expressed his astonishment at the singular disposition the count had made on his death-bed but all he could obtain from her, was a promise to come to the castle of Wartbourg, to see the female whom she destined for her son, and the one whom he had himself chosen; and probably to elucidate by her arrival so singular and complicated an affair.

Spring was beginning to enliven all nature, when Ferdinand, accompanied by Emily, the baron, and his daughter, arrived at the castle of Wartbourg. The preparation which the principal cause of their journey required, occupied some days. Ferdinand and Emily consoled themselves in the hope that the countess of Meltheim's presence would remove every obstacle which opposed their love, and that at sight of the two lovers she would overcome her scruples.

A few days afterwards she arrived, embraced Emily in the

most affectionate manner, and called her, her dear daughter, at the same time expressing her great regret that she could not really consider her such, being obliged to fulfil a promise made to her dying husband.

The baron at length persuaded her to reveal the motive for this singular determination: and after deliberating a short time, she thus expressed herself.

"The secret you are anxious I should reveal to you, concerns your family, Monsieur le Baron: consequently, if you release me from the necessity of longer silence, I am very willing to abandon my scruples. A fatal picture has, you know, robbed me of my daughter; and my husband, after this melancholy accident, determined on entirely removing this unfortunate portrait: he accordingly gave orders for it to be put in a heap of old furniture, where no one would think of looking for it; and in order to discover the best place to conceal it, he was present when it was taken there. In the removal, he perceived a piece of parchment behind the canvass which the fall had a little damaged: having removed it, he discovered it to be an old document, of a singular nature. The original of this portrait, (said the deed,) was called Bertha de Hainthal; she fixes her looks on her female descendants, in order that if any one of them should receive its death by this portrait, it may prove an expiatory sacrifice which will reconcile her to God. She will then see the families of Hainthal and Meltheim united by the bonds of love; and finding herself released, she will have cause to rejoice in the birth of her after-born descendants.

"This then is the motive which made my husband anxious to fulfil, by the projected marriage, the vows of Bertha; for the death of his daughter, caused by Bertha, had rendered her very name formidable to him. You see, therefore, I have the same reasons for adhering to the promise made my dying husband."

"Did not the count," demanded the baron, "allege any more positive reason for this command?"

"Nothing more, most assuredly," replied the countess.

"Well then," answered the baron, "in case the writing of which you speak should admit of an explanation wholly differing from, but equally clear with, the one attached thereto by the deceased, would you sooner follow the sense than the letter of the writing?"

"There is no doubt on that subject," answered the countess; "for no one is more anxious than myself to see that unfortunate promise set aside."

"Know then," said the baron, "that the corpse of that Bertha, who occasioned the death of your daughter, reposes here at Wartbourg and that, on this subject, as well as all the other mysteries of the castle, we shall have our doubts satisfied."

The baron would not at this time explain himself further; but said to the countess, that the documents contained in the archives of the castle would afford the necessary information; and recommended that Ferdinand should, with all possible dispatch, hasten every thing relative to the succession. Conformable to the baron's wish, it was requisite that, previous to any other research, the secret deeds contained in the archives should be opened. The law commissioners, and the next of kin who were present, who, most likely, promised themselves an ample compensation for their curiosity in the contents of the other parts of the records, were anxious to raise objections; but the baron represented to them, that the secrets of the family appertained to the unknown heir alone, and that consequently no one had a right to become acquainted with them, unless permitted by him.

These reasons produced the proper effect. They followed the baron into the immense vault in which were deposited the family records. They therein discovered an iron chest, which had not been opened for nearly a thousand years. A massive chain, which several times wound round it, was strongly fixed to the floor and to the wall; but the emperor's grand seal was a greater security for this sacred deposit, than all the chains and bolts which guarded it. It was instantly recognised and removed: the strong bolts yielded; and from the chest was taken the old parchment which had resisted the effects of time. This piece contained, as the baron expected, the disposition which confirmed the right of inheritance to the house of Meltheim, in case of the extinction of the house of Wartbourg: and Ferdinand, according to the baron's advice, having in readiness the deeds justifying and acknowledging him as the lawful heir to the house of Meltheim, the next of kin with regret permitted what they could not oppose; and he took possession of the inheritance. The baron having made him a signal, he immediately sealed the chest with his seal. He afterwards entertained the strangers in a splendid manner; and at night found himself in possession of his castle, with only his mother, Emily, the baron, and his daughter.

"It will be but just," said the baron, "to devote this night, which introduces a new name into this castle, to the memory of those who have hitherto possessed it. And we shall acquit ourselves most suitably in this duty, by reading in the council-chamber the documents which, without doubt, are destined to explain, as supplementary deeds, the will of Ditmar."

This arrangement was instantly adopted. The hearts of Emily and Ferdinand were divided between hope and fear; for they impatiently, yet doubtingly, awaited the *dénouement* of Bertha's history, which, after so many successive generations, had in so incomprehensible a manner interfered with their attachment.

The chamber was lighted: Ferdinand opened the iron case; and the baron examined the old parchments.

"This," cried he, after having searched some short time, "will inform us." So saying, he drew from the chest some sheets of parchment. On the one which enveloped the rest was the portrait of a knight of an agreeable figure, and habited in the costume of the tenth century: and the inscription at the bottom called him Ditmar; but they could scarcely discover the slightest resemblance in it to the frightful portrait in the state-chamber. The baron offered to translate, in reading to them the document written in Latin, provided they would make allowances for the errors which were likely to arise from so hasty a translation. The curiosity of his auditors was so greatly excited, that they readily consented; and he then read as follows:

"I the undersigned Tutilon, monk of St. Gall,[1] have, with the lord Ditmar's consent, written the following narrative: I have omitted nothing, nor written aught of my own accord.

"Being sent for to Metz, to carve in stone the image of the Virgin Mary; and that mother of our blessed Saviour having opened my eyes and directed my hands, so that I could contemplate her celestial countenance, and represent it on stone to be worshipped by true believers, the lord Ditmar discovered me, and engaged me to follow him to his castle, in order that I might execute his portrait for his descendants. I began painting it in the state-chamber of his castle; and on returning the following day to resume my task, I found that a strange hand had been at work, and had given the portrait quite a different countenance, which was horrible to look at, for it resembled one who had risen from the dead. I trembled with terror: however, I effaced these hideous features, and I painted anew the count Ditmar's figure, according to my recollection; but the following day I again discovered the nocturnal labour of the stranger hand. I was seized with still

---

1 An abbey in the town (and canton) of the same name, by Lake Constance and the Rhine, in north-eastern Switzerland.

greater fear, but resolved to watch during the night; and I recommenced painting the knight's figure, such as it really was. At midnight I took a torch, and advancing softly into the chamber to examine the portrait, I perceived a spectre resembling the skeleton of a child; it held a pencil and was endeavouring to give Ditmar's image the hideous features of death.

"On my entering, the spectre slowly turned its head towards me, that I might see its frightful visage. My terror became extreme: I advanced no further, but retired to my room, where I remained in prayer till morning; for I was unwilling to interrupt the work executed in the dead of night. In the morning, discovering the same strange features in Ditmar's portrait as that of the two preceding mornings, I did not again risk effacing the work of the nightly painter; but went in search of the knight, and related to him what I had seen. I shewed him the picture. He trembled with horror, and confessed his crimes to me, for which he required absolution. Having for three successive days invoked all the saints to my assistance, I imposed on him as a penance for the murder of his enemy, which he had avowed to me, to submit to the most rigid mortifications in a dungeon during the rest of his life. But I told him, that as he had murdered an innocent child, his spirit would never be at rest till it had witnessed the extermination of his race; for the Almighty would punish the death of that child by the death of the children of Ditmar, who, with the exception of one in each generation, would all be carried off in early life; and as for him, his spirit would wander during the night, resembling the portrait painted by the hand of the skeleton child; and that he would condemn to death, by a kiss, the children who were the sacrifices to his crimes, in the same manner as he had given one to his enemy's child before he killed it: and that, in fine, his race should not become extinct, so long as stone remained on stone in the tower where he had permitted his enemy to die of hunger. I then gave him absolution. He immediately made over his seigniory to his son; and married the daughter of his enemy, who had been brought up by him, to the brave knight Sir Adalbert. He bequeathed all his property, in case of his race becoming extinct, to this knight's descendants, and caused this will to be ratified by the emperor Otho. After having done so, he retired to a cave near the tower, where his corpse is interred; for he died like a pious recluse, and expiated his crimes by extreme penance. As soon as he was laid in his coffin, he resembled the portrait in the state-chamber; but during his life he was like the portrait depicted on this parchment, which I was able to paint without interruption, after having given him absolution: and by his command I have written and signed this document since his death; and I deposit it with the emperor's letters patent, in an iron chest, which I have caused to be sealed. I pray God speedily to deliver his soul, and to cause his body to rise from the dead to everlasting felicity!"

"He is delivered," cried Emily, greatly affected; "and his image will no longer spread terror around. But I confess that the sight of that figure, and even that of the frightful portrait itself, would never have led me to dream of such horrible crimes as the monk Tutilon relates. Certain I am, his enemy must have mortally wounded his happiness, or he undoubtedly would have been incapable of committing such frightful crimes."

"Possibly," said the baron, continuing his researches, "we shall discover some explanation on that point."

"We must also find some respecting Bertha," replied Ferdinand in a low tone, and casting a timid look on Emily and his mother.

"This night," answered the baron, "is consecrated to the memory of the dead; let us therefore forget our own concerns, since those of the past call our attention."

"Assuredly," exclaimed Emily, "the unfortunate person who secured these sheets in the chest, ardently looked forward to the hope of their coming to light; let us therefore delay it no longer."

The baron, after having examined several, read aloud these words:

"The confession of Ditmar." And he continued thus:—"Peace and health. When this sheet is drawn from the obscurity in which it is now buried, my soul will, I hope firmly in God and the saints, be at eternal rest and peace. But for your good I have ordered to be committed to paper the cause of my chastisement, in order that you may learn that vengeance belongs to God alone, and not to men; for the most just amongst them knows not how to judge: and again, that you may not in your heart condemn me, but rather that you may pity me; for my misery has nearly equalled my crimes; and my spirit would never have dreamt of evil, if man had not rent my heart."

"How justly," exclaimed Ferdinand, "has Emily's good sense divined thus much!"

The baron continued: "My name is Ditmar; they surnamed me The Rich, though I was then only a poor knight, and my only possession was a very small castle. When the emperor Otho departed for Italy, whither he was called by the beautiful Adelaide to receive her hand, I followed him and I gained the affection of the most charming woman in Pavia, whom I conducted as my intended spouse to the castle of my forefathers. Already the day appointed for the celebration of my nuptials was at hand: the emperor sent for me. His favourite, the count Bruno de Hainthal had seen Bertha—"

"Bertha!" exclaimed every one present. But the baron, without permitting them to interrupt him, continued his translation.

"One day, when the emperor had promised to grant him any recompense that he thought his services merited, he asked of him my intended bride. Otho was mute with astonishment;—but his imperial word was given. I presented myself before the emperor, who offered me riches, lands, honours, if I would but consent to yield Bertha to the count: but she was dearer to me than every worldly good. The emperor yielded to a torrent of anger: he carried off my intended bride by force, ordered my castle to be pulled down, and caused me to be thrown into prison.

"I cursed his power and my destiny. The amiable figure of Bertha, however, appeared to me in a dream; and I consoled myself during the day by the sweet illusions of the night. At length my keeper said to me: 'I pity you, Ditmar; you suffer in a prison for your fidelity, while Bertha abandons you. To-morrow she weds the count: accede then to the emperor's wish, ere it be too late; and ask of him what you think fit, as a recompense for the loss of the faithless fair.' These words froze my heart. The following night, instead of the gracious image of Bertha, the frightful spirit of vengeance presented itself to me. The following morning I said to my keeper: 'Go and tell the emperor, I yield Bertha to his Bruno; but as a recompense, I demand this tower, and as much land as will be requisite to build me a new castle.' The emperor was satisfied; for he frequently repented his violent passions, but he could not alter what he had already decided. He therefore gave me the tower in which I had been confined, and all the lands around it for the space of four leagues. He also gave me more gold and silver than was sufficient to build a castle much more magnificent than the one he had caused to be pulled down. I took unto myself a wife, in order to perpetuate my race; but Bertha still reigned sole mistress of my heart. I also built myself a castle, from which I made a communication, by subterranean and secret passages, with my former prison the tower, and with the castle of Bruno, the residence of my mortal enemy. As soon as the edifice was completed, I entered the fortress by the secret passage, and appeared as the spirit of one of his ancestors before the bed of his son, the heir with which Bertha had presented him. The women who lay beside him were seized with fear: I leaned over the child, who was the precise image of its mother, and kissed its forehead; but—it was the kiss of death; it carried with it a secret poison.

"Bruno and Bertha acknowledged the vengeance of Heaven: they received it as a punishment for the wrongs they had occasioned me; and they devoted their first child to the service of God. As it was a girl, I spared it: but Bertha had no more children; and Bruno, irritated to find his race so nearly annihilated, repudiated his wife, as if he repented the injustice of which he had been guilty in taking her, and married another. The unfortunate Bertha took refuge in a monastery, and consecrated herself to Heaven: but her reason fled; and one night she quitted her retreat, came to the tower in which I had been confined in consequence of her perfidy, there bewailed her crime, and there grief terminated her existence; which circumstance gave rise to that tower being called the Nun's Rock. I heard, during the night, her sobs; and on going to the tower found Bertha extended motionless; the dews of night had seized her:—she was dead. I then resolved to avenge her loss. I placed her corpse in a deep vault beneath the tower; and having by means of my subterranean passage discovered all the count's movements, I attacked him when unguarded, and dragging him to the vault which contained his wife's corpse, I there abandoned him. The emperor, irritated against him for having divorced Bertha, gave me all his possessions, as a remuneration for the injustice I had heretofore experienced.

"I caused all the subterranean passages to be closed. I took under my care his daughter Hildegarde, and brought her up as my child: she loved the count Adalbert de Meltheim. But one night her mother's ghost appeared to her, and reminded her that she was consecrated to the Almighty: this vision, however, could not deter her from marrying Adalbert. The night of her marriage the phantom appeared again before her bed, and thus addressed her:

"'Since you have infringed the vow I made, my spirit can never be at rest, till one of your female descendants receives its death from me.'

"This discourse occasioned me to send for the venerable Tutilon, monk of St. Gall, who was very celebrated, in order that he might paint a portrait of Bertha, as she had painted herself in the monastery during her insanity; and I gave it to her daughter.

"Tutilon concealed behind that portrait a writing on parchment, the contents of which were as follows:

"'I am Bertha; and I look at my daughters, to see whether one of them will not die for me, in expiation of my crimes, and thus reconcile me to God. Then shall I see the two families of Meltheim and Hainthal reunited by love, and in the birth of their descendants I shall enjoy happiness.'"

"This then," exclaimed Ferdinand, "is the fatal writing that is to separate me from Emily; but which, in fact, only unites me to her more firmly! and Bertha, delivered from her penance, blesses the alliance; for by my marriage with Emily, the descendants of Bertha and Ditmar will be reunited."

"Do you think," demanded the baron of the countess, "that this explanation can admit of the slightest doubt?"

The only answer the countess made, was by embracing Emily, and placing her hand in that of her son.

The joy was universal. Clotilde in particular had an air of extreme delight; and her father several times, in a jocular manner, scolded her for expressing her joy so vehemently. The following morning they removed the seals from the state-chamber, in order to contemplate the horrible portrait with somewhat less of sadness than heretofore; but they found that it had faded in a singular manner, and the colours, which formerly appeared so harsh, had blended and become softened.

Shortly after arrived the young man who was anxious to enter into an argument with Ferdinand on the explication of the mysteries relative to the portraits. Clotilde did not conceal that he was far from indifferent to her; and they discovered the joy she had evinced, in discovering the favourable turn Emily's attachment had taken, was not altogether disinterested, but occasioned by the prospect it afforded of happiness to herself. Her father, in fact, would never have approved her choice, had not the countess Meltheim removed all pretensions to Clotilde.

"But," asked Ferdinand of Clotilde's intended, "do you not forgive our having searched into certain mysteries which concerned us?"

"Completely," he answered; "but not less disinterestedly than formerly, when I maintained a contrary opinion. I ought now to confess to you, that I was present at the fatal accident which caused your sister's death, and that I then discovered the writing concealed behind the portrait. I naturally explained it as your father did afterwards; but I held my peace; for the consequences have brought to light what the discovery of that writing had caused me to apprehend for my love."

"Unsatisfactory explanations are bad," replied Ferdinand, laughing.

The happy issue of these discoveries spread universal joy amongst the inhabitants of the castle, which was in some degree heightened by the beauty of the season. The lovers were anxious to celebrate their marriage ere the fall of the leaf. And when next the primrose's return announced the approach of spring, Emily gave birth to a charming boy.

Ferdinand's mother, Clotilde and her husband, and all the friends of the family, among whom were the pastor who was so fond of music, and his pretty little wife, assembled at the *fête* given in honour of the christening. When the priest who was performing the ceremony asked what name he was to give the child, that of Ditmar was uttered by every mouth, as if they had previously agreed on it. The christening over, Ferdinand, elate with joy, accompanied by his relations and guests, carried his son to the state-chamber, before his forefather's portrait; but it was no longer perceptible; the colours, figure,—all had disappeared; not the slightest trace remained.

b. "The Death-Bride"[1]

—She shall be such
As walk'd your first queen's ghost—
SHAKESPEARE[2]

THE summer had been uncommonly fine, and the baths crowded with company beyond all comparison: but still the public rooms were scarce ever filled, and never gay. The nobility and military associated only with those of their own rank, and the citizens contented themselves by slandering both parties. So many partial divisions necessarily proved an obstacle to a general and united assembly.

Even the public ball did not draw the *beau-monde* together, because the proprietor of the baths appeared there bedizened with insignia of knighthood; and this glitter, added to the stiff

1 This is the story remembered by Mary Shelley in 1831 as "the History of the Inconstant Lover, who, when he thought to clasp the bride to whom he had pledged his vows, found himself in the arms of the pale ghost of her whom he had deserted" (354-55).
2 Shakespeare, *The Winter's Tale* 5.1.79-80.

manners of this great man's family, and the tribe of lackeys in splendid liveries who constantly attended him, compelled the greater part of the company assembled, silently to observe the rules prescribed to them according to their different ranks.

For these reasons the balls became gradually less numerously attended. Private parties were formed, in which it was endeavoured to preserve the charms that were daily diminishing in the public assemblies.

One of these societies met generally twice a week in a room which at that time was usually unoccupied. There they supped, and afterwards enjoyed, either in a walk abroad, or remaining in the room, the charms of unrestrained conversation.

The members of this society were already acquainted, at least by name; but an Italian marquis, who had lately joined their party, was unknown to them, and indeed to every one assembled at the baths.

The title of *Italian* marquis appeared the more singular, as his name, according to the entry of it in the general list, seemed to denote him of Northern extraction, and was composed of so great a number of consonants, that no one could pronounce it without difficulty. His physiognomy and manners likewise presented many singularities. His long and wan visage, his black eyes, his imperious look, had so little of attraction in them, that every one would certainly have avoided him, had he not possessed a fund of entertaining stories, the relation of which proved an excellent antidote to *ennui*: the only drawback against them was, that in general they required rather too great a share of credulity on the part of his auditors.

The party had one day just risen from table, and found themselves but ill inclined for gaiety. They were still too much fatigued from the ball of the preceding evening to enjoy the recreation of walking, although invited so to do by the bright light of the moon. They were even unable to keep up any conversation; therefore it is not to be wondered at, that they were more than usually anxious for the marquis to arrive.

"Where can he be?" exclaimed the countess in an impatient tone.

"Doubtless still at the faro-table, to the no small grief of the bankers," replied Florentine. "This very morning he has occasioned the sudden departure of two of these gentlemen."

"No great loss," answered another.

"To us—," replied Florentine; "but it is to the proprietor of the baths, who only prohibited gambling, that it might be pursued with greater avidity."

"The marquis ought to abstain from such achievements," said the chevalier with an air of mystery. "Gamblers are revengeful, and have generally advantageous connections. If what is whispered be correct, that the marquis is unfortunately implicated in political affairs—."

"But," demanded the countess, "what then has the marquis done to the bankers of the gaming-table?"

"Nothing; except that he betted on cards which almost invariably won. And what renders it rather singular, he scarcely derived any advantage from it himself, for he always adhered to the weakest party. But the other punters were not so scrupulous; for they charged their cards in such a manner that the bank broke before the deal had gone round."

The countess was on the point of asking other questions, when the marquis coming in changed the conversation.

"Here you are at last!" exclaimed several persons at the same moment.

"We have," said the countess, "been most anxious for your society; and just on this day you have been longer than usual absent."

"I have projected an important expedition; and it has succeeded to my wishes. I hope by tomorrow there will not be a single gaming-table left here. I have been from one gambling-room to another; and there are not sufficient post-horses to carry off the ruined bankers."

"And cannot you," asked the countess, "teach us your wonderful art of always winning?"

"It would be a difficult task, my fair lady; and in order to do it, one must ensure a fortunate hand, for without that nothing could be done."

"Nay," replied the chevalier, laughing, "never did I see so fortunate an one as yours."

"As you are still very young, my dear chevalier, you have many novelties to witness."

Saying these words, the marquis threw on the chevalier so piercing a look that the latter cried:

"Will you then cast my nativity?"

"Provided that it is not done to-day," said the countess; "for who knows whether your future destiny will afford us so amusing a history as that which the marquis two days since promised we should enjoy?"

"I did not exactly say *amusing*."

"But at least full of extraordinary events: and we require some such, to draw us from the lethargy which has overwhelmed us all day."

"Most willingly: but first I am anxious to learn whether any of you know aught of the surprising things related of the *Death-Bride*."

No one remembered to have heard speak of her.

The marquis appeared anxious to add something more by way of preface; but the countess and the rest of the party so openly manifested their impatience, that the marquis began his narration as follows:—

"I had for a long time projected a visit to the count Lieppa, at his estates in Bohemia. We had met each other in almost every country in Europe: attracted *hither* by the frivolity of youth to partake of every pleasure which presented itself, but led *thither* when years of discretion had rendered us more sedate and steady.—At length, in our more advanced age, we ardently desired, ere the close of life, once again to enjoy, by the charms of recollection, the moments of delight which we had passed together. For my part, I was anxious to see the castle of my friend, which was, according to his description, in an extremely romantic district. It was built some hundred years back by his ancestors; and their successors had preserved it with so much care, that it still maintained its imposing appearance, at the same time it afforded a comfortable abode. The count generally passed the greater part of the year at it with his family, and only returned to the capital at the approach of winter. Being well acquainted with his movements, I did not think it needful to announce my visit; and I arrived at the castle one evening precisely at the time when I knew he would be there; and as I approached it, could not but admire the variety and beauty of the scenery which surrounded it.

"The hearty welcome which I received could not, however, entirely conceal from my observation the secret grief depicted on the countenances of the count, his wife, and their daughter, the lovely Ida. In a short time I discovered that they still mourned the loss of Ida's twin-sister, who had died about a year before. Ida and Hildegarde resembled each other so much, that they were only to be distinguished from each other by a slight mark of a strawberry visible on Hildegarde's neck. Her room, and every thing in it, was left precisely in the same state as when she was alive, and the family were in the habit of visiting it whenever they wished to indulge the sad satisfaction of meditating on the loss of this beloved child. The two sisters had but one heart, one mind:

and the parents could not but apprehend that their separation would be but of short duration; they dreaded lest Ida should also be taken from them.

"I did every thing in my power to amuse this excellent family, by entertaining them with laughable anecdotes of my younger days, and by directing their thoughts to less melancholy subjects than that which now wholly occupied them. I had the satisfaction of discovering that my efforts were not ineffectual. Sometimes we walked in the canton round the castle, which was decked with all the beauties of summer; at other times we took a survey of the different apartments of the castle, and were astonished at their wonderful state of preservation, whilst we amused ourselves by talking over the actions of the past generation, whose portraits hung in a long gallery.

"One evening the count had been speaking to me in confidence, on the subject of his future plans: among other subjects he expressed his anxiety, that Ida (who had already, though only in her sixteenth year, refused several offers) should be happily married; when suddenly the gardener, quite out of breath, came to tell us he bad seen the ghost (as he believed, the old chaplain belonging to the castle), who had appeared a century back. Several of the servants followed the gardener, and their pallid countenances confirmed the alarming tidings he had brought.

"'I believe you will shortly be afraid of your own shadow,' said the count to them. He then sent them off, desiring them not again to trouble him with the like fooleries.

"'It is really terrible,' said he to me, 'to see to what lengths superstition will carry persons of that rank of life; and it is impossible wholly to undeceive them. From one generation to another an absurd report has from time to time been spread abroad, of an old chaplain's ghost wandering in the environs of the castle; and that he says mass in the chapel, with other idle stories of a similar nature. This report has greatly died away since I came into possession of the castle; but it now appears to me, it will never be altogether forgotten.'

"At this moment the duke de Marino was announced. The count did not recollect ever having heard of him.

"I told him that I was tolerably well acquainted with his family; and that I had lately been present, in Venice, at the betrothing of a young man of that name.

"The very same young man came in while I was speaking. I should have felt very glad at seeing him, had I not perceived that my presence caused him evident uneasiness.

"'Ah,' said he in a tolerably gay tone, after the customary forms of politeness had passed between us; 'the finding you here, my dear marquis, explains to me an occurrence, which with shame I own caused me a sensation of fear. To my no small surprise, they knew my name in the adjacent district; and as I came up the hill which leads to the castle, I heard it pronounced three times in a voice wholly unknown to me: and in a still more audible tone this strange voice bade me welcome. I now, however, conclude it was yours.'

"I assured him, (and with truth,) that till his name was announced the minute before, I was ignorant of his arrival, and that none of my servants knew him; for that the valet who accompanied me into Italy was not now with me.

"'And above all,' added I, 'it would be impossible to discover any equipage, however well known to one, in so dark an evening.'

"'That is what astonishes me,' exclaimed the duke, a little amazed.

"The incredulous count very politely added, 'that the voice which had told the duke he was welcome, had at least expressed the sentiments of all the family.'

"Marino, ere he said a word relative to the motive of his visit, asked a private audience of me; and confided in me, by telling me that he was come with the intention of obtaining the lovely Ida's hand; and that if he was able to procure her consent, he should demand her of her father.

"'The countess Apollonia, your bride elect, is then no longer living?' asked I.

"'We will talk on that subject hereafter,' answered he.

"The deep sigh which accompanied these words led me to conclude that Apollonia had been guilty of infidelity or some other crime towards the duke; and consequently I thought that I ought to abstain from any further questions, which appeared to rend his heart, already so sensibly wounded.

"Yet, as he begged me to become his mediator with the count, in order to obtain from him his consent to the match, I painted in glowing colours the danger of an alliance, which he had no other motive for contracting, than the wish to obliterate the remembrance of a dearly, and without doubt, still more tenderly, beloved object. But he assured me he was far from thinking of the lovely Ida from so blameable a motive, and that he should be the happiest of men if she but proved propitious to his wishes.

"His expressive and penetrating tone of voice, while he said this, lulled the uneasiness that I was beginning to feel; and I promised him I would prepare the count Lieppa to listen to his entreaties, and would give him the necessary information relative to the fortune and family of Marino. But I declared to him at the same time, that I should by no means hurry the conclusion of the affair by my advice, as I was not in the habit of taking upon myself so great a charge as the uncertain issue of a marriage.

"The duke signified his satisfaction at what I said, and made me give (what then appeared to me of no consequence) a promise, that I would not make mention of the former marriage he was on the point of contracting, as it would necessarily bring on a train of unpleasant explanations.

"The duke's views succeeded with a promptitude beyond his most sanguine hopes. His well-proportioned form, and sparkling eyes smoothed the paths of love, and introduced him to the heart of Ida. His agreeable conversation promised to the mother an amiable son-in-law; and the knowledge in rural economy, which he evinced as occasions offered, made the count hope for an useful helpmate in his usual occupations; for since the first day of the duke's arrival he had been prevented from pursuing them.

"Marino followed up these advantages with great ardour; and I was one evening much surprised by the intelligence of his being betrothed, as I did not dream of matters drawing so near a conclusion. They spoke at table of some bridal preparations of which I had made mention just before the duke's arrival at the castle; and the countess asked me whether that young Marino was a near relation of the one who was that very day betrothed to her daughter.

"'Near enough,' I answered, recollecting my promise.— Marino looked at me with an air of embarrassment.

"'But, my dear duke,' continued I, 'tell me who mentioned the amiable Ida to you; or was it a portrait, or what else, which caused you to think of looking for a beauty, the selection of whom does so much honour to your taste, in this remote corner; for, if I am not mistaken, you said but yesterday that you had purposed travelling about for another six months; when all at once (I believe while in Paris) you changed your plan, and projected a journey wholly and solely to see the charming Ida?'

"'Yes, it was at Paris,' replied the duke; 'you are very rightly informed. I went there to see and admire the superb gallery of pictures at the Museum; but I had scarcely entered it, when my eyes turned from the inanimate beauties, and were riveted on a lady whose incomparable features were heightened by an air of melancholy. With fear and trembling I approached her, and only ventured to follow without speaking to her. I still followed her after she quitted the gallery; and I drew her servant aside to learn the name of his mistress. He told it me: but when I expressed a wish to become acquainted with the father of this beauty, he said that was next to impossible while at Paris, as the family were on the point of quitting that city; nay, of quitting France altogether.

""""Possibly, however," said I, "some opportunity may present itself." And I looked every where for the lady: but she, probably imagining that her servant was following her closely, had continued to walk on, and was entirely out of sight. While I was looking around for her, the servant had likewise vanished from my view.'

"'Who was this beautiful lady?' asked Ida, in a tone of astonishment.

"'What! you really did not then perceive me at the gallery?'

"'Me!'—'My daughter—!' exclaimed at the same moment Ida and her parents.

"'Yes, you yourself, mademoiselle. The servant, whom fortunately for me you left at Paris, and whom I met the same evening unexpectedly, as my guardian angel, informed me of all; so that after a short rest at home, I was able to come straight hither.'

"'What a fable!' said the count to his daughter, who was mute with astonishment.

"'Ida,' he said turning to me, 'has never yet been out of her native country; and as for myself, I have not been in Paris these seventeen years.'

"The duke looked at the count and his daughter with similar marks of astonishment visible in their countenances; and conversation would have been entirely at an end, if I had not taken care to introduce other topics: but I had it nearly all to myself.

"The repast was no sooner over, than the count took the duke into the recess of a window; and although I was at a considerable distance, and appeared wholly to fix my attention on a new chandelier, I overheard all their conversation.

"'What motive,' demanded the count with a serious and dissatisfied air, 'could have induced you to invent that singular scene in the gallery of the Museum at Paris? for according to my judgment, it could in no way benefit you. Since you are anxious to conceal the cause which brought you to ask my daughter in marriage, at least you might have plainly said as much; and though possibly you might have felt repugnance at making such a declaration, there were a thousand ways of framing your answer, without its being needful thus to offend probability.'

"'Monsieur le count,' replied the duke much piqued; 'I held

my peace at table, thinking that possibly you had reasons for wishing to keep secret your and your daughter's journey to Paris. I was silent merely from motives of discretion; but the singularity of your reproaches compels me to maintain what I have said; and, notwithstanding your reluctance to believe the truth, to declare before all the world, that the capital of France was the spot where I first saw your daughter Ida.'

"'But what if I prove to you, not only by the witness of my servants, but also by that of all my tenants, that my daughter has never quitted her native place?'—

"'I shall still believe the evidence of my own eyes and ears, which have as great authority over me.'

"'What you say is really enigmatical,' answered the count in a graver tone: 'your serious manner convinces me you have been the dupe of some illusion; and that you have seen some other person whom you have taken for my daughter. Excuse me, therefore, for having taken up the thing so warmly.'

"'Another person! What then, I not only mistook another person for your daughter; but the very servant of whom I made mention, and who gave me so exact a description of this castle, was, according to what you say, some other person.'

"'My dear Marino, that servant was some cheat who knew this castle, and who, God only knows for what motive, spoke to you of my daughter as resembling the lady.'

"''Tis certainly no wish of mine to contradict you; but Ida's features are precisely the same as those which made so deep an impression on me at Paris, and which my imagination has preserved with such scrupulous fidelity.'

"The count shook his head; and Marino continued:—

"'What is still more—(but pray pardon me for mentioning a little particularity, which nothing short of necessity would have drawn from me)—while in the gallery, I was standing behind the lady, and the handkerchief that covered her neck was a little disarranged, which occasioned me distinctly to perceive the mark of a small strawberry.'

"'Another strange mystery!' exclaimed the count, turning pale: 'it appears you are determined to make me believe wonderful stories.'

"'I have only one question to ask:—Has Ida such a mark on her neck?'

"'No, monsieur,' replied the count, looking steadfastly at Marino.

"'No!' exclaimed the latter, in the utmost astonishment.

"'No, I tell you: but Ida's twin-sister, who resembled her in the most surprising manner, had the mark you mention on her neck, and a year since carried it with her to the grave.'

"'And yet 'tis only within the last few months that I saw this person in Paris!'

"At this moment the countess and Ida, who had kept aside, a prey to uneasiness, not knowing what to think of the conversation, which appeared of so very important a nature, approached; but the count in a commanding tone ordered them to retire immediately. He then led the duke entirely away into a retired corner of the window, and continued the conversation in so low a voice that I could hear nothing further.

"My astonishment was extreme when, that very same evening, the count gave orders to have Hildegarde's tomb opened in his presence: but he beforehand related briefly what I have just told you, and proposed my assisting the duke and him in opening the grave. The duke excused himself, by saying that the very idea made him tremble with horror; for he could not overcome, especially at night, his fear of a corpse.

"The count begged he would not mention the gallery scene to any one; and above all, to spare the extreme sensibility of the affianced bride from a recital of the conversation they had just had, even if she should request to be informed of it.

"In the mean time the sexton arrived with his lantern. The count and I followed him.

"'It is morally impossible,' said the count to me, as we walked together, 'that any trick can have been played respecting my daughter's death: the circumstances attendant thereon are but too well known to me. You may readily believe, also, that the affection we bore our poor girl would prevent our running any risk of burying her too soon: but suppose even the possibility of that, and that the tomb had been opened by some avaricious persons, who found, on opening the coffin, that the body became re-animated; no one can believe for a moment that my daughter would not have instantly returned to her parents, who doted on her, rather than have fled to a distant country. This last circumstance puts the matter beyond doubt: for even should it be admitted as a truth, that she was carried by force to some distant part of the world, she would have found a thousand ways of returning. My eyes are, however, about to be convinced that the sacred remains of my Hildegarde really repose in the grave.

"'To convince myself!' cried he again, in a tone of voice so melancholy yet loud that the sexton turned his head.

"This movement rendered the count more circumspect, and he continued in a lower tone of voice:

"'How should I for a moment believe it possible that the slightest trace of my daughter's features should be still in existence, or that the destructive hand of time should have spared her beauty? Let us return, marquis; for who could tell, even were I to see the skeleton, that I should know it from that of an entire stranger, whom they may have placed in the tomb to fill her place?'

"He was even about to give orders not to open the door of the chapel, (at which we were just arrived,) when I represented to him, that were I in his place I should have found it extremely difficult to determine on such a measure; but that having gone thus far, it was requisite to complete the task, by examining whether some of the jewels buried with Hildegarde's corpse were not wanting. I added, that judging by a number of well known facts, all bodies were not destroyed equally soon.

"My representations had the desired effect: the count squeezed my hand; and we followed the sexton, who, by his pallid countenance and trembling limbs, evidently shewed that he was unaccustomed to nocturnal employments of this nature.

"I know not whether any of this present company were ever in a chapel at midnight, before the iron doors of a vault, about to examine the succession of leaden coffins enclosing the remains of an illustrious family. Certain it is, that at such a moment the noise of bolts and bars produces such a remarkable sensation, that one is led to dread the sound of the door grating on its hinges; and when the vault is opened, one cannot help hesitating for an instant to enter it.

"The count was evidently seized with these sensations of terror, which I discovered by a stifled sigh; but he concealed his feelings: notwithstanding, I remarked that he dared not trust himself to look on any other coffin than the one containing his daughter's remains. He opened it himself.

"'Did I not say so?' cried he, seeing that the features of the corpse bore a perfect resemblance to those of Ida. I was obliged to prevent the count, who was seized with astonishment, from kissing the forehead of the inanimate body.

"'Do not,' I added, 'disturb the peace of those who repose in death.' And I used my utmost efforts to withdraw the count immediately from this dismal abode.

"On our return to the castle, we found those persons whom we had left there, in an anxious state of suspense. The two ladies had closely questioned the duke on what had passed; and would not admit as a valid excuse, the promise he had made of secrecy. They entreated us also, but in vain, to satisfy their curiosity.

"They succeeded better the following day with the sexton, whom they sent for privately, and who told them all he knew: but it only tended to excite their anxious wish to learn the subject of the conversation which had occasioned this nocturnal visit to the sepulchral vault.

"As for myself, I dreamt the whole of the following night of the apparition Marino had seen at Paris; I conjectured many things which I did not think fit to communicate to the count, because he absolutely questioned the connection of a superior world with ours. At this juncture of affairs, I with pleasure saw that this singular circumstance, if not entirely forgotten, was at least but rarely and slightly mentioned.

"But I now began to find another cause for anxious solicitude. The duke constantly persisted in refusing to explain himself on the subject of his previous engagement, even when we were alone: and the embarrassment he could not conceal, whenever I made mention of the good qualities that I believed his intended to have possessed, as well as several other little singularities, led me to conclude that Marino's attachment for Apollonia had been first shaken at the picture gallery, at sight of the lovely incognita; and that Apollonia had been forsaken, owing to his yielding to temptations; and that doubtless she could never have been guilty of breaking off an alliance so solemnly contracted.

"Foreseeing from this that the charming Ida could never hope to find much happiness in an union with Marino, and knowing that the wedding day was nigh at hand, I resolved to unmask the perfidious deceiver as quickly as possible, and to make him repent his infidelity. An excellent occasion presented itself one day for me to accomplish my designs. Having finished supper, we were still sitting at table; and some one said that iniquity is frequently punished in this world: upon which I observed, that I myself had witnessed striking proofs of the truth of this remark;—when Ida and her mother entreated me to name one of these examples.

"'Under these circumstances, ladies,' answered I, 'permit me to relate a history to you, which, according to my opinion, will particularly interest you.'

"'Us!' they both exclaimed. At the same time I fixed my eyes on the duke, who for several days past had evidently distrusted me; and I saw that his conscience had rendered him pale.

"'That at least is *my* opinion,' replied I: 'But, my dear Count, will you pardon me, if the supernatural is sometimes interwoven with my narration?'

"'Very willingly,' answered he smiling: 'and I will content myself with expressing my surprise at so many things of this sort having happened to you, as I have never experienced any of them myself.'

"I plainly perceived that the duke made signs of approval at what he said: but I took no notice of it, and answered the count by saying,

"'That all the world have not probably the use of their eyes.'

"'That may be,' replied he, still smiling.

"'But,' said I to him in a low and expressive voice, 'think you an uncorrupted body in the vault is a *common* phenomenon?'

"He appeared staggered: and I thus continued in an under tone of voice:—

"'For that matter, 'tis very possible to account for it naturally, and therefore it would be useless to contest the subject with you.'

"'We are wandering from the point,' said the countess a little angrily; and she made me a sign to begin, which I accordingly did, in the following words:—

"'The scene of my anecdote lies in Venice.'

"'I possibly then may know something of it,' cried the duke, who entertained some suspicions.

"'Possibly so,' replied I; 'but there were reasons for keeping the event secret: it happened somewhere about eighteen months since, at the period you first set out on your travels.

"'The son of an extremely wealthy nobleman, whom I shall designate by the name of Filippo, being attracted to Leghorn by the affairs consequent on his succession to an inheritance, had won the heart of an amiable and lovely girl, called Clara. He promised her, as well as her parents, that ere his return to Venice he would come back and marry her. The moment for his departure was preceded by certain ceremonies, which in their termination were terrible: for after the two lovers had exhausted every protestation of reciprocal affection, Filippo invoked the aid of the spirit of vengeance, in case of infidelity: they prayed even that whichever of the lovers should prove faithful might not be permitted to repose quietly in the grave, but should haunt the perjured one, and force the inconstant party to come amongst the dead, and to share in the grave those sentiments which on earth had been forgotten.

"'The parents, who were seated by them at table, remembered

their youthful days, and permitted the overheated and romantic imagination of the young people to take its free course. The lovers finished by making punctures in their arms, and letting their blood run into a glass filled with white champagne.

""'Our souls shall be inseparable as our blood!" exclaimed Filippo; and drinking half the contents of the glass, he gave the rest to Clara.'

"At this moment the duke experienced a violent degree of agitation, and from time to time darted such menacing looks at me, that I was led to conclude, that in *his* adventure some scene of a similar nature had taken place. I can however affirm that I related the details respecting Filippo's departure, as they were represented in a letter written by the mother of Clara.

"'Who,' continued I, 'after so many demonstrations of such a violent passion, could have expected the denouement? Filippo's return to Venice happened precisely at the period at which a young beauty, hitherto educated in a distant convent, made her first appearance in the great world: she on a sudden exhibited herself as an angel whom a cloud had till then concealed, and excited universal admiration. Filippo's parents had heard frequent mention of Clara, and of the projected alliance between her and their son; but they thought that this alliance was like many others, contracted one day without the parties knowing why, and broken off the next with equal want of thought; and influenced by this idea, they presented their son to the parents of Camilla, (which was the name of the young beauty,) whose family were of the highest rank.

"'They represented to Filippo the great advantages he would obtain by an alliance with her. The Carnival happening just at this period completed the business, by affording him so many favourable opportunities of being with Camilla; and in the end, the remembrance of Leghorn held but very little place in his mind. His letters became colder and colder each succeeding day; and on Clara expressing how sensibly she felt the change, he ceased writing to her altogether, and did every thing in his power to hasten his union with Camilla, who was, without compare, much the handsomer and more wealthy. The agonies poor Clara endured were manifest in her illegible writing, and by the tears which were but too evidently shed over her letters: but neither the one nor the other had any more influence over the fickle heart of Filippo, than the prayers of the unfortunate girl. Even the menace of coming, according to their solemn agreement, from the tomb to haunt him, and carry him with her to that grave which threatened so soon to enclose her, had but little effect on his mind, which was entirely engrossed with the idea of the happiness he should enjoy in the arms of Camilla.

"'The father of the latter (who was my intimate friend) invited me beforehand to the wedding. And although numerous affairs detained him that summer in the city, so that he could not as usual enjoy the pleasures of the country, yet we sometimes went to his pretty villa, situated on the banks of the Brenta;[1] where his daughter's marriage was to be celebrated with all possible splendour.

"'A particular circumstance, however, occasioned the ceremony to be deferred for some weeks. The parents of Camilla having been very happy in their own union, were anxious that the same priest who married them, should pronounce the nuptial benediction on their daughter. This priest, who, notwithstanding his great age, had the appearance of vigorous health, was seized with a slow fever which confined him to his bed: however, in time it abated, he became gradually better and better, and the wedding-day was at length fixed. But, as if some secret power was at work to prevent this union, the worthy priest was, on the very day destined for the celebration of their marriage, seized with a feverish shivering of so alarming a nature, that he dared not stir out of the house, and he strongly advised the young couple to select another priest to marry them.

"'The parents still persisted in their design of the nuptial benediction being given to their children by the respectable old man who had married *them*.—They would have certainly spared themselves a great deal of grief, if they had never swerved from their determination.—Very grand preparations had been made in honour of the day; and as they could no longer be deferred, it was decided that they should consider it as a ceremony of solemn affiance. At noon the bargemen attired in their splendid garb awaited the company's arrival on the banks of the canal: their joyous song was soon distinguished, while conducting to the villa, now decorated with flowers, the numerous gondolas containing parties of the best company.

"'During the dinner, which lasted till evening, the betrothed couple exchanged rings. At the very moment of their so doing, a piercing shriek was heard, which struck terror into the breasts of all the company, and absolutely struck Filippo with horror. Every one ran to the windows: for although it was becoming dark, each

---

1 A river that flows into the Adriatic near Venice.

object was visible; but no one was to be seen.'

"'Stop an instant,' said the duke to me, with a fierce smile.—His countenance, which had frequently changed colour during the recital, evinced strong marks of the torments of a wicked conscience.

"'I am also acquainted with that story, of a voice being heard in the air; it is borrowed from the "Memoirs of Mademoiselle Clairon;"[1] a deceased lover tormented *her* in this completely original manner. The shriek in her case was followed by a clapping of hands: I hope, monsieur le marquis, that you will not omit that particular in your story.'

"'And why,' replied I, 'should you imagine that nothing of a similar nature could occur to any one besides that actress? Your incredulity appears to me so much the more extraordinary, as it seems to rest on facts which may lay claim to belief.'

"The countess made me a sign to continue; and I pursued my narrative as follows:

"'A short time after they had heard this inexplicable shriek, I begged Camilla, facing whom I was sitting, to permit me to look at her ring once more, the exquisite workmanship of which had already been much admired. But it was not on her finger: a general search was made, but not the slightest trace of the ring could be discovered. The company even rose from their seats to look for it, but all in vain.

"'Meanwhile, the time for the evening's amusements approached: fire-works were exhibited on the Brenta preceding the ball; the company were masked and got into the gondolas; but nothing was so striking as the silence which reigned during this *fête*; no one seemed inclined to open their mouth; and scarcely was heard a faint exclamation of *Bravo*, at sight of the fire-works.

"'The ball was one of the most brilliant I ever witnessed: the precious stones and jewels with which the ladies of the party were covered, reflected the lights in the chandeliers with redoubled lustre. The most splendidly attired of the whole was Camilla. Her father, who was fond of pomp, rejoiced in the idea that no one in the assembly was equal to his daughter in splendour or beauty.

"'Possibly to satisfy himself of this fact, he made a tour of the room; and returned loudly expressing his surprise, at having perceived on another lady precisely the same jewels which adorned Camilla. He was even weak enough to express a slight degree of

---

1   Claire Josephe Hippolyte Léris de la Tude (1723-1803), *Mémoires d'Hippolyte Clairon* (1799).

chagrin. However, he consoled himself with the idea, that a bouquet of diamonds which was destined for Camilla to wear at supper, would alone in value be greater than all she then had on.

"'But as they were on the point of sitting down to table, and the anxious father again threw a look around him, he discovered that the same lady had also a bouquet which appeared to the full as valuable as Camilla's.

"'My friend's curiosity could no longer be restrained; he approached, and asked whether it would be too great a liberty to learn the name of the fair mask? But to his great surprise, the lady shook her head, and turned away from him.

"'At the same instant the steward came in, to ask whether since dinner there had been any addition to the party, as the covers were not sufficient.

"'His master answered, with rather a dissatisfied air, that there were only the same number, and accused his servants of negligence; but the steward still persisted in what he had said.

"'An additional cover was placed: the master counted them himself, and discovered that there really was one more in number than he had invited. As he had recently, on account of some inconsiderate expressions, had a dispute with government, he was apprehensive that some spy had contrived to slip in with the company: but as he had no reason to believe, that on such a day as that, any thing of a suspicious nature would be uttered, he resolved, in order to be satisfied respecting so indiscreet a procedure as the introduction of such a person in a family *fête*, to beg every one present to unmask; but in order to avoid the inconvenience likely to arise from such a request, he determined not to propose it till the very last thing.

"'Every one present expressed their surprise at the luxuries and delicacies of the table, for it far surpassed every thing of the sort seen in that country, especially with respect to the wines. Still, however, the father of Camilla was not satisfied, and loudly lamented that an accident had happened to his capital red champagne, which prevented his being able to offer his guests a single glass of it.

"'The company seemed anxious to become gay, for the whole of the day nothing like gaiety had been visible among them; but no one around where I sat, partook of this inclination, for curiosity alone appeared to occupy their whole attention; I was sitting near the lady who was so splendidly attired, and I remarked that she neither ate nor drank any thing; that she neither addressed nor answered a word to her neighbours, and that she appeared to have her eyes constantly fixed on the affianced couple.

"'The rumour of this singularity gradually spread round the room, and again disturbed the mirth which had become pretty general. Each whispered to the other a thousand conjectures on this mysterious personage. But the general opinion was, that some unhappy passion for Filippo was the cause of this extraordinary conduct. Those sitting next the unknown, were the first to rise from table, in order to find more cheerful associates, and their places were filled by others who hoped to discover some acquaintance in this silent lady, and obtain from her a more welcome reception; but their hopes were equally futile.

"'At the time the champagne was handed round, Filippo also brought a chair and sat by the unknown. She then became somewhat more animated, and turned towards Filippo, which was more than she had done to any one else; and she offered him her glass, as if wishing him to drink out of it.

"'A violent trembling seized Filippo, when she looked at him steadfastly.

"'"The wine is red!" cried be, holding up the glass; "I thought there had been no red champagne."

"'"Red!" said the father of Camilla, with an air of extreme surprise, approaching him from curiosity.

"'"Look at the lady's glass," replied Filippo.

"'"The wine in it is as white as all the rest," answered Camilla's father; and he called all present to witness it. They every one unanimously declared that the wine was white.

"'Filippo drank it not, but quitted his seat; for a second look from his neighbour had caused him extreme agitation. He took the father of Camilla aside, and whispered something to him. The latter returned to the company, saying,

"'"Ladies and gentlemen, I entreat you, for reasons which I will tell you presently, instantly to unmask."

"'As in this request he but expressed in a degree the general wish, every one's mask was off as quick as thought, and each face uncovered, excepting that of the silent lady, on whom every look was fixed, and whose face they were the most anxious to see.

"'"You alone keep on your mask," said Camilla's father to her, after a short silence: "May I hope you will also remove yours?"

"'She obstinately persisted in her determination of remaining unknown.

"'This strange conduct affected the father of Camilla the more sensibly, as he recognised in the others all those whom he had invited to the *fête*, and found beyond doubt that the mute lady was the one exceeding the number invited. He was, however, unwilling to force her to unmask; because the uncommon splendour of her dress did not permit him any longer to harbour the idea that this additional guest was a spy; and thinking her also a person of distinction, he did not wish to be deficient in good manners. He thought possibly she might be some friend of the family, who, not residing at Venice, but finding on her arrival in that city that he was to give this *fête*, had conceived this innocent frolic.

"'It was thought right, however, at all events to obtain all the information that could be gained from the servants: but none of them knew any thing of this lady; there were no servants of hers there; and those belonging to Camilla's father did not recollect having seen any who appeared to appertain to her.

"'What rendered this circumstance doubly strange was, that, as I before mentioned, this lady only put the magnificent bouquet into her bosom the instant previous to her sitting down to supper.

"'The whispering, which had generally usurped the place of all conversation, gained each moment more and more ascendancy; when on a sudden the masked lady arose, and walking towards the door beckoned Filippo to follow her; but Camilla hindered him from obeying her signal, for she had a long time observed with what fixed attention the mysterious lady looked at her intended husband; and she had also remarked, that the latter had quitted the stranger in violent agitation; and from all this she apprehended that love had caused him to be guilty of some folly or other. The master of the house, turning a deaf ear to all his daughter's remonstrances, and a prey to the most terrible fears, followed the unknown (at a distance, it is true); but she was no sooner out of the room than he returned. At this moment, the shriek which they had heard at noon was repeated, but seemed louder from the silence of night, and communicated anew affright to all present. By the time the father of Camilla had returned from the first movement which his fear had occasioned him to make, the unknown was no where to be found.

"'The servants in waiting outside the house had no knowledge whatever of the masked lady. In every direction around there were crowds of persons; the river was lined with gondolas; and yet not an individual among them had seen the mysterious female.

"'All these circumstances had occasioned so much uneasiness to the whole party, that every one was anxious to return home; and the master of the house was obliged to permit the departure of the gondolas much earlier than he had intended.

"'The return home was, as might naturally be expected, very melancholy.

"'On the following day the betrothed couple were, however, pretty composed. Filippo had even adopted Camilla's idea of the unknown being some one whom love had deprived of reason; and as for the horrible shriek twice repeated, they were willing to attribute it to some people who were diverting themselves; and they decided, that inattention on the part of the servants was the sole cause of the unknown absenting herself without being perceived; and they even at last persuaded themselves, that the sudden disappearance of the ring, which they had not been able to find, was owing to the malice of some one of the servants who had pilfered it.

"'In a word, they banished every thing that could tend to weaken these explanations; and only one thing remained to harass them. The old priest, who was to bestow on them the nuptial benediction, had yielded up his last breath; and the friendship which had so intimately subsisted between him and the parents of Camilla, did not permit them in decency to think of marriage and amusements the week following his death.

"'The day this venerable priest was buried, Filippo's gaiety received a severe shock; for he learned, in a letter from Clara's mother, the death of that lovely girl. Sinking under the grief occasioned her by the infidelity of the man she had never ceased to love, she died: but to her latest hour she declared she should never rest quietly in her grave, until the perjured man had fulfilled the promise he had made to her.

"'This circumstance produced a stronger effect on him than all the imprecations of the unhappy mother; for he recollected that the first shriek (the cause of which they had never been able to ascertain) was heard at the precise moment of Clara's death; which convinced him that the unknown mask could only have been the spirit of Clara.

"'This idea deprived him at intervals of his senses.

"'He constantly carried this letter about him; and with an air of wandering would sometimes draw it from his pocket, in order to reconsider it attentively: even Camilla's presence did not deter him.

"'As it was natural to conclude this letter contained the cause of the extraordinary change which had taken place in Filippo, she one day gladly seized the opportunity of reading it, when in one of his absent fits he let it fall from his hands.

"'Filippo, struck by the death-like paleness and faintness

which overcame Camilla, as she returned him the letter, knew instantly that she had read it. In the deepest affliction he threw himself at her feet, and conjured her to tell him how he must act.

"""Love *me* with greater constancy than you did her,"—replied Camilla mournfully.

"'With transport he promised to do so. But his agitation became greater and greater, and increased to a most extraordinary pitch the morning of the day fixed for the wedding. As he was going to the house of Camilla's father before it became dark, (from whence he was to take his bride at dawn of day to the church, according to the custom of the country,) he fancied he saw Clara's spirit walking constantly at his side.

"'Never was seen a couple about to receive the nuptial benediction, with so mournful an aspect. I accompanied the parents of Camilla, who had requested me to be a witness: and the sequel has made an indelible impression on my mind of the events of that dismal morning.

"'We were proceeding silently to the church of the Salutation; when Filippo, in our way thither, frequently requested me to remove the stranger from Camilla's side, for she had evil designs against her.

"""What stranger?" I asked him.

"""In God's name, don't speak so loud," replied be; "for you cannot but see how anxious she is to force herself between Camilla and me."

"""Mere chimera, my friend; there are none but yourself and Camilla."

"""Would to Heaven my eyes did not deceive me!"—"Take care that she does not enter the church," added he, as we arrived at the door.

"""She will not enter it, rest assured," said I: and to the great astonishment of Camilla's parents I made a motion as if to drive some one away.

"'We found Filippo's father already in the church; and as soon as his son perceived him, he took leave of him as if he was going to die. Camilla sobbed; and Filippo exclaimed:—

"""There's the stranger, she has then got in."

"'The parents of Camilla doubted whether under such circumstances the marriage ceremony ought to be begun.

"'But Camilla, entirely devoted to her love, cried:—"These chimeras of fancy render my care and attention the more necessary."

"'They approached the altar. At that moment a sudden gust of wind blew out the wax-tapers. The priest appeared displeased at their not having shut the windows more securely; but Filippo exclaimed: "The windows! See you not, then, that there is one here who blew out the wax-tapers purposely?"

"'Every one looked astonished: and Filippo cried, as he hastily disengaged his hand from that of Camilla,—"Don't you see, also, that she is tearing me away from my intended bride?"

"'Camilla fell fainting into the arms of her parents; and the priest declared, that under such peculiar circumstances it was impossible to proceed with the ceremony.

"'The parents of both attributed Filippo's state to mental derangement. They even supposed he had been poisoned; for an instant after, the unfortunate man expired in most violent convulsions. The surgeons who opened his body could not, however, discover any grounds for this suspicion.

"'The parents, who as well as myself were informed by Camilla of the subject of these supposed horrors of Filippo, did every thing in their power to conceal this adventure: yet, on talking over all the circumstances, they could never satisfactorily explain the apparition of the mysterious mask at the time of the wedding *fête*. And what still appeared very surprising was, that the ring lost at the country villa was found amongst Camilla's other jewels, at the time of their return from church.'

"'This is, indeed, a wonderful history!' said the count. His wife uttered a deep sigh: and Ida exclaimed,—

"'It has really made *me* shudder.'

"'That is precisely what every betrothed person ought to feel who listens to such recitals,' answered I, looking steadfastly at the duke, who, while I was talking, had risen and sat down again several times; and who, from his troubled look, plainly shewed that he feared I should counteract his wishes.

"'A word with you!' he whispered me, as we were retiring to rest: and he accompanied me to my room. 'I plainly perceive your generous intentions; this history invented for the occasion—'

"'Hold!' said I to him in an irritated tone of voice: 'I was eye-witness to what you have just heard. How then can you doubt its authenticity, without accusing a man of honour of uttering a falsehood?'

"'We will talk on this subject presently,' replied he in a tone of raillery. 'But tell me truly from whence you learnt the anecdote relative to mixing the blood with wine?—I know the person from whose life you borrowed this idea.'

"'I do assure you that I have taken it from no one's life but

Filippo's; and yet there may be similar stories—as of the shriek, for instance. But even this singular manner of irrevocably affiancing themselves may have presented itself to *any* two lovers.'

"'Perhaps so! Yet one could trace in your narration many traits resembling another history.'

"'That is very possible: all love-stories are founded on the same stock, and cannot deny their parentage.'

"'No matter,' replied Marino; 'but I desire that from henceforth you do not permit yourself to make any allusion to my past life; and still less that you relate certain anecdotes to the count. On these conditions, and only on these conditions, do I pardon your former very ingenious fiction.'

"'Conditions!—forgiveness!—And do you dare thus to talk to *me*? This is rather too much. Now take my answer: To-morrow morning the count shall know that you have been already affianced, and what you now exact.'

"'Marquis, if you dare—'

"'Oh! oh!—yes, I dare do it; and I owe it to an old friend. The impostor who dares accuse me of falsehood shall no longer wear his deceitful mask in this house.'

"Passion had, spite of my endeavours, carried me so far, that a duel became inevitable. The duke challenged me. And we agreed, at parting, to meet the following morning in a neighbouring wood with pistols.

"In effect, before daylight we each took our servant and went into the forest. Marino, remarking that I had not given any orders in case of my being killed, undertook to do so for me; and accordingly he told my servant what to do with my body, as if every thing was already decided. He again addressed me ere we shook hands;—

"'For,' said he, 'the combat between us must be very unequal. I am young,' added he; 'but in many instances my hand has proved a steady one. I have not, it is true, absolutely killed any man; but I have invariably hit my adversary precisely on the part I intended. In this instance, however, I must, for the first time, *kill* my man, as it is the only effectual method of preventing your annoying me further, unless you will give me your word of honour not to discover any occurrences of my past life to the count, in which case I consent to consider the affair as terminated here.'

"As you may naturally believe, I rejected his proposition.

"'As it must be so,' replied he, 'recommend your soul to God.' We prepared accordingly.

"'It is your first fire,' he said to me.

"'I yield it to you,' answered I.

"He refused to fire first. I then drew the trigger, and caused the pistol to drop from his hand. He appeared surprised: but his astonishment was great indeed, when, after taking up another pistol, he found he had missed me. He pretended to have aimed at my heart; and had not even the possibility of an excuse; for he could not but acknowledge that no sensation of fear on my part had induced me to move, and baulk his aim.

"At his request I fired a second time; and again aimed at his pistol which he held in his left hand: and to his great astonishment it dropped also; but the ball had passed so near his hand, that it was a good deal bruised.

"His second fire having passed me, I told him I would not fire again; but that, as it was possible the extreme agitation of his mind had occasioned him to miss me twice, I proposed adjusting matters.

"Before he had time to refuse my offer, the count who had suspicions that all was not right, was between us, with his daughter. He complained loudly of such conduct on the part of his guests; and demanded some explanation on the cause of our dispute. I then developed the whole business in presence of Marino, whose evident embarrassment convinced the count and Ida of the truth of the reproaches his conscience made him.

"But the duke soon availed himself of Ida's affection, and created an entire change in the count's mind; who that very evening said to me,—

"'You are right; I certainly ought to take some decided step, and send the duke from my house: but what could win the Apollonia whom he has abandoned, and whom he will never see again? Added to which, he is the only man for whom my daughter has ever felt a sincere attachment. Let us leave the young people to follow their own inclinations: the countess perfectly coincides in this opinion; and adds, that it would hurt her much were this handsome Venetian to be driven from our house. How many little infidelities and indiscretions are committed in the world and excused, owing to particular circumstances?'

"'But it appears to me, that in the case in point, these particular circumstances are wanting,' answered I. However, finding the count persisted in his opinion, I said no more.

"The marriage took place without any interruption: but still there was very little of gaiety at the feast, which usually on these occasions is of so splendid and jocund a nature. The ball in the evening was dull; and Marino alone danced with extraordinary glee.

"'Fortunately, monsieur le marquis,' said he in my ear, quitting the dance for an instant and laughing aloud, 'there are no ghosts or spirits here, as at your Venetian wedding.'

"'Don't,' I answered, putting up my finger to him, 'rejoice too soon: misery is slow in its operations; and often is not perceived by us blind mortals till it treads on our heels.'

"Contrary to my intention, this conversation rendered him quite silent; and what convinced me the more strongly of the effect it had made on him, was, the redoubled vehemence with which the duke again began dancing.

"The countess in vain entreated him to be careful of his health: and all Ida's supplications were able to obtain was, a few minutes' rest to take breath when he could no longer go on.

"A few minutes after, I saw Ida in tears, which did not appear as if occasioned by joy; and she quitted the ball-room. I was standing as close to the door as I am to you at this moment; so that I could not for an instant doubt its being really Ida: but what appeared to me very strange was, that in a few seconds I saw her come in again with a countenance as calm as possible. I followed her, and remarked that she asked the duke to dance; and was so far from moderating his violence, that she partook of and even increased it by her own example. I also remarked, that as soon as the dance was over the duke took leave of the parents of Ida, and with her vanished through a small door leading to the nuptial apartment.

"While I was endeavouring to account in my own mind how it was possible for Ida so suddenly to change her sentiments, a conference in an undertone took place at the door of the room, between the count and his valet.

"The subject was evidently a very important one, as the greatly incensed looks of the count towards his gardener evinced, while *he* confirmed, as it appeared, what the valet had before said.

"I drew near the trio, and heard, that at a particular time the church organ was heard to play, and that the whole edifice had been illuminated within, until twelve o'clock, which had just struck.

"The count was very angry at their troubling him with so silly a tale, and asked why they did not sooner inform him of it. They answered, that everyone was anxious to see how it would end. The gardener added, that the old chaplain had been seen again; and the peasantry who lived near the forest, even pretended that they had seen the summit of the mountain which overhung their valley illuminated, and spirits dance around it.

"'Very well!' exclaimed the count with a gloomy air; 'so all the old idle trash is resumed: the *Death-Bride* is also, I hope, going to play her part.'

"The valet having pushed aside the gardener, that he might not still further enrage the count, I put in my word; and said to the count, 'You might at least listen to what they have to say, and learn what it is they pretend to have seen.'

"'What is said about the *Death-Bride*?' said I to the gardener.

"He shrugged up his shoulders.

"'Was I not right?' cried the count: 'here we are then, and must listen to this ridiculous tale. All these things are treasured in the memory of these people, and constantly afford subjects and phantoms to their imaginations.—Is it permitted to ask under what form?'—

"'Pray pardon me,' replied the gardener; 'but it resembled the deceased mademoiselle Hildegarde. She passed close to me in the garden, and then came in to the castle.'

"'O!' said the count to him, 'I beg, in future you will be a little more circumspect in your fancies, and leave my daughter to rest quietly in the tomb.—'Tis well—'

"He then made a signal to his servants, who went out.

"'Well! my dear marquis!' said he to me.

"'Well?'

"'Your belief in stories will not, surely, carry you so far as to give credence to my Hildegarde's spirit appearing?'

"'At least it may have appeared to the gardener only. Do you recollect the adventure in the Museum at Paris?'

"'You are right: that again was a pretty invention, which to this moment I cannot fathom. Believe me, I should sooner have refused my daughter to the duke for his having been the fabricator of so gross a story, than for his having forsaken his first love.'

"'I see very plainly that we shall not easily accord on this point; for if my ready belief appears strange to you, your doubts seem to me incomprehensible.'

"The company assembled at the castle, retired by degrees; and I *alone* was left with the count and his lady, when Ida came to the room-door, clothed in her ball-dress, and appeared astonished at finding the company had left.

"'What can this mean?' demanded the countess. Her husband could not find words to express his astonishment.

"'Where is Marino?' exclaimed Ida.

"'Do *you* ask us where he is?' replied her mother; 'did we not see you go out with him through that small door?'

"'That could not be;—you mistake.'

"'No, no; my dear child! A short time since you were dancing with singular vehemence; and then you both went out together.'

"'*Me!* my mother?'

"'Yes, my dear Ida: how is it possible you should have forgotten all this?'

"'I have forgotten nothing, believe me.'

"'Where then have you been all this time?'

"'In my sister's chamber,' said Ida.

"I remarked that at these words the count became somewhat pale; and Ida's fearful eye caught mine: he however said nothing. The countess, fearing that her daughter was deceiving her, said to her in an afflicted tone of voice:—

"'How could so singular a fancy possess you on a day like this?'

"'I cannot account for it; and only know, that all on a sudden I felt an oppression at my heart, and fancied that all I wanted was Hildegarde. At the same time I felt a firm belief that I should find her in her room playing on her guitar; for which reason I crept thither softly.'

"'And did you find her there?'

"'Alas! no: but the eager desire that I felt to see her, added to the fatigue of dancing, so entirely overpowered me, that I seated myself on a chair, where I fell fast asleep.'

"'How long since did you quit the room?'

"'The clock in the tower struck the three-quarters past eleven just as I entered my sister's room.'

"'What does all this mean?' said the countess to her husband in a low voice: 'she talks in a connected manner; and yet I know, that as the clock struck three-quarters past eleven, I entreated Ida on this very spot to dance more moderately.'

"'And Marino?'—asked the count.

"'I thought, as I before said, that I should find him here.'

"'Good God!' exclaimed the mother, 'she raves: but the duke—Where is he then?'

"'What then, my good mother?' said Ida with an air of great disquiet, while leaning on the countess.

"Meanwhile the count took a wax-taper, and made a sign for me to follow him. A horrible spectacle awaited us in the bridal-chamber, whither he conducted me. We there found the duke extended on the floor. There did not appear the slightest signs of life in him; and his features were distorted in the most frightful manner.

"Imagine the extreme affliction Ida endured when she heard this recital, and found that all the resources of the medical attendants were employed in vain.

"The count and his family could not be roused from the deep consternation which threatened to overwhelm them. A short time after this event, some business of importance occasioned me to quit their castle; and certainly I was not sorry for the excuse to get away.

"But ere I left that county, I did not fail to collect in the village every possible information relative to the *Death-Bride*; whose history unfortunately, in passing from one mouth to another, experienced many alterations. It appeared to me, however, upon the whole, that this affianced bride lived in this district, about the fourteenth or fifteenth century. She was a young lady of noble family, and she had conducted herself with so much perfidy and ingratitude towards her lover, that he died of grief; but afterwards, when she was about to marry, he appeared to her the night of her intended wedding, and she died in consequence. And it is said, that since that time, the spirit of this unfortunate creature wanders on earth in every possible shape; particularly in that of lovely females, to render their lovers inconstant.

"As it was not permitted for her to appear in the form of any living being, she always chose amongst the dead those who the most strongly resembled them. It was for this reason she voluntarily frequented the galleries in which were hung family portraits. It is even reported that she has been seen in galleries of pictures open to public inspection. Finally, it is said, that, as a punishment for her perfidy, she will wander till she finds a man whom she will in vain endeavour to make swerve from his engagement; and it appears, they added, that as yet she had not succeeded.

"Having inquired what connection subsisted between this spirit and the old chaplain (of whom also I had heard mention), they informed me, that the fate of the last depended on the young lady, because he had assisted her in her criminal conduct. But no one was able to give me any satisfactory information concerning the voice which had called the duke by his name, nor on the meaning of the church being illuminated at night; and why the grand mass was chanted. No one either knows how to account for the dance on the mountain's top in the forest.

"For the rest," added the marquis, "you will own, that the traditions are admirably adapted to my story, and may, to a certain degree, serve to fill up the gaps; but I am not enabled to give a more satisfactory explanation. I reserve for another time a second history of this same *Death-Bride*; I only heard it a few weeks since: it appears to me interesting; but it is too late to begin to-day, and indeed, even now, I fear that I have intruded too long on the leisure of the company present by my narrative."

He had just finished these words, and some of his auditors (though all thanked him for the trouble he had taken) were expressing their disbelief of the story, when a person of his acquaintance came into the room in a hurried manner, and whispered something in his ear. Nothing could be more striking than the contrast presented by the bustling and uneasy air of the newly arrived person while speaking to the marquis, and the calm air of the latter while listening to him.

"Haste, I pray you," said the first (who appeared quite out of patience at the marquis's *sang-froid*): "In a few moments you will have cause to repent this delay."

"I am obliged to you for your affecting solicitude," replied the marquis; who in taking up his hat, appeared more to do, as all the rest of the party were doing, in preparing to return home, than from any anxiety of hastening away.

"You are lost," said the other, as he saw an officer enter the room at the head of a detachment of military, who inquired for the marquis. The latter instantly made himself known to him.

"You are my prisoner," said the officer. The marquis followed him, after saying Adieu with a smiling air to all the party, and begging they would not feel any anxiety concerning him.

"Not feel anxiety!" replied he whose advice he had neglected. "I must inform you, that they have discovered that the marquis has been detected in a connection with very suspicious characters; and his death-warrant may be considered as signed. I came in pity to warn him of his danger, for possibly he might then have escaped; but from his conduct since, I can scarcely imagine he is in his proper senses."

The party, who were singularly affected by this event, were conjecturing a thousand things, when the officer returned, and again asked for the marquis. "He just now left the room with you," answered some one of the company.

"But he came in again."

"We have seen no one."

"He has then disappeared," replied the officer, smiling: he searched every corner for the marquis, but in vain. The house was thoroughly examined, but without success; and the following day the officer quitted the baths with his soldiers, without his prisoner, and very much dissatisfied.

2. Lord Byron, "A Fragment" (1819)

June 17, 1816.

IN the year 17—, having for some time determined on a journey through countries not hitherto much frequented by travellers, I set out, accompanied by a friend, whom I shall designate by the name of Augustus Darvell. He was a few years my elder, and a man of considerable fortune and ancient family—advantages which an extensive capacity prevented him alike from undervaluing or overrating. Some peculiar circumstances in his private history had rendered him to me an object of attention, of interest, and even of regard, which neither the reserve of his manners, nor occasional indications of an inquietude at times nearly approaching to alienation of mind, could extinguish.

I was yet young in life, which I had begun early; but my intimacy with him was of a recent date: we had been educated at the same schools and university; but his progress through these had preceded mine, and he had been deeply initiated into what is called the world, while I was yet in my noviciate. While thus engaged, I had heard much both of his past and present life; and although in these accounts there were many and irreconcileable contradictions, I could still gather from the whole that he was a being of no common order, and one who, whatever pains he might take to avoid remark, would still be remarkable. I had cultivated his acquaintance subsequently, and endeavoured to obtain his friendship, but this last appeared to be unattainable; whatever affections he might have possessed seemed now, some to have been extinguished, and others to be concentred: that his feelings were acute, I had sufficient opportunities of observing; for, although he could control, he could not altogether disguise them: still he had a power of giving to one passion the appearance of another in such a manner that it was difficult to define the nature of what was working within him; and the expressions of his features would vary so rapidly, though slightly, that it was useless to trace them to their sources. It was evident that he was a prey to some cureless disquiet; but whether it arose from ambition, love, remorse, grief, from one or all of these, or merely from a morbid temperament akin to disease, I could not discover: there were circumstances alleged, which might have justified the application to each of these causes; but, as I have before said, these were so contradictory and contradicted, that none could be fixed upon with accuracy. Where there is mystery, it is generally supposed that there must also be evil: I know not how this may be, but in him there certainly was the one, though I could not ascertain the extent of the other—and felt loth, as far as regarded himself, to believe in its existence. My advances were received with sufficient coldness; but I was young, and not easily discouraged, and at length succeeded in obtaining, to a certain degree, that common-place intercourse and moderate confidence of common and every day concerns, created and cemented by similarity of pursuit and frequency of meeting, which is called intimacy, or friendship, according to the ideas of him who uses those words to express them.

Darvell had already travelled extensively; and to him I had applied for information with regard to the conduct of my intended journey. It was my secret wish that he might be prevailed on to accompany me: it was also a probable hope, founded upon the shadowy restlessness which I had observed in him, and to which the animation which he appeared to feel on such subjects, and his apparent indifference to all by which he was more immediately surrounded, gave fresh strength. This wish I first hinted, and then expressed: his answer, though I had partly expected it, gave me all the pleasure of surprise—he consented; and, after the requisite arrangements, we commenced our voyages. After journeying through various countries of the south of Europe, our attention was turned towards the East, according to our original destination; and it was in my progress through those regions that the incident occurred upon which will turn what I may have to relate.

The constitution of Darvell, which must from his appearance have been in early life more than usually robust, had been for some time gradually giving way, without the intervention of any apparent disease: he had neither cough nor hectic, yet he became daily more enfeebled: his habits were temperate, and he neither declined nor complained of fatigue, yet he was evidently wasting away: he became more and more silent and sleepless, and at length so seriously altered, that my alarm grew proportionate to what I conceived to be his danger.

We had determined, on our arrival at Smyrna, on an excursion to the ruins of Ephesus and Sardis,[1] from which I endeavoured to dissuade him in his present state of indisposition—but in vain: there appeared to be an oppression on his mind, and a solemnity in his manner, which ill corresponded with his eagerness to proceed on what I regarded as a mere party of pleasure, little suited to a valetudinarian; but I opposed him no longer—and in a few days we set off together, accompanied only by a serrugee and a single janizary.[2]

We had passed halfway towards the remains of Ephesus, leaving behind us the more fertile environs of Smyrna, and were entering upon that wild and tenantless track through the marshes and defiles which lead to the few huts yet lingering over the broken columns of Diana—the roofless walls of expelled Christianity, and the still more recent but complete desolation of abandoned mosques—when the sudden and rapid illness of my companion obliged us to halt at a Turkish cemetery, the turbaned tombstones of which were the sole indication that human life had ever been a sojourner in this wilderness. The only caravansera[3] we had seen was left some hours behind us, not a vestige of a town or even cottage was within sight or hope, and this "city of the dead"[4] appeared to be the sole refuge for my unfortunate friend, who seemed on the verge of becoming the last of its inhabitants.

In this situation, I looked round for a place where he might most conveniently repose:—contrary to the usual aspect of Mahometan burial-grounds, the cypresses were in this few in number, and these thinly scattered over its extent: the tombstones were mostly fallen, and worn with age:—upon one of the most considerable of these, and beneath one of the most spreading trees, Darvell supported himself, in a half-reclining posture, with great difficulty. He asked for water. I had some doubts of our being able to find any, and prepared to go in search of it with hesitating despondency—but he desired me to remain; and turning to Suleiman, our janizary, who stood by us smoking with great

---

1 Greek cities in what is now Turkey; the temple of Diana at Ephesus was one of the seven wonders of the classical world.
2 A driver and an élite member of the Turkish army, serving as an armed guard, respectively.
3 "Inn" (Farsi).
4 A literal translation of *necropolis*, the Greek word for cemetery; cf. Byron, "On the Star of 'The Legion of Honour'" (1815) 37-38.

tranquillity, he said, "Suleiman, verbana su," (i.e. bring some water,) and went on describing the spot where it was to be found with great minuteness, at a small well for camels, a few hundred yards to the right: the janizary obeyed. I said to Darvell, "How did you know this?"—He replied, "From our situation; you must perceive that this place was once inhabited, and could not have been so without springs: I have also been here before."

"You have been here before!—How came you never to mention this to me? and what could you be doing in a place where no one would remain a moment longer than they could help it?"

To this question I received no answer. In the mean time Suleiman returned with the water, leaving the serrugee and the horses at the fountain. The quenching of his thirst had the appearance of reviving him for a moment; and I conceived hopes of his being able to proceed, or at least to return, and I urged the attempt. He was silent—and appeared to be collecting his spirits for an effort to speak. He began.

"This is the end of my journey, and of my life—I came here to die: but I have a request to make, a command—for such my last words must be—You will observe it?"

"Most certainly; but have better hopes."

"I have no hopes, nor wishes, but this—conceal my death from every human being."

"I hope there will be no occasion; that you will recover, and—"

"Peace!—it must be so: promise this."

"I do."

"Swear it, by all that"—He here dictated an oath of great solemnity.

"There is no occasion for this—I will observe your request; and to doubt me is—"

"It cannot be helped,—you must swear."

I took the oath: it appeared to relieve him. He removed a seal ring from his finger, on which were some Arabic characters, and presented it to me. He proceeded—

"On the ninth day of the month, at noon precisely (what month you please, but this must be the day), you must fling this ring into the salt springs which run into the Bay of Eleusis:[1] the

---

1   The Bay of Eleusis, near Athens, is the site of the Eleusinian mysteries
    in honour of the goddess Demeter (Latin, "Ceres") and especially in
    honour of the return of her daughter, Persephone, from the underworld.

day after, at the same hour, you must repair to the ruins of the temple of Ceres, and wait one hour."

"Why?"

"You will see."

"The ninth day of the month, you say?"

"The ninth."

As I observed that the present was the ninth day of the month, his countenance changed, and he paused. As he sate, evidently becoming more feeble, a stork, with a snake in her beak, perched upon a tombstone near us; and, without devouring her prey, appeared to be stedfastly regarding us. I know not what impelled me to drive it away, but the attempt was useless; she made a few circles in the air, and returned exactly to the same spot. Darvell pointed to it, and smiled: he spoke—I know not whether to himself or to me—but the words were only, "'Tis well!"

"What is well? what do you mean?"

"No matter: you must bury me here this evening, and exactly where that bird is now perched. You know the rest of my injunctions."

He then proceeded to give me several directions as to the manner in which his death might be best concealed. After these were finished, he exclaimed, "You perceive that bird?"

"Certainly."

"And the serpent writhing in her beak?"

"Doubtless: there is nothing uncommon in it; it is her natural prey.[1] But it is odd that she does not devour it."

He smiled in a ghastly manner, and said, faintly, "It is not yet time!" As he spoke, the stork flew away. My eyes followed it for a moment, it could hardly be longer than ten might be counted. I felt Darvell's weight, as it were, increase upon my shoulder, and, turning to look upon his face, perceived that he was dead!

I was shocked with the sudden certainty which could not be mistaken—his countenance in a few minutes became nearly black. I should have attributed so rapid a change to poison, had I not been aware that he had no opportunity of receiving it unperceived. The day was declining, the body was rapidly altering, and nothing remained but to fulfil his request. With the aid of Suleiman's ataghan and my own sabre, we scooped a shallow grave upon the spot which Darvell had indicated: the earth easily gave way, having already received some Mahometan tenant. We

---

1 Cf. Pliny (c. AD 23-79), *Natural History* 10.31.

dug as deeply as the time permitted us, and throwing the dry earth upon all that remained of the singular being so lately departed, we cut a few sods of greener turf from the less withered soil around us, and laid them upon his sepulchre.

Between astonishment and grief, I was tearless.

3. P.B. Shelley, "Fragment of a Ghost-Story" (1816)

> A SHOVEL of his ashes took
> From the hearth's obscurest nook,
> Muttering mysteries as she went.
> Helen and Henry knew that Granny
> Was as much afraid of ghosts as any,
>   And so they followed hard—
> But Helen clung to her brother's arm,
> And her own spasm made her shake. (3:382)

4. P.B. Shelley, "Journal at Geneva (including Ghost Stories)" (1816)

Geneva, Sunday, 18th August, 1816.

SEE Apollo's Sexton,[1] who tells us many mysteries of his trade. We talk of Ghosts. Neither Lord Byron nor M.G.L. seem to believe in them; and they both agree, in the very face of reason, that none could believe in ghosts without believing in God. I do not think that all the persons who profess to discredit these visitations, really discredit them; or, if they do in the daylight, are not admonished by the approach of loneliness and midnight, to think more respectfully of the world of shadows.

Lewis recited a poem, which he had composed at the request of the Princess of Wales.[2] The Princess of Wales, he premised, was

---

1   Byron had called M.G. Lewis this in *English Bards and Scotch Reviewers* (1809) 268.
2   Caroline of Brunswick (1768-1821) was separated from her husband, the Prince of Wales; he would attempt to divorce her for adultery when he came to the throne in 1820. Lewis's mother was one of her ladies in waiting. The poem does not seem to have survived.

not only a believer in ghosts, but in magic and witchcraft, and asserted, that prophecies made in her youth had been accomplished since. The tale was of a lady in Germany.

This lady, Minna, had been exceedingly attached to her husband, and they had made a vow that the one who died first, should return after death to visit the other as a ghost. She was sitting one day alone in her chamber, when she heard an unusual sound of footsteps on the stairs. The door opened, and her husband's spectre, gashed with a deep wound across the forehead, and in military habiliments, entered. She appeared startled at the apparition; and the ghost told her, that when he should visit her in future, she would hear a passing bell toll, and these words distinctly uttered close to her ear, "Minna, I am here." On inquiry, it was found that her husband had fallen in battle on the very day she was visited by the vision. The intercourse between the ghost and the woman continued for some time, until the latter laid aside all terror, and indulged herself in the affection which she had felt for him while living. One evening she went to a ball, and permitted her thoughts to be alienated by the attentions of a Florentine gentleman, more witty, more graceful, and more gentle, as it appeared to her, than any person she had ever seen. As he was conducting her through the dance, a death bell tolled. Minna, lost in the fascination of the Florentine's attentions, disregarded, or did not hear the sound. A second peal, louder and more deep, startled the whole company, when Minna heard the ghost's accustomed whisper, and raising her eyes, saw in an opposite mirror the reflexion of the ghost, standing over her. She is said to have died of terror.

Lewis told four other stories—all grim.

1

A YOUNG man who had taken orders, had just been presented with a living, on the death of the incumbent. It was in the Catholic part of Germany. He arrived at the parsonage on a Saturday night; it was summer, and waking about three o'clock in the morning, and it being broad day, he saw a venerable-looking man, but with an aspect exceedingly melancholy, sitting at a desk in the window, reading, and two beautiful boys standing near him, whom he regarded with looks of the profoundest grief. Presently he rose from his seat, the boys followed him, and they were no more to be seen. The young man, much troubled, arose, hesitating whether he should regard what he had seen as a dream, or a waking phantasy. To divert his dejection, he walked towards the church, which the sexton was already employed in preparing for the morning service. The first sight that struck him was a portrait, the exact resemblance of the man whom he had seen sitting in his chamber. It was the custom in this district to place the portrait of each minister, after his death, in the church.

He made the minutest inquiries respecting his predecessor, and learned that he was universally beloved, as a man of unexampled integrity and benevolence; but that he was the prey of a secret and perpetual sorrow. His grief was supposed to have arisen from an attachment to a young lady, with whom his situation did not permit him to unite himself. Others, however, asserted, that a connexion did subsist between them, and that even she occasionally brought to his house two beautiful boys, the offspring of their connexion.—Nothing further occurred until the cold weather came, and the new minister desired a fire to be lighted in the stove of the room where he slept. A hideous stench arose from the stove as soon as it was lighted, and, on examining it, the bones of two male children were found within.

2

LORD LYTTLETON[1] and a number of his friends were joined during the chase by a stranger. He was excellently mounted, and displayed such courage, or, rather so much desperate rashness, that no other person in the hunt could follow him. The gentlemen, when the chase was concluded, invited the stranger to dine with them. His conversation was something of a wonderful kind. He astonished, he interested, he commanded the attention of the most inert. As night came on, the company, being weary, began to retire one by one, much later than the usual hour: the most intellectual among them were retained latest by the stranger's fascination. As he perceived that they began to depart, he redoubled his efforts to retain them. At last, when few remained, he entreated them to stay with him; but all pleaded the fatigue of a hard day's chase, and all at last retired. They had been in bed about an hour, when they were awakened by the most horrible

---

1   Thomas Lyttleton (1744-79), second Baron Lyttleton, known as "the wicked Lord Lyttleton." On the night of 24 November 1779, he dreamed that a bird flew into his room, turned into a woman, and told him that he had only three days to live. He died suddenly on the night of 27 November.

screams, which issued from the stranger's room. Every one rushed towards it. The door was locked. After a moment's deliberation they burst it open, and found the stranger stretched on the ground, writhing with agony, and weltering in blood. On their entrance he arose, and collecting himself, apparently with a strong effort, entreated them to leave him—not to disturb him, that he would give every possible explanation in the morning. They complied. In the morning, his chamber was found vacant, and he was seen no more.

3

MILES ANDREWS,[1] a friend of Lord Lyttleton, was sitting one night alone when Lord Lyttleton came in, and informed him that he was dead, and that this was his ghost which he saw before him. Andrews pettishly told him not to play any ridiculous tricks upon him, for he was not in a temper to bear them. The ghost then departed. In the morning Andrews asked his servant at what hour Lord Lyttleton had arrived. The servant said he did not know that he had arrived, but that he would inquire. On inquiry it was found that Lord Lyttleton had not arrived, nor had the door been opened to any one during the whole night. Andrews sent to Lord Lyttleton, and discovered, that he had died precisely at the hour of the apparition.

4

A GENTLEMAN on a visit to a friend who lived on the skirts of an extensive forest in the east of Germany lost his way. He wandered for some hours among the trees, when he saw a light at a distance. On approaching it, he was surprised to observe, that it proceeded from the interior of a ruined monastery. Before he knocked he thought it prudent to look through the window. He saw a multitude of cats assembled round a small grave, four of whom were letting down a coffin with a crown upon it. The gentleman, startled at this unusual sight, and imagining that he had arrived among the retreats of fiends or witches, mounted his horse and rode away with the utmost precipitation. He arrived at his friend's house at a late hour, who had sate up for him. On his

---

1 Andrews (d. 1814), a dramatist and friend of Lyttleton, claimed that the latter had appeared to him in a dream on the night of his death.

arrival his friend questioned as to the cause of the traces of trouble visible in his face. He began to recount his adventure, after much difficulty, knowing that it was scarcely possible that his friend should give faith to his relation. No sooner had he mentioned the coffin with a crown upon it, than his friend's cat, who seemed to have been lying asleep before the fire, leaped up, saying—"Then I am the King of the Cats!" and scrambled up the chimney, and was seen no more (P.B. Shelley, *Works* 6:207-12).

Appendix B: Contemporary Reviews

1. The Vampyre

a. *Edinburgh Monthly Review* 1 (1819): 618-20

THIS audacious catchpenny was announced by all the various artifices of puffing, as the production of Lord Byron. It first made its appearance as such in a periodical work. Some qualms of terror, however, seem to have shaken the parties; as it is understood, that the leaf which contained the original introduction to the article was cancelled: and this we should think very probable, from the circumstances of all the numbers of the work now alluded to, which we have seen, having a *loose leaf*, and the publication itself, in the separate state, not having his Lordship's name!

Had the publication possessed any merit, we should have supposed that it was a sinister and malignant stratagem of some enemy of Lord Byron, to degrade his genius, and to place on record the slanders which have been maliciously attached to his name and eccentricities; but it is so evidently a stupid effort of illiterate presumption, that it could not proceed from any such *machiavelli*.[1] It consists of three parts: *"Extract of a Letter from Geneva; the Vampyre, a tale; and, an account of Lord Byron's residence in the island of Mitylene.["]*[2] We believe they have all been evacuated from the same vulgar pen. The description of the residence appeared some months ago in the newspapers, and it is really a diverting performance, for it represents Lord Byron as dancing at country weddings, and distributing Greek Testaments among the poor children! Two things, both *naturally* and *morally* improbable.

The extract of the letter from Geneva is given by way of preface, for the purpose of inducing the reader to believe, that the filthy tale which follows, was written by his Lordship. We shall quote the passage in which the insinuation is made.

"It was afterwards proposed, in the course of conversation, that each of the company present should write a tale depending upon some supernatural agency, which was undertaken by Lord

---

1 Niccolò Machiavelli (1469-1527), author of *The Prince* (1532), became proverbial for deviousness.
2 Usually called Lesbos, an island in the Ægean Sea.

Byron, the physician, and Miss M.W. Godwin. My friend, the lady above referred to, had in her possession the outline of each of these stories; I obtained them as a favour, and herewith forward them to you, as I was assured you would feel as much curiosity as myself, to peruse the *ébauches*[1] of so great a genius, and those immediately under his influence."

There is not a word here about *the Vampyre*, nor in any other part of the work is it ascribed to Lord Byron, although it was puffed in every possible mode and manner as his composition.

The tale is introduced with some account of the superstition regarding Vampyres, and by way, we suppose, of leading on the reader to think that this "ugly story"[2] is Lord Byron's, we have a long quotation from his Lordship's poem of the Giaour, in which he describes *a vampyre* with that peculiar force and vividness which throw all his imitators at such an immeasurable distance behind. Did the wretched bungler, who has foisted his own mass of putrid sentiments on the public, not perceive, that by bringing it into immediate comparison with the living and glowing images of genius, he furnished the most effectual exposure of the imposition, which the admirers of Lord Byron's works could desire? But now for the tale. The opening furnishes a good specimen of the *elegance* with which it is written.

[The reviewer here quotes the opening sentences: "It happened ... could not pass" (39).]

A dead eye striking on a cheek is certainly a new idea, but the metallic addition is decidedly in the Bathos. Were Lord Byron able to pen such "monstrous rodomontade,"[3] what must be thought of those who have applauded him as the greatest poetical genius of the age?

Not only, however, in the style, but in the incidents, is the fraud manifest. It is well known that Lord Byron spent a long time, at different periods, in Athens. None knows the environs of that famous city better than his Lordship. But the author of the Vampyre has evidently never been there; or, if he has been at the town, he is ignorant of the country around it,—for he speaks of forests and other gener-

---

1 "Rough drafts" (French).
2 Possibly from Samuel Richardson (1689-1761), *Pamela* (1740-41), vol. 2: The Journal Continued: Friday; or M.G. Lewis (1775-1818), *The Castle Spectre* (1797) 1.1.
3 From the Introduction to *The Vampyre*.

alities of scenery which have no existence in its neighbourhood. Is it at all likely, that Lord Byron, who is so prone to give local descriptions, in which he excels, would have committed such a blunder as this? On the contrary, is it not probable that his Lordship, in laying a scene under the shade of trees in the environs of Athens, would have spoken of the celebrated and immortal olive groves? and that at least some local feature would have been noticed in incidents which are supposed to have happened in Greece? The following passage is the most correct in point of language in the book. Let our readers judge for themselves if such trash could have escaped from the poetical pencil of the author of the Bride of Abydos.

[The reviewer here quotes "Having left Rome ... of an epicure" (44-45).]

But why should we waste time in animadverting on a performance which, but for its slanderous gossiping, and the tricks used to attach it to a distinguished name, we should not have noticed. As a literary essay, it is void of all merit as to style, and the subject and incidents are quite odious. The fostering embraces of "the dead and alive" monster that it describes, could not be more disgusting. Let us have done with it.

b. *Monthly Review* 89 (May-August 1819): 87-96

THE origin of this tale, which has been improperly advertized with the name of Lord Byron as its author, is explained in an "extract of a letter from Geneva," inserted as a preface. After having stated Lord Byron's intimacy with several families in the neighbourhood of Geneva, the writer proceeds:

"It appears that one evening Lord B., Mr. P.B. Shelly, two ladies, and a gentleman who travelled with his Lordship as physician, after having perused a German work, entitled Phantasmagoriana, began relating ghost stories; when his Lordship having recited the beginning of Christabel, then unpublished, the whole took so strong a hold of Mr. Shelly's mind, that he suddenly started up and ran out of the room. The physician and Lord Byron followed, and discovered him leaning against a mantle-piece, with cold drops of perspiration trickling down his face. After having given him something to refresh him, upon enquiring into the cause of his alarm, they found that his wild imagination having pictured to him the bosom of one of the ladies with eyes, (which was reported of a lady in the neighbour-hood where he lived,) he was obliged to leave the room in order to destroy the impression. It was afterwards proposed, in the course of conversation, that each of the company present should write a tale depending upon some supernatural agency, which was undertaken by Lord B., the physician, and one of the ladies before mentioned. I obtained the outline of each of these stories as a great favour, and herewith forward them to you, as I was assured you would feel as much curiosity as myself, to peruse the *ébauches* of so great a genius, and those immediately under his influence."

The composition of the lady here introduced is the extrava-gant story of Frankenstein, which we noticed with brief censure in our Number for April 1818; and it was intended that we should consider the present tale as the *pic-nic* contribution of his Lordship: but a letter has been since published by Dr. Polidori, (the physician, we believe, mentioned in the above relation,) stating that the ground-work of the story only is Lord Byron's property, while the developement belongs to the Doctor.

The superstition, on which the tale is founded, universally prevailed less than a century ago, throughout Hungary, Moravia, Silesia, and Poland; and the legends to which it gave rise were not only believed, but were made the subject of learned disputations by the divines and physicians of the times. In Dr. Henry More's Philosophical Works,[1] and in Calmet's Dissertation on Appari-tions,[2] may be found many interesting particulars relating to this fancy; and in the latter is an ample account of its origin and progress. It was imagined that men, who had been dead for some time, rose out of their graves and sucked the blood of their neigh-bours, principally the young and beautiful: that these objects of their attack became pale and livid, and frequently died; while the vampyres themselves, on their graves being opened, were found as fresh as if they were alive, and their veins full of good and florid blood, which also issued from the nose, mouth, and ears, and even through the very pores of the skin. The only mode of arrest-ing the pranks of these tormentors was by driving a stake through the heart of the vampyre; a practice frequently adopted, and

1 Henry More (1614-87), author of *Philosophical Poems* (1647) and *Divine Dialogues* (1668).
2 Augustin Calmet (1672-1757), *Dissertations sur les apparitions des anges, des démons et des esprits, et sur les revenants et vampires de Hongrie, de Moravie et de Silesie* (1746).

during the performance of which, we are told, he uttered a horrid groan. The body was then burned, and the ashes thrown into the grave. The introduction states that this superstition is very general in the East, and is also common among the Arabians; and it contains the following account of a particular case of vampyrism, which is described as having occurred at Madreyga, in Hungary:

"It appears, that upon an examination of the commander-in-chief and magistrates of the place, they positively and unanimously affirmed, that, about five years before, a certain Heyduke, named Arnold Paul, had been heard to say, that, at Cassovia, on the frontiers of the Turkish Servia, he had been tormented by a vampyre, but had found a way to rid himself of the evil, by eating some of the earth out of the vampyre's grave, and rubbing himself with his blood. This precaution, however, did not prevent him from becoming a vampyre[1] himself; for, about twenty or thirty days after his death and burial, many persons complained of having been tormented by him, and a deposition was made, that four persons had been deprived of life by his attacks. To prevent further mischief, the inhabitants, having consulted their Hadagni,[2] took up the body, and found it (as is supposed to be usual in cases of vampyrism) fresh, and entirely free from corruption, and emitting at the mouth, nose, and ears, pure and florid blood. Proof having been thus obtained, they resorted to the accustomed remedy. A stake was driven entirely through the heart and body of Arnold Paul, at which he is reported to have cried out as dreadfully as if he had been alive. This done, they cut off his head, burned his body, and threw the ashes into his grave. The same measures were adopted with the corses of those persons who had previously died from vampyrism, lest they should, in their turn, become agents upon others who survived them."[3]

In the *Athenæum*, a periodical publication circulated a few years since, and the discontinuance of which was a source of regret to all who were acquainted with the liberality and talents displayed in it, an allusion was made to this tale, accompanied by the subsequent remark:

---

1 The universal belief is, that a person sucked by a vampyre becomes a vampyre himself, and sucks in his turn. [Note in the original.]
2 Chief bailiff. [Note in the original.]
3 For a fuller version of the story of Arnold Paul, see Barber 15-20.

"This horrible account caused a good deal of conversation about the time when it first appeared. In page 750. of the same volume, [of the *Gentleman's Magazine*, from which it was quoted,] we find a humorous number of the paper called the Craftsman, on the conceit that the whole story of the vampyres was but a political allegory: that Arnold Paul, the heyduke, was a minister of state, and his blood the treasure he had sucked out of the public funds, &c. &c. &c.; and in page 755. is a grave attempt to reason on the causes of so uncommon a superstition.

"It is certain that dead bodies have occasionally been dug out of the earth, which, after lying for as many years, or more, as the heyduke is said to have lain *days*, have exhibited appearances as extraordinary as those attributed to these vampyres."

If we remember rightly, the body of the unfortunate Charles I., when lately found in the vault at Windsor, bore some peculiar marks with regard to the running of blood from his neck, and the growth of his hair; which, had the discovery had been made in a more superstitious age, would have afforded matter for much speculation among priests and old women.[1]

The visitations of these vampyres were said to be sometimes unattended by the sucking of blood, and were then merely considered as ominous of the speedy death of the persons to whom they appeared. These were evidently nothing more than the visions of a distempered imagination; to be placed on a level with the stories of previous warnings of a similar nature, to which many persons even now, and particularly our friends in the North, unhesitatingly pin their faith.

That great naturalist, Linné,[2] was induced to give the name of Vampyre Bat to a particular variety of that animal, which he imagined to be the species that was stated to suck the blood of men and cattle. The late Dr. Shaw, in his Zoology,[3] says that it is generally about a foot long, with wings extending about four feet, but is sometimes found larger; and it has been reported that specimens have been seen of six feet in extent. It has four cutting teeth both above and below, and the canine teeth are large and sharp: the tongue is pointed, and terminated by sharp prickles; and this tongue it is supposed to insert into the vein of a sleeping

---

1 Cf. Byron, "Windsor Poetics," discussed in the Introduction (11-12).
2 Karl Linné or Carolus Linnæus (1707-78), founder of modern botanical taxonomy; author of *Systema naturae* (1735; 10th ed. 1758), *Genera plantarum* (1737), and *Species plantarum* (1753).
3 George Shaw (1751-1813), *General Zoology* (1800-12).

person in so peculiar a manner as not to excite pain; fanning the air at the same time with its wings, by which means the sleep is rendered still more profound.[1] Dr. Shaw observes that this extraordinary statement is so solemnly related, and seemingly so well authenticated, as almost to enforce belief; and he proceeds to mention the accounts of Condamine, respecting the large bats of America, which destroyed all the great cattle introduced by the missionaries: of Bontius and Nieuhoff, relative to those of Java; of Gumilla, concerning those of the banks of the Orinoco; of P. Martyr, who speaks in the same terms of the bats of the Isthmus of Darien; and, lastly, he adds that "the self-same faculty has been time out of mind attributed to the common European bats."[2]

Let us, however, return to the tale before us; in which the natives of England are now first made subject to the horrible attacks of Vampyres. This is not the only novelty, however, which has been introduced. As far as the present legends on the subject go, we do not find that these unwelcome guests pay more than solitary visits, or have been considered in any other light than as troubled spirits who make their offensive appearance and terrible attack, and then, nightly, return to their graves: but the author of

---

1 Polidori knew this account of the vampire bat's *modus operandi*; in "Chatterton to his Sister," he draws on it in an epic simile for the behaviour of seducers (in another example of his eroticization of vampirism):

> As vampire bat excites a breeze
> Soft, cooling, lulling to repose
> The child whose life's blood quickly flows,
> Feeding the filthy beast with all
> A mother's fondest name may call. (*Ximenes* 138)

2 Charles Marie de La Condamine (1701-74), French soldier, mathematician, and naturalist, who explored South America 1735-45 and published his *Journal du voyage* in 1751; Jacobus Bontius or Jakob de Bondt (1592-1631), Dutch physician and naturalist; Jan Nieuhoff ([1618-72], said to be the first person to put milk in his coffee), who travelled to China as Dutch ambassador in 1655 and published *An Embassy from the East-India Company ... to the Grand Tartar Cham Emperor of China* in 1665; Joseph Gumilla (1686-1750), Jesuit missionary, who travelled extensively along the Orinoco from 1716 to 1737, and published a natural and civil history of the region; Peter Martyr (1457-1526), who in 1516 published an account of the expedition of Vasco Nuñez de Balboa (c. 1475-1519) to Darien (1510-13) entitled *De orbo novo decades cum Legatione Babylonica*, or just "Decades."

this tale has made the vampyre-hero of it a bustling inhabitant of the world; restless and erratic; a nobleman subject to disappointments,—to pecuniary embarrassments, (p. 32. [41])—and even to death (p. 55. [51]). We have still another peculiarity in the description of his appearance. His face is depicted in the tale as of a *"deadly hue, which never gained a warmer tint;"* and this in direct opposition to the account of a vampyre's complexion, which is reported, by those who are learnedly cognizant of the fact, to be florid, healthy, and full of blood. For the gratification of such persons as have always made Lord B. the hero of his own tale, we extract the whole of this introductory picture; for which we doubt not they will say that he sat, when the writer formed the ground-work of the tale.

[A summary of the tale, with copious quotations, follows.]

Such is the outline of this tale; in which, whatever may be the opinion of our readers as to its general merit and interest, they will perceive several passages that are forcible, elegant, and effective. Criticism cannot look minutely on a composition produced as this was for a temporary and social purpose, with no view to be exposed to its scrutiny.

2. *Ernestus Berchtold; or, The Modern Œdipus*

a. *Edinburgh Monthly Review* 4 (1820): 727-35

DR. Polidori is aware that he cannot decently appear before the public, without making certain explanations, touching a transaction, in which it is hard to say, whether dulness or impudence was most conspicuous. The publication of that vile abortion, "The Vampyre," under the name of the greatest of living geniuses, was a wrong which we were among the first to expose, and which it will not be easy for the perpetrator to expiate. The attempt at explanation, made by him in his preface to the present volume, is quite unsuccessful. This doctor tells us, that he left his Vampyre with a lady, that "from thence,—to use his own immaculate phraseology—it appears to have fallen into the hands of some person who sent it to the editor, in such a way as to leave it so doubtful from his words, whether it was his Lordship's (Lord Byron's,) or not, that I found some difficulty in vindicating it to myself. These circumstances," this worthy person adds, "were stated in a letter sent to the Morning Chronicle, three days after the publication of the tale—but, in consequence of the publishers representing to me, that they were compromised as well as myself, and that immediately they were certain it was mine, that they themselves would wish to make the *amende honorable* to the public, I allowed them to recal the letter which had lain some days at that paper's office." We have no doubt, our readers are satisfied, by the perusal of these passages, that Dr. Polidori is both a very candid and a very elegant writer.

We cannot imagine what mental disease could induce Lord Byron to endure for a moment the uncongenial dulness of such an author as this, or how he should have been betrayed into the foolery of writing the fragment[1] published, along with Mazeppa,[2]—a composition which might have formed no unworthy companion to the Vampyre itself. Dr. Polidori, indeed, can get up a flat and feeble tale of preternatural horrors, which, in the simple particular of revolting combinations, shall outdo the inspired ferocity of the noble bard himself—but so could any assignable blockhead, who ruminates within the purlieus of Grub Street. Nothing easier than to catch the common-place and the grossness of these things—nothing more difficult than to extract their poetry. The fact is, that all our unimaginative dealers in monstrous things, are just dull grown-up persons, who fearlessly resume the dress of infancy to propitiate the weaker portion of their fellow adults—while the secret of the disciples of the new morality—for they are kindred schools of one great establishment of dulness—is that they boldly appear among well clothed persons, *in puris naturalibus*[3]—and give free utterance to the sentiments which linger about every imagination, but which it is the prime object of all moral training to subdue. There is nothing original or inventive about either; the one merely remembers what abler men would rather forget; the other only dares to express what better men blush even to feel. It may, and sometimes does happen, that men of great power stoop to a course so unworthy of them, and lavish on it the splendours of their genius; but even in their hands it fails of its aim—and while the display may extort our passing wonder, it will infallibly provoke our deep and lasting aversion.

---

1 Appendix A.2.
2 A poem by Byron (1819), to which his publisher, John Murray, appended his Fragment (Appendix A.2), to distinguish it from *The Vampyre*.
3 "Stark naked" (Latin).

The author before us is an avowed experimentalist in supernatural story; for he tells us, in his introduction, that he "had agreed to write a supernatural tale; and that does not," he adds, "allow of a completely every-day narrative." Now, we do not recollect to have seen a more tame or "every-day" narrative than this of Ernestus Berchtold. "I am afraid," the Dr. observes, "that though I have thrown the superior agency into the back ground as much as was in my power, still, that many readers will think the same moral, and the same colouring, might have been given to characters acting under the ordinary agencies of life,"—which is quite true; and the author himself confesses that it is so; but he "had agreed to write a supernatural tale." The *nec deus intersit*[1] is thus intrepidly violated—but it is well; for if there had been in his story a single knot which it was beyond the dexterity of the most inexperienced boarding-school miss to untie, Dr. Polidori is not the man to have called down a divinity adequate to its solution.

This story, which begins with a pretty extended course of wandering in the Alps—of which the ground has been so duly trodden, and the region so thickly peopled by the common scribblers of romance—ends with the attractive spectacle of a double incest consummated at Mittau—this being the delicate sort of interest which the students of strong emotion love to excite.— The mother of the hero Ernestus Berchtold, arrives, it matters not when, at the village of Beatenberg, on the lake of Thun, accompanied by an aged man, bleeding from his wounds, whom she carefully, but ineffectually tends; and soon after his death, she herself expires in giving birth to Berchtold and his sister Julia. The unfriended innocents devolve, of course, as a legacy on the worthy pastor of the parish, by whom they are adopted, and who afterwards explains to them the fate of their mother, over whose grave they hold many mysterious musings. The vicinity of the Alps makes Berchtold a hunter, of course—and has also tempted Dr. Polidori to indulge in much bad description and silly bombastic reflections. The French, in the mean time, opportunely invade Switzerland; and instantly the author overwhelms us with the novel details of partizan warfare—surprises, military tribunals, dungeons, moonlight deliverances by means of impossible excavations, and convenient boats,—mysteriously chained to the sides of lakes. In one of his excursions in the Wengern Alps,

---

1   "And let no god intervene [unless a knot come worthy of such a deliverer]" (Latin): Horace, *Ars Poetica* 191, tr. H. Rushton Fairclough.

Berchtold meets an aged man, accompanied by a young female, whose appearance makes so strange an impression on him, and is so incoherently described, that we really did not know for some time whether we had been introduced to a *bona fide* human creature, or to one of Dr. Polidori's "superior agencies." This delightful vision, however, finds a voice to address the intrepid hunter; and to reproach him with his supineness, while Switzerland was struggling with her fate. Such a monitor could not of course be disobeyed: Berchtold repairs to the rendezvous of Swiss patriotism—assumes the command of the peasantry of his native parish—performs at least the ordinary quantum of heroic exploit—sees Swiss valour extinguished by French discipline—and at last, by the treachery of a servant, finds himself safely immured in the deepest cell of a state prison, many fathoms beneath the waters of the surrounding lake. But neither nature nor art can oppose an obstacle to the wonder-working fancy of a romance writer. A file and a knife presented to him by a child, and a boat stationed by invisible hands, enable Berchtold to triumph over the terrors of his state prison—to pierce the solid rock, and pass the envious waters. He again reaches his native village—but only to witness the last solemn rites performed over his adopted father, and to find himself and his sister rendered orphans in the world. Fortune, however, again interposes in his behalf. Count Filiberto Doni, an Italian nobleman of splendid fortune, had a son, Olivieri, who, in the enthusiasm of youthful courage, had borne a distinguished part in Switzerland's unequal struggle—had fought side by side with Berchtold—and had more than once owed his life to the enterprise and valour of his companion. The grateful father resolves to supply the place of the deceased pastor to the orphans;—they remove to Milan, and share the splendours of his palace; and Berchtold is delighted to recognize in Louisa,—the daughter of Doni, and the sister of his friend,—the beautiful vision of the Wengern Alps, which had never faded from his memory, amid all the vicissitudes of fortune. But it is here his deeper sorrows begin. Olivieri, thoughtless and unprincipled, runs the full career of vice—seduces Berchtold into the abysses of gambling, and contrives, in the interim, to accomplish a yet more fatal seduction—that of Julia, whom he deserts, of course, in her shame, and leaves to die in a hovel. Then he joins a gang of banditti; is seized, and about to pay the forfeit of his crimes, when the forgiving hero of this well-constructed tale undertakes, at the solicitation of the elder Doni, a mission to save the life of his sister's destroyer,—and miraculously succeeds. Berchtold is at last rewarded with the hand of Louisa; but it is only to see her die of a disease, which deferred hope and the errors of her lover had implanted in her frame. Before this fatal event, an accident occurred, which led to the terrible development upon which the story hinges. Berchtold had brought out the portrait of his mysterious mother, to be placed beside that of the father of his Louisa; and Doni, on seeing it, is struck with despair—buries himself in his chamber, and soon after dies,—having first put into the hands of Berchtold, a paper narrating the history of his life, and revealing his fatal secret.

Doni, it seems, had in his youth become passionately attached to a lady, whose affections were previously engaged. He abandoned Italy, and proceeded to the east in quest of mercantile adventure and riches; became acquainted with the individual who possessed the affections of his mistress; joined with him in speculations which brought ruin upon both; was robbed by Arabs in an encounter in which his rival was severely wounded, and left on the field; saved from the sword of the marauders an aged fellow-traveller, who revealed to him the secret of his intercourse with a demon, which he had the power of summoning at any time to supply him with unbounded riches, upon the single condition that some dreadful domestic calamity should be the penalty of each conjuration. Doni closes with the terms of the old man, and his familiar spirit—becomes suddenly and immensely rich—returns to Italy elated with the prospect of gaining his mistress;—and for this purpose fabricates a nefarious story of the actual death of his rival—and succeeds in his object. But the dead man, as might have been expected, reappears, and has an interview with Matilda—that is the lady's name—of which Doni gets intelligence, and becomes frantic. This abused woman, unable to bear the presence of a man by whom she had been undone, resolves to quit Milan in the company of her father. Doni pursuing and overtaking the fugitives—and, mistaking his wife's companion for his own rival, fires into the carriage—mortally wounds the old man—and thus dispatches the bleeding and dying party to the village of Beatenberg, where they are found at the beginning of the book. The sight of Matilda's picture reveals to him the horrors which his guilt had wrought among his children; the double incest of Olivieri and Julia, Berchtold and Louisa;—and the author, with tragic gracefulness, thus disposes of his characters one after another by death, with the exception of the villain Olivieri,[1]

---

1 The reviewer evidently missed the account of Olivieri's death (142-43).

whose fate is left untold—and of the forlorn hero of the tale, who is made to tell his own story with appropriate anguish.

Such is this silly tale, of which the *disjecta membra*[1] lie scattered over any circulating library in the kingdom, and which assuredly stood in no need of that "superior agency" which Dr. Polidori imagines he has a talent for managing, but which is far, very far indeed, beyond his pitch. As this very stupid work seems to have been written with the express view of developing this peculiarity in the Dr.'s genius, it is proper that the reader should see what sort of thing it is—and duly admire the presumption of this exceedingly common-place person. We believe the following passages contain all the "superior agency" which the Dr.'s "agreement" to write a tale, "that does not allow of a completely every day narrative" has been able to produce.

[The reviewer here quotes from three parts of the narrative; pp. 123-24, pp. 132-35, and pp. 164-65.]

And this is the actual compass of Dr. Polidori's magic, to explain the very common occurrence, of a villain entailing disgrace upon himself, and bringing destruction on his offspring.

We have already alluded to the fantastic descriptions, and bad rhetoric of this author—and were it worth while, we could select paragraphs without number in proof of our assertion,—but the task would be an unprofitable one.

The perusal of this volume has, we confess, left a painful impression on our minds of the extent to which the vice of scribbling is carried in this our age—mingled too with a reasonable share of compassion for those who are seduced by the glare of literary reputation, from the honest beaten paths of life—and whom it were real mercy to chastise in their wanderings, if any chastisement could reclaim them. When we say this, we are not forgetful of Swift's ingenious story of the mountebank in Leicester Fields, and the corpulent individual who—while he occupied with his own person the space which rightfully belonged to his neighbour—was the most vehement to complain of encroachment.[2] We remember that we ourselves render no illiberal contribution to the general mass of printed intelligence—but our walk

---

1 "Scattered remains" (Latin): cf. Horace, *Satires* 1.4.62.
2 Jonathan Swift (1667-1745), Introduction, *A Compleat Collection of Genteel and Ingenious Conversation &c* (1738).

is less ambitious, and we should hope rather more useful, than that of persons who essay to climb the heaven of invention, and, like the author before us, tumble down with such melancholy and hideous ruin. It is indeed surprising, that while so many majestic spirits occupy the summits of the temple of fame, there should be found persons like the present, so presumptuous as to knock their addle pates against its base. The alternate pangs of difficult delivery and swift-coming disappointment, which they are fated to endure, render this class of persons the objects of the most sincere commiseration. The fancy of the poet alone can realize a Dr. Polidori in the agony of his supernatural parturitions, or the alternate anguish of deploring his still-born progeny.

> He gnawed his pen, then dashed it on the ground,
> Sinking from thought to thought—a vast profound,
> Plunged for his sense, but found no bottom there,
> Yet wrote and floundered on in mere despair.
> Round him much embryo, much abortion lay,
> Much future ode, and abdicated play;
> Nonsense precipitate, like running lead,
> That slipped thro' cracks, and zig-zags of the head,
> All that on folly, frenzy could beget,
> Fruits of dull heat, and sooterkins of wit.[1]

And for what reason is all this folly acted by a plain dull man, vainly endeavouring to escape from his own native sphere? Why, for the laudable purpose of raking together the sweepings of the Minerva Press,[2] and circulating libraries—of delighting and improving the world, by the delicate exhibition of a *partie quarrée*[3] of incest—and of nicknaming a stupid story, the modern Œdipus, only we suppose because Mr. Shelly has chosen to designate one of *his* reveries the modern Prometheus.[4]

---

1 Alexander Pope (1688-1744), *The Dunciad* (1743) 1.117-26.
2 A publishing house, established in 1790 by William Lane (1745?-1814), that was notorious for producing Gothic fiction.
3 "Four-handed game" (French).
4 Like many contemporaries, the reviewer assumes that P.B. Shelley had written the anonymous *Frankenstein*.

b. *European Magazine* 76 (1819): 534-36

IF it be one of the highest faculties of invention to combine the natural with the marvellous, and to develope the human charac-ter with the consistency of truth, in a sphere of action beyond the range of possibility, this extraordinary tale may claim no obscure place in the department of literature to which it belongs. In regard to the nature of its subject, it may be said to hold the same rank among novels which is assigned in the drama to the Œdipus Tyrannus of Sophocles, or to Horace Walpole's play, called "The Mysterious Mother."[1] But the case of Ernestus Berchtold differs essentially from that of the Theban prince, and is less revolting in its circumstances than that which forms the basis of Lord Orford's masterly, but dreadful tragedy. That subjects of this kind are more fitted for narrative than for dramatic representation, is a truth of which every reader will, we think, be convinced, who compares the impression left on his mind by the two plays above mentioned, with that which the present story is calculated to produce. It developes the origin and progress of an innocent love, which is blasted in its consummation by a sudden and accidental discovery, that the parties are connected through ties of consan-guinity, incompatible with a more intimate union. No moderate degree of skill was required to detail such a story in a manner consistent with the purest delicacy, and at the same time to render it capable of exciting strong sympathetic emotions, and of conveying an important moral lesson. In his aim at these impor-tant objects, Dr. Polidori appears to have eminently succeeded; and it is gratifying to observe with what ease he has vanquished those difficulties in his subject, which might have dismayed a less daring spirit.

The scene opens in Switzerland ...

[A summary of the plot follows, quoting "I determined once more ... confronted with him" (86-87) and "Louisa's image was ... her maid. She recovered" (126-28).]

The catastrophe has been already adverted to; and we shall only add, that although deeply pathetic, it is the only conclusion

---

1 Sophocles (496-06 BC), *Œdipus Tyrannus*, and Horace Walpole, later Earl of Orford (1717-97), *The Mysterious Mother* (1768). Byron was a great admirer of Walpole's tragedy (*CPW* 4:305).

to which the reader, on considering the peculiar circumstances of the case, can reconcile his feelings.

c. *Literary Gazette* 136 (28 August 1819): 546-48

THIS is another of the semi-sentimental semi-supernatural productions to which we are now so prone,—the prose Byroniads which infect the times. The style is good, and the story as horrible as the greatest lovers of raw-head and bloody-bones can desire. It relates to a double incest, which is indeed so readily foreseen in the earlier pages, that the second part of the title might have been spared, and into the author's mouth the words of Terence be put, "*Davus sum non Œdipus.*"[1] .

An introduction states Berchtold to be one (and we are happy to believe the last) of the three tales engendered by a travelling junto of our country-folks, who agreed to write each a story founded on some superstition. Frankenstein by Godwin's Daughter, Shelley's Wife, was the first; the Vampyre, of which we have a poor piece at the end of Mazeppa, and a surreptitious whole by Dr. Polidori, instead of its planner Lord Byron, in a separate form, the second; and this novel the third. Frankenstein described the adventures of a man who had succeeded in creating another human being: the Vampyre those of a mysterious monster which sustains a post-humated life by sucking the blood of virgins:—and Berchtold unfolds the wretched fate of one possessing the power of immeasurable wealth, at the cost, however, of a heavy calamity every time that he invokes the aid of the spirit which assists him. The Vampyre forgery is not very clearly or satisfactorily accounted for. Dr. P. seems, in the vulgar phrase, to have done the trick; or else he has been egregiously tricked himself: but we presume that all the parties made money by that transaction, and have no reason to complain even if the noble Poet takes leave to damn them to everlasting fame for their pains. They will deserve their niche much better than the British Review, which has indignantly repelled his Lordship's cruel and unjust insinuation of its being influenced by bribery.[2] This it utterly denies; and we must say, that such calumnies, if

---

1 "I'm Davus, not Œdipus" (Latin): Terence, *The Lady of Andros* (167 BC) 194. In context, the speaker uses this phrase to announce that he is not good at riddles.

2 Byron, *Don Juan* 1 (1819) 209-10.

unfounded, are too unprincipled and infamous to pass for jests. Character is all that review or man has of value, and he that robs either of that commodity by falsehood, is a robber of the basest kind. We deem it right to observe this much, because, being struck with the fact in Don Juan, and never questioning that it had truth for its basis, we admitted the charge against the British Review into our columns; and it is but candour to a contemporary, to give place to its utter contradiction. We now turn to the novel before us.

[The reviewer here summarizes the plot.]

Such is the outline of this romance; and, allowing for the improbability implied in the supernatural agency, it seems to us to be well constructed and ably written. The incidents are perhaps rather meagrely related, in comparison with the lavish display of language upon the sentiments: but this is the immutable genius of the school to which Berchtold belongs. Generally speaking, however, its delineations are powerful, and we are glad to say, that we observe little of those principles which we reprehended in the author's first work (On the Sources of Positive Pleasure: see Literary Gazette, No. 81, Aug. 8, 1818, page 502, in our volume for that year.)[1] That publication we have been assured, indeed, was rather a joke than the enforcement of genuine opinions; but it was too grave to pass muster in that way, and we do not regret that our strictures have induced Dr. Polidori to be more guarded, if not more moral.

We will now quote a few passages from the Modern Œdipus, to enable the public to judge how far our remarks are worthy of acceptation. When at Milan the tenets of the Swiss orphans are attacked by the philosophers of that place, and speaking of Olivieri, we have a spirited and fine defence of the Catholic religion in opposition to Atheism.

[The reviewer here quotes a passage from pp. 105-06 ("His opinions were ... and future hope.").]

Pursuing the argument we are told of Ernestus himself.

---

1 In this philosophical treatise, heavily influenced by *Childe Harold's Pilgrimage*, Polidori gave offence by arguing that the imagination was the only source of pleasure.

[The reviewer quotes "I at last was bewildered ... a man's faith in his existence" (107-08).]

This is the only one of the author's sophisms which we shall cite. Strange that a man of common understanding should not perceive that in comparison to *infinity*, the smallest particle is as great as a universe, and therefore a single individual as important as a nation of men! Among the suitors of Louisa is a portrait, which we think will be recognized, when it is called to mind that Dr. P. was the domestic or travelling physician with Lord Byron.

[The reviewer quotes the introduction of Count Wilhelm: "The apartment was ... in Doni's palace" (117-18).]

Julia watching Count Doni to discover his secret power, affords a fair specimen of the author's manner.

[The reviewer quotes "she hoped, if ... seeking her seducer" (132-35).]

In aiming at the utmost effect, we are sometimes disgusted by images loathsomely particular. For example, the death of Louisa:

[The reviewer quotes "She held my hand ... any longer there" (151), including "there were two flies already revelling on those lips, and she could not chase them."]

This resembles Lord Byron's dogs gnawing the dead[1]—but our readers will judge of the rest for themselves, as Berchtold is a book which we would recommend as original and interesting—therefore deserving of perusal.

---

1 Byron, *The Siege of Corinth* (1816) 454-65.

Works Cited and Recommended Reading

Primary

Works of John William Polidori

The Diary of John William Polidori, 1816, Relating to Byron, Shelley, etc. Ed. William Michael Rossetti. London: Elkin Mathews, 1911.

Disputatio Medica Inauguralis, quaedam de Morbo, Oneirodynia Dicto. Diss. Edinburgh, 1815.

Ernestus Berchtold; or, The Modern Oedipus. London: Longman, Hurst, Rees, Orme, and Brown, 1819.

An Essay upon the Source of Positive Pleasure. London: Longman, Hurst, Rees, Orme, and Brown, 1818.

The Fall of the Angels: A Sacred Poem. London: John Warren, 1821.

Sketches Illustrative of the Manners and Costumes of France, Switzerland, and Italy. Sketches by R. Bridgens. London: Baldwin, Cradock, and Joy, Hatchard and Son, 1821.

The Vampyre: A Tale. London: Sherwood, Neely, and Jones, 1819.

Ximenes, The Wreath, and Other Poems. London: Longman, Hurst, Rees, Orme, and Brown, 1819.

Reviews

The Vampyre

La Belle Assemblée supp. 20 (1819): 334-37.

British Lady's Magazine 3rd ser. 3 (July 1819): 31-34.

Edinburgh Monthly Review 1 (1819): 618-20.

Fireside Magazine 1 (1819): 231, 233-34, 265.

Kaleidoscope 1 (13 April 1819): 149-50.

Lady's Monthly Museum 3rd ser. 9 (1819): 282-87.

Literary Journal and General Miscellany 2 (1819): 214, 267-73.

Monthly Magazine 47 (1819): 345.

Monthly Review 89 (1819): 87-96.

Theatre; or, Dramatic and Literary Mirror 1 (1819): 149-52, 166-69.

Ernestus Berchtold

La Belle Assemblée ns 20 (December 1819): 280-83.
Edinburgh Monthly Review 4 (1820): 727-35.
European Magazine 76 (1819): 534-36.
London Literary Gazette, and Journal of Belles Lettres, Arts, Sciences, etc. (1819): 546-48.
Monthly Review ns 91 (1820): 215.

Edition

The Vampyre and Ernestus Berchtold; or, The Modern Œdipus: *Collected Fiction of John William Polidori.* Toronto: U of Toronto P, 1994.

Other Primary Texts

Aeschylus. *Plays: One.* Ed. J. Michael Walton. Trans. Frederic Raphael and Kenneth McLeish. London: Methuen Drama, 1991.

Byron, George Gordon Noel. *Byron's Letters and Journals.* Ed. Leslie A. Marchand. 12 vols. London: John Murray, 1973-82. Cited as *BLJ.*

——. *The Complete Miscellaneous Prose.* Ed. Andrew Nicholson. Oxford: Clarendon, 1991.

——. *The Complete Poetical Works.* Ed. Jerome J. McGann. 7 vols. Oxford: Clarendon, 1980-92. Cited by line numbers, or as *CPW.*

Calmet, Augustine [*sic*]. *The Phantom World: The History and Philosophy of Spirits, Apparitions, &c. &c.* Ed. Henry Christmas. Philadelphia: A. Hart, late Carey and Hart, 1850.

Coleridge, Samuel Taylor. *Poetical Works.* Ed. Ernest Hartley Coleridge. London: Oxford UP, 1967.

Dante Alighieri. *The Divine Comedy.* Trans. and commentary Charles S. Singleton. Bollingen Series 80. 6 vols. Princeton, NJ: Princeton UP, 1970-75.

Dryden, John. *The Works of John Dryden.* Gen. eds. Edward Niles Hooker, H.T. Swedenberg, Jr., Alan Roper, and Vinton A. Dearing. 19 vols. Berkeley: U of California P, 1956-84.

Frayling, Christopher, ed. *Vampyres: Lord Byron to Count Dracula.* London: Faber, 1991.

[Hone, William.] *Don Juan: With a Biographical Account of Lord Byron and his Family: Anecdotes of his Lordship's Travels and Residence in Greece, at Geneva, &c. Including, also, a Sketch of the Vampyre Family*. London: William Wright, 1819.

Lamb, Lady Caroline. *Glenarvon*. 1816. Ed. Frances Wilson. London: Everyman, 1995.

Lewis, Matthew Gregory. *The Monk: A Romance*. 1796. Ed. D.L. Macdonald and Kathleen Scherf. Peterborough: Broadview, 2004.

Mallet du Pan, Jacques. *The History of the Destruction of the Helvetic Union and Liberty*. 2nd American ed. Boston: Printed by Manning and Loring for J. Nancrede, 1799.

Merivale, John Herman. *Poems Original and Translated*. 1828. Rpt. Introd. Donald H. Reiman. New York: Garland, 1978.

Moore, Thomas. *Life of Lord Byron: With His Letters and Journals*. New ed. 6 vols. London: John Murray, 1854.

Rice, Anne. *Interview with the Vampire*. 1976. Rpt. New York: Ballantine Books, 1977.

Rousseau, Jean-Jacques, and Johann Gottfried Herder. *On the Origin of Language*. Trans. John H. Moran and Alexander Gode. Milestones of Thought. New York: Frederick Ungar, 1966.

Schiller, Johann Christoph Friedrich Yon. *Wilhelm Tell*. Trans. and introd. Gilbert J. Jordan. The Library of Liberal Arts. Indianapolis: Bobbs-Merrill, 1964.

Scott, Walter. *Guy Mannering; or, The Astrologer*. London: Dent, 1906.

Shelley, Mary Wollstonecraft. *Frankenstein; or, The Modern Prometheus*. [1818 ed.] Ed. D.L. Macdonald and Kathleen Scherf. 2nd ed. Peterborough: Broadview, 1999.

Shelley, Percy Bysshe. *The Works of Percy Bysshe Shelley, in Verse and Prose. Now first brought together with many pieces not before published*. Ed. Harry Buxton Forman. 8 vols. London: Reeves and Turner, 1880.

——. *Shelley's Poetry and Prose*. Ed. Donald H. Reiman and Sharon B. Powers. New York: Norton, 1977.

Sheridan, Frances. *Memoirs of Miss Sidney Bidulph, Extracted from Her Own Journal, and Now First Published*. Introd. Sue Townsend. Mothers of the Novel. London: Pandora, 1987.

Southey, Robert. *The Poetical Works of Robert Southey. Complete in One Volume*. New ed. London: Longman, Brown, Green, and Longman, 1853.

Stoker, Bram. *Dracula*. Ed. Glennis Byron. Peterborough, ON: Broadview, 1998.

[Utterson, Sarah Elizabeth Brown, trans.] *Tales of the Dead*. Ed. Terry Hale. London: The Gothic Society, 1992.

Wordsworth, William. *The Poetical Works of Wordsworth*. Ed. Thomas Hutchinson. New ed. Rev. Ernest de Selincourt. London: Oxford UP, 1950.

Zschokke, Henry [Johann Heinrich Daniel]. *The History of the Invasion of Switzerland by the French, and the Destruction of the Democratical Republics of Schwitz, Uri, and Unterwalden*. Trans. from the French of J.B. Briatte [by John Aikin]. London: T.N. Longman and O. Rees, 1803.

Secondary

Ariès, Philippe. *The Hour of Our Death*. Trans. Helen Weaver. 1981. Rpt. New York: Vintage Books, 1982.

Auerbach, Nina. *Our Vampires, Ourselves*. Chicago: U of Chicago P, 1995.

Barber, Paul. *Vampires, Burial, and Death: Folklore and Reality*. New Haven: Yale UP, 1988.

Barbour, Judith. "Dr. John William Polidori, Author of *The Vampyre*." *Imagining Romanticism: Essays on English and Australian Romanticisms*. Ed. Deirdre Coleman and Peter Otto. West Cornwall, CT: Locust Hill, 1992. 85-110.

Bonjour, E., H.S. Offler, and G.R. Potter. *A Short History of Switzerland*. Oxford: Clarendon, 1952.

Boone, Troy. "Mark of the Vampire: Arnod Paole, Sade, Polidori." *Nineteenth-Century Contexts* 18 (1995): 349-66.

Bowers, Fredson. "Textual Criticism." *The Aims and Methods of Scholarship in Modern Languages and Literatures*. Ed. James Thorpe. New York: MLA, 1963.

Budge, Gavin. "'The Vampyre': Romantic Metaphysics and the Aristocratic Other." *The Gothic Other: Racial and Social Constructions in the Literary Imagination*. Ed. Ruth Bienstock Anolik and Douglas L. Howard. Jefferson, NC: McFarland, 2004. 212-35.

Cantor, Paul A. *Creature and Creator: Myth-Making and English Romanticism*. Cambridge: Cambridge UP, 1984.

Cass, Jeffrey. "The Contestatory Gothic in Mary Shelley's *Frankenstein* and J.W. Polidori's *Ernestus Berchtold*: The Spectre of a Colonialist Paradigm." *JAISA: The Journal of the*

Association for the Interdisciplinary Study of the Arts 1 (1996):
33-41.

Day, William Patrick. *In the Circles of Fear and Desire: A Study of Gothic Fantasy.* Chicago: U of Chicago P, 1985.

——. *Vampire Legends in Contemporary American Culture: What Becomes a Legend Most.* Lexington: UP of Kentucky, 2002.

Derrida, Jacques. *Of Grammatology.* Trans. Gayatri Chakravorty Spivak. Baltimore: Johns Hopkins UP, 1976.

Farson, Daniel. *The Man Who Wrote "Dracula": A Biography of Bram Stoker.* London: Michael Joseph, 1975.

Godet, Marcel, Henri Türler, and Victor Attinger, eds. *Dictionnaire historique et biographique de la Suisse.* 7 vols. Neufchatel: Administration du dictionnaire historique et biographique de la Suisse, 1921-33.

Harse, Katie. "Melodrama Hath Charms: Planché's Theatrical Domestication of Polidori's *The Vampyre.*" *Journal of Dracula Studies* 3 (2001): 3-7.

Harson, Robert R. "A Profile of John Polidori, with a New Edition of *The Vampyre.*" Diss. Ohio University, 1966.

Macdonald, D.L. *Poor Polidori: A Critical Biography of the Author of "The Vampyre."* Toronto: U of Toronto P, 1991.

Marchand, Leslie A. *Byron: A Portrait.* New York: Knopf, 1970.

Mellor, Anne K. *Mary Shelley: Her Life, Her Fiction, Her Monsters.* New York: Methuen, 1988.

Morrill, David F. "'Twilight is not good for maidens': Uncle Polidori and the Psychodynamics of Vampirism in *Goblin Market.*" *Victorian Poetry* 28 (1990): 1-16.

Morrison, Ronald D. "'Their fruits like honey in the throat / But poison in the blood': Christina Rossetti and *The Vampyre.*" *Weber Studies* 14 (1997): 86-96.

Palmer, R.R. *The Age of the Democratic Revolution: A Political History of Europe and America, 1760-1800.* 2 vols. Princeton: Princeton UP, 1959-64.

Pasco, Allan H. "'Lovers of Self': Incest in the Romantic Novel." *Cincinnati Romance Review* 14 (1995): 58-72.

Punter, David. *The Literature of Terror: A History of Gothic Fictions from 1765 to the Present Day, Volume 1: The Gothic Tradition.* London: Longman, 1996.

Richardson, Alan. "The Dangers of Sympathy: Incest in English Romantic Poetry." *SEL* 25 (1985): 737-54.

Sedgwick, Eve Kosofsky. *Between Men: English Literature and Male Homosocial Desire.* New York: Columbia UP, 1985.

Senf, Carol A. "Polidori's *The Vampyre*: Combining the Gothic with Realism." *North Dakota Quarterly* 56 (1988): 197-208.

Skarda, Patricia L. "Vampirism and Plagiarism: Byron's Influence and Polidori's Practice." *Studies in Romanticism* 28 (1989): 249-69.

Stockholder, Kay. *Dream Works: Lovers and Families in Shakespeare's Plays.* Toronto: U of Toronto P, 1987.

Tancheva, Kornelia. "Vampires Are Them, Vampires Are Us." *Engendering Identities.* Ed. Susan Castillo. Porto: Universidade Fernando Pessoa, 1996. 81-91.

Telotte, J.P. "A Parasitic Perspective: Romantic Participation and Polidori's *The Vampyre.*" *The Blood is the Life: Vampires in Literature.* Ed. Leonard G. Heldreth and Mary Pharr. Bowling Green, OH: Bowling Green State U Popular P, 1999. 9-18.

Veeder, William. *Mary Shelley and Frankenstein: The Fate of Androgyny.* Chicago: U of Chicago P, 1986.

Viets, Henry R. "The London Editions of Polidori's *The Vampyre.*" *Papers of the Bibliographical Society of America* 63 (1969): 83-103.

Waller, Gregory A. *The Living and the Undead: From Stoker's "Dracula" to Romero's "Dawn of the Dead."* Urbana: U of Illinois P, 1986.